Dear Chris,

The order of things
is not always
as it seems. —
that's what makes
life interesting.

Saul.

2018.

THE
ORDER
— OF —
THINGS

BASIL GEORGIOU

BALBOA.
PRESS

A DIVISION OF HAY HOUSE

Balboa Press books may be ordered through booksellers or by contacting:

Balboa Press
A Division of Hay House
1663 Liberty Drive
Bloomington, IN 47403
www.balboapress.com.au
1 (877) 407-4847

Print information available on the last page.

ISBN: 978-1-5043-0820-5 (sc)
ISBN: 978-1-5043-0821-2 (e)

Balboa Press rev. date: 08/07/2017

ABOUT THE AUTHOR

Basil Georgiou grew up and received his education in South Africa. He graduated in law at the University of the Witwatersrand and joined the bar in 1981.

He and his young family migrated to Perth, Australia in 1986. Basil has practised law there ever since.

For Athena

A NOTE ON LANGUAGE

South African and non-English words are shown in italics the first time they occur in the text and are followed by a translation in parentheses. The italics and translation do not appear after the first instance, but meanings are given again in a glossary at the end of the book.

To preserve the Afrikaner flavour where Afrikaner scenes and characters appear, titles and terms of address follow the conventions of Afrikaner writing.

PART I

1930–1956

1

❖❖❖

On a cold winter night in 1930, Thomas Ngubeni stood shivering outside the mud-walled hut from which his wife had banished him. He knew Saleena was young and strong. Their first child arrived soon after the pain started, but some hours had gone by now. This second child was different.

Like candles at an outdoor feast, the flickering stars illuminated the black sky of the South African highveld. This was a good omen, he thought: no clouds, no storms. He paced up and down, trying to keep the cold at bay but not wanting to stray far. It should not be long now. But his optimism dampened as the frost settled into his threadbare pullover.

He selected some thorn-tree twigs he had stacked nearby and packed them into a rusted drum pocked with ventilation holes. Then he lit the kindle, bent low and blew the fire alive. He stood over the barrel for warmth, drawing comfort from the sweet acacia scent. This provided a temporary distraction.

The muffled moaning in the hut drew his attention again. Every time he thought there would be news, a lull followed. He sat down next to the fire, which crackled and spat as he kept feeding it. He wrapped himself in the thick woolly blanket thrown to him by their neighbour, acting as midwife, as she said, "This one's in no hurry,

Thomas." After feeding the fire again and again, he heard the groans from inside become more frequent, as did the sound of the midwife's encouraging voice.

Then he heard a different noise: the farm truck rattling and whining towards him. He got up and flung the blanket off when the truck lights emerged from the bush. It screeched to a halt two yards from the fire. He blinked the dust away from his eyes.

A voice roared from the cab, "Come on, Thomas. Get onto the truck. We must go now."

Thomas looked back. Before he could say anything, *baas* (boss) Herman Strydom added, "You can see your baby later. Hurry up, man."

To be near his wife was all Thomas wanted. If he could just pop his head into the hut and see what was happening—

"Come on, boy," ordered baas Strydom. "The market won't be there later. They'll close, and then we will have to come back with all the potatoes. And you don't want that."

"Yes … no, Baas." He ran to the truck. Saleena would realise he had to go.

Thomas climbed into the back of the Chevrolet and clambered on top of the cargo of potatoes. His neighbour, Alfred, was already there, clinging to the backboard, a shadow in the dark morning. They grunted a greeting to each other as Baas Herman crunched the truck into gear and put his foot flat on the accelerator, covering Thomas's family shack in a fog of fumes.

"I told him we didn't need you, but he insisted," said Alfred, pointing back towards the cab.

"I know." Thomas rubbed his hands and blew to warm them against the Transvaal predawn. He had known that Saleena might go into labour this week. He had taken Alfred with him on these trips over the last two months and had shown him what to do. He had even told the baas that Alfred could take his place and Thomas didn't have to be there. It was easy. He just checked the scales when the payload was weighed at the market. Once he was satisfied that the correct weight was written on the papers, he took the docket to Baas Strydom. Alfred could do that.

But there was no swaying his boss, who wanted the faithful Thomas with him when he delivered his cargo. Baas Strydom would have it his way.

The three men arrived in Nelspruit just as the sky was turning pink. Baas Herman went to the manager's office to have coffee and large, hard, dry, dunking *beskuit* (biscuit), while Thomas supervised three men unloading yesterday's crop of potatoes. Thomas checked the quantities recorded, doubled back, knocked on the window of the office, and held up the docket he had been given. Baas Herman opened the window and grabbed the receipt.

"Ja, this is about right," he said after examining the document. He turned to the manager. "I'd like cash this time," Thomas heard just before his boss shut the window.

He knew Baas Herman would gossip with the white manager for a while, so he returned to Alfred. They greeted arriving trucks from other farms in the district. Soon a small ring of black farm labourers huddled around a fire, breathing out wisps of morning frost, their hands extended as though they were patting the flames in a morning ritual.

The talk was centred on Thomas's child, who, they assured him, would have arrived by now and must be happy to be in Saleena's arms. "The longer the baby is kept away from your ugly face, the better for the child," said one of them, and they all laughed.

Thomas chuckled. "You're just jealous because you haven't got my royal nose," he said, lifting his chin towards the sky and tapping his prominent nose gently.

As the warm rays of the sun softened the bite of the morning chill, the men stood back and let the fire go out. By the time Baas Herman stepped out of the office, there was just a pile of warm ash.

"Come, boys, let's go," he commanded from a distance, marching towards the truck.

Some of Thomas's companions patted him on the back and others shook his hand. All wished him strength for his new responsibility and said they would wait for the good news and some home brew to celebrate when they next met.

Baas Herman's truck moaned briefly and then smoked to life. "Hurry up," he shouted as he drove towards the gate. The two black friends hopped on while the Chevy accelerated. They clung to the empty bed of the truck and dragged themselves towards the bulkhead where they sat, facing back, their legs flat against the floor. After a short bumpy trip, the truck pulled up at the general store just as the doors were swinging open for the day's trade.

"On time again. Let's hope he's quick. I want to get home and see what's happened," Thomas said to Alfred, making sure Baas Herman could not hear him.

Their employer disappeared into the dark shop, leaving them on the pavement outside, waiting to be summoned. Eventually he called them to load a couple of crates of provisions.

They did so in haste and then jumped in the back again, where they braced themselves for the jarring drive back to the farm.

Thomas smiled to himself: his friends could joke about his nose, but he had been told by his mother that this was part of the heritage of his ancestors. She had said many times that she was a descendant of the original rain queen, Maselekwane Modjadji. He was born during the reign of Queen Masalanabo Modjadji.

His mother once reminisced about her privileged life, which

had continued after her union with Thomas's father and the birth of Thomas, their only child, whose real name was Mpapatla.

Their future, as heirs to the enormous wealth of the Balobedu tribe, had seemed secure. She told him of the many cattle that fed on the vast Limpopo lands of the tribe. Their queen, who lived in the royal *kraal* (village), was waited upon by a close circle of royal women. She was revered as having powers to bring rain to her friends and drought to her enemies. His mother told him of the frequent visitors who brought gifts to the queen and daughters for the men of her tribe. In this way the Rain Queen extended her influence beyond her kraal.

Thomas's family had been part of the royal circle. And his mother recognised Thomas's nose as being distinctly from her family line. Knowing that, he was proud of it and hoped his children would inherit it too.

But their family suffered towards the end of the queen's reign, when her royal quarters were surrounded by white militia who demanded that she be handed over to them. Thomas's mother fled with a group of the women (and Thomas) towards the south, the real queen with them.

Other members of the tribe presented to the white aggressors an old dying woman as the queen. His mother never saw his father again and was later told that he died heroically in a skirmish with the whites.

The group of escaping women separated, intending to meet at the caves that were some way from the Limpopo. But his mother became confused and never found her way back. She walked and walked, hoping to find a familiar feature that would guide her home. After many days and nights, she found herself in the town of Lydenburg.

Thomas was too young to recall these events, but the life he knew was far removed from that of a royal household. His mother moved from job to job as a domestic servant for white families. Thomas and his mother lived in backyard quarters – overcrowded shacks – which they shared with other groups of black workers trying to earn a living in the white towns of the Transvaal. When his mother had no work, they slept on mats of newspaper under trees or in the corners of shop yards. The memory of sleeping outside in the winters, when the chill never left his bones, still haunted him. He was determined that his family would never be without a roof over their heads.

He cried for two nights when fever claimed his mother. At just 12 and with no family to care for him, he needed food and shelter. With nowhere to go, he walked the few streets of Lydenburg, not knowing what he was looking for or what he would find. It seemed better than doing nothing. He came across a makeshift military camp at the end of the main road entering the little town. Soldiers were stumbling in, on horseback, on foot, and in horse carts. All their uniforms were muddied and many were bloodied, especially those being carted in. He stood under a tree and watched. The soldiers had obviously been in a recent battle.

Luck was on his side: one of them beckoned to him. With that invitation, he became assistant to the camp cook for British forces engaged in the Second Boer War until they decamped three years later. By then the conflict between the two warring white factions had come to an end, and a sort of peace seemed to reign between the local farming community and the ruling forces.

After the job at the British camp, he managed to get low-paid work as a labourer but never had accommodation he could call his own. He shacked up with a group of young men in an abandoned shed that the military had used for storing guns and explosives. Although the place was overcrowded, he remembered those times with a smile. His companions were Zulus, Swazis and Sothos who, like him, were far from their people.

At the time, all of his friends spoke about their dreams of returning to their tribal homes. Thomas knew that, for him, this would not be possible. He could not remember enough about where he had come from and where to return to. His mother and father were dead. He knew his name, Mpapatla, and his mother had often used the name Ngubeni in reference to the family, but he had no way of tracing its origin and did not know of any other relatives.

He had decided that he would adopt Lydenburg as his permanent home. He worked hard and found a good job as a gardener at the Duitse Gereformeerde Kerk (Dutch Reformed Church), where he lived in a storeroom. He was treated well and was happy there; just pleased to have stable employment. He remained loyal to this position for almost twenty years.

But now he turned, as he often did, to that other strong memory: the day he first saw Saleena. In his late thirties at the time, and convinced that he would not take a bride, he was enjoying life with no responsibilities and no one to account to. But when he saw this beautiful young woman, his heart skipped a beat. This had never happened to him before. She looked twenty years younger than him. She would surely not be interested in him. But he was proud of his appearance and spent a fair portion of his wages on good clothing. He was tall and believed in the power of that regal look he had about him. She seemed poor. Maybe he could attract her.

For a few weeks he placed himself "accidentally" in her way and took every opportunity to get to know her. She smiled and spoke to him in a manner that gave the shy Mpapatla hope.

He made enquiries and found out that she and her brother were also orphans. She helped out at the Methodist church. Her brother, Samson, worked in a garage workshop.

Their relationship deepened and became serious. But if they married, he couldn't live with Saleena in his storeroom. Then he remembered that *meneer* (Mister) Herman Strydom, one of the church elders, had offered him a job at his farm, and a hut all to himself. He had declined, but Meneer Strydom had repeated the offer a few times and, the last time, promised more pay.

Within three months, Thomas had married Saleena and become a permanent farm hand with a hut of his own in the Strydom farm compound. But his boss said he couldn't call him "Mpapapapa … or whatever your name is. Your new name is Thomas, because you doubted me for so long."

Now Thomas was eager to see his second child.

Thomas and Alfred dozed off a few times, but, as they approached Lydenburg, Thomas stood up and leaned on the roof of the cab, peering ahead to look first for the farmhouse, then for his little hut that was hidden from view in the surrounding bush. Baas Herman pulled up outside the shed. "Right, boys. Unload the crates. After you hose the truck down you can go home," he ordered and walked to the homestead nearby, where he shut the door behind him.

The two of them heaved the crates off the truck. They carried the one with household items to the scullery door at the back of the house, and the other with farm provisions into the shed.

"Go now, Thomas. I'll finish up," said Alfred after looking around to make sure the master hadn't reappeared.

"Thank you, Alfred." Thomas ran the half mile to his hut. When the group of ramshackle structures that housed the black farmhands came into view, he heard the crying of his newborn baby.

Thomas entered the one-room hut. He looked in the direction of the soft snuffling sounds and saw Saleena's bright smile and eyes in the candlelit room. "It's a boy, Thomas. Just as you asked," she said.

"Number two. We have number two." He danced and drummed on the table.

"And this baby is strong and has a mind of his own already."

"Good. I think our Jeremiah here will survive all that the world has in store for him."

"Jeremiah? Where did you get that name?"

"From the Bible."

"But we haven't discussed this."

"Jeremiah was tough and overcame all kinds of hardship. Our Jeremiah will be tough too. In this world he will need to be strong."

"Hmm! I like the name. Je-re-mi-ah." Saleena nodded slowly in thought. "Yes, I like it."

As Thomas gently stroked the small bare head with his rough hand, Jeremiah let go of his mother's breast and looked up at his father, his eyes shining. Then he turned his head this way and that until he locked on to Saleena's breast again.

2

❖❖❖

A town south-west of London was not a good place to be in 1940 – not that young Neil Robertson had known anywhere better. This evening, as he looked down at the orange flower pattern on his dinner plate, he heard his father's heavy footsteps approach. He glanced up before the big frame of Milton Robertson entered the dark kitchen of their Guildford home like a black shadow. Milton pulled his chair back and sat down.

Mary shuffled from the stove with a saucepan and piled a generous portion of potato stew onto her husband's plate. Before she moved away, Milton Robertson shovelled a heap onto his fork and filled his mouth.

She then arranged Neil's portion on his plate. "Here, love," she said.

"Thank you, Mummy."

Milton Robertson's chewing stopped. Neil glanced towards him and then away again, but with enough time to catch a glimpse of his father's yellow regent moustache turning down as he acknowledged this exchange with a grunt.

Neil's mother's delicious meat and vegetable stews had become more and more potato as World War II dragged on. She tried to add flavour with gravy that Neil thought tasted like diluted Worcestershire sauce.

On this September evening, Neil could sense that his mother was upset. She looked pale and picked at the small serving she had given herself. "Wasn't today's attack on the Vickers factory in Brooklands horrific?" she asked rhetorically after resting her knife and fork on her plate. "Apparently over eighty were killed and four hundred injured." She paused. Milton filled his mouth again, but Neil froze, focusing on his mother. "It's terrible. They say the Germans simply followed the railway line to the aircraft assembly factory. The poor workers had no warning. The sirens didn't go off."

Neil's mouth dropped as she spoke. He had been following the newspaper and wireless reports with great intensity, especially those of the German air assault on Britain. Until now, he felt like a spectator. But today's events, and his mother's reaction, brought the war close to home.

"What's going to happen?" asked his mother, looking at Milton. "They'll call you up soon, dear. They're going to need more mechanics." She paused. "And what about the garage?"

At the mention of his business, Milton stopped eating. He looked directly at Mary. "Let's not get ahead of ourselves." As if sensing Neil's eyes on him, he turned to his son and forced a smile. "We must just carry on and see what happens."

Neil waited for Mary to continue. He sensed that she wanted to say something more to his father, but there was no further discussion.

For Neil, the proud sign announcing "Robertson's Garage" in bold black letters had always marked his father's domain. He was six when first required to help keep the workshop tidy. From that time on, he had felt the burden of the silhouetted slogan, "We Repair with Care", painted below the name. Its angled cursive sealed Milton Robertson's promise to his customers in scarlet, as if in the owner's blood.

At the start of business each day, Neil's father swung two big red doors open to reveal a high-ceilinged garage workshop with bays for two cars and a large yard beyond. Neil made sure he kept away from the deep oblong pit below floor level in the right bay. It was half the width of a car and long enough to allow his father to work from beneath, from bumper to bumper. When Neil peered into it, the dark depth seemed to draw him in so that he nearly lost his balance.

His father ran the place in the same way Mary Robertson ran her kitchen – clean, neat, organised, with every implement in place when not in use.

One night, just a few weeks before Mary raised the matter of the war and their business at dinner, Neil had crept to the kitchen for a glass of water. He heard his father talking in the lounge. "But Mary, he does all his duties without dirtying his clothing."

"He does the work, doesn't he? You should be glad he never brings all the grease back home. I certainly am."

"You've missed the point."

"What point, dear?"

"He needs to be tough. He should be interested in engines."

"He's still young, but he's a good boy."

"Hah. I know him better than that. He's no good for the garage, Mary. We'll have to find something else for him."

Tears came to Neil's eyes. His father had good reason to reject him – he would never be good at the things his father did. He'd known it for some time: how he loathed the thought of all that grease, grime, sticky sweat, and back-breaking labour. On that night it had become obvious to him that no matter how much he yearned for it, he was never going to earn his father's approval.

Once this knowledge set in, he felt increasingly awkward in his father's presence. He found it easier to make sure his duties were done and then to be seen as little as possible. He knew that Milton really wanted him to graduate from workshop cleaning duties to mechanic, but Neil preferred to assist Mary in the front office and with the driveway service. He enjoyed chatting to the patrons – just what Milton detested. He loved to run errands for the neighbours and use his cocky but endearing wit to spar with them. How could anyone enjoy the idea of spending hours and hours each day interacting with machinery that couldn't talk back? There just had to be an easier and cleaner way to make a living. *I'd rather deal with people than engines.*

Neil envied his father's strength. Tall and well built, Milton Robertson could do most jobs in the workshop single-handed, using a pulley system only for the heaviest objects. His wavy golden hair, neatly combed, made him look like the men advertising Chesterfield cigarettes in the newspapers that Neil read. But it was his strong blue eyes that Neil feared most. Milton Robertson didn't have to speak to Neil. A look with those eyes was all it took to know Milton's thoughts, and those glances conveyed the older Robertson's sadness that father and son were so different.

The silent glare hurt Neil as much as a slap in the face, except that the pain in his heart did not go away.

❖

After dinner, Milton sat in his armchair in the lounge and prepared to smoke his pipe. Neil was fascinated by this ceremony.

Milton first used a pipe cleaner and blew into the mouthpiece. Then he fingered some sweet, clammy tobacco into the pipe's bowl and pressed it down with his brown-stained thumb. Even though Neil saw the grocer's shelves emptying gradually as the war progressed, the old shopkeeper produced a packet of tobacco from under the counter every time his father sent Neil to buy some.

Neil looked on as his father lit a match, held it over the briar bowl, and sucked in deeply. After drawing the flame down into the tobacco, he released a dense cloud of smoke through his mouth. The flame leapt up into the air until he drew in again. When the tobacco was properly lit, Milton waved the match to and fro and into final submission. He sat back, closed his eyes, and breathed in the strong, bittersweet smoke. He seemed oblivious to the presence of Neil, who sat mesmerised in the room, intoxicated by the tobacco-scented atmosphere and his father's lapse into a mellower mood.

When Milton was done, he went outside, knocked the pipe on his shoe heel, blew, brushed it with his pipe cleaner, and restored it to its stand on the round table by his armchair for the next ritual.

Neil sometimes loitered a while, soaking up the musky sweet smell lingering in the room.

Notwithstanding his aversion to the workshop, Neil had always been attracted to the shiny motorcars that went through the business. He enjoyed getting behind the wheel and pretending to drive. It made him feel grown up. As soon as his body was long enough for him to reach the steering wheel and floor pedals at the same time, he felt adventurous and began to move cars forwards into the yard and backwards into the workshop.

When no one was watching.

His father would have been furious if he had suspected Neil was manoeuvring the precious cars that customers had entrusted to Robertson's. The driving occurred only when Neil was sure that his father was safely at home.

On one occasion, shortly before his twelfth birthday, Neil couldn't resist starting up Sir Roger Hackett's pristine Rolls Royce Phantom III to listen to the purr of the engine. He didn't realise that it was in gear. As he engaged the starter, the car leapt forwards a foot and knocked into an oil drum, denting the drum … and the Phantom's bumper.

Neil ejected quickly and used all the panic-induced strength he could muster to push the car back a foot. Then, heaving with his full weight, he managed to turn the drum so that its dent wasn't visible. He concealed the obvious part of the drum further by strategically placing a stack of grease tins and buckets around it.

Knowing Sir Roger had recently driven to London, he developed a plan to deal with the crisis.

When Sir Roger came to collect his car, Neil showed him to the driver's seat. But, just as Sir Roger was about to get in, Neil cleared his throat. "Sir Roger. May I please show you something that I'm not sure you're aware of?"

"What is it, boy? I've got to go now."

"It won't take long, Sir Roger." He walked to the front of the Phantom and pointed to the dent. "As you never mentioned it, I'm not sure you know this bump is here, sir." He looked at Sir Roger as if baffled by this blemish to the otherwise shining bumper.

"What? How did that get there?" Pointing at the dent, Sir Roger looked doubtful.

But Neil stood there unabashed. "I thought so, sir. I was quite sure you weren't aware this was here."

Sir Roger pinched his chin between his thumb and forefinger. "I don't understand …"

Milton Robertson came over to see what was happening. He also inspected the damage. Unaware that it had taken place at Robertson's "We Repair with Care" in his lunch hour, Milton was ingenuous when he said, "Good heavens, Sir Roger, who could have done this?" He knelt beside the bumper, examined the dent, and wiped it with his handkerchief.

Neil stood by as Sir Roger looked around. Milton was the only mechanic at Robertson's. Neil could see Sir Roger staring at his father and judging that Milton was honest and patently unaware of the origin of the damage.

Then Neil said, "Sir Roger, if it happened when you were driving, you would have known about it. Someone must have knocked her in London when you weren't there."

Sir Roger seemed to ponder for a moment. "Damn those bloody Londoners. It must have happened in the lane I parked in, near the club in Mayfair. Parking's rather tight there. Thank you for pointing it out to me, boy."

He handed Neil a penny and walked to the car door, shaking his head in disbelief. "Damned coward. He could have found me or left me a note."

Neil opened the door for Sir Roger. "Yes, Sir Roger. You'd think they'd be honest. You can't trust anyone nowadays, can you, sir?"

"No, you can't." He looked at Milton. "Clever boy you've got there, Robertson. Clever boy."

Mary gave pocket money to Neil every week, just two coins to rub together and jingle. That and a little cash from easy errands picked up here and there were enough for a treat at the general store twice a week. When really desperate for something more, he scaled the grocer's backyard fence when no one was looking, helped himself to a few empty, returnable drink bottles, and claimed the deposit for "returning" them.

With this self-help, he indulged in the occasional extravagance – a fresh doughy bun or some boiled confectionary.

Neil felt the excitement of the battles far away that he heard about on the wireless, but he also felt the terror of the air bombings that threatened the streets in their neighbourhood. His parents kept the business going, but many men were away at war, and then there was the rationing. Neil noticed that Milton's custom was dropping.

In 1942, not long after the incident with Sir Roger's Rolls Royce, Milton announced at dinner that he had received his military papers.

Neil had just filled his mouth with watery carrot and potato soup, with a smidgeon of bully beef for taste. He had been hungry but couldn't swallow the mouthful after hearing the news.

Mary nodded. She seemed resigned to this moment.

"As we discussed, Mary, we'll close the business temporarily. Better to close. There's no money in the fuel, and we don't know how long supplies will trickle in."

"I know, dear. Shop's been struggling for some time. If it wasn't for the workshop …"

They were quiet for a while.

Milton slurped a spoonful of soup. "There are some savings in the bank, and the war will soon be over." After a short pause he added, "I'll not be gone long."

And the next day he left them.

All perfect six feet of him.

Within thirteen months, Milton was returned to Mary – in a wheelchair.

Neil had held his mother's hand tightly when, in the previous month, they went to the hospital in London where his father lay – thin, pale and motionless, apart from his chest that heaved up and down slowly. Neil was silent, his eyes and mouth wide open, as he listened to the doctor. "Mrs Robertson, shrapnel has lodged in his cranium and his back. His condition is stable and could improve slightly without more surgery. But if we operate, he may never wake up."

Neil pulled the curtains aside every five minutes the day his father was due to come home. His mother sat him down and held his hand. She spoke softly as she warned him that his father couldn't walk and couldn't talk properly.

The rain dripped from a miserable sky as a grey army van drove up the road and stopped at the Robertson front gate. Neil didn't want to go out, but Mary led him to the vehicle. Neil was praying that no one in the street was watching. Two men loaded Milton from a stretcher in the van onto a wheelchair they had parked in the street. They adjusted his body on the chair, folding his arms on his lap and lifting his legs onto the flat plates for his feet. He grunted as they pushed him upright. Mary scurried around her husband, patting his arm and then holding his hand and then resting her hand on his shoulder.

"Come 'ere, boy. Be a good lad," one of the men said to Neil. He took Neil's right hand gently and placed it on the grip of the wheelchair. "Can ye drive? Take ye dad inside now." The way he said "dad" made it sound like "dud", and Neil froze in horror, his hand still on the handle.

"I'll try," he said after hesitating. He pushed with both hands, and the wheelchair moved forward slowly. He heaved his father up the short path. The men lifted the chair up the porch steps, and, wet with perspiration, Neil manoeuvred it into the sitting room. Then he left Mary and the men there and ran out into the overgrown garage yard next door. He could hold back the tears no longer.

Neil was relieved that Milton's bruises and external wounds healed. But his father's mouth sagged on the right, and his weak control of his tongue and saliva meant that he drooled constantly. With a look of embarrassment, the once-proud Milton was ever dabbing at his mouth with a handkerchief held in his right hand, which he rested on the arm of the wheelchair.

His loud, clear voice had been replaced with angry, impatient grunting. The inexhaustible energy had given way to lame legs, disjointed arm movements, and obvious frustration and despair.

Neil knew that the business could not be revived. It needed someone prepared to reopen the workshop, someone who could pull up his sleeves and roughen his hands. But Neil still had no love of engines and grease.

Neil hated being at home. He could hardly look at the once-imposing workshop master who now dribbled and had to be fed and cleaned. He felt helpless when his father's frustrated growls gave way to pitiful sobbing. At these times, nothing Mary could do or say would comfort Milton. Neil saw her withdraw into the small back garden and sob quietly, unaware that he looked on in tears himself.

Neil tried to escape the bleak mood and the heaviness inside the Robertson household. He took long walks, scheming of ways to escape and to find a life where he didn't have to feel guilty about wanting to avoid his father.

His father's sad eyes were always looking at him, pleading for him to say something, but he had nothing to say. His guilt was a stone in his heart.

❖

"Our savings are dwindling," Mary told Neil early in 1949. "The past five years haven't left us much, even though your father is eligible for an army pension. I've arranged with Mr Sprigg to supply his tearooms with my meat pies. But you'll have to find some real employment. These odd jobs you're doing around the neighbourhood won't give you a career, love."

"I've been looking for work, but there aren't any vacancies in Guildford. I'll have to try London." He looked at Mary – outwardly resigned, but inwardly excited.

"Why not?" She nodded. "There must be jobs there."

He went to the newsstand every day and paged through the paper, jotting down notes about job vacancies, week after unsuccessful week. He carefully wrote out and sent sixty-six job applications and received fifty-three rejections. He discussed the results with his mother. "Thirteen didn't even bother to reply. They're clearly not interested. Maybe I'm too young. I've even added two years to my age, saying I'm 20."

"Your birthday's still some way off—"

"I look 20, don't I?" His father's coat was loose on him, he knew, but it wasn't too long. He was approaching Milton's six feet of height and looked quite grown up, if a bit thin.

"Mm, yes. You do look like your father when he was a young man."

She encouraged Neil to consider a life in the New World. "There seem to be opportunities there, Neil. You could try Canada. They're right next door to America – surely on their way to prosperity."

"But it's so cold there."

"What about Australia?" And she showed him reports of fully laden liners delivering English migrants to Sydney. She called Neil to the wireless when Australians were being interviewed: "You can feel the warm southern sun radiate out of the speaker." He laughed with her at their casual phrases and their quaint accents. And he admired their sportsmen.

"But if I go so far away, can you cope with Father?"

"Of course I can. I have, haven't I? I'll extend my range of baking and supply other tearooms too. And Mrs James can continue to help me. She needs the extra money now that poor Mr James perished in the war. And once you're settled, wherever it is, you can send for us and we'll join you."

Neil knew she wasn't serious. Milton couldn't cross the road, never mind travel to the other side of the world. "Wherever I go, I'll send you money every month," he told her. "If you want to join me, of course you can."

3

Marius Strydom knew what it meant to be an heir of the Strydom and De Wet families. He had grown up learning how his pioneer ancestors, from as far back as the 1600s, had left their home countries of Holland, France and Germany – often for reasons of persecution – to become *boers* (farmers) in South Africa. And he knew how they had battled to establish their own language, which they came to call Afrikaans.

Marius and his older brother, Hennie, grew up on stories of the Groot Trek, the epic journey of the Boers leaving the British Cape Colony in the 1830s and '40s to set up the Boer republics. The Afrikaners had done this, he was told, to be free of the power of colonial masters. They had fought the black tribes for a share of their adopted continent. And they had fought the British. Marius loved to hear the tales of his family's great deeds in the battles for freedom against the British.

One of these family histories stood out in his memory, along with the manner of its telling. He was about 9 years old, and it was a Sunday. After the evening prayer, Marius and his father, Jacobus Strydom, remained at the dinner table as the rest of the family went to bed.

"Marius, I've never told you about my own suffering at the hands of the British."

"No, Pa."

"Do you know how Oupa (Grandpa) Herman fought the mighty British empire?"

"No … How?"

"They used the tactic of hit-and-run, and—"

"Hit-and-run?"

"Yes, Marius. They ambushed the British with quick attacks, then fled and hid."

Marius was all attention. The dining room was now very quiet but for Strydom's deep voice.

"They confused the British by firing from hidden positions on all sides. Then they disappeared into the bush. They knew the bush like their own little houses." He leaned back and pointed to the window. "Every crevice and *koppie* (hill), every river and rut, every bush and *boom* (tree) was like their backyard. They were one step ahead of the big British empire, and they were invisible, like ghosts." He spoke slowly and with emphasis as he made a special point. "Yes, Marius. They caused havoc."

"But weren't they outnumbered, Pa?"

"Of course they were. But they were stealthy, like the leopard."

"Did they kill any soldiers?"

"Oh yes," said his father with pride. "They shot at them, and the Boers won some battles, like the first one – the great Battle of Majuba. That was before I was born. Oupa Herman attacked telegraph poles so that the British couldn't send messages to their army, and he blew up railway lines so that they couldn't move their soldiers. We called the redcoats *rooinekke* (rednecks) because that's all that our heroes could see when the empire's soldiers ran away – those cowardly, pale English necks burnt red by the African sun … our sun, the Boer sun." He paused and leaned forward. "Then one night – when I was younger than you are now – your Oupa Herman and his two brothers mounted their big farm stallions to ride out and challenge the British, who were advancing towards our district." He cleared his throat and dropped his gaze.

Reacting to the tension in his father's voice, Marius sat forward with his elbows on his thighs and his chin in his hands.

Jacobus nodded. "They were coming to rip out our hearts and seize our green bush and golden veld." He twisted his right hand in the air as though grabbing an imaginary soldier and pulling him towards him with an angry grimace. "I watched my pa and uncles gallop away, confident that they would soon teach a lesson to the enemy in those silly bright-red army uniforms." Strydom's voice faltered slightly. "Oupa Herman joked at the dinner table the night before they departed. We all laughed when he said, 'The idiots couldn't make themselves more obvious a target if they tried.' Early the next morning they left the womenfolk and me, armed with my wooden rifle, to await their victorious return." Strydom looked up. "They were brave, Oupa Herman and his brothers."

Marius did not take his eyes off his father.

"But on that night, Oupa Herman's two brothers were cut down by British bullets, and Oupa went into hiding. He became a hunted man."

Now his father's voice became so soft that Marius strained to hear. "Around the same time, British soldiers were setting the veld alight. Our land, along with our farm, was swept by bushfire." He looked down again. "The English soldiers pulled down the door to one of the *kaffir* (indigenous African) shacks we were hiding in and grabbed us children and the women. With my mother and brother and thousands of other Boer women and children, I was thrown into hell: a concentration camp. It was a terrible place – a place of the devil. They never cared for us. We all got sick." Strydom swallowed hard. "The Lord shortened the suffering for your *ouma* (grandma)," he said as his green eyes moistened. "She died of typhoid, and so did many other good Afrikaans Christians." He dabbed his eyes with his khaki handkerchief. "Those who caused this were *not* Christians, Marius."

He waved his right index finger in the air as he spat out the words: "They were British soldiers."

He paused again and seemed to change his line of thought. "But the hand of God saved me and reunited me with my pa. He came to get me when he heard of Ma's death. Yes, Oupa Herman risked being caught to get me and your uncle Eben out of there."

"You were lucky, Pa."

"No, Marius. This was not luck. We survived for a reason, son. We were chosen because our fight is not over."

"Chosen?"

"We are chosen to lead our people. That is why God let me live and has given us wealth and special qualities. It is no coincidence that me and my pa survived the bitter war which killed my ma and many of our family." Strydom turned to Marius, his eyes red-rimmed but his look now composed and determined. "Your grandfather was there to counsel President Paul Kruger in 1900 to flee the British and leave his Transvaal Republic. With the Strydom and De Wet blood in your veins, you will be a leader one day, and you will turn this injustice on its head."

Marius was quiet in thought. After a moment he asked, "What must I do, Pa?"

"Oupa Herman and his brothers were prepared to sacrifice their lives for us. But they have not lost. We are here, are we not? And we will carry on when our turn comes. Meanwhile we will be patient, work hard and bide our time." He rose and ruffled Marius's hair. "You must just do your homework. Your time will come, Marius. Your time will come."

❖

Marius loved his grandfather, Oupa Herman. They frequently went for long walks on the farm and spent hours talking. His oupa sometimes spoke of the war against the British, but rarely of his own personal hardships during that time. Not until Marius was 11, a couple of years after his father's Sunday night story, did he ask Oupa Herman directly about his role in that war.

Oupa must have decided Marius was ready for specifics. He walked and talked with Marius for a long time. He began by describing how his brothers were shot and killed. He felt guilty for surviving and leaving their blood to soak into the land they had fought for, but what could he do for them? Nothing. So he hid from the British in the veld.

"I was very successful at hiding. But I felt I let my family down. You see, while I was safe, my wife and sons were suffering in those overcrowded camps." He let out a long sigh and shook his head. "When I heard of your ouma's death, I nearly went mad. I felt like going to the British headquarters to shoot everyone, even though I knew they would get me. I almost did. But then I thought of our two boys. They deserved a father. I disguised myself as an old man with a walking stick." He turned to Marius with a grin. "As a matter of fact, I must have looked the way I look now, but with a bigger beard." And he lifted his sturdy, polished wooden walking stick. "This is how I went to the camp to look for my family. I pleaded with the pink-faced guards at the gate to fetch my children, who I said were my grandchildren. My disguise was so good they believed me. I can be a good actor, you know.

"When I walked in to find them, the stench was terrible." He scratched his silver goatee beard and spoke softly. His green eyes darted left and right, just as if he were walking through the camp, absorbing the squalor and cruel conditions. "All the Afrikaners were very thin – women *and* children. Then I saw my boys, Jacobus and Eben. They were skin and bone. Their legs were as thin as *knopkieries* (African walking and fighting sticks)." He joined his thumb and forefinger, making a small circle in front of Marius. "Their knees were like the bumpy knob on this kierie," he said and pointed to the lumpy bulge at the top end of his walking stick. "It

25

was an unhealthy place, and both my boys were very sick. I nearly cried, but I had to be strong in front of them. There was little food and they needed to be fed. I was still a wanted enemy leader, and so my family got less than the other families.

"Barely an hour after I walked in through that gate, our neighbour Marie de Wet died of typhoid too. I took her children, including your ma, then a little girl. They let me because they thought I was a useless old man, and I suppose they didn't want so many orphans there. I left with them all, the Strydom and the De Wet children. Your pa and ma were younger than you are now."

Marius sat quietly, trying to picture the disguised old man followed by the two Strydom and five De Wet children. "Where did you go, Oupa?"

"Where else? I came here, back to the farm in Lydenburg."

"But wasn't it burned down?"

"Yes, all the fields were black. And only the blackened stone walls of our little house stood, like ancient ruins in the overgrown veld. Not the present farmhouse. No – the little one that's in the native compound now."

"Yes, Oupa, I know it."

"Some of our servants were still there. They knew we would come back. They had planted a few crops, and we ate their *pap* (maize porridge) and hunted game. Anything – rabbits, buck, bird, *dassie* (rock hyrax) – you name it, we ate it. I brought your father and mother and their brothers and sisters to this place here, where they grew up together. Years later they got married, and that's how you and your brother have this home. All of us. One family."

"How did you build our big farmhouse?" Marius asked, pointing to the rambling homestead.

"I had hidden a few gold sovereigns before I hid from the British, and these I found when it was safe to be me again. I called the farm Heiligdom (Sanctuary). This became my little world of freedom away from the English. With my bit of gold, I bought cattle and regrew the crops. And here it is." He looked at the healthy farm surrounding them. Marius looked around, turning full circle as he did so.

Marius wondered why, in all the stories told by his oupa and pa, the black tribes were hardly mentioned. Only once did Oupa Herman tell him, "The kaffirs are meant to be servants."

"The Voortrekkers put them in their place. We weren't alone, of course. The British fought the kaffirs too. Now we have a good supply of servants and we feed them. We take on our fair share of mouths to feed, and they work and live on the farm. And that's how it should be. Without us, they would have no jobs."

Marius sat in silence. "Yes, I see, Oupa," he said after some moments. "Our one family feeds all the kaffirs in the compound."

"That's right. But never forget that the British were our biggest enemy and remain a threat to our people."

One hot Saturday morning, when Marius was 12 and he and Hennie were kicking a rugby ball to each other, they heard shouting and screaming. They ran to the commotion at the shed nearby and saw their pa jump off a horse-drawn cart. He shouted instructions to some of the farmhands who were running behind him. They transferred the limp Oupa Herman to the back tray of the farm truck. Marius edged his way nearer and was next to the truck when one of the men jumped up and knelt alongside Oupa Herman. The thin black man ripped off his shirt and started wrapping his boss's leg tightly with it as Marius's father revved the Chevrolet truck.

Marius looked on until dust swallowed the truck as it shuddered off to Lydenburg a few miles away. He held his mother's hand and listened closely as the workers explained to her that the old baas had been bitten by a snake – "A black mamba," said one of them. Marius had heard of people who had been killed by a bite from this snake, and he burst into tears.

Martha Strydom pulled him towards her and hugged him tightly. "Marius, let's go inside and pray to our Lord to help Oupa. The Lord is merciful. Come, let us pray." She took Marius and Hennie into the dining room, where they held hands, prayed, and then read the Bible.

Three hours later, a grey-faced Jacobus Strydom returned alone. He joined his family around the table. "Oupa Herman has been taken by the Lord. Let us pray."

Jacobus and Martha Strydom inherited the family farm.

Marius could not help but notice the truckloads of produce leaving the farm for the markets of Johannesburg and Pretoria. And he saw his family prosper. He shivered with a sense of pride when he thought of his oupa and pa. Their determination had ensured that the well-run Heiligdom farm grew from its ashes and now buzzed with the hardworking industry of the Strydoms and their army of African workers. He felt that their piece of the continent was blessed by God with the plentiful resources of Africa – specifically for the rise of the Afrikaner nation.

Two windmills churned lazily, drawing cool, sweet water from the depths below. There was more than enough water for the herds of cattle, and the large fields were soaked with mineral-rich nourishment. Most of the produce was sold to the market, with only a small proportion kept to feed the family and workers. Marius's mother was in charge of rations for the black labourers and their families living in the compound.

It did not escape Marius's inquiring mind that his father ran the enterprise like an army. On one occasion Marius held his brother's hand as they watched Strydom line up all the staff and single out one of the men. Strydom shouted at the man for taking fruit from the orchard without Mrs Strydom's permission. Marius winced as Strydom then whipped him in front of everyone.

He explained at dinner that night. "I make a law and the kaffirs obey. If they don't, they must be punished. Otherwise they will help themselves to more and more. We must keep them under control. You will see – no one will challenge my rules again."

Marius's older brother, Hennie, was being groomed by their pa during the school holidays to become farm foreman. At first Marius felt left out when Strydom spoke to Hennie about the farm. "The best way for you to learn, Hennie, is to see what I do and understand why I do it. Then one day you can take over."

Marius knew his bounds with Hennie, whose legs and arms were twice as thick as Marius's. He seemed to have the strength of an ox. It bewildered Marius that the differences between them could be so great. Hennie didn't like studying and preferred to be out hunting or playing his beloved rugby. Though only three years older than Marius, he already had the attitude of the new boss. Marius could not bring himself to order the farmhands about with the same air of authority as their father. Some of them were as old as Oupa Herman had been when he died.

But Marius heard Hennie swear viciously at the Africans, something that his religious and disciplined pa never did. Hennie mocked the developing teenage girls of the compound, calling them fat cows, and he took every opportunity to kick or hit a farm boy. "Get on with it, lazy pig. You haven't got all day!" Marius could see that they were simply exhausted from the hard digging, lifting and carrying, and he felt uncomfortable, but Hennie was his brother.

Strydom's encouragement to Marius was different. "You're a

clever boy. You've got a way with words. You should follow in Oom (Uncle) Eben's footsteps."

Marius hero-worshipped his uncle Eben, a successful *advokaat* (trial lawyer) in Pretoria. Oom Eben was also a scholar of the classics and peppered his language with foreign phrases, which he said were Latin or Greek, and translated them for Marius. Marius often laughed uncontrollably at his witty anecdotes.

He loved it when his uncle came to the farm for a weekend or more. Oom Eben had never married and always brought something from Pretoria for Marius: an expensive toy, a colourfully illustrated book, a fashionable jersey, or – for his birthdays – a bicycle or a watch. Some of the books were by Afrikaner authors. Marius enjoyed hearing his uncle recite Afrikaans poetry and loved to discuss with him the last book Marius had read. Oom Eben made him feel very grown up, especially when he once said, "You will become an Afrikaner leader one day, son."

Marius began to see how Lydenburg was remote enough for his father to become a leader in the Afrikaner cause, away from the prying eyes of government. Strydom was an active member in the anti-British militant group of renegades called the Ossewabrandwag or Ox Wagon Sentinels. He was indifferent to the general perception that this was a fanatical movement of diehard Boer descendants whose main aim was to ensure that South Africa would be ruled by Afrikaners for Afrikaners.

He instilled in Marius and Hennie the belief that the Afrikaner *volk* (people) had been "planted in South Africa by the hand of God". Divine Providence must therefore still be behind his people's actions and decisions, guiding them.

"The rooineks have England and their colonies. Let them go back to where they came from. This is *our* land."

As a young boy, Marius soaked up any news about World War II. He adopted his parents' dislike of the government of General Jan Smuts, who supported the British. Strydom and his group, the Ossewabrandwag, were pro-Germany. Marius saw how just the mention of Smuts's name seemed to make his father's blood boil. "That Smuts is a traitor to his Afrikaner roots," Jacobus would say. "Has he forgotten what the English did to our women and children?"

Countless times he told Hennie and Marius, "This is God's country and we are God's chosen people. Never forget that."

When Marius reached the age of 13, a meeting that he would never forget took place on the Strydom farm. It was late in 1943, and Jan Smuts was dealing with the demands of World War II.

The boys were told that their father would hold an important prayer meeting in the dining room, but it was to be kept secret. The women and children had supper early and were sent to bed.

Hennie and Marius, excited by the air of mystery, sensed that this was more than just a prayer meeting. After dark they crept out of the bedroom they shared and looked on as three sedans and two open-bed trucks full of Boers pulled up beside the barn. About twenty-five men of varying ages gathered in the front yard.

Jacobus Strydom gave instructions to eight of the older men to pair up and patrol the perimeter of the homestead. "You know how to whistle like the scops owl," he said, and they dutifully hooted to show the signal. "Now, men. Signal if anyone should approach. Karel will sit on the *stoep* (front veranda) and relay your warning to us. If we hear you signal, we will continue with our … *prayer meeting.*" Everyone chuckled and the four pairs went off.

Hennie and Marius stood motionless in the dark, formal sitting room that was usually out of bounds to them. Through a crack between the double doors that connected the two rooms, Marius could see the men enter the dining room and take their places around the solid-mahogany table. His father sat down at the far end. Three candles threw flickering shadows of the congregation against the walls. The bitter, sweaty, tobacco smell of the men overpowered the usually sweet and clean aroma of wood polish.

Strydom opened the fourth meeting of the district's Ossewabrandwag. Each man had a Bible. The meeting started with a prayer conducted by the Reverend Cloete, followed by an oath recited by two new recruits who were confirmed as members: *If I retreat, kill me. If I die, avenge me. If I advance, follow me.*

Strydom spoke. "We must destabilise Smuts and his rooinek government. Then we will get support from the Afrikaner people for the cause – to rid South Africa of foreign rule. We have all lost family in the Boer Wars, especially the last one. It's now up to us. And you know what the prize is, gentlemen of the guard?" Marius watched his father pause and survey them all. "It is the power to govern. To govern our land. To avenge our forefathers. Under the hand of God, we will fight to get rid of Smuts. And then? Then we have control over the gold of this country, which we will use for the people of South Africa, not for the King of England!"

"What if innocent people die?" asked one of the older men.

Strydom sat erect with his lower arms resting on the table and his fisted hands pointing forward. He looked at the questioner. "Did they not kill our women and children?" Then he turned his head, scanned the faces of the others, smiled, and spoke in a softer voice, almost friendly. "We are not aiming to kill, but there is sometimes a price for freedom. The Bible is full of battles between good and evil."

"What if we are caught, meneer Strydom?" asked one of the new recruits in a voice so soft, Marius could barely hear the question.

Strydom gave the young man a kind smile. "Thank you for that question, Dawie. Let me place our mission in perspective for the benefit of our younger members." The smile disappeared, his eyes narrowed, and a frown tracked his rutted forehead. "Our task is minor compared with the obstacles that faced our fathers and grandfathers. They didn't ask whether they would be caught. They were prepared to die." He knocked on the table with the knuckles of his right hand at the last word. The clear bang sounded like a gunshot to Marius, who strengthened his grip on his older brother. Strydom then spoke slowly. "Is our task so difficult? Are we not up to it? The decision is yours." He pointed in the air and said loudly, "Either you're in or you're out."

No one said he was out.

By the end of the meeting, Strydom had delegated duties for carrying out attacks on government installations, using dynamite on electrical power lines and railroads, and cutting telegraph and telephone lines, all at night and in remote locations. "Most of the police around here are our friends, so we will be tipped off if someone smells our plans. Just make sure no leaks come from you," Strydom warned.

The meeting was concluded in prayer led by the Reverend Cloete.

The words and the disciplined leadership of his father were stamped on Marius's soul. He prayed in silence for the success of the mission – the ousting of Jan Smuts and freedom for his people from the ruthless British.

Heiligdom stretched beyond the horizon. A stream feeding into the mighty Olifants River crossed through the land and brought life to the farm. It was the main artery for a large dam teeming with trout.

On the river bank upstream, three giant weeping willows massed together, forming an airy, vaulted cathedral. To Marius, the main tree covering most of the width of the river was like an altar. Its branches reached down and touched the rippling stream gently. The other trees' long drapes of delicate leaves shimmered like green lace curtains flowing to the ground. These parted and then embraced Marius when he entered the domed hall. The willow fronds decorated the chamber walls and, like stained glass, admitted soft, filtered light. Marius loved to breathe in the fresh incense steaming off the leaves. Malachite sunbirds were the congregants providing music to accompany the cicadas' choral chants.

Marius observed that his father often spent time in this special place, the "God-created Church of Willows", as Strydom called it. There he sought divine guidance. After his discussions with God, he always appeared to return brimming with confidence and strengthened in his belief in the purity and justice of his cause.

One afternoon, as he drove Marius home from school, he patted him on the knee and smiled. "Marius, you are 13 years old and fast becoming an adult. I am going to tell you a secret that you mustn't tell anyone. I believe you are responsible enough to share in these things now. Do you understand?"

"Yes, Pa."

"This secret is very important for the things Oupa Herman and our heroes fought for. You can't even tell Hennie and your friends. Is that clear?"

"Yes, Pa."

"I have been invited to become a member of the *Broederbond* (Brotherhood)."

"What's that, Pa?"

"It is a very important club. You have to be invited to join. I think the Broederbond will become the inner circle of Afrikaner power. We intend to penetrate the halls of power at various levels in the civil service – the police, the schools, the municipal authorities, and the provincial governments, right up to the central government. We will get rid of that turncoat Smuts. And we will appoint judges. Son, I am paving the way for you."

In the fertile surroundings of the Lydenburg district, Marius often thought about his pa's words, and his Afrikaner soul grew strong and patriotic.

4

Jeremiah Ngubeni was often told by his parents that he was the same age as *Kleinbaas* (Little Boss) Marius Strydom, a link which he felt gave him a special claim to the attention of the little baas. He knew that his parents had married just before they began working for the Strydoms, and that he and his brother were born in the same hut where they now lived. But he felt that his family extended to all the black workers who lived in the farm compound, a few hundred yards away from the main homestead but out of sight.

He enjoyed his life in the compound – playing among its familiar assortment of corrugated iron shacks, mud-clad rondavels, and run-down permanent structures that his father once told him had been built for the Strydom family when they first established the farm. The rondavel where he lived with his parents and older brother, Petrus, needed regular insulating against the wind, rain, and sun. He frequently climbed the walls to help his father patch the roof by adding to its thick layer of reed thatch bound together with grass and supported by interwoven branches.

He remembered the day that his father came home and told his mother that Mrs Strydom had asked for Saleena to help in the homestead. Thomas and their neighbour Alfred sang around the fire that night as they consumed Alfred's home brew of maize and sorghum beer until well after Jeremiah's usual bedtime. Saleena became one of four maids who could enter the Strydom house to help with the cooking, baking, washing and cleaning.

At 13 years old in 1943, Jeremiah was taller than other boys of his age. He was fast on his legs, and his movements were nimble. He roamed the compound freely. His young and bright eyes saw everything. They were sharp and quick, like those of an impala, always on the lookout. But whereas the impala searched for danger to see when the herd must run away from predators, Jeremiah was looking to perform a prank and make sure he wasn't caught.

He loved teasing the older girls and startling them. He spied on them when they chattered together. After dark he made noises in the bush or threw mud clods near them, terrifying them, and then laughed when they fled screaming.

When he played ball with the compound children, they used an old, worn ball that the baas's sons had thrown away. It more or less kept its shape after being tossed and kicked around for hours, but thudded to the ground instead of bouncing.

Jeremiah sought out chores in the compound to earn some reward – a *mielie* (corn) cob, an apple, or, on rare occasions such as when he helped build a thatch hut for a new family, a sweet. He was dressed in patched clothing, passed from Petrus and older members of the compound as they outgrew them. Then, when he outgrew the hand-me-downs in turn, Saleena passed what remained of them to younger neighbours.

In the evenings the family gathered around the outside fire where Saleena or Thomas cooked. On one occasion, his father explained that he had picked up some cooking skills as a young boy when helping the British feed their troops in the Second Boer War. At first Jeremiah was impressed, but he became confused when Thomas forced him to swear to keep secret his father's role in feeding the British troops. He understood the problem when his father explained that the British were fighting against "the Boers, like Oubaas Herman Strydom, whose brothers were killed by the British." He didn't want to get his father into trouble and resolved to keep silent on the matter.

Jeremiah enjoyed those evenings – the comforting, sweet, smoky smell of the dry bush-wood combined with the aroma of whatever was cooking over the fire. It was the best way to end the day.

On one of those days, as they were all gazing at the sky and watching the sun go down, his father said, "Our country has the best sunsets in the world."

Saleena laughed. "Yes, Father, and you have seen the whole world."

"No, I haven't, but I've been told this by Father Michael at the missionary school, and he wouldn't lie. He told me they hardly see the sun in London, which is where the King of South Africa lives. That's funny, isn't it? You'd think he would come and live here, where we have sun every day."

"This king should come and see our sun," said Jeremiah.

There was very little that scared Jeremiah. He pushed his mother to the limits with his attempts to bring pets home. Saleena shrieked and then shouted at his rabbits, porcupines, lizards and snakes, and frequently ordered him to keep the creatures out of their hut.

He caused havoc when his baby warthog escaped from the enclosure he had made for it. With tail erect, it screeched past every door in the compound, avoiding an army of children squealing in pursuit. Eventually they cornered it in the barn, where Petrus caught it in a thick blanket. While thus wrapped up, it protested strongly until Petrus let it loose in the nearby bush, with Jeremiah and the other children looking on. The little warthog took off like a bullet until well clear of them, then stopped, turned around, and grunted. Feeling free, it calmly trotted to the left and right, its tail proudly pointing toward the sky like an antenna beaming its location to its mother.

"Jeremiah, you can't separate a little animal from its family," his brother said. "Shame on you, man. Leave it to go find them." Petrus was always obeyed. Though just two years older than Jeremiah, he seemed far more mature and was hero-worshipped by all the younger children.

As Jeremiah grew up, he helped in the compound and eventually also on the farm, mainly tending to the farm animals. Initially he helped with the dogs and chickens, and later on with the large herd of cows. He was not paid, and Strydom did not have him on the strict working roster that he applied to the other workers, so Jeremiah had more time off than the others.

Jeremiah never went into the Strydom farmhouse. That was out of bounds.

Marius had enjoyed playing with Jeremiah from as far back as he could remember. They were the same age and liked the same games.

It had been drummed into Marius that he was a Boer and "Jeremiah is a kaffir". He knew that his pale European skin, dull like parchment, was unlike Jeremiah's shining mahogany skin. He sometimes envied Jeremiah's bristly hair that didn't have to be combed. When Marius woke in the mornings, his own straw-coloured mop stood up like tufts of African veld-grass. He could read Jeremiah's eyes like windows to his moods, while his own green eyes were unchanging and impenetrable. Marius was intrigued that each of their noses, quite different, resembled those of their respective fathers: Marius's short, thin nose ended in a triangle, but Jeremiah's long nose was high and broad. And why did his own narrow lips, almost invisible, mask and contain his feelings, whereas he could tell Jeremiah's temper at any time simply by glancing at his lips and supple cheeks?

It seemed to Marius that they were opposites in every conceivable way. And yet they got on like Kaiser and Blitz, the Strydoms' elegant, pedigreed German shepherd and lively, sleek Doberman, who were inseparable. Marius and Jeremiah were often accompanied on their adventures by the two dogs, who played along with them, sometimes enjoying a side romp together. Kaiser and Blitz backed one another up when confronted with unwelcome intruders such as porcupines, civets, foxes, rats, and snakes. Marius always felt safe with the dogs around.

On a hot summer day, he and Jeremiah were following the low river that intersected the farm. They were far from the homestead when the dogs suddenly took off together, barking frantically. Marius recognised their bravado turning to fear and panic; the tone of their yelping scaled up. Then he saw the leopard. He and Jeremiah called for the dogs to come back. The stealthy cat's eyes locked on to the dogs, who were not responding to the boys' calls. Sides heaving and noses fixed to the scent, the dogs burst into the grassy clearing and raced towards the big cat.

Marius and Jeremiah screamed louder. The leopard crouched low and tensed his body. He could have stood his ground but did not seem desperate enough to engage with the two frenzied canines. He turned to a tree and climbed the trunk with slow moves. On a large branch, he lay with his tail and left leg dangling, teasing Kaiser and Blitz. They barked and jumped up, trying to snap at him.

Marius ran home panic-stricken, the quicker Jeremiah a few paces ahead of him. He saw Jeremiah go straight to Thomas for help in retrieving the dogs. Before Jeremiah could get the full story out, the dogs galloped towards them and arrived panting, their long, thirsty tongues hanging loosely to the side through their teeth.

It happened often that Marius could think of nothing better to do than seek out his farm friend, Jeremiah, for playing and hunting together. Marius was accurate with a shotgun, able to blast the head off a snake from forty paces. But no matter how much he practised, he couldn't match Jeremiah's skill with a homemade knife. Jeremiah was able to peg a rabbit to the ground from twenty paces.

It seemed natural for Marius to ride and cavort naked with Jeremiah on a flying fox or the "foofy slide" rigged up by Hennie and his friends from neighbouring farms. They slid at great speed down a cable mounted on a large blue gum on the banks of the dam, and dropped like bombs with a colossal splash into the water below.

He and Jeremiah swam together, fighting for the large, worn tractor-tyre tube that floated around the dam. Its numerous patches told how often it had been repaired.

They paired up in games against Hennie's older gang. Particularly good at hide-and-seek, Marius and Jeremiah could never be found, yet were able to ferret Hennie's bunch out with no difficulty. But their games with the aggressive Hennie often turned nasty. He was unnecessarily rough with the younger Marius and, especially, with Jeremiah, who soon learned his boundaries.

When Marius and Jeremiah were on the foofy slide, Hennie and his friends ambushed them with a *kleilat* (pellet hurling) attack. They stung their unprepared victims with clay pellets flung from carefully selected pieces of green cane. From the tips of the yard-long shafts like fishing rods, the clay projectiles flew at whiplash speed to inflict maximum pain. Hennie's expert flick, strong arm, agile wrist and springy stick worked together so well that the fearsome missiles found the tummies of their defenceless prey. Marius and his tough friend were painfully branded many times as they hovered on the cable before crashing into the water.

Marius warned Jeremiah not to dare give Hennie the excuse to flog him for insubordination – even during play. They had seen Hennie beat compound children at the slightest provocation. They were there when Hennie broke one of Petrus's front teeth and his nose because he laughed when Hennie slipped in the mud outside the workshop.

"*Basie* (little boss), your brother … aai. He is too rough. He and his big friends attack me and the children when we play. We run away, but they catch and whip the slow runners."

"And you? Have they whipped you?"

"No. I'm always quick enough to escape and hide."

"That's good. Just keep away from him. I can't do anything about it. He will hit me too if I tell my pa."

Marius competed with Jeremiah as they fished from the dam and caught trout, which they gave to the compound residents in return for a slingshot or catapult or some other prize. They didn't like trout. Jeremiah agreed with him that there were "too many bones".

Jeremiah taught him how to make clay figurines – oxen, horses, lions, elephants, zebras and buck. They used clay warriors, no larger than four inches tall, to stage battles, backed up by their oxen and horses and, occasionally, the elephant. Marius set up the Boers, while Jeremiah planned and executed the battles for the British.

Under the willows, they killed rabbits and birds, which they either skinned or plucked. These they *braai'ed* (barbecued) over an open fire. Marius sneaked a box of matches from the kitchen to light the fire. He looked on as his nimble friend skewered the meat on strong twigs, which they held over burning firewood gathered in the bush.

Marius spent a lot of time in the workers' compound, running in and out of the workers' homes, playing tricks on them – quite at home there with Jeremiah. He enjoyed playing tok-tokkie on the unsuspecting residents: they knocked on doors or windows, ran away to hide behind bushes, and then giggled when the occupants came out saying, "Yeesss, who is it? … Who's there? … Aai, those naughty boys!"

And he chuckled behind his hands when they threw little stones on the corrugated iron roofs of the huts from a distance, avoiding detection by the angry inhabitants. They mixed up clothing on the various washing lines dotted throughout the compound, causing much confusion until Saleena found out. Jeremiah told Marius the next day that they had been caught. "My mother gave me a hiding, Basie. We can't do this anymore."

"Oh well. Maybe we'll leave it for a while. She'll forget in a few months." He knew she wouldn't raise her voice at the little white master.

He felt accepted by the people in the compound. He admired the toys they made him with wood and with clay, just as he saw them make for their own children. Some of the woodwork was painstaking and detailed, the faces full of expression: languid leopard and lazy lion, trumpeting elephant and guarded buck, looking and listening for danger. Marius hugged Thomas when Thomas gave him a lifelike vervet monkey. It looked so real in the shade of the stoep where Marius had placed it that Mrs Strydom took to it with a grass broom.

When the political commitments of the Strydoms took the couple to Pretoria, Marius would escape the homestead and camp in the bush with Jeremiah. They made a campfire with Marius's matches and cooked up some mielie meal, the stiff porridge made from crushed maize boiled and stirred in water or, better still, milk. When it was thick and firm enough, they clawed the clumps out of the pot with their fingers. Sometimes, if Saleena had some meat, she would give it to them to braai over a fire, or Marius would take some from the kitchen.

They took kudu skins with them and laid these on the ground to insulate themselves against the damp earth. Marius overlapped his with Jeremiah's so there was no bare earth between them. Thick, heavy blankets kept his body warm in the crisp night air. He and Jeremiah covered their heads with woollen skullcaps. He often found himself huddling up against Jeremiah in the frosty early mornings. At night, looking up into the vivid sky lit with the bright, flickering lights of heaven, they chatted for hours and hours.

such as fixing roofs, water pipes, taps, and household tools. Everyone on the farm knew that they could bring anything that broke to Alfred and he would fix it. Nothing was discarded unless Alfred declared, "This one's for the cemetery."

Alfred stressed to Jeremiah the importance of proper maintenance too. He showed him how to check the rubber hoses, and grease and oil the moving parts of the farming equipment. Jeremiah developed a fondness for the aging John Deere tractor that made the work on the farm easier and faster. They kept "Johnny" and his gadgets and trailers in crisp working order and were rarely called out to fix a broken part in the fields.

Working closely with Alfred through his teen years, Jeremiah fast acquired many skills of the mechanic. Although he had not attended school much, by school-leaving age he had become the person everyone turned to for repairing anything.

One day, as Jeremiah sat by the fire outside their hut with his parents, Alfred came over.

"Thomas," he said, "this young boy, he's clever."

"What do you mean? He hates school," responded his father.

"That's not everything, you know. His brains are for using his hands, for making machines well again. Don't worry about school. His future will be for fixing things."

"You tell Father Michael that," said Thomas with a chuckle and a wink at Jeremiah.

5

With barely twenty years of life behind him, all of it limited to the town of Guildford, in 1950 Neil bid farewell to his parents. Milton's eyes swelled with tears as he blessed his son's departure, slurring the words, "May the Lord be with you, my son." When Neil shook hands with him, he awkwardly pushed a clump of pounds into Neil's pocket.

Neil could barely see Milton's tears through his own blurred eyes as he said goodbye. He could not reconcile his alienation from his father with his heartbreak now at leaving him behind and so dependent. He could hardly recall the day his father had left for the war, tall, strong, and in command. Those indistinct memories were overshadowed by the pitiful sight before him.

Yet Neil respected him. He knew his father to be hardworking and honest, also faithful – to his family and his country. It was Milton's nature to be reliable and dutiful, if not passionate or spontaneous, just as it was Neil's to be entrepreneurial. His father was not to blame for the distance that had grown between them over the years, but Neil's understanding of this now only made the parting harder. He sensed that his father, too, knew this was their final farewell. At Milton's weeping, Neil broke down and hugged him for the first time ever – and the last.

Neil was expecting Mary to be more emotional, but when their eyes met, she quickly looked away. She did not say much to him. During the last ten minutes or so before he left, she was speaking to Mrs James. The speed and volume of her words increased as she looked over the other woman's shoulder, as if it was critical for Mrs James to complete the full set of pie recipes she was copying into a notebook.

When his uncle, Chapman Crook, came to collect Neil, Mary held her head high. Neil felt that his closeness to his mother enabled them to come through this parting just as they had lived. They had experienced their ups and downs and had simply got on with it. Although they had not articulated it, there also remained an underlying hope of being reunited after Milton passed away. Perhaps the day would come when Mary could join him. Neil knew it was only a matter of time.

❖

Neil managed to get a position as a waiter on the recently relaunched mail ship, *Pretoria Castle*, set for Cape Town. He looked to a future in a continent where "life is easy", or so a friend had told him of South Africa.

"Father's cousin works for the mines," his friend said. "He's made a fortune in no time. He has a huge house with housemaids and waiters at his beck and call, and gardeners for his massive garden. Acres and acres. He isn't coming back to England."

And Neil's cousin Henry, older by five years, was there too. Chapman Crook had sent his son to an uncle in Cape Town shortly before Henry's war papers arrived. Mary had later written to Henry, asking whether he could assist Neil.

"I know you're not overly fond of your cousin," she told Neil after sending off the letter, "but he's the only person we know in South Africa. Help of any kind will be better than nothing."

"I suppose you're right."

She had told him one afternoon about his father's attraction to her sister before she and Milton were married.

"You mean Aunty Jane?"

"Yes. Your father went out with her for some time. Always came to the house to pick her up. That's when I first saw him. But she was too flighty for him, and it came as no surprise to me when she got bored with him. I hated the way she hooted with laughter when she told me how clumsy your father was on the dance floor."

Neil's brow furrowed at the surprising revelation. It was obvious to him that his father and Aunty Jane were not suited to each other. "How on earth could he think—"

"Then she went off with Chapman Crook," she interrupted. "He was a band singer from London at the time – that was more her style! Well, she got what she was asking for. She never could appreciate the steady, honest ways of your father. Ooh, he really didn't like Chapman. 'Crook by name, crook by nature' is what he's always said about him."

"Yes, I do remember Father saying a couple of times, 'Jane got her crook all right'."

Mary smiled and nodded. "After they got married, I saw more of Milton, and two years later it was our turn. The rest you know."

The two families were not close, but they kept in touch for Mary's sake.

A few weeks after the letter was sent off to Henry Crook, mother and son were surprised to receive an envelope addressed to "Aunt Mary Robertson". It looked stiff and expensive, and bore a South African postage stamp. Henry's address was on the reverse. Mary ran to Neil's room, waving the envelope. They tore it open.

The first thing they found inside was a photograph of Henry in a smart suit, standing with one foot on the front bumper of a long American car. Then there was the letter. On fancy paper, Henry confirmed that South Africa was "the land of milk and honey, where servants do all the work". He was sure Neil wouldn't look back. He ended with the words, "Don't worry, Aunt Mary, I'll look after Neil." They read the letter three times, twice aloud for Milton to hear. Neil examined the photograph. "That's a Cadillac, Father!"

Mary nodded. "There you have it. Cousin Henry has paved the way for you."

Milton seemed unimpressed. "Not him ... useless boy. Yank car ... ghahh! Show-off!" he was able to say. "Watch out, Neil. Can't trust him, my boy," he spluttered. "He still owes us the money your mother lent them for his fare to South Africa. If he's got so much money, why hasn't he paid back the loan? Get him to pay you the money he owes us, Neil," said Milton, managing a distorted but sly smile.

In the first few days on the Atlantic Ocean, Neil's excitement at everything new helped him put Guildford behind him. From time to time he did think of Mary, who just might one day follow him, and of his father, who surely would not survive long.

Neil was keen to explore the ship with its many passages, rooms and closets. When not performing his duties as a waiter, he took walks around the ship and peered into every corner like a child playing hide-and-seek.

On the third day, he followed a crew member to the engine room. The smells reminded him of his father's workshop. But the similarities ended at the pipes, bolts and engine blocks – these were all massive and seemingly with lives of their own, like powerful animals heaving with all their might. The sounds of the pounding machines deafened him. The Robertson workshop had been a far cry from the soul-shuddering droning around him, but his thoughts went to his father. Milton, he knew, would have been in awe before the giant hall of toil and the synchronised technology driving tons of steel through deep, resisting waters.

His home had begun to feel far away, but now he knew with a jolt that it really was. And that he should not look back. He would prove that his mother's confidence in him was justified. He could not let her down.

He befriended one of the officers and asked to see the bridge. The hard, spotless edges of the narrow room stretched from one side of the ship to the other. Up on deck, he was overwhelmed by the infinite outlook beyond the ocean's powerful swell that constantly challenged the ship's resolute forward thrust. He felt powerless – not like the ship, more like a cork bobbing in the sea. What did his ambitions count for against this endless backdrop? *I'm not prepared for this. I have no trade, no skills and no experience.* But then what good could come of these doubts? Henry would be waiting for him in a Cadillac. Henry had had no better preparation and seemed to have done well enough.

The slow pace of the journey gave him time to think. He tossed and turned in his cot at night as his mind spun with the thoughts of what he wanted to achieve: a position in business that commanded respect. But he didn't know how. Anxious and impatient, he felt the need to do more about this now. The trip wasn't a pleasure cruise, he reminded himself. He decided to find a way to earn extra money.

Neil's tasks on the *Pretoria Castle* included assisting with the entertainment on board. He soon became one of the organisers and edged his way into the activities for the elderly in first class. He fussed about them, supervised the bingo, and helped them as they moved from the deck to their cabins or to the dining room. With his wit and jokes, he changed the hospital-like first-class decks, sealed in thick coats of sterile white paint, into lively congregations of elderly passengers playing cards, dancing, and laughing together during the sing-alongs he arranged for them.

Before long he knew which of the travellers were wealthy and generous. He took special care of them, even during his rest times, and earned more in tips during the trip than the aggregate of all the pocket money his mother had sequestered for him over the years. His confidence grew with his savings.

Neil had written in advance to Henry, telling him the date and details of his arrival. He had made a note of Henry's address in Cape Town. He had brought with him the photo of Henry beside the Cadillac, and upon arrival, he searched the dock and its surrounds for Henry and the car. They were nowhere to be seen.

"Henry's lost his money again," said the manager of the hostel located at the address on Henry's letter. "He's a good fellow but, you know, he gambles. On top of the world when he wins, on the bones of his arse when he loses. I've no idea where he is. If you want my advice, keep away from him, or you'll end up like him, son."

Neil stayed there for a week, hoping Henry would turn up. In the meantime he looked around for jobs. He had no specific skills and found the search more difficult than he had expected.

Until he saw a sign written neatly in black capital letters in a window of the Dromedaris Beerhall:

INGLISH SPEEKING BARMAN NEEDED

He observed the bar for a few hours. By the end of the night, the owner was exhausted after a busy evening's trade. Neil had obtained a little information about the proprietor from two of the patrons, who seemed to know him well and were obvious regulars. Neil, looking mature for his age in his father's suit, walked in and extended his right hand in greeting as confidently as he could.

"Mr Van der Westhuizen, my name is Neil Robertson. I read your sign. I speak English well and am a good worker."

Hans van der Westhuizen's bear-like clasp swallowed Neil's hand as they shook hands. The man was a tough and hardy descendant of

Dutch stock. "Hello, Meneer Robertson. I hope so, 'cause I want to increase my business."

"That's good, sir. How can I help?"

"Well, you see. It's like this. Generations of my family fight against the British. Now is my time to be ... how you say ... prag ... er ..."

"Pragmatic."

"Yes. That. I want more Iglish customers. That's where you come in. You be the Iglish barman. You speak the language. Make them feel like ... home. They spend money. Here." He pointed at the bar counter.

"That's easy," said Neil with a smile.

"I hope so, 'cause I look a long time for a Iglishman to work here. You carry on talk like Iglishman and get them to drink more."

Neil accepted Mr Van der Westhuizen's offer as a temporary solution. It gave him the opportunity to bide his time until he worked out how to make his fortune and maybe find Henry. With a job at the Dromedaris, at least he wouldn't starve.

❖

Neil relished joking with the customers but soon learned a lesson that Guildford had not prepared him for.

One evening he moved away from an Afrikaner patron to serve a customer waiting at the door. Over the weeks Neil had grown fond of the elderly man, who always stood at the doorway and beckoned to Neil. By now he knew that the old black man came to buy a bottle of gin for his boss. "Wait, sir," Neil said to the Afrikaner, who was so big that his hindquarters drooped over the bar stool, "until I serve this man who has been waiting a while, and then I'll return to you."

Inebriated, and by then on a short fuse, the Afrikaner stared for a moment and pointed at Neil. His round pink face turned tomato-red as he raised his voice. "You redneck *kaffir-boetie* (kaffir-brother), go back to England where you belong!" Nostrils flaring, the bovine-like patron stood up, knocking the bar stool over. He pursued Neil and aimed for his well-sculpted nose. Neil ducked, managing to protect his nose, but the powerful punch struck his forehead. He fell to the floor, temporarily stunned. Realising he was no match for the burly drunk, he lay hunched on the floor, immobile. He was relieved to see through his fingers meneer Hans van der Westhuizen rushing over with a rifle, yelling at the attacker. Neil lifted his head to see his boss prodding the customer out of the saloon-style doors with the barrel.

When the drunkard was gone, Van der Westhuizen turned around and faced Neil. "You lucky, my boy," he said, waving the heavy rifle that looked like a toy in his stocky hand. "You never serve no one before the whites. Rule number one is whites are first! And watch out for the Afrikaners; they don't like you rooineks. In fact, they don't like anyone except themselves."

This sounded a bit strange to Neil coming from Hans van der Westhuizen, a staunch Afrikaner. But then meneer Van der Westhuizen had been good to him.

Neil enjoyed the bar trade, where he could earn some extra money for himself by cajoling the customers into parting with more of their hard-earned cash. He wasn't past a little self-help; to his tips he added extra pennies when a patron was too drunk to realise he was being charged a small premium on the stated price. These coins Neil skilfully pocketed.

One of his tricks worked well on some patrons, and he had a good excuse to fall back on if caught out. He had encouraged meneer Van der Westhuizen to allow him to pack nuts in bags to sell for a penny. Neil strategically placed one such packet on the bar counter. When he assessed he could get away with it, he added a penny to the cost of the order and pocketed that penny for himself. He did this to the patrons he judged would not check their change. If he was challenged about it, he knew he could say that he thought the patron had placed the nuts there.

But he found himself in a jam when a penny-counting English army corporal, one Francis Harvey, didn't have enough for a sixth beer. Though quite drunk after the fifth, Corporal Harvey had carefully allocated his spending money. "Hey, what's happened here?" he slurred. "I'm a penny short." His little black eyes locked on to Neil. He was quivering in anger. He frowned and pointed a shaking finger at him. "You've short-changed me."

"I did not, sir. You must be mistaken."

Neil was so bold and confident that Corporal Harvey hesitated. In his less than sober state, he began to doubt himself. He checked his wallet again, turned it upside down, and searched his pockets carefully. "You must be wrong. I know how much I came in here with, how much I drank, and how much I have left. You've short-changed me, you little bugger. I know I had enough for six beers. But I'm a penny short." Much shorter than Neil, he raised his fists at the lanky young barman towering over him. From his stance, Neil realised he'd had some boxing training. "I am a penny short and you've got it! Give it back or I'll teach you a lesson." He was sobering up by the second and becoming progressively more hostile, placing his wound-up body at an angle, bending his knees, and rotating his fists a few inches under Neil's chin.

Neil realised this was the moment to call on his back-up plan. "But sir, what about the nuts you bought? You forgot to add the nuts, and they cost a penny."

"What nuts?"

"Those nuts there, on the counter, right where you were standing when you ordered the last beer. Look, they're still there."

He looked to where Neil was pointing. "I don't want them. They're not mine," said Corporal Francis Harvey, looking back at Neil.

"Oh, gosh, Corporal Harvey. I'm very sorry, sir. They were right here where you were standing. I thought you wanted them. Someone else must have left them there."

Corporal Francis Harvey looked down at the nuts again. "I didn't buy them. I never put them there."

"No harm done, sir." Neil opened the cash drawer, removed a penny, and held it between his index finger and thumb in front of the corporal's eyes. "Here's your penny, and I'll return the nuts to their rightful place in the box, here."

Corporal Harvey raised his right eyebrow and reclaimed his penny. Neil lifted the packet of nuts, held it up, and then patted it neatly into its box with the others. The little soldier was, by then, sober enough to want to avoid a fight. Harvey left the bar with his penny and his suspicions.

Neil felt relieved that, by his deft talk and air of self-assurance, he had been able to squirm out of the situation, but he'd already pocketed the penny. He replaced Corporal Francis Harvey's penny in the cash box as soon as it was safe to do so. He didn't want to cheat on his employer. That was not a good idea – you didn't steal from your boss, especially when he was meneer Hans van der Westhuizen.

With his enthusiasm to get rich quickly, Neil's savings soon built up, even though he sent money to Milton and Mary every month, hoping to repay within a couple of years the thirty pounds Milton had given him.

By 1951, Neil, approaching 21, was a strapping English South African, heir to Milton's blond-haired, blue-eyed good looks and athleticism, if not his muscular build – mainly because Neil didn't exercise much. All the manual work was done by African labourers. He had no steady relationship and tended to be frugal. His focus was on working up a good income, not on having a good time.

He spent well over a year at the Dromedaris Beerhall, benefitting from generous tips from the tipsy prosperous patrons and helping himself to some extras. His expenses were low because he lived in the drinking house's cellar, which he had cleaned and converted to a bedroom.

But before long he understood that there was more to South Africa than the so-called mother city. The real action was in Johannesburg. Most of what he saw coming through the Cape Town docks was destined for that city.

Neil had saved enough to keep himself going for a few months, but in Cape Town he was just treading water. It was time to move on. He began to look around for his ticket to the City of Gold.

6

Marius played with Jeremiah more than with his school friends. That was the way he preferred it.

But Marius felt hemmed in by his routine. It wasn't that he minded being driven to school in the mornings or participating every afternoon in after-school sports. He loved sport. He was happy to attend training sessions or to represent the school in interschool rugby and tennis competitions, often travelling many miles to neighbouring towns. But the activity left him no time to himself. Even when he returned home, he went straight to his homework and then dinner, prayer and conversation with his family.

While Marius attended school during the week, Jeremiah passed as much time as he could with Alfred in the work shed. He spent hours exploring the depths of the farm's cavernous corrugated-iron workshop that had accumulated decades of discarded materials. To him they were treasures. The shed was cold in winter and hot in summer, but this did not deter him. He found broken tools and toys, which he repaired with Alfred's help. He sought Alfred's permission to recycle two worn car tyres into compound toys that gave much pleasure to the youngsters, who chased them around the paths and used them for weekend tyre races.

He also resurrected two old copper and tin bed warmers, which he filled with hot water he had secretly heated over Alfred's fire next door. These he proudly presented to his parents on a cold winter's night.

On weekends, Marius found Jeremiah early on Saturday morning. They separated just in time for Marius to report for dinner in the dining room. Sundays, which the Strydoms dedicated to the Lord, found them attending church and returning home for a formal lunch, often with guests and sometimes with Oom Eben. After a restful afternoon of discussion or reading, they joined the Sunday evening congregation of Afrikaner families and then came home for a lighter meal and retirement.

In between these activities, Marius escaped to the dam, the veld, or the workers' compound, spending as much time as he could with Jeremiah. Marius knew his father was annoyed by his absence from the family gatherings when Hennie came to find his younger brother. Marius lost track of time when he was with Jeremiah. He scolded himself every time Hennie came to fetch him, and he undertook not to let it happen again.

It came as a surprise to Marius when, one Sunday night after their evening meal, Hennie called him. "Pa wants to see you, Marius. He's in his office," he said.

Strydom's large office was dominated by a heavy mahogany desk. Marius knew that one entered this room only by invitation, and not for a social chat. On that Sunday, he felt assailed by the breathless atmosphere and the stale smell of old furniture polish and the oiled-leather bindings of books. It made him nervous. The scene appeared to be set for some kind of severe communication, though he could not imagine what it might be about. Hadn't he just been with his father in the dining room? Why must he see him again so soon?

He found his father reading the Old Testament. He looked up when Marius came in. Before his son could sit, Strydom spoke. "Marius, you and Jeremiah must not play together again. You must keep apart. It is unseemly for you two to be so close, son. He is black and you are white."

"But Jeremiah works for us, Pa. He's in the garage all the time. We see him every time we go to the car."

"That's different. I don't speak to him like a friend. He's a kaffir."

"Yes, Pa. He is, but we do things together. I learn from him because he's good with his hands. He can fix anything. And he's good with his knife too."

"The kaffirs can't teach you what you need to know. Your future is not with these people or the farm, my son. You're not destined to fix things with your hands and fight with kni—"

"But, Pa, he still calls me baas."

"Don't interrupt me, son. You see? You're even forgetting your manners as you learn their ways."

Marius could see his father's anger reflected in the darkening redness of his face.

Then his father smiled at him. It was the same smile he had seen at the Ossewabrandwag meeting. And his pa spoke softly, as he had spoken then. "You need to understand the order of things, Marius. There are big things waiting for you in Pretoria. We will soon be in government. The sky is the limit. But not here on the farm with the animals. Let *me* take care of them."

Strydom's decrees were never questioned in his household. Marius dropped his head. "Yes, Pa," he said, not much louder than a whisper.

Seeing his son's disappointment, Strydom added, "I have plans for you. Just do your schoolwork and get good marks. You'll see. Oom Eben is a famous advokaat. He is getting briefed on big cases for the government. Your turn is coming, my son. Just do well at school."

And that became Marius's priority – to excel at school. He was athletic, too, and played rugby for the first team. He attended church regularly and read his Bible.

Faithfully obedient to his father's orders, Marius never went back to the compound. He saw Jeremiah on the farm and around the workshop but never approached him. He didn't mix with any of the farmhands or their families. He left the running of the farm to Strydom and Hennie. He didn't like Hennie's aggression towards the workers but felt it wasn't his place to do anything about that.

Marius became caught up in the political mood surrounding his father. Between 1946 and 1948, their beloved National Party, under the leadership of the Afrikaner Broederbond, rose to a political force to be reckoned with. Elections were for whites only. Marius could feel his father's excitement and drive. "We've got him now, Marius. Prime Minister Smuts has turned on his people, the workers – and now they will turn on him through the unions," Strydom said to a captivated Marius.

Strydom had predicted a change of government, and his dreams were fulfilled when Smuts's United Party was defeated in the 1948 election. Strydom had gone to Pretoria for a week, and at dinner on the first night of his return, his talk was of nothing else. The boys said little, but listened intently.

"We have kicked him in the pants, this *Generaal* Field Marshal or whatever-he-calls-himself Jan Smuts. Turncoat is what I call him. Good riddance to the United Party. United? What rubbish! The Divided Party is what I call it. The Englishman's party."

Mrs Strydom chimed in. She had met General Smuts, she declared, a few times at events in Pretoria. "And all I heard him speak of was the king and queen of England. Who are they, after all they've done to us in the past?" She shook her head. "This is a good lesson to traitors. I hope you children remember this day," she added, looking directly at Hennie and Marius. "The day our people won."

"Yes, Martha." Strydom nodded slowly. "Hah! We even kicked

Smuts out of his own seat." He chuckled. "We are finally getting our revenge. And yes, Ma, we must remember our women and children who died in those concentration camps." They sat quietly for a moment, and Marius thought of his oupa saving the ill and starving Strydom and De Wet children.

Martha Strydom brought the focus back to the present. "And this," she said, "is just one way of honouring the sacrifices of Oupa and Ouma Strydom and Ouma Marie De Wet. The Bible teaches us to forgive, but we will never forget."

The conversation soon turned to their new hero, Dr Danie Malan, in charge of an ambitious and well-organised National Party machine. The boys knew that their father was not the only Afrikaner stalwart who belonged to the party. A number of others were likewise former members of the Ossewabrandwag, and Marius suspected that some of these were now members of the Broederbond. A sense of privilege came to him with what felt like insider knowledge.

On one occasion some time after that successful election, Strydom went to his Church of the Willows and prayed to God. On his return, he called the family to the dining room, where they held hands and gave thanks to the Lord. Then he told them, "This is just the beginning. We have begun a campaign to put Afrikaners in place to teach and be the principals in schools, to be in charge of the police force and in the top positions in the civil service. We promised to look after the working class against the greedy English mining magnates and the Satan English empire," he sermonised.

Marius felt his father's grip conduct the prayer to his soul, like an electric current. He opened one eye and shut it fast when he saw his pa's determined frown, bowing before the Lord.

The messenger of God continued, "They have stolen our country's wealth for their kings and queens for so long! We fight for the workers of this country. For our Afrikaner people."

Marius knew that black people were not included in his father's political plan.

"This is God's country. This is the victory we have prayed for. That our fathers fought for. God has responded by giving us the government of South Africa, proving that we are God's people. Thank you, Lord. Amen."

Marius swallowed hard as though drinking his father's words. Yes, this had to be the work of the Lord. How else could the Boers have succeeded in taking the government from the mighty British? In his father's message, he sensed the part he would play in the future of an Afrikaner-dominated South Africa. It was a role he was hungry to fill.

Unwavering in the belief that he needed to be ready, Marius was a good student. At the age of 18, he stood before his father with a smile that reflected his pride. "I have been accepted to study law, Pa."

"I know, son. Well done. I've arranged for you to board at the student hostel at the Afrikaner University of the Highveld in Pretoria. You will make many friends there. With people like us."

Jeremiah's job in the workshop was ideal for him. He was learning from Alfred and he enjoyed the work, which was far better than the work in the fields. He avoided Hennie, who had whipped and kicked a number of the farmhands for "being lazy". Hennie was disliked within the compound. Word had got around that he was unpredictable. "Keep your head down when he approaches you," Thomas told Jeremiah. "Try to be invisible."

Jeremiah had developed an aversion for the Strydoms after he sensed Marius avoiding him. Marius had not done anything bad to Jeremiah. He had just cut off all communication without any explanation. Hennie and his antics incensed Jeremiah even more. He wasn't scared of Hennie and wanted to challenge him, but that would make life worse for him – and the others in the compound. So he walked away with bitterness in his heart when he saw Hennie shouting at someone.

If he saw Hennie approach the workshop, he would escape out the back entrance, believing that avoidance was the best way for his family to survive. "Just keep away from that ox," he told himself. "Alfred can see to him.'

On one occasion, when he was under a cart, repairing its damaged axle, he didn't see Hennie come in. The sharp pain of a strong kick at Jeremiah's protruding thigh confused him. Before he could say anything, he heard, "Wake up!" It was Hennie. "Don't sleep, you lazy *skelm* (rascal)!"

Jeremiah edged out from under the cart. He had been working with a big monkey wrench. He stood up slowly and held the spanner at a 45-degree angle to his right thigh. He and Hennie were about the same height.

Having left school, Hennie no longer played sport or exercised. He rode around the farm in the old Chevy truck. His former toughness was turning to flab. But he was aggressive and dangerous. Any of his blows that found its target could cause serious injury.

Jeremiah, still in his teens, was developing a muscular, athletic build. He had the agility and stealth of a leopard, fully aware of his surroundings. His shirt was off and his taut, sweaty skin glistened in the low light of the workshop.

There was no one else in the shed. Jeremiah stood three paces from Hennie. Their eyes met. "I … have … not … been … sleeping," Jeremiah said slowly.

"Don't lie. I saw you lying there. Are you calling me a liar?"

"I'm saying that I wasn't sleeping. Otherwise why have I got this in my hand?" He was within striking distance and lifted the long, solid iron wrench shoulder high.

"Put that down! Down!" Hennie shouted, pointing to the ground.

"Oh, I'll put it down. That won't make a difference. My hands are strong enough." Jeremiah's voice was soft and low. He could feel the beads of perspiration gathering on his forehead. He licked his lips.

As he put the spanner slowly on the ground, keeping Hennie in his sights, Hennie grabbed a spade from the cart. Just then Alfred entered. Jeremiah realised that Alfred couldn't quite see what was going on while his eyesight adjusted from the outer brightness to the dark workshop.

"Hello, kleinbaas," Alfred said to Hennie. "Can I help?"

Jeremiah was not deterred. It was now or never, he thought. He moved towards Hennie slowly, ready to pounce. He so wanted to land that perfect blow, despite that spade in Hennie's hand. Dammit! Alfred would have seen the spade by now, and must be feeling the tension in the air … but oh, how Jeremiah wanted to attack Hennie!

"Jeremiah, your father needs help at the water tank. Go." Alfred's voice was low and steady but his tone urgent.

Jeremiah looked across at him and then back at Hennie.

"*Now!*" Alfred shouted at him.

Jeremiah stepped a few paces backwards.

Hennie threw the spade into the cart, turned around, and walked out without saying a word.

Alfred sighed deeply. "I arrived just in time, Jeremiah. You must *pasop* (beware). Hennie will kill you. I'll have to tell your father what happened here. He must know. You must tell him too."

"It's a matter of time, uncle. A matter of time," Jeremiah mumbled and walked out the back door.

Jeremiah knew everyone in the compound, including a woman who was a few months younger than him.

One day he saw her with Petrus in a remote part of the compound.

They were walking towards the riverbank and did not see him. Like Jeremiah, Petrus was athletic and handsome.

But this sighting with Rachel confused Jeremiah. His brother was steady with – and promised to – Harriet, who also lived in the compound with her parents. They were to get married later in the year. *What was Petrus doing?*

Later that day Jeremiah told Petrus that he saw them together. "If anyone else had seen you there would be a scandal. All three families will be hurt."

Without betraying any concern, Petrus said that it was a just a close friendship. "It's not romantic," he said. "Harriet is my only love. Don't spread false rumours," he threatened.

Jeremiah was not so sure. He had heard Petrus and Rachel talking like love birds and then he saw them holding hands.

His suspicions were confirmed when he asked Rachel about them. He told her that Petrus's promise to Harriet could not be broken. "I know," she said. "But I love him. I try to put my feelings for Petrus aside. But, I just can't."

"This can't end well for you."

Tears filled her eyes.

Jeremiah put his right arm around her shoulder. "You'll find someone better. You must try to forget him."

They sat without talking for a while and she composed herself. But Jeremiah felt his heart beating fast.

After that day he made a point of seeking her out and spending more time with her and she seemed to like being with him. He enjoyed their long walks: holding hands, talking, giggling, and sometimes just walking quietly.

Now and then they disappeared together for hours on end, especially on Sunday afternoons.

By 1951 Jeremiah had left the farm.

His departure was not planned or chosen by him. He fled following an incident during one of Marius's university vacations. The episode started when Jeremiah passed Marius briskly one day. Each looked the other way without acknowledgement. Marius walked towards the large tomato garden where Jeremiah knew that Rachel was picking tomatoes for the market. Jeremiah was on his way to his family's hut to collect a broken brazier grill for repair.

As he came out of the hut, he almost collided with Rachel. She was in tears. Surprised to see him in the compound, she tried to turn and run away, but he caught her by the arm. "What happened, Rachel?"

"Nothing. I fell." She tried to cover her left breast with her torn dress.

"Don't lie. I can see you're lying!"

"It's true."

"I can tell you're lying. How could you fall and cause that kind of tear without dirtying your clothes? I can see what happened. Someone attacked you! Who was it?" He searched her eyes for an answer.

"No, no. Basie just touched me like this and my dress tore."

Jeremiah realised that she had inadvertently let slip the identity of the culprit in her attempt to minimise the severity of the incident. But he didn't see the incident as minor. How could Basie Marius treat Rachel with such contempt? And, he wondered, did Marius even know about him and Rachel?

He became convinced that not only did Marius perceive him, Jeremiah, as not good enough to be his friend any more, but now he was adding this insult of abusing Jeremiah's girlfriend and dishonouring her – and him – by fondling her breasts. And who knew what Marius would have done if Rachel hadn't run away?

Jeremiah felt his pulse beat and his head throb. Shaking with anger, he raced back to the tomato garden where he found Marius, Hennie, and a number of farmhands installing a new trellis.

He pointed at Marius. "How dare you attack my girlfriend?" he shouted.

"What are you talking about? I didn't do anything."

"You lie. You lie." He tried to stop his finger quivering. "You attacked Rachel. She said Basie tore her dress *by mistake*. You made her cry. You—"

A couple of the farmhands came up to Jeremiah and pulled him away. He shook them off and stepped towards Marius.

"Who said that? Listen here," said Marius. "I didn't. I don't know what you're talking about. You're making a big mis—"

Jeremiah's punch hit him full in the face. Marius fell to the ground like a sack of potatoes and lay still, unconscious.

For the briefest moment, Jeremiah stood staring down in surprise.

But then Hennie kicked at Jeremiah. "I'll get you for this, you fuckin' kaffir! I'll get you." He missed. Jeremiah was too quick and dashed away. After a brief chase Hennie gave up and stooped with his hands on his knees, panting for breath.

Jeremiah ran to Thomas and explained what had happened. "Go to Alfred's hut," said Thomas. "Stay there. I'll speak to you later."

Thomas judged that an escalation of the issue could see confrontation and bring the matter to the attention of Baas Strydom. That, he thought, was something no one wanted, least of all Marius.

He went to Marius. "Kleinbaas, I don't know what happened and why it happened," he lied. "But I am very sorry. I am sending Jeremiah to his uncle in Johannesburg. He will be gone tomorrow. I'm not going to say anything to Baas Strydom about the incident." He calculated that Marius wouldn't want his father to find out why he was sporting a black eye and would also want to conceal the fact that a Strydom tore the dress of a black farm girl.

Marius didn't look him in the eye, but Thomas was relieved when the young man said, "I also will say nothing to my father about this incident. But Jeremiah shouldn't have done this. He's made a big mistake. Tell him he must never come back. He said some very wrong and bad things about me. He should know me better than that. If he is so violent, he can't come back. I don't want to see him on this farm, ever."

"Yes, kleinbaas." Thomas retreated. He felt some satisfaction after seeing the purple around the half-closed left eye that had avoided looking at him – just like a guilty man. The little swine had been taught a lesson. He judged that a knock-out punch in the face in front of others was punishment enough for Kleinbaas Marius.

He also knew that Jeremiah should look for another life in the city, a better life, especially with his skills in mechanics. He hoped that, in due course, he would be able to work on reversing the banishment of Jeremiah from the farm.

As it happened, Thomas had been considering asking Saleena's brother, Samson, to find Jeremiah a job in Johannesburg. It was, after all, the biggest city in South Africa. Samson worked at a car repair shop. If anyone could find a job for Jeremiah, he could. But in the light of this latest incident, there was no time for arranging anything in advance. Jeremiah would have to leave within a day and find his uncle.

The next day, Thomas dispatched Jeremiah with a few pounds collected from workers on the farm, who could see the wisdom of letting Jeremiah go. They all knew what had happened and were willing to make sure that there were no repercussions for Jeremiah – or for themselves.

Baas Jacobus Strydom didn't enquire about Jeremiah until he noticed his absence some ten days later. He asked Thomas where his son was. Thomas said that Saleena's brother had found a job for him in Johannesburg and had sent for him.

That night Marius noticed a smirk on his father's face when they sat down at the dinner table. "Have you heard?" his father asked, turning to him. "Jeremiah has left us without even saying goodbye. After all we did for him. Now you know what kind of people these are. No loyalty." Marius and his brother kept silent.

Marius's position in the household remained that of the obedient son whose black eye was due to a mishap while helping to install the trellis. "I told you, Marius. You're not made for this kind of work. You stick to the law," his father said with a proud laugh.

At first Jeremiah was very upset that he had to leave. After all, Marius had got what he deserved. But after boarding the bus for Johannesburg, he observed the well-dressed and prosperous-looking black villagers returning to their work in the city. He began to feel hopeful and slightly less resentful.

The journey seemed unending. When night came and darkness enveloped the bus, Jeremiah's apprehension returned. After many hours and stops along the way, he saw the city lights in the distance. As they grew bigger, Jeremiah liked what he saw. He began to feel sure those lights must stand for the opportunities in his future, waiting for him.

He hadn't wanted to stay on the farm his whole life. This could be the break he deserved. The opportunity of a lifetime perhaps.

Thank you, Basie Marius.

7

Neil was eager to leave Cape Town, but the trip to Johannesburg would be costly. He had worked and earned some money during his passage on the ship. Why not find a way to be paid in full for his travels now?

After asking around among some of the beer hall customers, he found that way: he would hitch a ride to Johannesburg by offering to help load a truck transporting goods there. The "goods" turned out to be liquor shipped from England. In truth, there wasn't much work for him. The truck was loaded by the time he arrived, and packers would be on hand to offload on the other side.

The hardest job was to keep Jimmy Doyle, the Irish driver, awake on the long stretches through the searing Karoo heat. Jimmy was about thirty. Thin and short, to Neil he looked like a most unlikely choice for a truck driver. He could hardly reach the pedals and sat at the edge of the worn seating, its sponge flesh oozing out of the wounded upholstery. He leaned his shoulders over the large black steering wheel, and when he turned the corners, his whole body followed the wheel as if it were steering him. He just managed to floor the pedals with not an inch to spare.

It was obvious to Neil, when he first saw the former army transport truck, that the vehicle had seen better days. Neil wasn't sure if it would get them to the end of the street with all its shivering and shaking. But Jimmy had it worked out, revving the engine high at stops to prevent it from stalling. Occasionally it would emit black smoke in a cough that sounded like its final gasp or an attempt to rid itself of some evil force within. The cab was a faded dusty brown. The canvas pulled over the distorted frame was torn in places and frayed at the edges, but it still provided a canopy for the precious alcoholic payload.

From the way it rattled and shook, Neil had the impression that the 1930s Bedford was on its last legs. But whenever Jimmy's "Old Girl" threatened to come undone at the next stop, somehow all her parts seemed to take Jimmy's cue and pulled together to haul the coveted cargo to Johannesburg.

Some of the roads weren't sealed, and the truck took a hammering from Jimmy, who hardly slowed down for ruts. "She's a tough old girl. This is nothing for her, Neilie, my friend. We don't want to be late."

"Late for what? Are you getting married?"

"Oh, that's funny. You're a real joker, you are. No, we've got urgent business at the pub on Saturday. There's a lot of talent in the Golden City, my friend! And I know where to find it."

Neil was soon accustomed to the vibrations of the old girl and the odours of fuel and oil in the black fumes she emitted. As they got further away from Cape Town, he heard, felt and smelt less of her, and was able to behold and breathe in the serenity of the large empty tracts of land that stretched as far as the eye could see, a view interrupted only by the small towns that dotted the journey.

As he looked out over this land, he began to think that "empty" was not the right word. The flora and fauna were too abundant. Even the dry Karoo was carpeted with stunning natural bouquets. Neil saw hare, two types of buck, mountain zebra, wild ostrich, and many types of bird. Jimmy seemed to know something about the birdlife.

He told Neil the names of some, explained their habits and even imitated their calls. "There's plenty more, but you can't see them. This country is full of birds, my boy. Bird paradise, it is."

Every little town they passed through had at least one church, a post office, a general store and a petrol station. Yet each seemed to have a unique character. As Neil saw it, the wealth of the district was reflected in the number and grandness of the churches in this God-fearing land.

Jimmy drove for hours and hours, hardly stopping. "We have things to do, Neilie. The bright city lights are awaiting you. There's no time to dawdle."

Of course he got tired, and Neil had to engage him in discussion to keep him awake, asking him questions about his life and experiences and telling him stories. At some stage they both dozed off. The shuddering of the old girl as she hit the stones beside the road jolted Neil awake. "Jimmy, wake up! Wake up!"

Jimmy flung his body over the steering wheel and swung it right and left, his head and shoulders moving like a compass trying to find north. When he finally brought them back onto the road, he and Neil relaxed slightly, but both remained on the edge of the bench seat.

Neil's grey face was drained of colour. Mouth dry from the potential disaster just avoided, he could barely talk. "You're going to kill us, Jimmy. Let me drive; then we'll take it in turns."

"No, my friend. Your Jimmy will get you there."

The next time, Neil was able to warn Jimmy before they careened off the road. Again Neil asked to help with the driving. ""Hell, Jimmy, you'll kill us! I can drive, you know. I worked in my father's garage and drove the cars around the yard all the time."

"This is a truck and this is an expensive load." Jimmy pointed to the back.

"I've driven Sir Roger Hackett's Rolls Royce Phantom III. That's an expensive load!" He didn't mention the damage he had caused it.

"Okay, Neilie-boy. Let's see. And you'd better not let the liquids in the back find any way of getting out of their safe bottles!"

Even with stops along the way, they made good time. By sharing the driving they kept the Bedford going through much of the night and arrived in Johannesburg mid-morning on Friday, more than half a day early. "Great!" Jimmy said. "We can have a quick nap, and I'll start showing you the bright spots of Johannesburg tonight."

Jimmy reversed into the yard of the jail-like warehouse of Imperial Liquor & Beverage Distributors & Wholesalers (Proprietary) Limited. An army of black labourers stripped the old girl's canvas dress, exposing her valuable cargo. Like a synchronised military operation, they passed the crates down, throwing them from the truck with perfect timing and to the rhythm of their harmonised baritone songs. The crates were handed along to the edge of the warehouse, where more men built high stacks. Their pulse and the song were so engaging that Neil watched in awe.

Within an hour the old girl stood bare, her frame all bent like a carcass that vultures had picked at, leaving only the skeleton. It was unimaginable that this spent force could be resurrected, but the workers soon had her dressed in her worn covers. At Jimmy's first touch of the starter, she exploded back to life.

Jimmy took them to a boarding house, where a Mrs Botha let rooms to single European men. On the way, Jimmy explained, "I've met people from all over Europe here. I hear their sad stories and their dreams of wealth. All of them found jobs."

"Really? What jobs?"

"I've met welders, plumbers, electricians, painters, bricklayers and so on."

"But I've got no qualifications."

"Lots of them didn't either. They just said they did and were snapped up – just like that!" Jimmy snapped his fingers. "Some of my friends without any skills got jobs on the mines. They were white – that's all they were. You'll pass that test!" He chuckled. "They need Europeans to supervise the thousands of blacks on the mines. They pay you to look at the natives work! You'll see."

"But I don't know what to do."

"Agh, don't worry about that. They train you or you simply learn on the job. It's not that hard. The natives do the labouring. Pay's good. Much better than you'll get back home. Gone are the days of being frugal, my boy. You'll be wealthy sooner than you think!"

Mrs Botha's boarding house was a single-level red-brick building. Lining its front walls, several hydrangea bushes bursting with huge purple-blue flower clusters gave it the look of a family home. A fence of white wrought iron in a pattern of curves and twirls kept the public out.

Jimmy opened the matching gate. Neil followed along a narrow path of patterned ceramic tiles to a shining green stoep and then into the small entrance hall. A coat and hat stand with a mirror inlay was the only furnishing. They went to the kitchen. Through the open back door, Neil noticed that two wings extended to the rear of the property, making the house U-shaped. This couldn't be seen from the front.

The high-ceilinged kitchen, although large, was dominated by the rotund woman leaning over the stove and stoking the coals beneath a lifted hotplate. When she stood erect, her body extended to a greater height than Neil had expected. She was imposing, and clearly ruled over her domain.

"Neilie, this is Mrs Botha," Jimmy said.

She stood motionless, the poker in her right hand pointing ominously at Neil.

Neil could see that Mrs Botha had been beautiful in her twenties. She was now a matriarch in her fifties. Her sapphire eyes scanned Neil from head to toe. Her yellow hair was greying and had been drawn into a tight bun that proclaimed discipline. Each wisp of hair was in its right place. Every crease and wrinkle of her moon-shaped face bore witness to a life of struggle. A plain pink collar framed the high neckline of her dress which had a matching blossom print. The inexpensive and crisply ironed material fitted tightly around her large bosom. Her skin was plump, pale pink, slightly freckled and very soft, as evidenced by her large elbow dimples. She wore rubber-soled closed shoes, low and comfortable.

"Mrs B," said Jimmy, "I have a new customer for you. This is Neil. Now, don't forget my commission."

"Listen, Missterr Doyle," she boomed. "Don't you play games with me. First, don't 'Mrs Bee' me. My name is Missus Botha, proenounced Booetta." She pronounced the "t" strongly, in a full plosive with a silent "h". "Second, I should charge *you* commission for taking in your riffraff."

Mrs Botha spoke English with a distinct and heavy accent that Neil knew to be the influence of Afrikaans.

Turning to Neil, Mrs Botha said, "Did Mr Doyle tell you my rates?"

"Yes," said Neil with a forced smile.

"I bet you he hasn't told you the rules: no drink, no girls, and no noise. Otherwise I'll kick you out. Breckfiss is porrich and the best *koffie* (coffee) you ever had. Just help yourself or ask Ennie to get it for you." She looked in the direction of the adjoining scullery, where Neil could see a stocky African maid washing pots in the large sink. Then Mrs Botha pointed to the coal stove, where a brew was boiling away in the biggest kettle he had ever seen. Neil had felt pleasantly welcomed by the coffee aroma as soon as he entered the front door.

He took off his hat and extended his hand to Mrs Botha, bowing slightly. "Mrs Booetta," he said, careful to pronounce her name correctly. "Very pleased to meet you." He turned on his most charming voice.

She stared at him.

"Your koffie smells very good. I would be most grateful if I could have a cup now."

A knowing smirk shifted her wrinkles aside as though she had just won their first battle. She ambled over to an enamel-green kitchen cabinet with open shelves and removed a leaf-green mug. Into it she poured the muddy syrup until there was about half an inch to spare. She placed it on the large trestle table in front of Neil. She then brought him two matching pieces: one a bowl of sugar, the other a jug of creamy milk covered by a lace doily with beads around the edge. She pointed to the kitchen chair nearby.

"Mr Neil," she said, "now you know where everything is. You can help yourself at any time, *if*—" she added slowly "—I take you in. Now, let me see 'bout that."

"I'm going to have a quick sleep, Neil. See you later." Jimmy abandoned Neil to negotiate with Mrs Botha.

After some hard bargaining, Neil gave eight weeks' rent in advance. Mrs Botha wouldn't budge on that requirement. "That is 'cause I doesn't know you yet, Mr Neil." In return, he got a small room with a window facing the courtyard. She had shown him a number of rooms, all of them spotless. Furnishings consisted of a lumpy bed covered with a crocheted woollen bedspread in two tones, a bedside table and a wardrobe. Nothing else could fit in. He chose the cheapest and the smallest – the one with the bedspread made of green and yellow squares.

By the time Neil had finished his third mug of Mrs Botha's koffie and four of her beskuits, he had charmed her with his acknowledgement that it was indeed "the best koffie I have ever had" and with his gift of getting people to talk about themselves. He discovered that she had grown up in a family that had fought the English in both Boer Wars.

She had lost her husband in a mining accident. "He was the boss of a team of miners. They went underground, and they weren't blerrie-well told there was another team going to blast rocks near them. Bang." She clapped her hands and the fat of her arms shook. "A big underground rockfall. I swear I feel it ten miles away, in my feet and in my heart, Mr Neil. Dead. Thirty-two of them. My Koos was the first to die. He was the boss down there. But they dirrent look after them. And they dirrent looked after us, the Englishmen miners."

As she spoke there was no change in her diction, no moisture in her eyes, no vulnerability. Blame, yes. Anger, yes. Surrender, no.

"That was nearly eight years ago. He left me with six children. I just got on with life. Do you know how I manage to survive?"

Before Neil could respond, she answered her own question. "I was helped by an Englishman. The same people who fought against my family, who were so cruel to my people in those wars, and who then killed my Koos. I dirrent want to take charity from Major Charters. But I had no choice. He says to me, 'Mrs Botha, you can use this house. Pay me rent and collect as much as you can, but keep it neat, clean and painted.' Sometimes I coorrent pay the rent and he just say, 'Pay me when you can, Mrs Botha.' Can you believe it? My enemy treat me like that? He's a good Christian, Mr Neil. May the Lord Jesus bless him and forgive him and his people their sins. I added those eight rooms down your passage. We live that side," she said, pointing to a passage going to the right side of the courtyard.

Neil made a point of telling her he came from a family that had a petrol station and motor car repair shop in England. She paused and sat back. Then she looked at him and up to the ceiling. "Mr Neil, the good Lord Jesus bring you here."

"What do you mean?"

"Mr Van Tonder has a garage that does just that, you know … petrol and fixing cars. He's not well, and Mrs Van Tonder is looking for someone to manage for her. Maybe there's a job for you orreedy. I send the boy to give her a message." She stood up and put her head out the back door. "Piet! Piet! *Kom hier* (Come here)," she shouted.

Neil said, "I'll go. I need to see it first. What is the address?"

There was a knock on the back door. A voice from the doorway said, "*Ja* (Yes), Miesies?" To Neil's surprise, the "boy" was an elderly grey-bearded African, who appeared to be well into his seventies. He was thin and tall and dressed in faded brown working clothes. He stood just outside the doorway, slightly bowed, his cap in his hands.

"No, no, Mr Neil. It's quite far. It's the other side of town. Let Piet go. He can ask her if she still wants someone. If she does, then you go."

But Neil wanted to do a bit of reconnaissance. He was able to persuade Mrs Botha that he needed to see Johannesburg and wanted to go, after which "the boy" was dispatched back to the yard, shaking his head in obvious confusion as to why he had been summoned in the first place.

After three strong koffies and with the prospect of a job, Neil had no inclination to lie down. He went for a quick wash in the "guest bathroom" – an outhouse in the courtyard – and changed into his only suit. When he came out, Piet appeared from the shadows of the yard and approached him.

"Baas," he said, looking at the ground between them, his cap in one hand and a piece of paper on the other.

Neil stopped and looked at him. "Yes?"

Piet delivered the note to Neil with both hands as a sign of respect.

The note, on plain cheap paper, was from Mrs Botha, addressed in very neat handwriting to "*Mevrou* (Mrs) Magdalena van Tonder, Top Star Garage, Eloff Street, Johannesburg". Piet explained in broken English that Mrs Botha had gone to the shop and left this for "the baas".

"Thank you, Piet." He gave Piet a farthing. Neil left the hostel, intending to walk alone to the Top Star Garage via the city centre. Piet followed him. "Piet, there is no need to come. I'll find it."

"Miesies Botha, she say I go with."

"That's not necessary. You stay here."

"No, baas. Miesies Botha. She say I go."

"I'll explain that I told you to stay. Go back now."

"Sorry, baas. Miesies Botha is my miesies. I follow. That way."

He pointed in a direction and Neil marched as instructed, with Piet in tow.

8

Uncle Samson drew back, clearly surprised to be greeted by the young man who stood at the gates of his workplace at day's end.

Someone at the central Johannesburg bus station had told Jeremiah, "You can walk to Oxford Motors. Rosebank isn't far."

"Walk?"

"Yes. You're a strong boy. It's only a few miles north of the city centre. You'll find it. If you get lost, everyone knows Oxford Road. Just ask and walk north."

The walk was farther than he thought, but he found Oxford Motors easily and sat on the pavement across the road until the end of the workday.

A group of workers he approached as they were leaving pointed out his uncle, who was in conversation with a couple of men. Jeremiah waited until the men left, and then called to his uncle as he walked through the gate.

Seeing his confusion, Jeremiah went right up to him and said, "Uncle Samson, I am Jeremiah, your nephew."

Samson frowned. "Who? Who are you? My nephews live on a farm."

"I am Jeremiah, Saleena's son."

"Haaoow, Jeremiah!" Samson's face broke into a jovial smile that resembled Saleena's. But then Uncle Samson paused and frowned again. "But what brings you here, nephew? What've you done wrong?"

"Aai, Uncle. You know too well. I'm wrongly accused. I hit the bastard, but he denied he touched my girl. I know it's him."

"Who ... what?"

"It's a long story, but Kleinbaas Marius attacked a girl I know, and I punched him. Wasn't that the right thing to do?"

"Well, I don't know. That's what you tell me, but look what's happened?"

"What's happened? I'm in Jo'burg. This is my new life. This is the best thing that's happened to me."

"Are the police looking for you?"

"No. He was wrong. But I couldn't stay on the farm."

There was another pause in which his uncle seemed to come to terms with this unexpected visit. Jeremiah shuffled his feet as the older man looked long and hard at him. Samson shook his head, drew a deep breath, and let out a long two-toned whistle. "Life isn't easy here. It's hard work and no money."

"I can work as a mechanic. You know how good I am in the workshop? I know Baas Strydom's machines back to front – even his beautiful Buick."

Samson shook his head again. "We're all just workers here. Only the whites are paid like mechanics."

"That's okay, Uncle. I will work like you." Jeremiah's voice remained strong and unwavering.

"Yes, but the city isn't for a farm boy. They will eat you alive here."

"Weren't you a farm boy before the city? In any case, I'm a fixer. Give me something to fix and you'll see." He extended his hands towards Samson, palms up, as though about to receive his first engine part to repair.

Samson waved his right index finger. "No, no, no, my boy." Then he stopped and looked at his young nephew, who had not flinched. "Listen here, Jeremiah. This is the big city. There are many *tsotsis* (rascals). Don't trust anybody. Of course I'll try to help you, but be careful. You must have eyes in the back of your head."

"Okay, Uncle. I understand you." He turned and looked behind him as if demonstrating his ability to be on guard. "See? But I've got nowhere to stay. Can I sleep at your house for a while?"

"Haaauw. What house? I haven't got a house. You can't just turn up and say you want me to give you a house. This isn't the farm, my boy."

"Where can I sleep?"

"You see? This is the big city. It's different here."

Jeremiah sensed that Samson was holding back, or was it that he found it awkward to explain the situation? But Jeremiah pressed on. "What's different? I can stay where you stay."

"Where, Jeremiah? I work in the white town. There's no house for me here."

"So, where do you sleep?"

"I am very lucky. I have a friend whose boss lets her sleep in a backyard room. I share her room with her."

"Oh." Jeremiah's voice faltered for the first time when he realised that Samson shared a bed with his girlfriend.

"Yes, you see. Agnes has a room in the servants' quarters at the house she works in. She is a maid for a rich family in the white suburb of Houghton. Fancy house in a fancy area, but we can only work there, not live there."

"Oh. Do they let you sleep there too?"

"Only because they never see me. I creep in and out. I keep quiet and never cause trouble. Sometimes I help to fix things over at the house."

"I can do that. I can fix things for them too."

"But where will you sleep? Not in Agnes's room. I won't even ask her."

"Oh. I see."

"I told you, you're a farm boy. Only the whites have their own homes here. But I'll see what I can do. You'll have to come with me. Let's see what we can arrange for a short while, until we can find something for you somewhere else. Tomorrow we'll ask my boss whether he will give you a job."

"Thank you, Uncle. Thank you very much."

"Now, I'm catching a bus. Have you got money for the fare?"

"Yes, Uncle. My father gave me some."

"Show me."

Samson looked on when Jeremiah produced the few pounds that Thomas had mustered to see him through until he could find a job. Jeremiah held the precious notes and coins in his palm. Samson quickly grabbed the money before Jeremiah could protect his cash. "What did I tell you? Never trust anyone. Now, I hope you've learned that lesson well."

Jeremiah looked at him in shock, his mouth gaping.

Samson laughed aloud. "Have you learned your lesson? Have you? What are you going to do?"

Jeremiah regained his composure. "I now see I can trust nobody." He wanted to hit his uncle in the face just as he had punched Basie Marius. But he sensed it would be better to bide his time. Maybe he could get the better of his uncle in due course. Right now, it would do him no good to make an enemy of the only person he knew in Johannesburg. "But Uncle, as you know, this isn't my money."

Samson took his hand, held it firmly, and thrust the money back. "It *is* your money. Money your father has worked very hard for. You also will work hard and get some money. You must look after it because no one else will. Do you understand?"

Jeremiah burst out laughing and pointed at his uncle. "You clever man, you clever uncle. You wise old elephant. You taught me my first lesson in Jo'burg. I can feel many more lessons coming along. But I see I can trust you!" He quickly put the money into his pocket, took his uncle in both his big arms, and hugged him tightly. "We are going to have a good life together."

From the look on Uncle Samson's face, he wasn't sure that Jeremiah had learned anything, but he warmed to the reaction. "We are family and we have each other. But listen, Jeremiah …" He pointed his right index finger at Jeremiah and poked it into Jeremiah's chest with each word. "Don't … trust … anybody."

Jeremiah nodded slowly and gave back a look of earnestness that seemed at last to satisfy his uncle.

"Now, come. I'll pay your bus fare. Today only, Nephew." He turned round and walked away.

"Thank you, Uncle." Jeremiah followed with extra bounce in his step.

They did not go to any bus station, but walked less than the distance Jeremiah had walked from the city, to Houghton, the exclusive whites-only suburb about three miles north of the centre of Johannesburg.

"Where is the bus?"

"No bus, Jeremiah. We can walk all the way. That's why I'm paying the fare." Samson laughed in a way that made Jeremiah think of his mother.

"Ha ha, Uncle. I'm learning very fast."

They went down leafy avenues of tall trees. As they immersed themselves deeper in the well-heeled suburb, the houses swelled in size and the jade-coloured spaces between homes grew, abounding in trellises, trees and other vegetation. Jeremiah looked around him and thought he was in paradise. It was calm, serene, and country-like. The occasional large motorcar passed by or entered a large, open gate and then drove up a meandering driveway towards a stately mansion.

Jeremiah followed Samson through a functional picket side gate into an immaculate garden. The gate was painted cream, the same colour as the thick three-foot-high rendered wall into which it was built. A large double-gated entry for vehicles interrupted the wall further along. His eyes took in those iron gates, painted green and wrought in the shape of vines, leaves and flowers weaving up and down, with a fat flower in gold here and there. Of course! He'd heard Marius call them proteas. A lane of polished slate led from a matching gate to the house. He recognised pink flowers, just like those Miessies Strydom planted every year. Here they bordered the lane right up to the homestead, which was set back a distance of some seventy or eighty yards from the road.

He had never seen a building like this. Painted in various shades of white to cream, its walls were smoother than mud. Round windows looked down from the second storey, and made Jeremiah wonder what was behind them. Was anyone up there looking at the two of them? He felt like an intruder being peered at by all the occupants from every pane.

Then he saw the stylish semicircular veranda entrance with a half-round roof supported by solid off-white columns. He stopped to examine the large white double door inlaid with glittering silver, grey, white and sparkling yellow stained-glass panels of rectangles and squares – some corrugated, others with a cloudy texture, and a few of smooth glass. Haauw, he thought. A door of jewels!

"Come on," said his uncle a few paces ahead of him.

They walked right past this palace and went behind the garden bushes, becoming invisible to the masters as they made their way to the servants' quarters. A shrunken and less graceful clump of outbuildings in the same colours was hidden behind thick shrubs. It was almost concealed from the manor. These quarters consisted of three rooms.

One small room had Agnes's iron-rimmed bed. The looped bed legs stood on two bricks each, raising the bed above the height of the *tokoloshe* (bogeyman). Jeremiah recognised the attempt to keep this African spirit at bay. He had been told from childhood about this little man spirit who was too short to perform his evil deeds on those out of reach on raised beds.

The room also had a wardrobe, a table, one old, chipped wooden chair, and a timber crate on its side, doubling as kitchen closet and bench. Against the wall on the table, a newspaper-lined wooden tomato crate served as the only store for foodstuffs. Next to it, powered by paraffin, was a primus stove for heating water and cooking.

The next room was a crowded storeroom, packed from floor to ceiling with cartons, bottles, tools, household equipment, and odds and ends. One corner had been cleared. Here, a three-legged wooden bed was wedged up into the corner, the three legs on two bricks each and the fourth corner of the bed supported by eight bricks to make it approximately level. This was the gardener's bed.

The last room had the servants' toilet and a basin for washing. There was no shower or bath.

These rooms had no electricity or hot water. Light came only from candles stuck to chipped saucers with their own wax.

Shortly after arriving, Samson and Jeremiah were joined by a woman in a servant's pink dustcoat with buttons down the front. Samson stood up. "Agnes, this is my sister's child, Jeremiah."

Agnes greeted Jeremiah and he returned the greeting.

"Jeremiah, go and see Johannes, the gardener, next door while I speak to Agnes for a while."

Jeremiah went outside, but as soon as he was out of sight, he listened carefully. He knew they would be talking about him. As far as he was concerned, he had a right to know what was being said.

Samson pleaded with Agnes to let Jeremiah stay there as a temporary solution. "This is my sister's son. I can't leave him in the streets. He's only a farm boy, barely 20 years old. They'll eat him up alive out there. I'll find another place as soon as I can. I'll ask around at work and maybe up and down the roads here. Someone may need help in the garden. He can work there on weekends for them."

She gave in, after seeing there was no other solution. "But you must promise to find him a bed somewhere else by the weekend. Mrs Katz will shout and may even kick you out if she finds I have your whole family here."

"It's not my whole family. It's just my nephew from the farm."

That night Johannes agreed to let Jeremiah sleep on boxes they rearranged into a cot in the storeroom.

Samson also found Jeremiah a job as a general hand in the same car repair shop he worked in. Being the youngest, Jeremiah became the person to whom jobs that no one else would do were given. Jeremiah showed them he was capable, and in no time the mechanics gave him complex tasks that required special care.

He also charmed Mrs Katz, Agnes's boss, who was quite happy to let the strong Jeremiah do jobs around the large garden and look after the dogs – two large German shepherds. They could be vicious enough to tear apart an intruder, but soon found a best friend in Jeremiah. He was lucky, he thought, that they were being fed when he first arrived at the house. If they had approached him and Samson on that first afternoon, he would have run off and climbed a tree. That would have made his uncle laugh.

Although he enjoyed a few weeks in the Houghton yard, he wanted to experience more of the Jo'burg life all his workmates spoke about. "There are plenty of clubs where they play music and we jive," boasted Dizzy, a co-worker whose company he enjoyed. "There is drink and plenty of girls. It's all good fun." Jeremiah couldn't have fun with his uncle around all the time.

When Oxford Motors was broken into and thieves got away with the cash box and some tools, Jeremiah seized the opportunity. He went to the boss shortly before closing the next day. "Baas, I'm happy to keep an eye on the place at night. If I sleep here, the tsotsis will see me and go somewhere else. Somewhere where there's nobody to worry about. And if they try with me … well, I can look after myself." He expanded his well-built chest and stood erect, towering over the boss.

"There's no room for you here, boy."

"I don't need much. Look here. I'll clean this place up and use this." Jeremiah pointed to an underutilised bin area that was gathering rubbish.

"Yes, I see. Okay. We'll try it out. But, you can't bring anyone onto the premises; otherwise you'll have to leave."

"I don't know anyone here. Don't worry. The place is safe with me," he said, patting himself on the chest. "You can trust me."

Jeremiah was quick to convert the bin area into his bedroom. He felt free. For the first time in his life, he lived alone and had electricity, using an extension cord pilfered from the workshop. He even had hot water, which he rigged up from the kitchen geyser, plumbing installation being another skill he had picked up while working with Alfred at the farm.

He sent money to his father every month. He calculated that he would repay all the money Thomas had given him within eighteen months.

Jeremiah hung out with a group of single young men in their early twenties, all of whom had come from country towns and villages. Like him, they did not have anyone to account to.

He enjoyed their nights of liquor, tobacco and the clubs, where there were girls. He spent most of his week's earnings on the weekend, and sometimes the lot. Tomorrow was another day. As long as they went to work during the week, he and his friends could spend all their money on the weekends. They regretted it on Monday when their pockets were as empty as their heads were sore.

Except one Monday. Not only was Jeremiah's head sore – so was his manhood. He was shocked. He didn't know what the problem was and made discreet enquiries at the workshop.

But he couldn't fool the Jo'burgers. "You've been given a little present, man. Little Jeremiah has been where he shouldn't," teased one of them, "and someone has given little Jeremiah a very sore head. It's off to the doctor for you or else the doctor will take it off."

"No, no. It's not for me I'm asking," Jeremiah mumbled. "It's for my friend." But their words had hit home. He knew he had a problem and went outside for fresh air. His legs felt like jelly. He had to lean on his hands against the wall to avoid falling. He started shaking, and the perspiration beaded on his forehead.

This was all witnessed by Samson, who helped him to sit. He explained that Jeremiah needed treatment for the clap. "You must go now to the doctor, and it will pass."

Jeremiah looked Samson in the eyes earnestly. "And will it still work, Uncle?" He pointed to his crotch.

"I think so."

He felt relieved. He was glad that his uncle's attitude was caring rather than reproachful, and that Samson didn't repeat his earlier advice about not trusting anyone.

Jeremiah didn't know who had given him the disease, and he didn't want to find out who might have got it from him – he'd been with a few girls in recent weeks. The next two months' pay went towards injections followed by a dose of antibiotics.

In that time, he worked hard during the day and stayed in his room every night. He only went beyond the perimeter of the yard to buy food.

9

They threw Marius's limp body on the backseat of his Buick Roadmaster convertible. His hair was stained dark with clotted blood from a gash across the hairline above his forehead. Vomit was caked on his face and chest. He groaned in distress.

"Help me, help me," he moaned. Marius was aware of the two men around him. But he was unable to sit up.

"Fuck!" said one of them, the one who grabbed the Buick's keys from Marius's trouser pockets. "His old man will kill him if he finds out."

"And what about us? He'll kill all of us," said the other as he got into the front passenger seat.

"Shall we take him to hospital?"

"No. He'll be fine."

"What about his head? The gash looks blerrie bad."

"Nah. It looks worse than it is."

Marius was trying to imagine what he looked like and felt the stinging cut on his forehead. "Let me out – I feel sick," he groaned.

"God, you were acting like a real pisspot. You shouldn't have mixed your drinks," said one of his friends.

"Yes," said the other. "Fuckin' cheap wine, then beer ... and then that brandy! Even I wouldn't do that."

"And as for your solo act ..." said the other.

"But that ending wasn't meant to be part of it!" Now Marius recognised the voice of his university friend, Gerhard. He tried to answer him, but only threw up again, this time over the backseat of his Buick.

God! Three years at the Afrikaner University of the Highveld, and he was turning out like this? Not that any of them would have missed the law school's revue. Nearly every student took part in it at the end of third year.

Like his fellow students, Marius had been aware of just how conservative the campus was. The university, after all, was highly regarded by the Afrikaner elite. The most radical action the students ever took was to poke polite fun at lecturers at these end-of-year revues. They were restrained, and everyone was expected to behave with respect and dignity. It was supposed to be clean and clever. Then they retired to the boarding houses for their more salutary fun.

Many of them were from country families, folk who didn't drink alcohol and were too demure to joke much either. Marius knew all too well that as the son of an Afrikaner farmer who was an established church elder and government powerbroker, he was supposed to be a conventional well-behaved student.

And indeed he had been. He had excelled at his studies, had been conscientious, and had kept to tradition. He'd sat on various university committees: the Afrikaner Christian Boys Youth League, the National Party Youth Committee (of which he was university president), and the Law Students' Council. In sport, he'd played fly-half for the university's first rugby team. At five foot nine and a half, he wasn't built for the front line of the scrum, but he *was* strong and quick. And he could kick the ball far with accuracy, having had plenty of practice on the farm.

Marius had been a teetotaller until things changed rapidly midway through his second year of studies. Now, through the alcoholic haze, he vaguely recalled what had triggered this new behaviour. His rugby team had lost an acrimonious game against the team from the English-speaking rival Johannesburg university, Wits. They were beaten by one point. Marius missed an easy penalty in the dying minutes of the game and blamed himself for his team's bloody defeat.

As he emerged from the showers after the battle, his friend Gerhard, who was also a teammate, produced a bottle of brandy. "Here, Marius. Have a *dop* (shot). You'll feel better."

Without thinking, he took a swig from the bottle, and then a few more, on an empty stomach and a constitution unaccustomed to liquor. He soon felt tipsy, light-headed and light-hearted. That was the first time.

Marius was a happy drunk who joked and fooled around. What did it matter if he never harmed anyone?

Without his father nearby, he felt free and his inhibitions lifted. He embraced smoking and drinking, often to excess.

And he had fun.

Unaware of these antics, his father had shown pride in Marius's achievements by rewarding him at the end of his second year with a handsome allowance and new car. The latest model Buick, the two-door Roadmaster convertible, attracted everyone with its beautifully clean off-white colour, four prominent ventiports on each of the front fenders, skirts over the rear bumpers, and red trim on the sun visors. The Buick did indeed master the roads. It glided over them like an aeroplane on its wide white-walled wheels.

With his wealth, charisma and pedigree he counted on being excused his excesses.

But on the night of the revue, he wanted to get drunk. He had had wine earlier in the day. At the auditorium, Gerhard took a bottle of beer away from him. "Later, Marius. Do your show first."

"I'll just say my 'Ode to Professor Barnard' and then come off," he said. He turned around, grabbed a bottle of brandy from his duffel bag, and downed a few gulps directly from the bottle. Gerhard dimmed the lights and then led Marius to the stand on the stage and introduced him.

Marius started with his "Ode to Professor Barnard", a well-rehearsed satirical take-off of his favourite lecturer. He had never failed to raise hysterical laughter from those fortunate to see him practising.

But he felt free and abandoned the podium for the front edge of the stage, where he performed his "Ode" with vulgar animation. Then, overcome with the copious cocktail of liquor, he ejected the contents of his stomach over himself and the front row of the audience. At that point he fell off the stage, choking on his vomit.

Shuffling Marius out of the car, Gerhard examined the head wound again. "This is deeper than I thought, Marius. I'm taking you to hospital."

Marius winced as the nurse shaved the hair around the wound. The doctor sewed six stitches above his hairline, branding Marius for a few weeks.

Marius felt relieved that it was the end of the academic year. He could sit his examinations in November and then flee Pretoria, the campus and his peers, to take refuge on the farm.

But that refuge entailed explanations. "Gerhard didn't see me behind him when he closed the door in my face, Pa."

"Hmm ..." Strydom looked at Marius's scarred cranium without further comment. Marius turned scarlet when he realised that the wound was not consistent with being hit by a vertical door. *I should have had a better explanation.*

"Son, one must learn one's lessons in life. Those who don't will find life is more difficult as they repeat the same mistakes over and over again." That was all Strydom said. His tone was emotionless.

Then he walked away. Marius was initially relieved at his father's muted reaction. But then he felt guilty.

He recuperated, but although his physical injury was soon healed, his mental equilibrium recovered more slowly. He had let his father down. He knew that his father knew it. Strydom also knew that Marius had lied – though not that it was for a second time. Marius thought back to the first time, when Jeremiah had given him a black eye and he told his father it was due to a mishap whilst installing the trellis. Dishonesty was against his strict upbringing, and it ate away at Marius's conscience.

He spent days under the hallowed willow domes, praying and reading. He read parts of the Old Testament and the New – and some of the witty wisdom of Herman Charles Bosman, which he loved to read aloud. He enjoyed the short stories that usually revealed a twist in the unexpected ending. And Bosman's poetry was so strong. Marius could not read *Vernietiging* (Annihilation) without thinking of Oupa Herman and the oumas he never met.

He cleansed himself in the river waters and under God's sunrays. Intense and dazzling, they illuminated the path ahead. He felt them point him to his New Year resolutions before the commencement of his fourth year at university.

He smelled the damp river bank and the rotting vegetation as it decomposed to feed the riverbed. He saw nature die and rot, to do good again.

After almost five weeks of soul-searching, there came one day when he stripped and walked down to the water's edge, his arms extended like Jesus nailed to the cross and his palms up. He walked to the altar of the Church of the Willows and kept going, whispering as he submerged himself. "God, I lost control. Satan took my soul."

He continued walking. Soon the water was waist high, then up to his neck. Finally he was completely submerged. He relaxed when he floated freely. Then his feet touched the riverbed, and his body folded into a foetal position. He felt the cold water around him seep into his skin, his bones, his whole body. The deafening sound of silence under the water insulated him from the world outside. Totally immersed, he felt a peaceful calm overtake his body, until he could hold his breath no longer. He opened his mouth.

Then he pushed hard on his feet and propelled himself into the brilliant blue sky. Above the water, he took in the sweet breath of life and let out a loud cry.

It was still not enough – he must do it again. Three times he immersed himself and thrust himself towards the heavens. Only then could he wade to the shore under the willows and climb up the river bank. The water flowed and then dripped off him as he made his way slowly to the biggest willow.

"God, I have received your word. Under your trees, cleansed by your sun, and purified by your water. In your presence, I reject the temptations of Satan. The scar you have given me on my head is there to remind me of my weakness – the demon of alcohol. I pledge to you that I will never partake of it again. I pledge to you, O God, that I shall, from now on and forever more, use my head, my body and my soul wisely."

He dressed, gathered up the Bible and Bosman, and went back to the farmhouse.

❖

Marius returned from the wilderness of the farm to the university after forty days. He withdrew from many of his extracurricular activities, continuing only as an active member of the Afrikaner Christian Youth League, and concentrated his efforts on his studies. Now he saw a different future stretching out ahead of him.

10

On the afternoon of his arrival in Johannesburg, Neil walked west towards the city centre. In his pocket was the note from Mrs Botha to Mrs Van Tonder, the woman he'd been told was struggling to keep the Top Star Garage running while she attended to her ill husband. Piet, "the boy", kept up behind him, unwavering in his duty to Mrs Botha. When they came to the corner of Eloff Street, Piet tugged at Neil's sleeve and pointed left. They turned towards the southern fringe of the city centre.

Neil was impressed with Johannesburg, which was bigger and busier than he had anticipated. He was surprised to see so many buildings of substance, not the corrugated iron shacks he had assumed must dominate this mining town. The abundant display windows proudly told of fully stocked stores within. The customers seemed to be only white and were all very well dressed. He saw a marked contrast with the native African pedestrians, who wore work attire and carried packages or stood relaxed at street corners, chatting. Even when apparently on errands, they were unhurried and seemed unstressed.

Trams, motorcars, bicycles and delivery vehicles moved up and down the neat streets in an orderly fashion. He saw similarities with England. But it was warm and sunny, more casual and less crowded, he thought. He noticed that there were relatively more American automobiles than in England. Large Chevrolets and American Fords were just as popular as the British Austins and small Ford Prefects; the rarer Cadillacs and Buicks were just as numerous as the Jaguars and Humbers.

There must be wealth in this city, he concluded. He found some of the grand buildings impressive. The large Supreme Court building in the centre of the city had a distinctly British colonial influence, in contrast to the modern His Majesty's Theatre. Then there was the Royal Milner Club – conservative and unmistakably influenced by the private men's clubs of London, and set up exclusively for the well-heeled, he thought, not without envy. *Maybe one day.*

As they walked farther south, the grandness gave way to practical buildings, accommodating less affluent retail businesses, warehouses, workshops and finally, as Neil could see from a worn and faded sign, Top Star Garage. In all, they had walked west for over an hour from Kensington, up Pritchard Street, to Mrs Van Tonder's ailing business.

Neil crossed the road to get a good view of the establishment. He stood looking and thinking, taking in every detail. *Hmmm, that petrol station driveway could be improved – five natives attending to just two cars.* He guessed that the cash box was manned by Mrs Van Tonder in the small building tucked behind the driveway. There was a workshop on one side where three motor vehicles were being serviced. It certainly seemed to Neil as though the business had customers.

He observed for about half an hour and took in the lethargic service, impatient customers and the indifferent Mrs Van Tonder, who did not communicate with her staff. It wasn't going to be hard to make a difference to this business. And it seemed to have potential.

"Come, Piet. Let's say hello to Mrs Van Tonder."

"Not me, baas. Piet not allowed inside shop."

Neil went into the shop. Piet sat on the curb, his feet in the gutter. At a small table behind the counter sat the slightly built Mrs Van

Tonder, reading a newspaper. She was smartly dressed in a heavy navy-blue cardigan with undone gold buttons up the front, a light blue blouse, loose pleated charcoal skirt and delicate silk stockings. Elegant medium-heeled shoes adorned her feet. Her wavy grey hair was neatly combed, commencing at the fringe, up, and to the sides, forming stiff curls to the left and right of her forehead.

She didn't look up when Neil entered.

He cleared his throat. He had just been taught by Piet how to greet Mrs Van Tonder in Afrikaans. "*Gooie middag* (good afternoon), mevrou Van Tonder."

She removed her thick spectacles and looked at him. Her tired hazel eyes showed no emotion. "Ja, Meneer?" she acknowledged him, her expression unchanging and unsmiling.

Neil handed her the note from Mrs Botha. She replaced her spectacles on her petite nose, read the message and started speaking to him in Afrikaans.

He held up his right hand. "Sorry, mevrou Van Tonder. I am afraid I've exhausted my knowledge of Afrikaans. Do you speak English?"

She went into the workshop and returned with a white man in his thirties. Over his clothes he wore a heavily stained dustcoat that had once been white, but had not been washed for quite some time. His thinning, curly, black hair, combed back, was Brylcreemed to his skull. He frowned at Neil, eyes bloodshot, nose red-veined.

"I'm Karel Prinsloo, Mr Neil. I am the workshop foreman." He was reading Mrs Botha's note.

"How do you do, Mr Prinsloo. Neil Robertson is my name."

"Robertson, hey? It says here Mr Neil."

"Oh, that's what Mrs Botha calls me. I grew up in a business like this in England and would love to help out while Mr Van Tonder is ill."

Mr Prinsloo and Mrs Van Tonder had a discussion in Afrikaans. Then Mr Prinsloo looked at Neil. "Mr Robertson, you doesn't speak our langwich and Mrs Van Tonder wants one of *us* to run the gurrage. Not a Englishman, you know. But Mrs Van Tonder say you can train somebody else." He expanded his chest and stepped between Neil and Mrs Van Tonder. Neil could smell tobacco and alcohol on his breath. "So, she will give you job for two weeks at one pound ten a week. If Mr Van Tonder get better, you're out. And if not, you muss train me, so I can be manager if he don't get better. Then you can look somewhere else." He pointed his thumb to the street.

That was barely more than Neil's rent and what he would need for food, but he had a stash and an idea. "It's a deal, Mr Prinsloo." He shook Prinsloo's hand, turned to Mrs Van Tonder, and nodded. "*Dankie* (thank you), mevrou Van Tonder." This was the second and last phrase he had learned from Piet, anticipating that he might need to thank her. "When can I start, Mr Prinsloo?"

"Monday morning."

By the time he and Piet arrived at Mrs Botha's again, it was dark. She was in the kitchen. "So, Mr Neil. Have you got a job?"

"Thanks to you, Mrs Botha, I have," and he kissed her on the cheek.

She chuckled, pulled away and said, "Thank the Lord, Mr Neil. Not me."

Neil was relieved that Jimmy wasn't there. Mrs Botha said that he had gone off with a friend.

By the dim beam of his bedroom light, Neil wrote a letter to Mary, reporting his arrival and employment in Johannesburg. When he switched off the light, his mind would not stop, but kept churning as he thought of the Top Star garage. Eventually, sleep took over. A deep sleep.

The next night was Neil's first Saturday in Johannesburg, and Jimmy wanted to show him around. He drove them into the city centre, where all businesses were closed except for hotels and the odd beer hall. There was more activity closer to the main railway station. They drove to a suburb immediately north of the city, towards Hillbrow, where Jimmy pointed out more clubs and bars.

Jimmy parked the truck in a cleared lot, and they walked to the first club. They took a small table near the stage. The place stank of stale beer and acrid tobacco. Dark lighting did not hide the bad decor. The timber floorboards were black with grime.

A skimpy barmaid collected the empty glasses left on the table by previous patrons. She wiped the table with a dirty damp cloth, spreading the spilt beer instead of removing it. No wonder Neil's elbow stuck to the table when he leaned forward.

They ordered a beer each. Jimmy downed the pint in two gulps and then called for another.

The floor show started after Jimmy's fourth and Neil's second. Jimmy whistled sharply as dancers jiggled to lively tunes. The entertainers showed curves and crevices, flesh and flab which, as the drinks were consumed, appeared less attractive to Neil, not more attractive. The crass movements seemed to have the opposite effect on Jimmy and most of the others in the hall.

Neil became restless. "Let's go somewhere else," he said to Jimmy. "This place is too loud."

Jimmy looked at him in astonishment. "Why? Look here. Is there anything better than this?"

"Come on, Jimmy. I've seen this place now. Show me another club. Somewhere with a bit more class."

"But the beer here is the cheapest in town."

"Take me somewhere else. I'll pay for the drinks."

"Well, why didn't you say so? I'll show you a classy joint."

"With no floor show."

"If that's what you want, that's what you'll get. Let's go. I know just the place for you."

Neil walked with Jimmy to another establishment that was two blocks away. Thick royal-blue carpets and azure velvet drapes welcomed Neil to the serene gentlemen's bar. He made his way to two comfortable wing-backed lounge chairs on either side of a carved mahogany side table. He sank into the crimson velvet upholstery and relaxed in the subdued crystal lighting and piano music.

"Well, Neilie," said Jimmy, spoiling the ambience, "seeing that you're paying, I'll have a whisky. Neat, thank you." The drinks cost a bit more, but there were fewer costly distractions. They sat back as Neil nursed a beer and Jimmy emptied four whiskies down his gullet in between telling Neil about his journey from Ireland to Cape Town. He then slowed down and sipped the fifth. He spoke more softly and slowly, slurring as he tried to tell Neil about his hard life. Then, in mid-sentence, his head fell to the side of the wing-back chair, and he fell asleep.

As Neil savoured the quiet, celebrating his arrival in Johannesburg, he saw a group of several young men and women enter the stylish restaurant adjoining the bar he was in. They were loud and arrogant and disturbed Neil's peaceful contemplation. One of them shouted for service: "Waiter! Waiter!"

A curly-haired waiter scurried towards them and, with a strong Southern European accent, responded, "Yes, serr, 'scusa me, serr. Can I help you?"

The man who had shouted said, "My dear man. A waiter's job is not to make the *customers* wait, you know. Now, bring a round of sherry and your menus."

How rude, Neil thought. He stared at them in disgust. The rowdy fellow looked his way and shouted, "Hey you, what are you staring at?"

Neil was about to look away when he recognised something familiar. He looked at the man carefully again and then said, "Well, if it isn't Cousin Henry."

He recognised his cousin from the one and only photo of him they'd received – taken beside the American automobile. Neil was in no doubt, even though Henry had not turned up once in all the time Neil stayed in Cape Town.

"Blow me down. You aren't Cousin Neil, are you? Grown up and feeling sorry for yourself in the pub, are you? It won't help, my boy. Come and join us. Learn from your cousin Henry. Life is to be lived!"

Neil walked over to Henry. Before Neil could ask why he didn't meet him in Cape Town, Henry pulled him closer and hugged him. Then he turned to his companions. "This is my cousin Neil. I thought he was in Cape Town, but he's come to find his gold in our city." He lifted his hands and clapped them loudly. "Waiter! Drinks all round – make it a bottle of your good champagne."

Neil had nothing better to do. Jimmy would be out for a while. Besides, he couldn't ignore his cousin, who might still be able to give him some assistance … and even pay back the loan. Henry was obviously doing well. His companions looked well groomed, including the three very attractive ladies. The smell of money clung to Henry's group. Neil joined their table.

The ladies asked him a lot of questions, and the men included him in the rounds of alcohol, treating him as one of the group. He enjoyed the attention lavished upon him and felt especially flattered by the compliments from the young women.

After another two bottles of champagne, three bottles of wine, and steaks all round, they were quite inebriated.

Neil went to relieve himself in the men's toilets. Henry joined him at the urinal. "Say, Neil, do you have enough money to fall back on should the need arise? You really need a buffer here in Johannesburg."

"Yes. I have saved about thirty pounds, and I still have some of the money Father gave me."

"Good. You shouldn't carry it with you. You must stash some in a safe place."

"I only ever carry ten pounds and have the rest at my lodgings."

"Good man. That's very wise, cousin."

They returned together to the table. Desserts of crepe suzette soon flamed there, and port followed. Henry and his friends selected a cigar each from the cigar box that was wheeled over to the table at Henry's request. "Have one, dear cousin. This is good stuff. Imported, you know."

"No thanks, Henry. Not for me."

"Okay, suit yourself. I thought I could show you another of life's pleasures."

They finished off their cigars, and the waiter delivered the bill. Henry thrust forward dramatically, grabbed the bill, and said, "It's on me. To welcome my young cousin Neil to Johannesburg." They all cheered. "Neil, here's to many more celebrations," he said. He raised his glass and swallowed the last of his port.

He searched frantically in his jacket, then his trouser pockets. "Bugger. I changed suits and didn't transfer my wallet," said Henry with a frown. "Neil, could you lend me eight pounds, please? I'll return it tomorrow. Jot down the address of your lodgings here," he said, handing Neil a piece of paper and a pencil, extending the other hand for the money which both he and Neil knew he had.

Neil, still tipsy, gave Henry eight pounds and scrawled the address of Mrs Botha's boarding house as requested. Henry paid the bill and pocketed the balance.

They all thanked Henry and bid Neil another welcome to Johannesburg. With a "farewell old chap", the men shook his hand and patted him on the back, and the women kissed Neil lightly on each cheek. "See you again, Neil dahling." "Isn't he a dear? So cute." The six of them sped off in a shiny green Oldsmobile driven by Henry. They left Neil on the pavement outside the restaurant, wondering what had happened.

He made up his mind that when his cousin came by the next day to repay the eight pounds, Neil would get to know Henry better and ask his advice and for repayment of the loan. He would learn from Henry all about how he had made his money.

Neil found his way back to the still-sleeping Jimmy, who did not appear to have stirred, to judge by his position on the chair. Neil roused him just enough to bundle him into the Bedford. The old girl must have steered her own way home, because Neil wasn't in a sober state to drive and later could not recall the journey. When he saw her the next morning, he didn't understand how she had landed with one wheel on the pavement and her front bumper a hair's breadth from the stout mulberry tree to the right of Mrs Botha's pathway.

11

It was a Saturday. Jeremiah, dressing up for his weekend night out, was satisfied that the new clothes fitted him perfectly. With the money he saved during his convalescence, he had bought his dapper black sports jacket with nautical gold buttons, and had chosen a white shirt to give prominence to a shiny pearl-coloured tie with shimmering red and green circles framed in golden ovals like exotic jewels. A gold-plated tiepin inlaid with green enamel was complemented by matching cufflinks. He looked tall and athletic in his gold-brown slacks and wide-rimmed, two-tone, Jarman-style shoes that he had polished to a shine.

Besides the sports jacket, all these items had been purchased over seven months. His shopping excursions took place on the Saturday mornings after paydays, when he was still flush with cash. He would set out to look for something new from the Indian-owned businesses on the retail strip at the west end of the city. Each merchant presented the "highest quality", offered his wares at the "very best prices", and provided service fit for Savile Row in impeccable and heavily accented Indian-English, which, in itself, enhanced the occasion.

They made him feel special, and he enjoyed these outings. Sometimes he took his co-worker Dizzy along with him. Sometimes he went on his own.

He entered the exotic shops as if he were entering a magnificent cave full of gold coins and dazzling gems, like in the stories his father used to tell. He was drawn by the intoxicating, sweet smell: fabrics heavily laced with incense. His eyes feasted on the variegated colours. The thickly piled clothing absorbed all echoes, making conversation soft, personal, effortless and elegant.

The shirts and jerseys were in neatly packed boxes – one on top of the other, more than thirty high – and came in all sizes and colours. In the shop he frequented most, the graceful, immaculate Indian patriarch would nimbly extract a box near the bottom and reveal its contents to Jeremiah. One time it was a golden jersey preserved in a cocoon of soft tissue paper. Mr Lalloo presented it to Jeremiah with "Pure wool, sir. Just your size." He held the article as though it were a fragile golden egg in a bird's nest.

Shirts, cufflinks, ties and bow ties looked out from spotless glass-topped counters. There were more piled on top for the senses to feast on. Everything was neat and clean, like the handsome Lalloo family. They maintained a discreet presence in the background, ostensibly busy with a chore, until they appeared from the depths of the premises like magic with a garment that Mr Lalloo had secretly signalled to them was just the article Jeremiah was looking for.

Row upon row of trousers, jackets and suits hung densely, double height. From these Mr Lalloo had selected the nautical blazer and dressed him in it before Jeremiah could ask the price. "Look, sir, a faultless fit. It was made just for you," he said to Jeremiah, his delicate fingers stroking the shoulder. Then he gently patted Jeremiah's waist. "It hangs perfectly, sir."

On another shopping excursion, Jeremiah wanted to purchase underclothes but was too embarrassed to ask. He had seen them in the shops before and had noticed, while briefly staying with Samson and Agnes in her boss's backyard, that the spunky Johannes, the gardener, wore some. Since then Jeremiah had been on the lookout for them, and now caught sight of a pair that was neatly folded in a drawer under a glass counter.

He walked up to the counter and looked through the glass at the neighbouring drawer, which had a rainbow of handkerchiefs. Pretending to examine them, he cast his glance to the left and let it linger on the delicate, white, perforated underpants.

Too shy to take this purchase any further, he asked Mr Lalloo for two pairs of black socks inlaid with white diamond outlines to match his two-toned shoes. After laying these gently on the brown wrapping paper, Mr Lalloo produced two pairs of white Jockey underpants, arranged them on top of the socks and wrapped them all in the one parcel. "These are very comfortable, sir. Your size. You can pay for them next month."

Jeremiah mumbled a relieved "thank you".

Jeremiah didn't buy something every time. He seldom bought more than one item at a time, and then only after viewing the patterns and colours up close, touching the soft, smooth materials, inhaling the intense smell of the dyes, and listening to the swish of the fabrics. He tried his proposed purchase on, checked it out in the mirror and received commentary from the expert and supporting family members. Jeremiah was always pleased with his acquisitions, which he wore with pride.

And he knew without a doubt that he could carry off such elegant clothing, enhanced by his muscular, tall physique and smooth, handsome looks.

No matter what it cost, Jeremiah was determined to leave the farm boy behind.

On this particular Saturday night, Jeremiah smelt of fresh Lifebuoy soap and looked crisp and dashing. He was ready for a good time.

He met up with Dizzy, so called because of his love for jazz and his talent at mimicking the famous Dizzy Gillespie. Dizzy blew an expert air trumpet, his healthy lips and fat cheeks ballooning convincingly. The effect was topped up by his thick, black-framed spectacles. When Dizzy had a jukebox as his backing, you could be forgiven for thinking you were at the Apollo in Harlem, watching the real thing.

They were joined by a few co-workers and went to a jazz club in Sophiatown. Jeremiah took an immediate liking to this suburb on the western fringe of Jo'burg. Here American jazz and American cars were all the rage. Dizzy told him about the great musicians playing at the clubs and sometimes pointed out a black political leader or two in deep discussion over a drink at a secluded table.

Dizzy showed Jeremiah a number of shebeens: establishments selling illicit alcohol. He knew which served the best homemade brews of *skokiaan* or *babaton*. And Dizzy knew where to go every weekend for the best entertainment.

That night Jeremiah bought beer at the Bad Boy Jazz Club and joked with his friends. His attention was frequently drawn to the pretty girls. He complimented almost every one of them as he passed by.

An attractive young woman came over to him. He surveyed her, from her straight black hair down to her stiletto shoes. Stunning. Her dark skin gleamed like an elegant Buick. Her shimmering silver dress gave him a thrill. She was all shadows and mystery in the low club lighting. Her generous breasts mesmerised him – he felt like a rabbit caught in the headlights of a V8. She purred at him, stroked his chin, whispered into his ear, and pressed down on his crotch. "Hello, baby. Do you mind if I sit here? There are no empty chairs."

His heartbeat quickened as his head and groin pulsated. "Sure, gorgeous. I think you'll fit very neatly into my lap." She sat on his thighs and slid her dress up. "I'll hold you to make sure you don't fall." He folded his arms around her, his right hand brushing, and then resting on, her left breast. She shivered. He felt light-headed. "Ooh, this dress is lovely and smooth." He stroked her lower back and, lower … lower, he explored her shapely thighs. He kissed her neck. The contact and temperature between them increased. She caressed his inner thighs and moved her hands to his bulging groin. She pressed all the right buttons and so did he.

"Come, baby," he whispered. "Let's go outside."

He led her out and around the corner to an alley and pushed her up against a wall. He embraced her tightly. He kissed her and she him as they became intertwined, breathing heavily. Her hands guided his to her breasts, encouraging him. She pulled his shirt up, rubbed his lower back, and caressed his hips, exploring with her fingers inside his trousers toward his firm buttocks.

"Ohh, my love, yesss," she sighed when he lowered her neckline and kissed her neck, edging towards her now-exposed breasts. Her fingers went to the front of his pants and started rubbing him. It felt so good that he was struggling to remain on his feet.

Suddenly, he felt a sharp pain shoot through his head into his eyes. He couldn't control his balance and fell to the left, taking his new friend with him. All sounds around him were muffled and his sight went blurry. He couldn't understand what was going on until he felt a warm, thick liquid flowing down his face and a second sharp pain, this time across his shoulders.

He heard his companion scream and felt himself being repeatedly hit from behind. He curled up in a ball, realising that if he turned to face the attacker, he risked full frontal assault and worse danger. As long as he could hold his head and take the blows on his back and arms, he might survive the unrelenting onslaught.

She ran away screaming. His attacker shouted at him, "You filthy son of a whore! I'll make sure you never fuck again, you dirty bastard!"

The alley filled with people, shouting and hitting. Jeremiah couldn't move. He was barely conscious, but could sense that he was in the middle of a battle.

After the commotion subsided, he turned over and saw that he was surrounded by his bloodied friends, knives drawn, ready to repel any further attack.

Dizzy was leaning over him. "Are you okay, man?"

"I think so. What happened?"

"It was Simon."

"Who is Simon?"

"Don't tell me you don't know who Simon is."

"I don't, Dizzy. Who's he? Why the hell did he attack me?"

"He said you gave his sister the clap, man."

Jerry stared at him, not comprehending.

"Weeks ago, man. Now he's after you."

"Oh, shit."

"Yes. And guess what? He's dangerous. You've got him way too angry – it wasn't a good idea to give his sister your problem."

Jeremiah gripped Dizzy's hand. "Help me up."

Dizzy pulled him to his feet. "Listen here. Simon's got many cousins. They're walking around with knives, pangas and I think I saw one with a gun. They're scary, man. They said tonight they came to cut your cock off because of what you did to his sister." He straightened Jeremiah's jacket. "Are you okay?"

"No. I'm not." Jeremiah paused and leaned forward, holding himself up with his hands on his thighs. Then he almost shouted, "Hell, Dizzy! Now what?"

"We were lucky to have the numbers tonight – three of the tough mechanics from Oxford Motors. And they had friends."

"So that's how I survived."

"Yes, but Simon and his family are out to get you. There's a group waiting for you at the garage tonight. They'll take you to Simon for the punishment."

"You mean I can't go back to the garage?"

"Not unless you want trouble."

"I don't want trouble. I'm innocent."

"They don't think so. I'll see what I can find out, but maybe you'll have to pay for her doctors."

"No, I'm not paying anything. Someone gave *me* the disease. I have an idea who his sister is, but hey, that was ages ago. Anyway, she's a big girl who can look after herself. I didn't force her to do anything. In fact, she threw herself at me."

"But, Jeremiah, she didn't know you would pass your problem on to her."

"I didn't know I *had* a problem. Well, I did, but I didn't know it would pass to her."

"You see? You're an idiot. What do you expect?"

"What can I do? Where can I go? I know nobody except you guys and Uncle Samson. Hell! Uncle Samson ..." he repeated with a groan and held his head. "He'll go crazy with anger. Where can I go?"

"My sister. She will help you. She lives across town. Far enough from Simon."

They spoke for a while, trying to decide what Jeremiah should do. He must hide, they agreed, at least until things cooled down a bit. Jeremiah memorised an address in a distant suburb where Dizzy's sister worked.

"Go there tomorrow morning. She works on Sundays. She'll contact me."

They walked together for a while. Dizzy looked around all the time to make sure that they weren't being followed. Then they separated, scarcely saying goodbye.

Jeremiah had nothing but the soiled clothing he was wearing and the little money he had on him – his main stash being hidden in a jam tin underground at a spot in the workshop yard, known only to him.

Never mind. He could find it later. His life and manhood were more important. His injuries hurt, but no more than his ego as he thought about what he should do. And now, to make matters worse, he was lost. For hours he walked in the direction he thought Dizzy had pointed him, but the landmarks he was supposed to come across were not there.

He couldn't hide forever, but if Simon was as vicious as Dizzy had told him, then he could not expect his friends to risk their lives for him.

He got as far as the southern part of Eloff Street and collapsed in an alleyway near a workshop.

12

◈◇◈

At university, Marius became a member of the National Party and attended many political rallies addressed by the Afrikaner prime minister and other government ministers in Pretoria.

In articles he wrote for the university's student law journal, he justified the government's right to make laws that kept black and white apart. He thought it was a good idea for the black tribes of South Africa to have their own homelands and their own governments. The blacks would have jobs in the white towns and cities, he reasoned, but their presence there would be temporary because they would have homes to go back to. This was a solution that should satisfy everyone. And it provided the whites with a logical basis for retaining most of the land, since the tribal lands had become small dots on the map.

He repeated these arguments to himself many times. The blacks outnumbered the whites by more than five to one, and so could not be allowed to vote for members of the South African parliament. Giving blacks the vote would mean handing power to them. If such a thing were ever to happen, the whole system would break down.

He also wrote a paper on the meaning of treason. He felt strongly that the black political movements claiming the right to vote and own property were a threat to Afrikaner rule and to the elected government.

And they were rallying against the government, threatening violence. *This* was the treason, he thought. But he felt uncomfortable when he recalled how his father had promoted sabotage against the Anglophile Smuts government in the 1940s, and he decided against publishing the paper.

The farm provided a quiet refuge while he developed his beliefs – it even contributed to them. He saw how well everything worked. His father and Hennie imposed a strict regime on the black farmhands, resulting in good yields from the land, with more than enough for all to eat. His family were the masters, he thought. Without them, would the farm workers have jobs? And did his family not help them to feed theirs? *We are educated and they aren't.*

So whites provided for blacks, and blacks worked for whites. He recalled arguments being made about the cross being carried for Jesus by a black man on the way to Calvary. It was God's message confirming that blacks must serve whites. There was an obvious and natural logic to all this. It was simply the order of things.

When at the farm, he shunned contact with the farmhands except in a strictly master-servant context, and then usually to give instructions. He never spoke to Thomas or Saleena about Jeremiah and never visited the compound. Unlike Hennie, he was at least civil. Nevertheless, he was still aloof with the staff.

Marius took long walks on the farm, rode the farm horses, and went hunting for rabbit and buck. He swam in the dam, read books and wrote essays. He hosted friends from the university and shared these activities with them too.

On one of his weekends at home, he led a hunting party to find a leopard that had attacked a calf. Marius went with Gerhard and two others to follow the spoor to a cluster of trees. Marius combed the scene with his binoculars and then the rifle scope, checking every branch of every tree, but the leopard was nowhere to be seen. He inched forward without making a sound and signalled with his hand, ensuring obedience from his group, who followed him quietly. He was expecting to find the leopard in the trees.

But then he saw it camouflaged in the veld grass. Marius's trained eye could make out its spotted coat. He followed its sleek body line to its head. He shivered when he saw its golden eyes and felt as though they were staring into his own. *He has us in full view.* Crouching not far off, the cat was edging towards them. He realised it was preparing to spring.

Marius stood still with his left foot forward and the other at a right angle to it. He steadied his rifle against his shoulder and pointed it as he focused through the scope. The leopard tensed on its haunches and then sprinted towards him.

Marius froze. The leopard closed in and leapt. It flew through the air. Everything seemed to be happening in slow motion, and he knew he was running out of time. When the target was so close and big that he felt he couldn't miss, he fired one shot. "Run!" he shouted, and stepped to the side.

Marius's pale and trembling friends gathered around the once-beautiful animal, its head torn apart in mid-flight by Marius's shot. "Fuck, Marius! Why wait so long?" panted Gerhard.

"I knew I had only one go. It was him or me."

Later Marius skinned the leopard and kept the headless pelt. He did not consider it a trophy so much as a reminder that the choice to survive might sometimes mean destroying something as beautiful and powerful as a leopard.

Marius had put his wild university days behind him and had become a solemn student who was earnest about the politics of the country. Mindful of his father's politics and ambitions for him, he had no time or appetite for partying. At home he had lengthy discussions with Jacobus Strydom about religion and entrenching the power of the

Afrikaner. Marius felt that there would be a time for him to stand up for his people, just as his oupa and others had before him.

Oom Eben was the only one who lifted the heavy frown from Marius's forehead with his witty anecdotes and interesting stories. Marius could not restrain his laughter at his uncle's retelling of humorous moments during cross-examination in murder trials, or the latest political joke. Oom Eben had the knack of picking out a moment from a serious occasion – a mannerism of the judge, a gesticulation of opposing counsel, or an answer of a witness – and depicting it as though it were in an episode of *The Three Stooges*.

But he could also be serious. In his talks with Marius, Oom Eben questioned some of the hateful rhetoric that some Afrikaner leaders were espousing. "It is a pity that people don't really learn from history," he said one day. "How unjust it was when our people were being hunted for standing up for our cause. We turned to fighting. Now we are the hunters. Such a shame, such a shame."

"What do you mean, Oom? Who are we hunting? We're just governing."

"Oh, my boy. We're doing more than that. We're governing for our people. We're not thinking ahead … and we're not listening. We're not listening to the voices out there. Instead, we're arresting them and throwing them in jail."

"Who, Oom? Who are you referring to?"

Just then Jacobus Strydom entered the room. "I hope Oom Eben isn't poisoning you with his voice of doom, Marius."

"No, Jacobus. Not a voice of doom. I'm just telling my nephew that ears are made to listen, not just to hear. And eyes to look, not just see."

Strydom frowned at his brother. "Yes, and our hearts are made to feel and our memories to remember. We will never allow others to govern us."

"*Twak* (nonsense), Jacobus! There's more at stake here than us and the English. Wait and see."

"We're taking care of that too, Eben. We're taking care of the kaffir tribes. Don't worry."

"How? By arresting them? By banning them? By making sure we can't read their words in the newspapers? By forcing them to violence like the Brits did to our pa?"

Marius looked on, confused. He had thought that Oom Eben supported the government.

"Their words won't go away, you know. You're just hiding them, Jacobus – hiding them from yourselves and our people. And from your family – from Marius."

"That's enough, Eben. Don't fill Marius's head with your silly theories." Jacobus Strydom turned to his son. "We know what's going on, and we're dealing with it. And we're making sure the kaffirs have their say. We're restoring them to their tribal homelands, where they'll have rights. Black and white. We'll all be separate – as it should be."

Oom Eben got up and went for a long walk.

Marius's friend, Gerhard, was glad to put his studies behind him and looked forward to being an attorney in the real world. He was proud of his final year results released in December. He was prouder still when he received an invitation to do articles at one of the leading Afrikaner law firms in Pretoria, commencing in the first week of the new year.

A group of friends was going to the distant seaside city of Durban for the Christmas holidays, but he couldn't afford to join them. His father was a train driver and his family had sacrificed a great deal to finance his education and residence at the university hostel.

He could hardly contain his delight when Marius invited him

to the farm for two weeks before Christmas. That was perfect, he thought: the Strydom farm was the ideal place to rest and recharge, especially after the intensity of sixteen-hour days of study. And then he could join his parents on Christmas Day.

Marius was at the station to collect him.

"Thanks for the invitation, Marius. I was at a loose end and really felt like a break. I nearly killed myself preparing for the finals."

"Me too. That's behind us now. We can be kids again for the next two weeks." Marius led his friend to the shining Buick convertible.

For the next few days, the two of them rode horses on the tracks around the farm. They armed themselves with shotguns and belts of bullets, and then went hunting for buck. Even though tracts of the farm had been cleared for farming, large sections remained wild. They swam in the dam to relieve the heat of the day. Gerhard enjoyed playing around with the farming equipment, especially Johnny, the old tractor.

The day before he was to go back to Pretoria, he and Marius went for a jaunt on the tractor around the farm, far away from the farmhouse. Gerhard was at the wheel and Marius sat on the left wheel guard.

"Watch out, Gerhard! You're going straight for that fence!"

"Oh!" His pull to the right coincided with the large left tractor wheel thumping into a foot-wide rut on the gravel track. The combination of actions threw Marius to the ground. He came to rest with a thud just as Thomas appeared with a horse and cart loaded with tomatoes.

The scene before Gerhard seemed to take place in slow motion. His concern became alarm when he saw Thomas pull out a knife without provocation and fling it in Marius's direction. "Hey! Hey!" Gerhard yelled. "What are you doing, kaffir? Are you trying to kill him?" Gerhard stared in shock. He was confused and scared.

"Look there," Thomas shouted and pointed towards Marius. Gerhard felt threatened by the deep frown and dilated eyes that made Thomas look wild.

He tried to start the stalled tractor, but Thomas came to him and held him and looked him in the eye. "Listen, Baas." The old man's grip was starting to hurt Gerhard's hand. "Baas Marius has been bitten by a snake. A snake."

What was he saying? There was no snake. *Marius has fallen off the tractor and is injured – that's all. The man's gone mad.* Gerhard tried to pull away from Thomas's clenched hold of him. "Leave me, kaffir, let go! I haven't done anything to you."

Thomas shook him hard. "I need your help to save the baas." He pulled Gerhard off the tractor and towards Marius, who lay unconscious. Now Gerhard began to comprehend something of what Thomas was saying. Could the man be trying to help? Where was the snake?

"Look, look!" The wiry fingers pointed to a green-grey narrow shape partially concealed in the long grass next to Marius's right hand. But it lay still and lifeless with its head severed from its body by the knife Thomas had thrown in Marius's direction.

"Look! Basie's hand." Gerhard saw two distinct puncture marks between Marius's right thumb and finger. "Black mamba – look at the black mouth," said the man.

"Oh, fuck! Fuck, fuck, fuck!" Gerhard felt faint and unsteady as the blood drained from his face.

"Baas, maybe we've got one hour." Thomas appeared unruffled while Gerhard tried to regain his composure. "Maybe just an hour … if I was quick enough with the knife and if the snake hasn't bitten him somewhere else. But I need your help, Baas."

"Yes, yes. What must I do?"

"Is the tractor's tank full?"

"No, it's nearly empty."

"Oh. Then make the tomatoes level on my cart. Level with the side panel. His arm must lie out and down."

Gerhard ran to the cart. He had noticed that Thomas was removing his frayed shirt. He turned his attention to rearranging the tomatoes and glanced at Thomas from time to time. The man was tearing his old shirt into long strips. Using one as a bandage, he bound Marius's injured hand. When Gerhard returned, Thomas was fastening the improvised bandage between the two bite punctures and the thumb knuckle.

Gerhard remembered a cowboy film he had seen not long before. "Shouldn't we bite the poison out?"

"No, Baas," said Thomas as he twirled the bandage up Marius's arm, leaving no gap. He tightened it and linked it with the next strip of shirt until the entire arm had been constricted by the bandages. He then immobilised the arm with a splint made of a branch that he broke to the length of Marius's arm.

"Help me, Baas," he called to Gerhard.

They lifted Marius onto the back of the cart. "Let his arm hang down. It must be lower than his heart. Keep it still." The young man hopped onto the trailer near Marius's head, which was supported by the thick bed of tomatoes.

Thomas got on the small bench seat and willed the horse to go as fast as was possible.

"Where are you going? This isn't the way to the house," shouted the young lawyer.

Thomas responded over his shoulder. "No, Baas. It will be quicker to cut through this field and get to the main road. We'll take a shortcut, straight to the doctor's rooms."

"Are you sure?"

"Yes. Going back and then driving the long road from the farmhouse will waste time. And what if there's no car ... or no one to drive?"

"You'd better be right."

Once on the road, Thomas whipped the reins, urging the horse faster towards the town.

❖

Thomas tried his best to keep calm, but the enormity of his decision to bypass the farmhouse weighed heavily on him. He knew it was the right decision, but what if Baas Marius died? He would surely be blamed.

Marius began to stir. Thomas looked back. "Try to keep him calm and still," he said to Gerhard. Thomas had no idea what injuries Marius had suffered by the fall, but he knew that those injuries, and the snakebite too, would do less harm if Marius remained immobile.

They arrived at the doctor's rooms after twenty minutes, though it seemed longer.

"Stay here with Baas Marius. If he comes awake fully, tell him the doctor is on his way." Thomas jumped up the stairs to the entrance and sprinted past the reception area, going straight to the doctor's consulting room. He did not want to be stopped at the reception. It would take too long to explain what was happening, and he would rather use the time explaining this to the doctor.

Thomas remembered where the doctor's consulting room was; he recalled carrying Marius's grandfather into that very room when he had been bitten by a black mamba some years before. On that tragic day, Baas Jacobus Strydom had taken his father to the farmhouse first and then rushed him to the doctor's by truck. They had been too late for Oubaas Herman.

Thomas knew he was going against all the rules, but he flung the door open without knocking. Before the doctor could protest against the intrusion, Thomas explained that he had an unconscious Marius who had been bitten by a black mamba. The doctor listened and nodded. "Where is the young man?" he asked, pushing past Thomas.

"In the cart out the front."

The doctor ran towards the road, yelling instructions to the nurse as he did so.

Thomas followed and turned to Gerhard. The boy's clothes were soiled with tomatoes. His face was pale and he was shaking.

Gerhard's eyes were enlarged. Thomas realised he was in shock.

"Baas Gerhard, we must tell Baas Strydom."

There was still no response.

Thomas left him and ran inside again, this time going to the kitchen. He gave instructions to the maid to take some sugar water to the young baas and see to his shock. Then he returned to the receptionist and requested her to telephone the Strydom farm and tell Baas and Miesies Strydom to come quickly.

He went outside and looked on as the doctor administered antivenin whilst Marius was lying in the cart. "Since Oubaas Herman's death, I keep enough serum to treat two major bites," he said to Thomas.

Thomas could see that Marius's breathing became difficult and shallow. Vomiting and convulsions were starting.

"Doctor, Baas Marius also fell from a tractor, and there may be other injuries."

"Oh, I see. Did you bring him on this thing?"

"Yes, Doctor."

"Take us to the clinic immediately then. I want to move him as little as possible. That will speed up the spread of the poison. We may need help if he gets worse and also if something is broken." The doctor got into the tomato cart and sat next to Marius. Thomas drove them a few blocks and turned the corner to the little hospital. Still bare-chested, he helped the doctor and two nurses move Marius onto a stretcher and carry him into the whites-only clinic.

The nurses stripped Marius to his underpants, and the doctor checked his whole body for injuries. He examined a bump on the head. "That's from the fall from the tractor, Doctor," said Thomas.

"Yes, this could have knocked him out at first. There seems to be no permanent damage here." He appeared to be talking to himself, but Thomas leaned forward and cupped his hand over his ear to listen.

The doctor examined the bandaged arm. "This is a pretty good job. It has really slowed down the poison," he said to the nurses. "Leave the bandages and the splint in place." Marius's breathing started getting more even. "That's good, the serum is working," said the doctor.

Thomas left the clinic and waited for Baas Jacobus Strydom on the pavement outside. He stood up when he saw the Strydoms' Buick speeding towards the clinic. The car drew up with a screech. Miesies Strydom was in tears when she ran past Thomas towards the clinic's entrance. Baas Strydom followed her. He paused and looked at Thomas with a deep frown, which Thomas had learned to recognise. To that mood, silence was the best response.

"Why didn't you bring him to the farmhouse rather than dawdle with that thing?" Strydom pointed to the cart. Before Thomas could answer, he added, "If he doesn't make it, there will be hell to pay!"

Strydom rushed after his wife into the clinic. Thomas followed in the shadows and could hear their panicked questions. "How is he, Doctor? I believe it's a black mamba again – just like my pa. The black hand of Satan took my father. Now he wants my son too."

"Meneer Strydom, I think he will be all right. He's very lucky someone who knew what he was doing bound his arm so well. They didn't try to bite into the snakebite and suck out the poison like you did with your pa. The bandage and splint worked well, and they brought him straight here. That kaffir saved Marius's life."

"What kaffir?"

"The one who brought him and told me what to do. He's a bloody good snake doctor. I should give him a consulting room here!"

At this point, Thomas went to the cart and took up the reins to leave. He saw Hennie speeding up the road in Marius's convertible. Thomas quickly jumped off the cart and hid behind it.

Baas Strydom had warned him verbally. Hennie's warning was likely to be more violent. Thomas made himself invisible.

Hennie ran past and jumped the three stairs into the clinic.

With Hennie safely inside, Thomas drove the cart back to the doctor's rooms, where he found Gerhard sitting on a bench under a thorn tree in the garden. He was not as pale as before, but his shirt was blood-red from the emergency transportation in the tomato cart. The kitchen maid was taking away a teacup. "He's better now. He should go and have a good bath and change of clothes."

"Thank you. Come, Baas. Let's go."

"What about Marius? How is he?"

"We were in time. He's okay, I think. I can take you to the clinic if you want, but you do not look well."

"I should go there. Take me there."

They got on the cart bench and Thomas drove to the clinic. Both Strydom cars were still there. It was getting dark, and the lights inside the clinic shone a dim yellow. "Wait here. I'll see what I can find out," said Gerhard.

Just then Hennie came out and lit a cigarette. He puffed hard, blowing smoke as though his life depended on it. Thomas hid away again, keeping well out of Hennie's sight and range. As soon as Gerhard saw his friend's older brother, he ran to him. "Hennie, how's Marius? Will he make it?"

"Thank Jesus, he'll be okay. You guys got him here in time. He broke his arm, though. What the hell happened? He got bitten by a snake, broke his arm, and had concussion – there's quite a knock on his head." He inhaled deeply on the cigarette and blew out puffs of smoke through his mouth and nose. "What were you guys doing?"

"I'll explain later. I'm not feeling well. Thomas will take me back to the farm."

"No, leave the kaffir. I must go back. I can't do anything here. I'll just tell Pa I'm going back. You come with me."

Gerhard went over to Thomas, who sat behind the cart. He had heard the conversation. "I'm going with Baas Hennie. He'll take me. You go back now." Gerhard turned to go, hesitated, and turned back to Thomas. "Marius's arm is broken, you know. It wasn't the splint, was it?"

"No, Baas. It's the other arm. I saw he broke the other arm. We had no time to fix that."

Gerhard walked back to the clinic to wait for Hennie.

Thomas drove the cart back to the farm and went straight to his hut. While telling Saleena of the day's events, he felt his arms and head grow heavy. He got up and dropped onto his bed without undressing.

13

◈◇◈

Cousin Henry approached Neil's lodgings at Mrs Botha's. It was the Monday after they had met, and he had waited until he saw Neil leave for work. He hoped that Neil had explained to Mrs Botha that his cousin was expected.

He knocked on the door.

A large, matronly woman opened and looked at him with a frown. "Yes?"

"Good morning, madam. You must be Mrs Botha." Henry extended his hand in greeting.

"Yes, I am," she replied. "What do you want?" She did not accept his proffered hand.

Henry dropped his arm. "Is my cousin, Neil Robertson, at home?"

"No, Mr Neil is not here. He has gone to work."

"Did he leave an envelope for me?"

"No, but he say his cousin will give me some money for *him*."

"Oh, yes. I have it here." Henry produced from his inside jacket pocket a sealed envelope addressed to Neil. Mrs Botha took the envelope, examined it and held it tightly in her plump hand.

"I give it to him." She looked at Henry and then turned to dismiss him. "Goodbye, sir."

"Excuse me, madam. But what about the package he said he would leave me?" Henry looked at her.

She hesitated and frowned again at him. "He dirrent say nothing about a package."

"Well, maybe I should look in his room. It may be there."

She stood in the doorway, holding the envelope in one hand, resting her other fist on her hip. "No. He never say nothing about a package. I can't just let everybody from the street in his room. You come back when he's here. Then he give you … whatever he say he'll give you."

"But madam, I have to have it now. I'm leaving for Pretoria soon and must take it with me."

"Well, why dirrent he give it to me? Or tell me?"

"I'm sorry, madam. I can't explain that. He promised me I could collect it. He must have forgotten to tell you about this." Henry sensed he must tread softly. He did not want to antagonise this stern matriarch on her territory. She glared at him for a while and looked him up and down.

Then she looked beyond him and saw the gleaming Oldsmobile near the pathway. "Is that yours?"

"Yes, madam. That's my car."

"Humph. Okay. Come, we go look together." She beckoned to him and led him to a neat room.

Henry guessed that Aunty Mary might have shown Neil how to stash his money in the same place as his mother, Jane, had told him. Maybe it was a family hiding place for valuables. He took a chance and went straight to Neil's wardrobe and fossicked amongst Neil's socks. He found a pair of balled-up socks that felt thick and stiff. Henry breathed a sigh of relief, but he saw that it did not go unnoticed by the vigilant Mrs Botha. "Here it is, madam. I've found what he left for me. Tell Cousin Neil I'll see him next week, and please don't forget to give him the note."

"Not so fast, Mister Cousin-of-Mr Neil. This envelope should have money, not a note." Mrs Botha had picked up on Henry's last word and now repeated it emphatically, drawing out the "o" and amplifying the "t". She blocked the doorway with her wide girth while she tore the envelope open and read the note aloud. Henry looked on, with Neil's stash in his hands and his escape route sealed off by the solid Mrs Botha.

"Dear Neil," she read pointedly, "I have to go to Pretoria and am in a rush." She looked up at Henry, and then continued. "I have borrowed a bit more from your stash, which I will repay. See you next week. H."

Her penetrating eyes pierced right into Henry's core. "So, Mister H. There's no money in this envelope." She paused for barely a moment. "And what's in those socks?" she yelled. She lunged forward, knocked Henry off his feet, and grabbed the socks from his hand. As she dug around in the socks with her fingers, Henry bolted for the door. Although she was twice his size, he was twice as fast.

"You thieving *vuilgoed* (dirty goods)! With cousins like you, who needs robbers?" she bellowed and chased after him. He fled from the house, slamming the front door shut behind him. But she was in full flight, yelling obscenities at him in Afrikaans. She got as far as the front gate, hurling curses at Henry that he knew he would not have understood, even if he could have heard them more clearly.

He was nimble on his feet and quick to get into the Oldsmobile. He screeched off as if Mrs Botha would single-handedly blockade him if she had been fast enough to stand astride the narrow road.

❖

That night Mrs Botha described the episode to Neil with dramatic effect. She explained not only what had happened, but also what had been going through her mind. "Yes, Mr Neil. Your very own cousin could not fool this old *Boerevrou* (Boer lady). I see through his roving eyes straight to his thieving heart. I dirrent want to fight your cousin, sir. So I was prepared to let him prove me right. And when he say he has a *note* and not *money*, the *skelm* (thief) prove me right."

Then she demonstrated how she had grabbed the balled-up socks, and continued until she was out of breath. "I nearly grab him by the neck through the open window of his getaway car." She thrust her thick arms out and was about to demonstrate by grabbing Neil by the throat, but then checked herself. "But I had your money and dirrent want to risk losing it. Besides, I coorrent really lock him in the storeroom until you come home. So I let the sack of manure go."

"Just as well you had my socks, Mrs Botha. I really need that money to pay my rent here."

"Ja, you see. I knew what I was doing."

"I'm ever so grateful to you. I can't believe he tried to take my money. Everything I've saved. I won't be telling Mum about this."

"But Mr Neil, you *must* tell her. She must know what her own flesh and blood do to you," Mrs Botha said. "Or try to do to you," she added, and swotted a fly that had rested on the sugar bowl.

"It'll just worry her and create ill feeling between her and her sister. And Father won't make it any easier. No, I'll just keep this to myself and catch up with Henry later."

"Suit yourself, Mr Neil. It's a free country."

Neil soon had free reign of the Top Star Garage. Mr Van Tonder's health deteriorated, and Mrs Van Tonder stopped checking on the business. Neil reported to her daily on his way to work about the previous day's trading. He told her the garage would need substantial upgrading to keep afloat.

"Mrs Van Tonder, without careful management, this business could lose money." He met with her at her home for her convenience, and got her maid to translate, as her English was not up to the level of discussion he needed to have with her. "I would like to train Mr Prinsloo to manage it, but he's a mechanic, Mevrou. He's no businessman. You'll lose the lot. I've done a bit to increase the profit. See here. Here are the figures. They don't lie."

He brought her Mr Van Tonder's bookkeeper's letter paper with the figures for the past twelve months, other figures in her husband's writing, and then his own figures that showed a very small profit.

In truth, the profit was greater. Neil had understated the closing fuel stock figure, inflating the cost of sales slightly. And he had incurred a number of one-off costs that increased the expenses, such as uniforms for all staff and expensive new car-lifting equipment.

"Ja. Karel Prinsloo isn't good with figures. But I'm happy with a small profit," she said.

Neil knew that Mr Van Tonder's condition was deteriorating. He had tried to galvanise the staff to work better, but he had had only marginal success in this area. He did manage to make a few improvements in the workshop, bringing the Milton Robertson order to the layout, tool storage, tool maintenance, and car service schedule. The workshop was now running more efficiently. What he needed at this point was more time and freedom – and some money to spend on making improvements.

One day a few weeks after Mr Van Tonder passed away, Neil collected Mrs Van Tonder from her house and took her to the garage. He called Prinsloo and asked him to translate.

"Mrs Van Tonder, some things will need a lot of money to fix up. Look here. This door is broken. There, the roof is rusted and must be changed. We also need to invest in new equipment to get the cars through quickly. New pumps in the driveway, for instance." He gestured towards the pumps. "These won't last long, and they're so slow." He kicked a particularly battered one and the side panel fell off, revealing the rusted skeleton behind. "Nearly dead. And wages are going up. Mr Prinsloo will tell you wages are higher."

Neil had given him a raise the week before, and he nodded in agreement.

"This business will soon be making a loss," Neil continued, "unless you put a lot of money into it. I've picked up the turnover, but the expenses have gone through the roof. At your age, I'm sure you don't need the worry. I have a healthy proposition for you. I will buy your business. The business has served you well, and you can retire on what I will pay you."

"But Mr Neil, why is it good enough for you and not me?"

"Because I am young and starting out. I will have many years to pay off the money I will be borrowing to give this business what it needs. I'm the one who will have the sleepless nights."

"But I need the income. I need to live."

"I will put myself in debt and give you more than the land and the business are worth. You should be able to retire comfortably." He paused and watched her growing look of concern. "I heard that Mr Joffe is going to open up down the road. He runs the garage in Kensington."

At the mention of the name Joffe, Mrs Van Tonder's eyes froze. "Really? That's a worry, you know." Through Prinsloo, she went on to tell Neil how she and her husband had been good friends of "poor old Danie Potgieter" who had a garage in Kensington. When Joffe started his business just across the road from Danie's, that closed him down. It was terrible. He died a broken man.

Neil had heard the Afrikaner version of these events from Mrs Botha. There had been rumours that Joffe was interested in opening near Top Star. Nothing had come of them so far, but Neil knew the added advantage of their mention here. "I'm not sure I can survive against Mr Joffe, but I want to take the chance. At your age, though, how can you take him on? And do you even want to?"

Even Prinsloo panicked at the mention of Joffe and had a discussion with Mrs Van Tonder in Afrikaans. Neil could make out that he was encouraging Mrs Van Tonder to ask for a bit more and accept.

"I'll speak to our bookkeeper," she said.

The next week she counter-offered, and the price she named still fell slightly short of what Neil was prepared to pay. Within weeks of his initial offer and shortly before his twenty-second birthday, Neil became the owner of the Top Star Garage and Service Station.

Neil persuaded a bank manager into valuing the land for 50 per cent more than its current value, enabling him to pay Mrs Van Tonder in full. This was a risk, but Neil was aware of the garage's income and knew that the existing revenues could just service the debt. He had plans to secure more corporate custom by approaching businesses to open accounts for fuel purchases and car servicing. And he had ideas to make his staff proud of their work, to improve the service and his business.

Neil advised Mrs Van Tonder to invest her money in Barclays, Anglo American and De Beers shares and to live off the dividends. He knew that would yield more than she could spend, and the shares would grow in value to make her a substantially wealthy lady.

14

After escaping the attack by Simon's family, Jeremiah slept the night in a yard behind a pharmacy. His face throbbed and puffed up like a boxer's after a fight. Gaping pink wounds disfigured the side of his head. His back ached as if run over by the loaded farm cart. When he removed his shirt, he found purple blotches of trapped pain on his sides, as far back as he could see. From the way he felt, he knew his back must be more indigo than brown. A black stain shone through his golden trouser, as though car oil had bled from his thigh, and it felt as if a knife blade were still lodged in the muscle.

He knew exactly how this looked and how it would affect his efforts to find work. *Who will give a job to someone who looked like a failed gangster?* He lay back and sighed through his teeth.

He survived the Sunday in the pharmacy backyard. On the Monday morning, the pharmacy's cleaner discovered him under some newspapers and cardboard boxes behind the toilet block.

By then, he was struggling to open his swollen eyes. Through his lashes, he could see enough to make out a kind face and a look of concern. He felt his own face, knowing it must be grotesque. *She must think from my expensive, torn blazer and my bloody tie – oh, and my cufflinks and tiepin – that I am a tsotsi.*

He told her that he had recently moved from a farm near

Lydenburg, and was still looking for a job. He was not a tsotsi, he stressed. But in telling his story, he exaggerated some aspects and left out others. He made sure to paint himself as a farm boy who became an innocent bystander, and he asked her to help him. Some of these wounds could become infected, he told her. All he needed was an ointment to treat the open wounds. He wasn't worried about the rest.

She looked on as he uncovered some of his cuts and bruises. He could see that she was apprehensive, but her concern for his injuries got the better of her. She went into the pharmacy and returned with some antiseptic and dressing supplies. He couldn't move without aggravating the pain, so she helped him set up a sturdier refuge behind the toilet block. It couldn't be seen from the back lane, and she concealed it from the rear door of the pharmacy with a pile of cardboard cartons.

On the first day, she sneaked out of the shop four times to check on him. He was dozing but seemed settled.

During her lunch break, when she had a bit more time to assess his injuries, she checked again. He lay naked to the waist on the cardboard floor she had helped him prepare earlier. She couldn't spend too much time with him: there were chores to do in the shop, and she didn't want the owner to come looking for her. If her boss discovered him, he'd be chased away and her boss would shout at her. She did not have to be told that permitting this man to sleep in the yard would cause trouble for her, especially a man who had been in a fight.

He stirred when she applied antiseptic to his head wounds. The sores had not fully scabbed, and some were still weeping blood. She got him to turn slowly so that she could check his body wounds too, mostly on his back and sides, where there were dark bruises.

"I'm okay." But when he tried to sit up, he winced in pain.

"It will be sore for a few days. I hope you have no damage inside. You should go to the hospital, just in case, you know."

"No, I think I'm okay." He lay back.

Her eyes lingered on his unscathed chest, which was heaving from the exhaustion of the painful effort to sit up. He was very attractive, she thought, and forced her attention back to his wounds.

"What about the thigh wound? There's some fresh blood. Look, your trousers are full of blood there." She pointed and tried to lift the cuffs of his trouser leg high enough to see, but couldn't reach the wound. "It could get infected. I need to see what to do. You had better take your pants off." She tried to sound businesslike. She was embarrassed to make this request, but her concern for infection overtook her timidity.

"What, so quickly? I don't know you well enough," he teased with a toothy smile. It quickly turned to agony when he tried to lift his body to push his trousers down. "I can't. Can you help me?"

"Don't be silly. I will not fall for this, boy. You have injuries and you need my help. If you don't stop your nonsense, I'll leave you to die here. In the gutter."

"Okay, okay, but … actually … I can't. It is too painful. You're quite safe – I couldn't do anything to you even if you wanted me to."

She could see he was teasing her and was not fooled when he put on his vulnerable look again. But she knew his injuries must be causing pain. "Okay. You loosen the buttons in the front and then I'll help you."

He obeyed, undoing his fly buttons, and she tried to slide his pants from under his buttocks. Slowly, his perforated white Jockey underpants were revealed, and she was careful not to lower them too.

As she leaned over him, she felt uncomfortably close. Although she tried to look at the back of the trousers she was pulling down, she couldn't help but see the large mound restrained tightly by the Jockeys, his long and round shapes visible as they filled the thin undergarment.

She gasped and then diverted her attention to the business at hand. A deep cut in the thigh oozed blood. She was almost out of breath from the exertion … or the closeness. Jeremiah looked at her as if to say that it couldn't take that much energy to lower his pants.

She examined the wound. "Haauw! This is a big cut. No wonder it's bleeding. You may need stitches. You must go to the hospital."

"No, I can't move from here."

"But it's bad. And I'm worried it won't get better."

"If the wound was smaller, what would you do?"

"I'd apply antiseptic and bandage it up tightly."

"Right. Please do that. Can you get some bandages?"

"But … it could go bad. You will need to keep a good eye on it."

"*We* will have to keep an eye on it," he said, leaning on his left elbow, pointing with his right index finger to her and then in the general direction of his thigh – or crotch. She looked him over, his bulging Jockeys, bulky chest and broad smile, and her heartbeat jumped. Her facial expression didn't change, though.

She applied the antiseptic, burning him into submission, and was pleased when he hissed. She went into the shop for a short while and returned with a length of bandage, which she threaded around his thigh, lifting his leg as she did so – around the back and between his legs, unintentionally brushing against his tight underpants. She became aware that through all the pain, Jeremiah was battling arousal, and she feared the closeness might excite him. He tried to lighten the moment with humour: "Hey, be careful, madam. It's the thigh, remember?" He smiled.

She pulled the bandage tighter, turning his grin into a wince.

❖

As Jeremiah's eyesight improved over that lunch break, so did his view of his attendant. He found her very striking, although the stiff work clothing she wore didn't do justice to her figure.

Her strong eyebrows drew him to her deep eyes. They were soft and caring, and made his heart skip a beat every time he looked into them. Yet she avoided his. A set of flawless teeth shone through her generous smile. Her figure was disguised by the straight, light-blue dustcoat she had been issued by the pharmacy. But this could not hide her soft breasts that brushed against him occasionally as she tended to him. He caught glimpses of her black skin, smooth and firm, and drew deep breaths to inhale her soapy smell.

He looked at her hips again when she walked back into the store. Despite the constraints of the blue outfit, she looked sexy as she walked, revealing her curves. He imagined her shapely legs, invisible behind the curtain of her garment. Its swaying told of her sensuous saunter.

He compared her to the Sophiatown club dancers he had seen. They came out in their sexy tasselled clothing, exciting the audience by leaving little to the imagination. They drove men to a frenzy with their motion and the shimmering of their skimpy, tight outfits, and shed layers to reveal more of themselves. They were vulgar.

This lady was at another level entirely. She was graceful, and her uniformed body made her more desirable to him.

But the throbbing ache in his crotch subsided as his other pains returned, and he fell back, groaning.

Later in the day, when she dabbed the cut above his eye with antiseptic, her cheeks not five inches from his, he could feel his heart pounding.

❖

On the third day, after the pharmacy closed, he removed his shirt for her inspection of his bruises and cuts. Once again his chest was exposed: muscular, taut and smooth. He could tell she was struggling to draw her gaze away from it.

Then it was time to check his thigh wound, an exercise that

could not be delayed any longer, as she had reluctantly conceded during the lunch break. He removed his pants and lay there in only his underpants.

She tried her best to check how the healing had progressed. Even though she said nothing he could feel that she seemed satisfied. After checking all wounds she rubbed ointment on his bruises.

His vision blurred as his head pounded. Trying to mask the emotions swirling through him, he held his breath, but this only made him feel light and dizzy. Unable to hold back any longer, he raised himself up, and touched her lips with his. She pulled back.

"I'm sorry, I couldn't hold back," he whispered.

"I don't know you or who you are. I don't even know your full name."

He lay there for a while, breathing slowly and thinking. "I am Jerry Ngubeni," he whispered, and looked into her dreamy eyes. "I don't know your name either."

"Grace. Grace Bakwena." Her voice and the rhythm of her name caressed his soul like a love song.

"A beautiful name for a beautiful woman," he sighed in her ear.

He decided there and then to shed "Jeremiah" and plant his roots in this neighbourhood as Jerry, a name that seemed to express his new life in this area of Johannesburg – near Grace and away from Simon, who, with any luck, wouldn't find Jeremiah.

Jerry's wounds healed quickly. He soon looked presentable in clothing acquired from clotheslines about a mile away.

He had by then befriended an assistant packer at the nearby liquor store. The man told Jerry that he was an amateur boxer. He looked like one, with thigh-size arms, big fists and a thick chest. "My friends call me Joe, after Joe Louis," he said when he first introduced himself.

"Joe, I need a big favour."

"What is it?"

"I can't go to Rosebank, but I need to get a message to my uncle at Oxford Motors."

"That's about ten miles from here."

"No, it's not that far."

"It's the other side of Jo'burg, Jerry."

"Yes, but still not that far."

Jerry managed to persuade him with a five-shilling reward. Joe borrowed the store's three-wheeled delivery cycle and was back soon after his lunch break. "Your uncle is not very happy with you – not happy at all. And I also met Dizzy, who told me all about you. He's coming here after work today."

That evening, Dizzy arrived. "Simon and his cousins are patrolling the area for you, Jeremiah. It's not safe, man."

"They know me here as Jerry. And I'm not going back to Oxford. I'll find work here soon. I no longer look like a gangster. I am just sorry about Uncle Samson. He did his best for me, and I let him down." He looked at his feet. Then he looked at Dizzy. "But I really want to stay. I've met this great girl, and she's looking after me."

"I'll tell your uncle that you're well. He has been worried, but I'll give him a good version of what I see. Don't worry, man. I won't mention the girl because he'll just think you're following your cock again."

"I'm not. I can feel this place is right for me. And so is she. Tell my uncle that I have a job. He won't be so worried then. I will have a job by next week this time. Guaranteed." He didn't feel so sure of this, but his words were enough to convince Dizzy.

"Okay Jeremiah – er, Jerry."

15

It was Uncle Eben who arranged for Marius to do pupillage at the Pretoria Bar. "My friend, Advokaat Frik Mostert, will teach you, my boy. Take in everything you can learn, and within six months you will become a trial lawyer yourself. Then we'll make sure you get briefs from the state attorney to represent the government."

Day after day Marius sat in Advokaat Mostert's chambers. He saw how his master planned trial strategy, and was present in court when the wily cross-examiner tore witnesses apart. The six months felt like six weeks, and at the end of his pupillage, Marius felt he had learned a great deal. He still had doubts about his ability to make it as an advocate, but he would let his father down if he didn't try.

His chambers were fitted out with a solid mahogany desk, studded leather chairs, a scarlet thick-pile rug and floor-to-ceiling bookshelves. His father had done that for him.

Within days Marius was acting for the government when it seized property from a black community who was to be resettled away from white suburbs. He could not help thinking that the people had occupied that land for generations, but the government was passing laws to advance the policy of racial segregation. After a few weeks, he was briefed to defend the eviction of blacks from the multiracial cultural hub, Sophiatown.

The black people persisted in seeing these as forced relocations and did not seem to understand that they would be accommodated in new townships established for them to the southwest. Yes, these were a few miles out of town, but he knew there was no choice if the government was to achieve its policy of separating non-Europeans from the white suburbs. And that was what mattered, after all.

Marius fully understood the government policies that his family supported. And yet, in a discussion with the state attorney, he once surprised himself by asking whether the new townships had the facilities to accommodate all those being resettled. The state attorney, an influential member of the Broederbond, answered without hesitation, "Of course, Marius."

Not long after that discussion, which Marius saw as informal, Jacobus Strydom came to his son's chambers. "Marius, I have heard that you are questioning the policy of separating the black peoples from us whites."

"No, Pa. I'm not." Then he realised what had happened. "I just want to make sure we're not creating new problems. We're taking land from people who have been there for years and years. We must still make sure they are looked after."

"Son, we have fought in many wars against many enemies to get to where we are. It is now our time to govern. We must remember the sacrifices made by Oupa and many others. If you keep this in mind, you will have a big part to play in the future of this country. If you don't, you will make too many enemies among your own people. And remember this: those who are not your own people don't care about you. That is something we have learned the hard way."

"I'm a lawyer, Pa. Everyone is entitled to representation, and I will comply with my professional obligations."

"Just remember, your professional obligations apply to *your* people and *your* government. The other people can take care of their own."

A few days later, the state attorney sent Marius a brief to advise on a challenge made to a government eviction notice issued to a resident of Sophiatown. Marius politely returned the brief with the note, "Thank you for thinking of me. I am currently involved in a major criminal defence which is taking all of my time, and unfortunately will not be able to give this matter the attention it deserves."

Within twenty-four hours, Strydom stormed into Marius's chambers in Pretoria. "What's the matter with you? You're committing suicide."

"I've got a criminal trial on the go. I'm busy."

"The way you're going, you won't be busy for long!"

"Pa, I really do have this other case. But I have come to realise that I am more interested in commercial cases and in real criminal trials. That's why I've decided to move to Johannesburg and to join the Johannesburg bar. There are plenty of advocates in Pretoria who can take on the types of cases I'm getting here."

"Marius, think about this very carefully. There is a big future for you here. Not only in law, but also in government. This is where the power is. This is just your time to earn your reputation and – one day – reach right up to the top. Please, I beg you, don't throw it away."

"Pa, I won't dishonour you, but I think it's best for me to earn my reputation in the biggest commercial city. The biggest cases are in Johannesburg."

"I hope you know what you're doing, because I don't know what the hell you're talking about. Just don't be stupid. Don't forget, Smuts will be remembered as a traitor. I will not allow my own flesh and blood to be a traitor, Marius. Not after all the blood we have spilled. This has to blerrie well stop now. As your father, I insist that you obey me."

"I have to do this. For me. I need to prove myself in Jo'burg."

His father's frown froze and his eyes locked on to Marius. "I will let you go to the God-forsaken Johannesburg," he said slowly, "but *don't* take cases against our government. Also, keep your blerrie mouth shut. Leave the politics to me."

Marius could see Strydom was furious. His father had never spoken so harshly to him, had always been stern but in control of his language. This time, Strydom had lost his temper as never before.

Meekness was the wisest response. "Yes, Pa."

Within three months, Marius had packed up his chambers in Pretoria and joined the Johannesburg bar, where he was introduced to a new experience. The majority of the members were English and Jewish South Africans; the Afrikaners formed a small minority. The big commercial matters were briefed by the large English-speaking law firms.

Marius received a number of criminal briefs to defend charges of fraud, theft, assault, rape and murder. He did not accept cases against the government.

He followed the government's legislative programme restricting movement of the blacks. Strydom's party was diligently, if impatiently, fulfilling its policy of entrenching segregation of the races.

Marius informed himself about the history and culture of law practice in Johannesburg. The Afrikaner law firms in and around that city were still in the minority, but he discovered that after the National Party won the 1948 election, several of them had begun to enjoy a healthy flow of work from the growing number of Afrikaner-controlled municipal authorities, the burgeoning Afrikaner business community, and the government itself. These firms briefed him in commercial cases for their clients.

As previously in Pretoria, his court skills were noticed by others. Mr Isaac Landau was the first Jewish partner in Ambrose, Archibald & Co., a law firm established in 1888 to serve British business in Johannesburg. The firm was one of the largest in the city and still counted among its clients mining houses, banks, insurance companies, and the English-speaking business end of town.

Landau briefed Marius to give legal opinions on large-scale matters of a commercial nature. Although Marius had developed his reputation as a good criminal lawyer, Landau gave him the opportunity to extend that reputation to the highly coveted big commercial disputes.

As time passed, he saw more of Mr Landau. The two of them would often lunch together at Landau's favourite tearooms in Pritchard Street, near the Supreme Court and Marius's chambers. Landau would have wine with the meal while Marius drank lemonade. Marius looked forward to those lunches with the well-informed older man. He realised that Landau made it his business to know what was happening in Johannesburg.

A day came when Mr Landau spoke about his family. "My father emigrated from Russia many decades ago. There was no future there."

"Why did he leave?"

"They were being harshly discriminated against, even though they had been there for hundreds of years."

"Hmm."

"He started a men's clothing store and has done quite well. The old man worked very hard to give me a future here."

"Yes. This country has been good to many."

"That's true. Even though we are immigrants, I had opportunities, more than many around us. My father told me that education is the one thing no one can take away from you."

"That's true, but your father's property is safe here. Our government is looking after him."

"In Europe it has been very different. Jews escaped from Germany with just the clothes on their backs. My father helped many of them who arrived here with nothing. Many lost their families there."

Marius, acutely aware of his family's influence in the pro-Nazi Ossewabrandwag, felt his ears burning and his face reddening. "Yes, Mr Landau. It is the case that each must look after his own kind." Then he changed the subject. He decided that politics would remain off the table in their future lunches.

16

While Jerry was recovering in the pharmacy yard, he realised that the little cash he'd had with him would fast run out. He couldn't have asked for a better piece of luck than being found by Grace. She was feeding him and seeing to him without accepting his money.

He was apprehensive about the streets of Jo'burg and was reluctant to venture too far from his cardboard hideout. No one knew him here, and he felt that it was best to steer clear of Simon's jurisdiction north of the city.

Impatience was getting the better of him. He hated being idle in the small space behind the pharmacy toilet block. How long would this continue? He could be out of a job for a while. He needed to get out and look at the world around him.

During a reconnoitre of the neighbourhood early one morning, he walked past the corner store. His attention was drawn to the garage located almost directly opposite. He stopped to observe it and then sat on a low wall near the store, easing the lingering soreness in his limbs while he surveyed the business. It looked good. Here was a potential source of employment almost right under his nose. Given his skills, the Top Star Garage just might be worth a try.

Jerry was interrupted in his observations when he caught sight of the corner store's delivery man departing on his three-wheeled cycle.

A mound of cartons loaded with groceries filled the crate over the front two wheels.

Jerry's stomach growled. Although Grace was looking after him well, he felt he could provide a little extra food for himself on this bright morning. He had already assessed the corner store's security, or lack of it, during his rare sorties.

His hunger pangs sharpened, but he didn't want to part with the little cash he had. He looked around. There was no one in the store's backyard. It took little effort for him to quickly scale the fence and help himself to four empty soft-drink bottles. After hopping back onto the pavement, he checked about him, and then adopted an easy stroll that took him around the corner to the front of the shop. There he entered through the main door, relaxed and casual. He handed in the empty bottles for a refund, which he spent on two buns. He soon came swaggering out of the shop, munching on the fresh, doughy softness.

Unnoticed, he thought.

It had been more than a year since Neil's night out with his cousin and Henry's thwarted attempt to make off with Neil's stash. Neil sometimes recalled the incident with a mixture of embarrassment and anger, and a feeling that it was not the last he would hear of Henry. *I'll be glad to give you a piece of my mind if ever we cross paths again, cousin.* But he felt that to go looking for Henry would be a waste of time. If anything, the experience had strengthened his resolve and brought his own business plans into clearer focus. Already he had increased the turnover at Top Star and was still making changes to increase his profit margin.

Today, as he stood by the window of the shop, he thought about further changes he could make. The business still wasn't running smoothly enough. He'd been missing something. What was it? That driveway service area could still do with an upgrade – and not just physical. The men at the pumps did what they had to do, but it was all very mechanical. They had no enthusiasm.

His thoughts were interrupted by the distracting sight of a well-built and neatly dressed black man hopping over the side fence of the store across the road. The man soon reappeared with empty bottles and then went to the store's main entrance. Before long he emerged with two buns, chomping happily on one of them.

Neil chuckled to himself. He felt a surge of empathy with this spunky young African.

Neil was surprised when, the very next week, this same young man walked into his office.

"Mr Robertson," he said as if he had known Neil for many years, "I am Jerry Ngubeni, and I am the best mechanic in Johannesburg. Not only that, sir, your garage is very badly run, and I can help you."

Neil was taken aback. This was a bit arrogant. He'd never been approached by anyone in such a way. Then again, hadn't he been drawn to the boldness of this man the week before? He was sure this was the same person he'd seen stealing from the store across the road. There was no knowing what this man could do to him ... *But he's got attitude. I'll give him that.*

"Well, Jerry, that's very interesting. And how do you think you can improve the way I run my business?"

"Ah! I'm not your worker yet, Mr Robertson, sir. And I won't give away my secrets until you give me the job. But you won't be disappointed – that *I* can promise *you*." With these last words, he gestured first to himself and then to Neil.

Neil felt some connection with Jerry – they did have in common their deft way of exploiting the bottle refund exchange. But if he was going to follow his instinct and try Jerry out, he had to start by showing him who the boss was.

"But I don't have a vacancy. This isn't a charity. I can't take you on your say-so that you are the best mechanic. I have a workshop full of good mechanics."

"I know exactly what you've got in your workshop already, sir. Some are good and some need a kick up the backside. But if you haven't got a place for me, I have a solution that solves everyone's problem."

"Oh, what's that?"

"I offer my services at the pump – at no charge to you. But you must make me the boss boy, in charge of all the pump attendants. My pay will be from tips only."

There was something ingenious here, a spark of inventiveness that once again touched a chord.

Without hesitating, Neil went for the gamble. He took Jerry on.

Jerry was so enthusiastic at the pump that he developed a distinctive style of service – joking with customers, offering to do oil checks, and encouraging the use of the Top Star maintenance and repair shop. Without asking, he took it upon himself to select young men with a bit of humour to man the pumps. He also trained them to smile and be playful, but respectful, with the customers.

He got Neil to give the pump staff their own uniforms, which were spotted, and he called them "the Top Star Cheetahs". The name gave this neglected group of workers a level of prestige and pride that no other service station offered. He told them they were the face of the business: they were the ones who had direct contact with the customers. Then he began brief training sessions for them on how to serve and how to sell other products. "If they come in for petrol, make them feel special," Jerry drilled into his team. "Sell them oil and tell them our workshop is the best in Jo'burg."

He organised all the pump attendants so that they pooled the tips and he got the lion's share.

But Jerry also walked through the workshop, where he complimented the good mechanics and jovially pulled up the lazy ones, inspiring them to put their hearts into their work. "You do a good job and the customers come back. You don't and they don't. Then what will happen to this business? What will happen to us? There'll be no job for you."

He was formally the leading pump boy, but he became the informal leader of all the black staff at the garage.

So good was business for Neil that within one year he extended both the repair shop and the petrol station area. Jerry had a team of fifteen young black pump attendants spread over three shifts, all chosen by him for their personalities and customer skills. By this time Jerry was on the payroll as boss boy of all the African staff.

Neil had kept the old staff employed by Mr Van Tonder, but Jerry outperformed them. Neil still felt he had no choice but to keep foreman Prinsloo as the manager, even though the man sat around, smoked continually, and drank cheap brandy from the bottles he kept wrapped in brown paper at the back of the workshop.

Neil noticed that when challenging problems appeared in the repair shop, the black staff went to Jerry to help solve them. But Jerry told him that he didn't want to work as a mechanic. He relished his new status of boss boy.

Occasionally he also identified sellers of cars and matched them with buyers, all for Neil's profit. "Hey, boss," he said to Neil one day, "why don't you sell cars there?" He pointed to the empty land next door.

"Well, Jerry. Isn't that a coincidence? I was thinking exactly that myself. I've already made enquiries about that land and worked it all out. With the support of the service station, we can offer warranties for cars we sell and then keep the customers for repairs later."

Within another two months, Neil had bought the land and extended the operation into a saleyard for second-hand cars.

Top Star Garage and Service Station soon became Top Star Motors – *"Your one-stop shop for all your motoring needs"* – with Neil as owner, Prinsloo as manager in title only, and Jerry as the boss boy. Neil could see that Prinsloo was ineffective and even that he deferred to Jerry much of the time. But Neil couldn't fire Prinsloo: it was important not to alienate the Afrikaner staff, and he was their senior man. Because Prinsloo was white and Jerry was black, Prinsloo was the highly paid manager and Jerry the worker on a lower pay rate. But what could Neil do? *That's the way it is in South Africa.* He had a business to run.

Neil employed Prinsloo's niece, Brunelda, as an office clerk. It made Neil angry when, one day, he saw her order Jerry to purchase stamps and clear the wastepaper bin. Even though Jerry had many other duties to perform, he complied with a grunt and no thanks from Brunelda.

Neil wanted to reprimand her then and there, but couldn't do so in front of Jerry and the other staff. He decided to speak to her later. She was no older than 19. She could not have appreciated how critical the black staff were to the success of the business.

Neil was pleased with Jerry's leadership and left him, in his Top Star Cheetah overalls with the Top Star motif, to run the engine of the whole operation.

Except for the saleyard.

Neil was in charge of the second-hand car sales business. As buyer, he selected carefully, and then always sold at the right price, turning the inventory around quickly and at a handsome profit.

By 1955, with Jerry selecting all the black staff and training them to follow the culture he had set up, the Eloff Street business had been supplemented by branches in the east, in Kensington, and in the west, in Melville. The only important area Neil had not yet tackled was in the north. He was keen to set up in Oxford Road, Rosebank, which was the artery to the wealthy northern suburbs. But he couldn't understand why Jerry kept telling him he would not work in Rosebank.

Neil felt that he treated Jerry well. He had given him a good job, was paying him slightly more than the other black workers, let him keep the lion's share of the tips, and now provided him with accommodation – a converted storeroom behind the Kensington branch. This was not far from where Neil lived, and he often dropped Jerry off at the end of the day.

Neil still rented a room from Mrs Botha, but by this time he occupied one of the larger rooms facing the street. It had a bed, a wardrobe, a desk that he had purchased, and a comfortable armchair. He usually ate with the Botha family and spent time with them in the courtyard. Even though he wasn't much older than Mrs Botha's oldest son, a policeman, Neil was now seen as a benevolent uncle.

As his business grew, he bought the younger Botha children clothes and luxuries they couldn't afford. He was just as happy as they were when he gave them toys, watches, and radios. He sourced a good, cheap second-hand car for Constable Koos Botha when the young man was ready to buy his first car.

Neil was well known in the licensing department too, and at Christmas handed out gratuities as a token of his appreciation for the "efficient" attention they gave "the public".

"I am the public," he explained to Jerry.

When Neil spoke about his contacts at the licensing department, Jerry's eyes glowed. "Boss, can you get me a driver's licence?" he asked Neil one day. "I can drive very good, you know."

"You're joking, Jerry. Where did you learn to drive?"

"On the farm. There was a Buick. I knew that car better than anyone, and I could park her into tight spots – not a scratch. Here, let me drive. I'll show you."

"All right. Let's see what you can do."

Neil got into the passenger seat of his sporty Austin Healey. Jerry took the wheel. He crunched the gears once only and the car jerked twice, almost stalling. But for someone who hadn't driven this car before, he managed well. "Hmm ... Not perfect, but okay."

Within a week he'd brought Jerry his driver's licence certificate, embossed with the official stamp. Jerry didn't even have to go for a test. "This cost me a bottle of brandy, Jerry."

"Thank you, boss. Just tell me where you want to go and I'll be there. But ... you know, boss, you'll get more out of me if you give me a car. I can check the branches out for you."

"And who is going to check *you* out? No thanks, Jerry," replied Neil.

Neil found out that Jerry often pulled rank on the saleyard staff and drove newly acquired second-hand stock out the yard "to see if it needed fixing before being put on sale". Neil turned a blind eye – Jerry did sometimes report problems with the cars he took. And they were always returned within a day or after the weekend. Neil could see that Jerry would not be deterred. Somehow, a car was coming to him.

17

Neil decided to work on becoming a sales agent not just for second-hand cars, but for new cars as well. He was convinced that one day every family in South Africa would have at least one car. Such a big business opportunity came once in a lifetime. He'd have to be a fool, he thought, to miss this one. And he had what it took – he knew how to sell.

Within a short time he had the dealership agency for Austin and was selling more of the new British cars from his showrooms than anyone else in the city. These display yards were luxurious extensions of his "one-stop car centres" covering areas to the east, west and south of Johannesburg.

He wrote letters to his mother, giving her his news, and she replied telling him how well she was coping. She also explained that she didn't need the money orders he was sending. But he continued the monthly payments. It made him feel as though he was fulfilling his duty to them. He still dreamed that Mary would join him, but she reported that Milton was doing well, if not well enough to leave Guildford.

Then, one night, his mother telephoned him. Her voice was shaky. "Neil, your father has taken a turn for the worse." She paused. "He has had a stroke and is semi-paralysed. The whole of the left side of his body can't move – even more than before. His face has dropped."

"I'm so sorry, Mum. What can I do?"

"I don't know. That's up to you. The doctors say he is rather bad." Her voice sounded weak, or was it the long distance call? "They're trying to keep him stable, but they're worried about internal haemorrhaging if they strengthen the blood thinners. I think he wants to die." He could hear her sniffing.

"It's amazing he's lasted so long. I didn't give him one year when I left."

"If you want to see him, you'd better come soon, love."

"I can't, Mum. The business needs me. It's too big to leave. I'm on my own. Too many people here depend on me every day."

"Of course, dear." She was disappointed and Neil could feel it.

"I can't drop the business every time he takes a bad turn. He can go on like this for years. I will visit soon, but I can't leave now."

"Yes, dear."

"Please tell him I'm thinking of him. My business employs a hundred and sixty men, and I have three outlets. Tell him that. I'm sure he'll like that."

"Yes, dear. I'll tell him. Bye, love."

After ringing off, Neil stared at the telephone, unsure of his decision to stay in Johannesburg. That niggling doubt was forced from his mind when the telephone rang again and his attention was taken up by the manager at the Kensington branch.

A week later, Neil received a telegram.

DEAR NEIL STOP FATHER PASSED AWAY IN SLEEP TODAY STOP FUNERAL ON TUESDAY STOP LOVE MUM STOP

Neil had been expecting this news for years, and yet now it hit him like an electric shock. He sat in his office with the telegram in his hand and reread it. He barely remembered the athletic, strong mechanic reduced to an invalid – the man in charge who was later to become someone unable to care even for his personal hygiene. The image imprinted on his mind was the sad farewell and the emotion shown by his father, a man he thought had no capacity to love. Yet Neil had felt the love that day.

He regretted not going over to say farewell one last time. He wondered, should he go to the funeral? It wouldn't make a difference now that his father had gone, he told himself. *It will look false if I go and stand in the front of the church when I effectively abandoned him to Mum.*

He sent a telegram back.

DEAREST MUM STOP SO SAD AND UPSET FOR YOU STOP YOU WERE HIS STRENGTH AND SAVIOUR STOP THOUGHTS ARE WITH YOU STOP WILL SEND MONEY FOR FUNERAL STOP LOVE NEIL STOP

Again there were the temporary pangs of guilt at not seeing his father one last time and at not being there for Mary. And again these were soon pushed aside, overtaken by the demands of his business.

Neil had cultivated a good relationship with Walter Blair, the senior manager of British Motors in Johannesburg. Blair telephoned Neil one day. "London has told me that they are thinking of giving a dealership for Austins and Morris vehicles in Rosebank to someone else. A decision has been made at the top not to give you a chance for the dealership."

"What? How can this be, Walter? I know I haven't been an agent for very long, but in that time I have built up three of the most successful Austin sales and repair businesses in the country."

"I know, but I am helpless because this decision was made by the head office in London."

"Please see what you can find out about this. I'll be at your office in half an hour. Who made the decision? Please find that out for me."

Within the hour Neil was standing across the desk from Walter. "What's going on? I've been so loyal. And I've increased your share of the market in Johannesburg."

"I'm sorry, Mr Robertson. There has been an adverse report from London, and there is some suspicion around you. Someone has expressed distrust of you."

"What do you mean?"

"There's a note that came with the instruction. Here it is, from a Mr Francis Harvey, acting deputy manager of the sales division for the Union of South Africa. The note says, 'Mr Robertson is not to be trusted, as he is less than honest.'"

"What? Let me see."

He looked at the note and the name on it. And with the force of a blow, the memory came back to him of his previous encounter with Francis Harvey, at that time the penny-counting Corporal Francis Harvey. He could not believe this absurd coincidence. The pedantic little nitpicker from a few years ago in Cape Town had found a position with British Motors in London, dammit! With power over South Africa. So this was what it was all about! *That bloody nutcase remembers my little nut trick.*

But he would not be put off by such a petty twist of fate. He gave a slightly modified version of events to Walter Blair. "That damned Harvey tried to get away with some free nuts, and I caught the little man out. I embarrassed him, and now he's trying to get his revenge. Surely you as the manager here in Johannesburg can override him,

Walter. That Harvey's got the brain of a pea and is so crooked he couldn't lie straight in bed. I don't want to make a scene for you and him in London."

"What do you mean?"

"You know I'm the best car salesman in this city. Only I can get you a big piece of the action in the north of Jo'burg. But if Austin doesn't want me, I'll take the message, and you can forget about the south, east and west too. Austin is on notice. I'll switch to General Motors. Opel has approached me because they know I've got the best positions for new car sales. But you know, I'm English. I like the British cars. I'm willing to be loyal, and you've already seen proof of that. Now you have to be loyal to me. Can we arrange to bypass this report?"

The manager sat there, squirming in his worn mustard chair behind his two-tone grey steel desk. Neil looked at his dark suit with its sheen from long wear, and his thin dim-maroon tie. Walter Blair exuded an anxious air of discomfort. Perspiration collected on his reddening brow above thick black-rimmed spectacles. He wiped his forehead with a faded brown handkerchief and shuffled uneasily on his squeaky chair. He was clearly distressed about Neil's confrontational manner and attitude, which left him under no illusions: Neil was angry and wouldn't take no for an answer.

"Listen here, Walter. I have other friends in London. Is there a way we can cut Harvey out of the loop? I'll use my contacts and you use yours. I'll make sure they know you helped find our location in the west. And that you helped us with our approaches to the city council that increased our sales of Austin vans to the various municipalities. Surely both of us are stronger than pea-brain Harvey?"

"I don't know. Mr Harvey seems to have some power ... and powerful friends."

"What do you mean? Aren't you the boss of South Africa?"

"I am, but I fall under London, and he's based there."

"We can join forces. With your support, we'll pull this our way. I'll make sure it's worth your while. In fact, I always budget a 5 per cent fit-out fee that you will earn for Rosebank because getting the agency is part of the set-up."

"I don't know, but I'll see what I can do. I also don't fancy someone else moving into our territory. I'll make a few calls."

Neil was relieved at Blair's compliant approach. He didn't have to resort to plan B, which he had up his sleeve in case he was accused of dishonesty.

"Thank you, Walter. You won't regret this."

Neil left, but he certainly wasn't going to leave anything to chance. He returned later with two gold Omega watches, one for Walter and one for Margaret Blair.

❖

Walter Blair managed to make an appointment for Neil to see a member of the board of directors of the British Motor Company. Neil dropped everything and flew to London. He used his membership of Johannesburg's exclusive Royal Milner Club, which had reciprocal arrangements with the very private St Hugo's Club in Mayfair – the club of the board member he was to meet, Sir Julian Hackett.

He spared no effort, ensuring that he and Sir Julian received treatment reserved for royalty. He presented Sir Julian with engraved gold cufflinks and a necklace studded with Kimberley diamonds for Lady Edwina Hackett.

Neil had also done his homework. "Sir Julian. Our families go back a while."

"Really?"

"Yes. My father, Milton, had Robertson's Motors in Guildford. I recall him caring for a Rolls Royce Phantom III that belonged to your late father, Sir Roger."

"Well, well, Robertson. That is a coincidence. I remember Father commenting once about Robertson. 'An honest good man, who paid a heavy price in the war,' he told me. How is your father? Still unwell, I expect."

"I'm afraid he passed away recently, Sir Julian. But it was a relief. He hadn't been well for years."

"I'm sorry to hear that. Father was never happy with the many mechanics he tried with his Rollers later, you know. He told me that the secret with Robertson was his passion for the machines, even though they didn't belong to him."

"Oh yes. Father was a very passionate man," Neil commented, pinching his ear. "He passed on that ethic to me, and I apply it in my businesses in South Africa today."

"Good. Good, Robertson. Well done."

Within a month, Neil was appointed agent for British Motors' Austin and Morris cars in Rosebank. By then he had also put in an offer on premises adjacent to Oxford Motors in Oxford Road.

Neil's visit to London came less than three weeks after his father's funeral. He didn't tell Mary; he was in a rush to get back to the business.

Within two months of his return, he received a telegram.

DEAR NEIL STOP YOUR MOTHER PASSED
AWAY IN HOSPITAL STOP CANCER FINALLY
BEAT HER STOP DEEPEST SYMPATHY STOP
AUNT JANE STOP

Neil's heart fell and he could think of nothing else. He hadn't even known his mother had been ill. He immediately got through to the exchange, found Aunt Jane's telephone number and called her.

"Oh, Neil. It's you." Her voice was steady and cold.

"What happened? Was she ill?"

"Neil, she's been ill for three years."

"What do you mean?"

"She's had breast cancer and had both breasts removed about two years ago."

"I didn't know. Why didn't—"

"She didn't want you to know. She wanted you to live your life. She knew they were both on their way out and—"

"But I would've come. I could've helped."

"How? Milton was almost a vegetable. She took care of him with the help of Mrs James. Even when she was very sick, the two of them did their best for Milton."

"I could have seen her. I would have sent for her."

"She wasn't going anywhere, Neil. In fact, I wasn't sure she would outlast Milton. She kept herself going just for him."

"Oh, my God. I wish someone had told me. I could've seen her two months ago." He was emotional.

"Well, then, maybe you should have. You should've seen her earlier. Your mother didn't want you to see her like that. She wanted you to remember her the way she was before. But I don't know why you never came to see her."

"When is the funeral?"

"Well, that depends on whether we wait for you. Are you coming?"

"Yes. Yes. I'm coming. I'll be there on Wednesday."

Neil flew to London, borrowed an Austin from the head office, and drove to Guildford for the funeral. He arrived at the family home next to what used to be Robertson's Motors, now long abandoned, to find Mrs James in the sitting room. The walls and furniture greeted him with the scent of his father's pipe tobacco. The ceilings had turned a smoky yellow.

"Jane told me you were coming today and I didn't know what time, so I just stayed home, waiting."

"Thank you, Mrs James, but that wasn't necessary."

"No, Neil. I moved in to help Mary and Milton. You see, your mother did her best. But *her* health weakened too, over the last couple of years. She was fine until about eleven every day, and then she got tired. I used to come in and help. The evenings were a problem for Mary. So I offered to move in. She was relieved."

"I don't know how to thank you, Mrs James."

"There's no need. If you want to stay here, I'll move out. But I have no home any more. I gave up my council home when I moved in here, you see. I may be able to stay with my cousin."

Neil realised she had taken over his bedroom. "No, Mrs James. You've carried our family enough. You keep your room, and I'll go to a hotel."

"Are you sure, love?"

"Yes. Also, Mrs James, unless Mum has made other plans, this house is yours for the rest of your life. I'll keep it going, and I'll pay the rates and taxes."

❖

Aunt Jane came to the funeral. She sniffed into a lace handkerchief. "Neil, your mother was so disappointed you never came to see them."

"She didn't want me to know about her illness. You said so yourself."

"Yes, but you could have come to see them." She had stopped sniffing by then. "You were their only child!"

"Aunt Jane, I sent them money every month." He felt a knot in his throat and fought to hold back his tears.

"It's not the money, Neil. They lived for you, not your money," she said and pushed her balled handkerchief up her left sleeve.

"Yes, they did." Neil paused and swallowed. He leaned forward and said, "By the way, when did Henry last come to see you?"

Jane stared at him. When she burst into tears, Neil regretted what he'd said. Of course Henry hadn't been back to see his parents either. All the more reason not to make such a hurtful remark. And how could anything Henry did excuse his own near-neglect of his parents?

Later that night, Neil found Milton and Mary's last will in a locked drawer of the bureau in their bedroom. It was the "Joint Will and Testament of Mary Eleanor Robertson and Milton Neil Robertson". He read: *"We leave and bequeath all our property to our beloved son, Neil, who we are both so proud of. We want him to know that we did not expect him to look after us as we aged. We were happy until the end and did not regret that he has made a successful life overseas. Our future is his."*

He looked at the date on the legal document. It was a recently prepared will signed by Mary and Milton three months before Milton's death. He saw in his father's tobacco-stained finger smudges, all over the legal document, evidence that Milton had paid attention to every word.

18

On weekends Jerry emerged from his Kensington storeroom well dressed and eager for fun.

Dizzy was still his closest friend and, even with his thick glasses, one of the best mechanics Jerry had worked with at Oxford Motors. It wasn't long before Jerry had arranged a job for him at Top Star. A short while after that, they had found a new group of men to hang around with when they sought amusement.

They cruised around the black townships on the outskirts of Johannesburg, looking for entertainment and seeking out the shebeens. There was no shortage of suggestions from their new friends about where to find the best homemade liquor. Jerry was excited by the thought that the shebeens were unlawful, and he enjoyed the drinking, laughing and dancing. And, as far as he could tell, so did the young women they went about with or picked up along the way.

Since he had moved to Kensington he and Grace had drifted apart. They courted for a couple of months, but it soon became clear to Jerry that Grace did not trust him. She had even told him that, as a handsome and securely employed young man, he would be a target for many young ladies. And she was right.

Young women were seduced by his looks and his light-hearted

approach to life. He just could not put the brakes on his pleasure-seeking. He was all too willing to take what he could get. He soon found himself pushing aside the lessons of his previous promiscuous experiences.

Without Grace's temperate influence, Jerry's weekends had no limits.

On most Friday nights he selected a car from the stockyard of second-hand vehicles that were still in the process of being tested and made ready for sale. He had already begun to take them "for checking". Now they were part of his nights out.

He usually selected a large American automobile – the more chrome, the better – and provided transport for his group of friends. These huge "Yank tanks" with wide front and backseats like long sofas could comfortably seat six passengers, but packing in eight allowed them to get closer and more intimate, which suited Jerry and his friends just fine.

The majestic cars and spunky occupants never failed to impress the gaggles of giggling girls who were out and about. Starting at someone's house in the township, they sometimes collected one girl for each friend. Then they prowled the neighbourhoods, looking for a party, a club or a shebeen. Sometimes they went without girls, hoping to find new acquaintances at their destination.

❖

In the same week that the new Top Star Motors opened in Rosebank, Dizzy told Jerry that a popular jazz band was to perform at a club belonging to Mama Elizabeth, known as "the Queen of Thokoza". The black township was some twenty miles south of Johannesburg. This was too much for Jerry and his friends to miss. They agreed to go to Mama Elizabeth's to unwind after the arduous effort of preparing for the first day of trade in Rosebank.

The opening was a success. Jerry had trained over twenty new

Top Star Cheetahs and had helped in the selection of forty men to work in the shop. He insisted that, apart from the formal ceremony (for whites only) where Neil would cut the ribbon at the front door, he would take care of a grand inauguration for the black staff. That Friday morning, the repair shop was invaded by the smell of braaied meat instead of oil and grease. Laughter and banter replaced the tinker of tools and hissing of machines.

When their stomachs were full, the men sang. Initially groups competed with clan songs from their respective tribal memories. By the time the "whites only" party abandoned their festivities to investigate the melodious roar from the back, the hundred or so black voices resonated as one. They had formed a large semicircle around Jerry, and his heart vibrated with their rhythm.

Prinsloo came up to him after the first song in the presence of the VIPs and whispered, "That's enough. Tell them to get back to work."

Jerry scanned the small group of whites for Neil. There he was, focused on Jerry. Their eyes met. Instead of the approval Jerry expected to see, Neil's unsmiling countenance pierced the bubble of Jerry's joy and pride.

Jerry was baffled. Why would his boss not want them to celebrate so spontaneously?

He was still searching for an answer when the men broke out into a stirring hymn, which drew Jerry back to the choir. Tears gathered in his eyes as he saw Dizzy conducting them, the spotted Top Star Cheetahs in the front and, behind them, the mechanics in their brown overalls – all chanting for him.

He had done his best for his boss.

He had thought a few times that, as an immigrant, Neil had been given more opportunities than he ever had. Jerry could not even dream of having a business of his own. Sure, Neil had grabbed the chances he was given. This new workshop was part of Neil's success. Why did he not want Jerry and the black staff to enjoy it too?

The week had been tense for Jerry in another way. The new Rosebank branch was in Simon's neighbourhood. Jerry had reminded Dizzy, and asked him to keep a lookout, in case Simon turned up. He mentioned it again on the day.

"Don't you worry, man," Dizzy told him on the way to Rosebank. "I heard yesterday that Simon was badly injured in a fight a few months ago. And there is a rumour he's in jail."

"Really? Who was he fighting with this time?"

"I don't know. No one is saying. His friends are keeping a lid on it."

Jerry was relieved that Dizzy turned out to be right. There was no trouble at the opening.

On that Friday afternoon, Jerry checked out a Buick from Top Star's second-hand yard. When he saw it, he knew he wanted *that car* for the weekend. It was the same model as Baas Strydom's Buick that he'd loved so much as a boy. How long had it been since he helped Alfred look after that other car? It had to be some twelve or thirteen years. He inhaled the faint whiff of the interior. *My God! This car still has the smell of sweet heaven!* When he saw the three-spoked steering wheel, inlaid with the silver horn rim and the Buick logo, he chuckled.

Now he sat up against the door, one arm controlling the steering wheel, his other arm out the window. He followed the long chrome Buick bullet at the tip of the bonnet as he swished along the streets, collecting his boys. He drove it with pride and joy, even though it wasn't his. "I'm going to get the boss to give this car to me. Do you like this car, Dizzy?"

"Jerry. I luuuuve this car. This is the car of my dreams."

"Really? It's mine too."

"Let me drive."

"I can't. It's not mine yet, you know."

"Please, man. You're not the only one at Top Star. I'm a mechanic, remember. I can also *test* it, you know. Please."

"Okay. Here. You take over. But that means you must drive us home too, because tonight … I'm going to get drunk."

"It's a deal." They changed places.

Jerry slumped back into the seat and said, "My shoulders are beginning to feel lighter. I spent most of the day ironing out the creases and dealing with that Prinsloo, who was trying to show off to the boss. Tonight I will unwind."

Dizzy had heard from the young men about the training Jerry had given them that day. He chuckled. "Show off your personality. Make them come back so that your job is safe. *And* you will get a *biiig* tip!" They laughed at Dizzy's accurate mimicking of Jerry's voice.

They passed through the crowded Thokoza township, where the streets looked like ghettos. "Where do all these people work? Look how packed it is," Dizzy said as the stench of rotting rubbish invaded the Buick.

Jerry looked at the squalor surrounding them. "They've been thrown here to work in the white town nearby, Alberton, to provide labour."

"It's so dark. It's scary."

"Yes, there's no electricity."

They arrived at Mama Elizabeth's shebeen. It was a long, rectangular house with brick walls and a corrugated iron roof. Jerry thought it looked well maintained. Although plain, it stood out like a palace among the squalid surroundings of dilapidated shacks, lean-tos, sheds, and other haphazard structures that the Thokoza residents had erected in their battle to provide roofs over their heads.

Dizzy parked the Buick at the side of the dusty street adjacent to the shebeen, and they clambered out. The night was warm and balmy. A large, neat lounge at the entrance of the house was empty. It had a long bench for use as a bar counter in bad weather. They followed the sound of music through a kitchen and towards a back door, passing a long passage to the left with about four doors leading from it.

They stepped from the house into a large courtyard sheltered by a massive acacia tree growing out of a circle of red earth in the concrete floor. There was no electricity. The lighting came from gas lamps set around the perimeter, and candles. Large timber cable reels and the occasional oil drum served as tables to sit at or lean on. People sat on wooden drink and milk crates mixed with random chairs, stools and benches.

The band had been set up in a corner adjacent to a cleared area. That space would become the dance floor as the drinks flowed and the music tempo went up a notch.

Trumpeter Big Joe Mkhonza, "big" because of his size and his sound, led the band. He was accompanied on his right by a sunglassed drummer and, on his left, by the saxophonist. A dexterous percussionist on the triangle, tambourine and maracas stood to the far right. A buxom singer, in a crimson body-hugging dress with elegant side slits that revealed her long silky brown legs, waved and winked at Dizzy as they arrived.

"Haauw! Who's that sexy woooman, Dizzy?"

"That, my dear friend, is Lady Luckylips Twala."

"I can see why."

"Jerry, she's my third cousin. I should protect her from you, but if you want—"

"Yes, introduce me when they have a break. I want to meet your cousin."

She blew kisses at Jerry as she whispered the 1952 hit, "When I Fall in Love".

Drinks were for sale at a counter: two long planks over empty oil barrels painted yellow, red and green.

Everything happened under the watchful eye of Mama Elizabeth. Like an eagle seeking prey, she looked out for trouble. Looking larger than life, she was dressed in flowing sheets of green, red, and yellow. A golden *duku* (cloth head-covering), wrapped above her frown with a powerful bowknot to the side, completed the impression of royalty.

Dizzy explained to Jerry that her shebeen was legendary for her *skomfani* skokiaan, a home brew with a high alcohol content made from sugar, yeast and warm water. "I'm told she adds *a bit* of meths to give it an extra kick," said Dizzy with a pump of his arms, "and pineapple skin for taste."

Dizzy was astonished at how quickly Jerry unwound after the first three drinks. Jerry's voice volume increased a few notches as he called out to Lady Luckylips during her songs.

Dizzy got a little nervous when Mama Elizabeth frowned at Jerry. At first Dizzy couldn't understand why she then sent more of her skokiaan over and smiled as Jerry gulped it down with relish. He raised his glass to her. "Cheers, Mama," he shouted from one end of the courtyard to the other, to Dizzy's embarrassment.

Only when Jerry relaxed even further and there was a lameness to his voice and movements did Dizzy realise what Mama Elizabeth was doing. She had pegged Jerry as a possible troublemaker; Dizzy was sure of it. The kick of the alcohol had rammed home in poor Jerry's head. Dizzy began to feel concerned about what they should do with Jerry. Should he try to hold up the drinks that kept coming at speed? Or just leave Jerry alone? *Maybe we should take him home.*

Within a short while, Dizzy noticed that the strength had gone out of Jerry's arms. He lost control of his limbs, his eyes looked heavy and he started slurring his words. Dizzy looked at their friends, trying to attract attention.

By the time Jerry's body had gone completely limp and he had passed out with his head flat on the table, Dizzy knew it was too late to do anything. What would be the point of trying? They might as well stay and have some fun. Jerry would wake up soon enough.

Mama Elizabeth came over to Dizzy and the others. "Excuse me, gentlemen. He will soon want to vomit. May I suggest that you lead him to the gate there and let him expel what he can? It will make him feel better later."

Dizzy and one of the others helped Jerry to the outside gate as he groaned semiconsciously. They encouraged him to throw up outside the gate, which he did. But he was still barely conscious, and he rocked on his feet as they supported him back into the yard.

Mama E beckoned to them. "Come here. Come inside the house. There is a room for your friend to lie in while you men enjoy the night." She led them to one of the rooms and they laid him on the floor. "There, now. Sleep well and your friends can take you home later," she said to the incoherent Jerry. Then she turned to Dizzy. "You boys go outside and enjoy yourselves. He'll be all right there."

Dizzy couldn't tell whether Jerry had fallen into a deep sleep or passed out, but he trusted the advice of the Queen of Thokoza. He and his friends returned to the party, where the music was louder and the tempo lively.

The yard was quite full. Every now and then Dizzy glanced at Mama Elizabeth as she surveyed her domain. Dizzy attributed her smile to her satisfaction that she had everything under control, and her expectation of another profitable night.

When Dizzy walked towards the bar counter to get another round of drinks for himself and the boys – their fourth – he looked back to make sure he didn't attract the ire of Mama Elizabeth. She wasn't there. As he moved up to the counter, a large man, almost six feet tall, obstructed his way and even began to resist him. Sensing the tension, Dizzy edged around the hulk, who continued to stare at him. Dizzy didn't know the man. What was his problem?

At that moment, to his relief, Mama Elizabeth reappeared and went straight up to the man. "Sorry, Sonny. You can see we are full."

"Oh, Maaama. It's my biirrrthday," the man said, half singing.

"But we don't want to attract the police. We're full, and I don't want people outside on the pavement."

"You're not full. Look there … and there." Sonny pointed to an empty table and the dance floor that was not yet in use. "I tell you what, we'll just have one drink."

"Just one. Then you go." She walked away from them.

While Sonny stood at the counter, ordering the barman to get drinks for his friends, Dizzy had a good look at him. Sonny was dressed in a black leather bunny jacket that hung open to reveal the ivory handle of a flick knife protruding from his horizontal trouser pocket. His immaculate black slacks were held up by a snakeskin belt clasped with a gold-plated skull buckle. His contrasting crimson, silky shirt was a tight fit and opened low enough to reveal his well-built torso, flaunting its muscle tone. A thick gold chain hung around his neck. His socks matched his shirt, and his shoes were of the same snakeskin as his belt. A scar that cut across his right eyebrow added a human chink to his good looks and bore testimony to a previous altercation. His eyes were small, alert and evasive, and his mouth was locked in a sneer. Dizzy could see that his group deferred to him.

"Hey, Sonny," Dizzy heard one of them say. "Where'd you get the snakeskin belt, man?"

"From the veld. I killed the snake and had the belt made." Sonny laughed.

Dizzy tried to edge through Sonny's men to attract the attention of the barman, and found himself next to Sonny again, who was at the end of the bar, near the band.

Sonny leaned on the bar counter and shouted in the direction of the band. "Hey, Lady Luckylips! What's wrong with your voice? It seems dry and needs a bit of juice. How about you get your lucky lips around my cock, and I'll inject some lubrication."

Dizzy could not help hearing and was stung by the crass verbal assault on his cousin. "Hey. What did you say?"

"I said I can help the lady improve her voice."

"That's filthy. Leave her alone."

"Shut up, you worm. Go read your books. I want this woman, not you."

Dizzy stood behind his thick black-framed spectacles and made himself as tall as he could, pushing out his chest. He lined up with Sonny's gold chain and looked up at his respondent. "Listen, man. You can't treat—"

The blow to his stomach was swift. Dizzy doubled over, and gasped for breath. Still winded, he looked up, and saw Sonny with his knife drawn. "Come, boy. Come to Sonny," he said.

Dizzy's friends rose to his aid, and Sonny's men took up positions alongside him in battle formation, bearing their arms of chains and knives. Some were breaking beer bottles against the bar counter, holding them by the tops and wielding the serrated glass edges.

Dizzy, now barely standing, but still struggling to regain his breath, saw what happened next in slow motion. He heard Mama Elizabeth shout for order, but no one seemed to take any notice. Even Dizzy could barely hear her voice over the din. The whole shebeen joined in the fight. After a little more than five minutes of pandemonium, Dizzy's friends got the upper hand and Sonny fled with his friends. Dizzy couldn't believe this, but then he realised that he had gained the support of the other patrons. One of them told Dizzy later that most of the locals had seen what was brewing from the time Sonny entered, and knew that Sonny was the aggressor.

19

The excited talk during the aftermath of the shebeen brawl revealed to Dizzy that he had stepped where no one else would.

He found out that Sonny was infamous in Thokoza. He was the leader of a feared group of men who terrorised the streets with their taunts and attacks on young women. No one had been brave enough to challenge them before. People preferred to take refuge indoors when they drove up and down the streets, looking for trouble in their Chevrolet Fleetmaster. Someone told Dizzy that Sonny had removed the Chevy's muffler to ensure the loudest noise and inflict maximum terror on the defenceless community.

"Aai, aai. I didn't realise what a hornets' nest I stirred up."

"Yes, you did. But we're all pleased," said one of the men who had supported Dizzy's boys in the fight. He wiped his bloody hands. "Maybe now Sonny has been taught a lesson."

As they checked on the damage after the dust had settled, Mama Elizabeth cried out. "Oh, my goodness. We've got trouble."

Dizzy ran over to her. She looked down on a man slumped in a pool of blood against the yard wall. She knelt down and checked his pulse and his wounds. "He has been stabbed. He's dead."

One of Mama Elizabeth's minders looked at the dead man. "Aai, aai, aai. This is one of Sonny's men."

Dizzy didn't recognise him. "Come, boys, let's go. The bastard deserved it."

"No, you don't," boomed the matronly Mama Elizabeth. She had moved over to the other side of the outdoor area, where the hose was located, and was now surrounded by six members of staff who looked like big bodyguards. Dizzy was in no doubt that the men were capable of doing anything at the click of her tongue.

"You will not kill someone here in *my* home and leave me with the mess. The police will come, and that will be the end of my shebeen. Get him out of here and clean up!" She was wielding the hose, about to flood the courtyard.

"But it wasn't us," pleaded Dizzy.

"No? Who was it then? I saw you fighting with him." She pointed at him.

"I didn't. I've never seen him before."

"Listen here. You're all in trouble unless you get him out of my yard Now go! Make him disappear. We'll finish cleaning and no one will know anything happened. Sonny won't know who stabbed him. Get him out and leave the police to me."

Leaning with his hands on his thighs, Dizzy stooped over the dead man. He turned around and saw Mama Elizabeth and her men cleaning the yard. She commanded some of Dizzy's friends to help with moving the crates to neighbouring shacks and wheeling the cable reels to the back lane.

He didn't know what to do. What was he supposed to do with a dead man? He approached one of her helpers, who was taking alcohol to Mama Elizabeth's truck. "What can we do with the body?" he asked.

The helper put a crate of beer bottles on the floor. "Come, I'll show you," he replied. Following his instruction, Dizzy and his companions placed the dead man in the boot of the Buick. "Take him there." The man pointed.

"Where?" asked Dizzy. "The line?"

"Yes, over the tracks, man. There is an early train, just before five o'clock," the minder said. "It will look as if the train killed him." He was so matter-of-fact that Dizzy suspected it wasn't the first time he'd done this.

By five o'clock Dizzy and the Buick were safely on the other side of Jo'burg. He shivered as he imagined a train smashing the body and breaking it into pieces. It would be happening about now, or had already happened.

Dizzy assumed that, as with most crimes in the townships, the police would be far too busy to investigate. What would be the point of looking further into what appeared to be a train accident? After all, the deceased had been drinking. He could easily have passed out on the railway line.

Later that Sunday morning, Mama Elizabeth rose from her breakfast table to answer the loud banging on her front door. "Open up! Open up!"

A composed Mama Elizabeth opened the door. "Hello, Constable." She looked carefully at the policeman. "We haven't met. I know many of your colleagues."

"I'm Constable Visser. Me and my colleague here has been transferred to Thokoza recently."

"How can I help you and your colleague, Constable?" With a wide smile locked on her face, she was determined to present the picture of innocence. She ignored Sonny and two of his men, who stood behind the constables.

"We reeseef reeports that there is a shebeen here and that there was a fight and a murderr here … last night."

"A murder!" She pushed her neck back and transformed her face into an indignant frown. "Constable, I don't know where you get this nonsense from."

"Therr is plenty witnesses."

She stood erect in her doorway, her chest out and her hands on her hips, and looked down upon the police on the concrete pad at ground level, two steps lower.

"See, Constable. This is my *house*. You can see it is very clean. There was no murder here last night, no fight here the night before, no fight here last week or last year."

"She's lying," said Sonny. "I was here and so was Panga, my good friend. Panga is dead and I last saw him here."

"Oh, did you now? You last saw him here, did you?" She scowled at Sonny as if to say, *I'll show this flea.* "If you did, where was Panga when you left, Sonny? Did you leave your good friend behind? If you were both here, Panga must have left with you." She pointed at Sonny. "And how do you expect me to know what happened after that? It looks like you were the last person to see him." Her voice dripped with sarcasm.

"Let's look around," said the policeman in charge. "I'll soon find out what's happened."

They searched the house from room to room and found Jerry passed out in the back room. Mama Elizabeth had been under the impression that Dizzy had collected him when they left, but she realised that Dizzy must have been so spooked by events that he had forgotten all about Jerry. And so had she.

Constable Visser kicked Jerry a few times as he lay on the floor and then shook him hard. Slapping him in the face, the constable shouted, "Wake up! Wake up!"

Slowly, heavily, Jerry stirred awake.

"What arr you doing here, kaffir?" asked Constable Visser.

Sonny pointed at Jerry. "He was here last night. He was one of the attackers! You son of a bitch. You killed Panga, man." He went to Jerry and kicked him hard in the guts, winding him.

"What arr you doing here?" repeated Constable Visser.

"Can't you see this man is sick?" said Mama. "Now you've winded him. Leave him alone." She didn't want them to suspect he had been drunk.

"Shut up," said the constable.

"Leave me alone. I've got a bad headache. I must go home." Jerry coughed as he regained his breathing.

Constable Visser pressed him for answers as to why he was there and whether he took Panga to the railway line.

"I don't know who Panga is. I've never seen this boy here." He pointed at Sonny.

"He's right. He's sick and was fast asleep before Sonny got here," said Mama Elizabeth.

"Oh, I see. So there was something happening here." Constable Visser scanned the room. "What happen here, kaffir?" He kicked Jerry again in the guts.

"I don't know. I was asleep. You just woke me. Isn't that obvious?" Jerry wheezed back at him.

"You lying kaffir."

"I was asleep."

"I've heard that beforr. You all say that. We get the truth out of you. I'm taking you in. Get up and come with us, you filth."

They led Jerry to the police van outside and threw him into the caged back, where he hit his head on the sharp corner of the steel bench. When he arrived at the police station, the gash on his head was bleeding.

Constable Visser and another policeman pushed him into a holding cell. They kicked and beat him and starved him of food and water. He had nothing to tell them. Eventually they realised he wasn't going to reveal anything new.

Then they locked him in a packed police lock-up and left him there unattended – bloody, sore, and queasy, his clothing soiled with vomit and dried blood. The little cell was crowded. About eight others had been arrested for being involved in weekend brawls, to be dealt with on Monday. He huddled up against a wall and slept, too tired to speak to any of them.

As Neil approached the gate of the Top Star car park on Monday morning, he was greeted with the sight of Dizzy and some of Jerry's friends all lined up at the entrance and looking grave and awkward. Dizzy was shuffling his feet and looking at his shoes sheepishly. Neil noticed Jerry wasn't with them. He stopped his car and opened the window. "What's the matter? Where's Jerry?"

Dizzy explained the situation, or the gist of it, and added after barely a pause, "Baas, we never killed this man, but we panicked and forgot Jerry there. We were all afraid and had to get out of Thokoza fast. By the time I realised and drove back he was arrested."

Neil listened in disbelief. He was shocked by the events, but especially by the attempt to disguise the knifing as a rail death. And the car – how could they have been so thoughtless as to go to a shebeen in a Top Star Buick and, worst of all, use it to transport the body? "My car has got the dead man's blood all over it, Dizzy! What were you thinking?"

"Sorry, boss. We weren't thinking straight. We never killed this man."

Neil was astonished that they had taken the Buick and left Jerry behind. Jerry, certainly no angel, was clearly innocent of this crime. But now, to cap it all off, he was in jail!

Neil called his lawyer and arranged for Jerry to be granted bail.

"I slept through the whole thing. Honestly, boss." Jerry was uncharacteristically humble as he walked out of the police station to Neil's car, much the worse for wear. His spunky clothes were soiled and filthy. His face was swollen from the gash he'd suffered in the police van and also from Constable Visser's interrogation methods.

Jerry had pieced together what was being alleged against him. "I can't believe it, boss. We would not start a fight. We just have fun, like always. Looking for girls. But it wasn't me. I was out. Out cold."

Neil didn't respond, but just looked at him. In that look, Jerry saw that the best approach was to keep quiet.

The charge of murder dominated Jerry's life. He lost his energy and his enthusiasm. At work he stayed in his corner of the shop and tried to avoid talking to anyone.

One morning, he was brooding on what to do when Neil walked into the workshop. "Jerry, come to my office at eleven."

"Why, boss?"

"Just be there. My lawyer's coming to help you defend yourself against the charge of murder."

Jerry was worried. At eleven on the dot, he approached Neil's office. He walked past Prinsloo's niece, Brunelda. The young clerk's dresses were too short for her, he thought. He'd often seen her staring into space at a table near the stationery storeroom. When not at that table, she was walking empty-handed in the direction of Mrs Hammond, Neil's secretary. Was she capable of anything that required intelligent thinking? Unless it was guarding the stationery, he couldn't quite work out what she did.

Now, as he entered Neil's office, Brunelda came and stood near Mrs Hammond. Jerry guessed she had seen the lawyer arrive and didn't want to miss out on the action. He felt affronted by the way she glared at him.

He ignored her and turned to Mrs Hammond. "I have a meeting with Boss Neil," he said.

"Yes, Jerry. He's waiting," Mrs Hammond responded in her usual officious manner and led him to the closed office door. She opened it and went in, and he followed, embarrassed and looking down at the carpet.

"Jerry, this is Mr Landau, my attorney. Mr Landau has kindly used his influence to bring his recommended defence lawyer to my office."

Jerry looked at the small, well-dressed Jewish attorney. The bearded, balding professional nodded at him and turned to the man on his right.

Neil continued, "And this is Advocate Marius Strydom. He will defend you. He says you have a good chance of getting off."

Jerry looked at the man at the edge of Neil's desk. On hearing the name, he avoided eye contact, but not before catching a glimpse of him. Advocate Strydom was shuffling his papers, not looking up. Jerry barely recognised the grown-up Marius in his suit, and only just managed to rein in his astonishment. He was impressed in spite of himself. *Marius has become a real lawyer, just as he always said he would.*

Still, it was obvious to Jerry that Marius did not consider it worth his while to look for long at the native he would be defending. Jerry could detect no sign of recognition on his part. Why should Marius care who he was? This was just another law case against a black man. Besides, Marius had known him as Jeremiah ... only ever just as Jeremiah. *I don't think he even knows my family name.*

It was almost five years since they had last seen each other. Jerry had grown from an innocent farm boy in worn, borrowed clothing into a man about town, even though he was now dressed in the Top Star Cheetah uniform and cap and was still bruised from the police questioning and his face wound had not yet fully healed.

He didn't want Marius on his case. If his parents got wind of this ... No. He couldn't bear to think about it. Given his limited contact with them and the farm after his exile, that was the last thing he wished for. With the little he'd told them about his urban life, he knew they still thought he was under the care of Samson. He sent them money occasionally, but not as often as he felt he should do. Jerry shook his head. The less they found out about him, the better.

He looked up, addressing Neil. "What do you mean, I have 'a chance to get off'? I didn't do it. If Advocate Whoever-he-is can't get the charges dismissed, let's get someone else, boss."

Jerry's reply was cheeky and delivered in English, a language he had never used before with Marius, further ensuring he wouldn't be recognised. The language of the farm was strictly Afrikaans. "Yeah! Let's get someone else, boss," Jerry repeated.

Jerry saw Neil look at him, then at Marius, and then at the floor, clearly embarrassed. He could see that his boss was about to react to what was clearly a rude and disrespectful rant from his native worker, who had overstepped the line between master and servant in South Africa. This attitude was unheard of. Jerry knew it and was surprised at his own boldness. When Neil looked as if he was about to speak, Jerry expected to be reprimanded and pulled into line.

But his boss was beaten to the cue.

"Well, Mr ... er ... Ngubeni," Marius said, looking at his papers to check his new client's surname. "You must be very special to Mr Robertson. Mr Landau doesn't do cases like this. And I don't get requested by Mr Landau to go out to clients like this. They usually come to my chambers, you know." He paused as he looked at the briefing papers on Neil's desk. He spoke in clear English with an Afrikaans accent. "I will do my best of course, Mr Ngubeni. But you will have to tell me what happened, and then we'll see what I can do for you."

Jerry didn't look at Marius. Instead he looked straight at Neil. "Boss, he can't do anything for me. He's just here for your money."

Mr Landau then spoke. "Advocate Strydom is an excellent criminal lawyer. He knows the system, the police and the prosecutors. If anyone can do something, he can. Don't worry, Neil."

"That settles it then. Jerry, this is your legal team. You must tell Advocate Strydom what he wants to know. By the way, it's not my money he's here for. It's yours, Jerry. You'll repay me from your wages … if you don't go to jail."

"Your decision, my money, and my life, boss," Jerry said. "Where's the justice? Don't I have any voice?"

Neil pointed at Jerry, his finger shaking, his face reddening. "Yes, Jerry. You have a voice. Now use it with your advocate!" Neil was shouting. "I'm leaving you here with the lawyers, and you tell them your story."

Jerry had never seen him so angry before. Neil stormed out of his office, leaving the three of them behind.

Marius took notes on a writing pad as Jerry told him what had happened. He asked Jerry a few questions and jotted down the answers without looking up. Jerry looked more often at Mr Landau, as if addressing him. There wasn't much to tell, he said, since he'd been asleep throughout the brawl and had seen none of it. Jerry made sure the advocate's view of him was partly obstructed by keeping Mr Landau in between them.

Jerry heard a call over the workshop intercom: "*Jerry, report to Mr Robertson's office. Jerry to Mr Robertson's office immediately!*"

It was a month after the meeting with the lawyers. The announcement by Mrs Hammond had Jerry hastening to comply. Mrs Hammond let him in, with Brunelda looking on. Neil was at his desk. Jerry stood on the opposite side, pulled his cheetah cap off, and held it in his hands like a schoolboy in the principal's office.

"I've just received a call from Mr Landau," Neil said without greeting Jerry. "Mr Strydom felt there was no evidence against you. He made representations for the charges to be dropped and was successful."

Neil looked at Jerry, but his face was deadpan. "Sorry, boss. I don't understand," said Jerry, searching Neil's expression for whether this was good or bad news.

"You won't be prosecuted. They've dropped the charges."

Jerry's head felt light as he started to appreciate the impact of what Neil had told him. He was swaying on his feet and grabbed the back of the chair in front of him. "Jeez, boss. I can't believe it." He drew breath and whistled. "Are you sure?"

"Yes. It's over."

Jerry lifted his cap to his eyes and pressed the tears away. He took a few deep breaths and gathered his thoughts. Images of Marius, the advocate in his suit, flashed through his mind. And then his parents at the farm. "I am not guilty, boss. You know that. I was a victim of injustice. I went to the shebeen for some fun ... that's all."

"You bloody idiot. You have everything going for you. Look what you have. You nearly threw that all away. You could have been hanged!" Jerry felt uneasy as the volume of Neil's voice rose. "You and your friends could have got us all into trouble using a Top Star Buick to cover up the crime. We're fuckin' lucky the police didn't find out about that!"

Jerry stood without moving.

Neil's chair squeaked as he sat back. After a brief pause, he went on. "All right. Listen here, Jerry." His voice was calmer. "You're young, smart, good-looking, and you have a good job. I believe in you. You have the pick of the bunch, and you still seek out the sluts. You had a fine woman in Grace. What happened?" There was silence for a while. Neil stared at Jerry. "Has what I've been saying begun to sink in?"

Jerry stared back, unflinching. Neil got up and walked around the desk.

"Now, you go and make up with Grace. Go to the pharmacy right now and tell her how sorry you are. Go on, go on." He waved Jerry in the direction of the door. When Jerry did not move, Neil laid his hand against Jerry's back and steered him.

Jerry wanted to reply but was given no chance to backchat him. He was starting to get angry when Neil pulled him back and spoke again. "You are not allowed to take any of my cars out of the garage until I am satisfied that you're back with Grace. I'll be checking. If you don't obey, I will issue that instruction to all the staff at all the saleyards. You don't want that, do you? They will know you've blown it, my boy. You won't be the boss boy anymore. Oh, and by the way, here's a nice necklace that you bought from your wages for Grace."

Jerry was speechless as his boss thrust an eight-inch-square jewellery box covered in red velvet in his hand. He glanced at it. It looked stylish and was embossed in gold with the words "*By Elegance Jewellers*". In smaller writing underneath, he read, "*Elegantly crafted by our own jewellers*".

Jerry left Neil's office without a word.

But he knew he would comply – not because Neil told him to, but because the message *had* sunk in, long before his boss's sermon. He'd been thinking for some time that he had to pull his life together. The images of the police holding cell and the possible impact of a guilty finding had haunted him ever since he was detained. He couldn't sleep at night. He had let his parents down. And what about Uncle Samson? He was embarrassed to be in his uncle's presence.

Even before the events of that night, it had occurred to him a few times that he needed to settle down, but the criminal charges had made him put his life on hold. He couldn't even think of a serious relationship until the case was behind him. How could he expect Grace to take him back with the possibility of jail or worse?

Now he could look forward again. His boss's words only crystallised his own intentions. He had never lost his feelings for Grace. Now he was ready to commit to her, if she would have him back.

He paused just before entering the workshop and looked inside the velvet case. *Can I afford this?* He studied the silver necklace of flat rectangles. A larger, heavier square, inlaid with an open rose, gold streaked into its petals, was suspended in the centre. *But can I afford not to do this?*

Another thought niggled at him: he couldn't let his boss get away with what Neil had done. He knew Neil cared about him. Jerry cared about his boss too, in his way. Time for payback, and the only way was to pay him in kind. He started brewing something for Neil.

20

Within a week of Neil's lecture, Jerry and Grace were together again.

Just two weeks after that, Jerry raised a matter with Neil as he drove him to the Eloff Street branch. "Boss, you know the pharmacist that Grace works for, Miss Angelique?

Neil did not answer.

Jerry persisted. "Grace tells me that she likes you."

"Who?" But Neil blushed. He knew exactly who Jerry was talking about.

Neil had been so busy with his commercial advancement that he hardly thought about his personal life. Since the pretentious petals in Henry's entourage, he had had no women in his life – other than Mrs Botha. She had assumed the role of surrogate mother, advising him regularly of the "evil elements" of Johannesburg. After the episode when Henry tried to appropriate Neil's savings, Mrs Botha had become convinced that Neil needed protecting. "Mr Neil, there is a thief behind every bush here. You can't trust your own flesh and blood in this city of sin. It corrupts everyone. Even your cousin became a crook."

But on this day, it seemed that Jerry saw it as his turn to give Neil a bit of advice. "You know, boss. The chemist down the road. The Greek girl. Miss Angelique. She's very pretty, and Grace says she cooks well. She brings in this food to eat and the whole place smells like a restaurant. That's what Grace says. What else can you want?"

"Oh, shut up and drive, Jerry."

"Okay, boss. But we need some plasters for the garage. Go and buy some … and check her out."

"What do *you* know? You just concentrate on the road and don't bother about me."

"She's really nice, know what I mean? It's worth a try."

Neil looked out the window and said nothing. He began to feel that he wouldn't mind knowing more about the woman Jerry was referring to, and he was flattered that someone had expressed an interest in him. But he wasn't going to show it.

Then hard upon the heels of that reaction came another feeling, even more sudden and unexpected. He felt alone. Going to his room and having no one to share the day with had begun to take its toll. He had Mrs Botha, but she was the one who did the talking.

And what he needed was not a mother. For so long the care he'd put into making his fortune had masked the need that was beginning to assert itself. He had noticed the young pharmacist on more than one occasion, but had never let the vague sense of attraction be taken further.

For the rest of the day he tried to busy himself with the affairs of the garage, but his mind kept returning to what Jerry had told him. There was even a sense of urgency that he could not put aside: it was time to look around for a serious relationship.

Neil could also sense his ego and curiosity getting the better of him. What harm was there, after all, in a little trip to the pharmacy, just to see Miss Angelique up close? He'd only ever seen her at some distance in her white dustcoat, and from what he could recall, she wasn't bad. An image came to him of olive skin and a classical nose. But what had most drawn his attention in the past was her pitch-black hair, with big curls lacquered into place. She had that sculptured appearance he liked to call striking Grecian looks – a bit like Maria Callas, he thought.

◆

On the day Jerry told Neil about Angelique, Grace was delivering a mid-morning cup of tea to her employer, just the way she liked it – strong and sweet. Grace knew there was no room for blandness in the life of this progressive lady in her early thirties.

"Madam, you know the handsome garage owner up the road? Jerry's boss?"

Angelique Kalonides glanced at Grace as if not understanding what she was saying. Then, when she registered Grace's meaning, she sniffed dismissively and took a sip of tea.

She knew who Grace meant, but only because he was Jerry's employer, and she had seen all too much of Jerry. Why did Grace bother with that young man? He was forever loitering outside, waiting to talk to Grace, and she remembered him trying to impress Grace with his dandy clothes, strong cologne and extravagant presents.

Only recently Grace had whooped for joy at the front door of the pharmacy when Jerry gave her an impressive necklace. They had been going out together some time back, but Angelique had noticed how Grace became moody and how her energy had declined when the two became estranged for a few months. The young person with her zest for life and smiling face had been replaced by a glum and pedestrian woman.

This changed and Grace's temper lifted the moment Jerry walked into the shop and presented her with his velvet-boxed gift. All the staff had gathered round. Angelique was concerned at how easily Grace gave in to Jerry. "Grace, get back to work. This isn't a nightclub where any man can just walk in from the street and demand the attention of the staff for his own gain."

She turned to Jerry with her hands on her hips. "And you? Where have you been? Have you had an interruption of your fun and games at the railway line and rediscovered your love for this poor woman?"

"Madam—"

"No, don't answer that. Don't make it worse. Just leave. We work here, you know. This is a business and this is working time."

She had warned Grace to be careful, as the neighbourhood was rife with stories of Jerry and his antics – the railway death being the incident that worried Angelique most. "Where there's smoke there's fire," she warned Grace. "And what about all the other stories? They say he's got a girl at every bus stop."

"Madam, he doesn't catch the bus. He drives the master to and from work every day. That's just jealous gossip."

"Well, you know what I mean. Don't say I didn't warn you."

Angelique was as surprised as anyone that Grace and Jerry had got together again. But she told herself it would not last, not once Grace realised what she was dealing with. And Angelique was certain Jerry wasn't going to turn over any new leaf. *A leopard doesn't change its spots.*

Now here was this question from Grace today. Where could it be leading? What did Jerry's boss have to do with any of this? Surely Grace did not delude herself – she knew that Jerry was not in Angelique's good books.

"Jerry is very close to Master Neil, and told me he was asking about you. Jerry reckons he likes you, ma'am."

"Oh, don't talk nonsense. Besides, I'm Greek. He won't want me, and my family certainly won't want him! Isn't he English?"

"I don't know what he is. Anyway, if he's a good man, why should it matter what he is?"

"Oh, believe me, Grace. It matters. I'm Greek and it matters. Forget about him. Now get on with it. Take these soaps and pack them on the shelves."

But Angelique found herself recalling how far she had gone against her father's wishes. From the early days of her tertiary studies, she had insisted to her parents that she wanted a career, not a husband.

Mr George Kalonides had been emphatic. "No."

But that hadn't stopped her. Angelique had been intractable and determined. She studied pharmacy against her father's wishes, earning his acquiescence by topping the class. After graduating, she opened her own business, Kos Pharmacy, so named to placate her reluctant father, who was born on the Greek island of Kos. He had surrendered eventually to her dogged resolve – not that she gave him a choice. She was going ahead with her plan to open a pharmacy in any case.

She accepted a shop in one of his buildings in Eloff Street, rent-free for a year. "Okay, *Baba* (Dad), but I'll arrange to fit it out my way," she insisted. She noticed that, even though he initially objected – as though he felt it was his duty to say no – his protestations changed to support as he arranged for the tradesmen and paid them. She could see his pride when he told the toyshop owner next door that this would be his daughter's pharmacy.

Mr Kalonides stood on the pavement and viewed the pharmacy on the day she took over. "My darling," he said, "you've got your business. Now get a good Greek husband!"

"Yesss, Babaah," she hissed, "but only when I'm ready. And I'm not ready yet."

Kalonides sighed and shook his head. "You've made all my hair grey with your independent ways. You're going to make it all fall out."

When Neil entered the pharmacy, he looked for Angelique at the counter and saw only a waiting customer. Then he walked straight into her as she stood up suddenly in front of him. She had been bent over, getting powdered milk from a low shelf for a customer. Neil knocked her off balance. When he instinctively grabbed her to stop her from falling, he got an accidental solid grip on her breasts. He felt a pulse flow through him as though he received an electric shock. "Oops! Er … sorry."

Angelique tried to regain her posture and her left hand gripped his right arm. In doing so, she clutched onto his taut muscles. Blood rushed to her head and her legs turned to jelly. He held her up, and she seized him tightly.

She looked up at him, lost for words, just as he seemed to be. He supported her rather clumsily. Her right hand was wedged between them, clasped tightly against his firm breast. Again, that current charged right through her, from her right hand to her toes.

"Oh, my!" Neil exclaimed, finding his tongue. "I am very sorry."

Angelique remained speechless. Now with both hands on his chest, she pushed him away. She looked at where her hands had been and then at his clear cobalt eyes and blond hair. Without thinking, she repeated the words she had trained the counter staff to use: "Good morning, sir. How may I help you?"

He was still processing the feel of her breasts and upper arms, and her dark, goddess looks. For a while he was mesmerised by her strong olive-black eyes, which her long, powerful eyebrows dramatically accentuated. "Sorry, ah … I meant to go to the post office." He felt his own surprise at this senseless and feeble response; the post office was a few blocks away.

He swivelled around on his heels and left the shop, turning right, back to Top Star Motors, the post office being in the other direction.

❖

The next day, Neil saw her at the post office. She had just turned to leave the counter with a page of stamps, when Neil walked in. "Mr … er …"

"Robertson. Neil Robertson's my name. How do you do, Miss … or is it Mrs …?"

"Miss Angelique Kalonides. Mr Robertson, I do hope you're not following me."

"Miss Kalonides, how could you think that? Of course not. Good day." He went to the counter to purchase stamps. He did not tell her that he had never been to the post office before, or that he had rushed there when he saw her enter.

Two days later, he saw her go into the general store opposite the garage. He ran across the road, slipped in and immediately veered to the right. He navigated around the high rotary comic stands, and slowly made his way towards the rounded glass cabinets where she was viewing a display of confectionary. He approached her from deeper within the shop, as she was still near the entrance.

"Miss Kalonides! I do hope you're not following me."

"Oh, Mr Robertson. How could you think that? I didn't see you. Good morning." She blushed.

"Into the sweets, are you?"

"One of my weaknesses. I have a very sweet tooth. I sometimes crave chocolate, toffee, or, like today, I'm inclined to get some liquorice all-sorts." She stooped to look at the multicoloured, layered cubes of candy.

"I'm quite partial to chocolates," he said.

They both paused.

He cleared his throat. "Miss Kalonides … would you be offended if I invited you to dinner?"

She stood straight and frowned at him, angling her head down and pulling her neck back. "Mr Robertson, I'm Greek." She responded as though that would put an end to this topic.

"So what? I'm English. It's just dinner, you know."

"Is it really? Is that what you think?"

"I'm not sure. I don't know what I think at the moment. What do you think?"

Before she could answer, the shopkeeper interrupted. "Angelique, are you okay? What would you like, my girl?"

"Oh, hello, Uncle Thanassi. I'll have half a pound of your liquorice all-sorts. Thank you, *theio* (uncle)."

The old man behind the counter took a paper bag, filled it with the colourful candy, and handed her the bulging bag without weighing it. "So how is my good friend George? Tell him I haven't seen him for a while. He must come in for a coffee." Uncle Thanassi walked to the front of the counter and, with his back to Neil, pecked her on the cheek.

"Yes, theio. I'll tell Baba." She tendered the money.

"No, my child," he said. "You have my blessing." He turned around and looked Neil directly in the eye as if to say, *I'm her guardian in the absence of her father, and you must leave her alone.*

"Thanks, theio." She faced Neil. "Mr Robertson, please call me at the pharmacy in half an hour." Then she walked out.

Uncle Thanassi said, "And how can I help *you*?" He looked at Neil without a smile.

Neil was taken aback. He hadn't come to purchase anything. "I'll have half a pound of liquorice all-sorts too, thanks."

The shopkeeper's mouth was turned down as he dug a clump out of the cabinet with a small tin scoop, placed them in a small brown paper bag and weighed them carefully, removing one and then checking the weight again. Satisfied, he folded the bag closed. "That'll be one shilling." His voice was flat.

"Thank you." Neil paid and walked out without looking back. He wondered at the events that had just taken place in that shop, all utterly beyond his control, it seemed. What had he been doing in there? He bent his head and put his hand to his brow. *And I don't even like liquorice.*

Exactly half an hour after their separation, Neil telephoned the pharmacy.

"Mr Robertson, is that you?"

It was her voice.

"Yes," he breathed. The answer came out more softly than he intended. He cleared his throat. "Yes, Miss Kalonides. It's me. How did you know?"

"Well, it's half an hour after I left the shop, so I guessed it must be you. I'm free for a cup of tea tomorrow after work. We can go to the Splendid Tearoom."

Neil tried to keep his voice strong and level. "Okay, shall I pick you up?"

"Yes, thank you. I'll wait for you here, at the pharmacy. But we can't be too long as I must get home."

"I can drop you home if you like."

"No, thank you. I do drive, you know."

"Oh, I didn't know that. It's not common … you know … for women to drive."

"Well, I think you'll find I'm not your common woman. You can pick me up, but drop me off at the shop and I'll drive home – to my parents' house."

Neil took her to the Splendid Tearoom. The next night after work, he took her out again, for a hamburger at the trendy Tampico Roadhouse in Alberton, and then for lunch on the Sunday at the classy African Pavilion restaurant. This was followed by the theatre and dinner the next weekend. By then they were enjoying each other's company; she called him Neil and he called her Angelique.

Neil knew he wanted her. And didn't he always meet with success when he put his mind to something? But it would surely be a mistake to approach her as a business acquisition.

He settled on sending her a large box of chocolates every Friday "for your sweet tooth" and a bouquet of roses every Monday morning "to bring colour to your customers". He also spent some time at Elegance Jewellers, selecting at first a stylish bracelet, which he gave to her in the third week, then matching earrings, then a matching necklace, and finally an engagement ring.

All within six weeks of departing for the post office.

❖

But Neil did have his work cut out for him getting past her father. Mr Kalonides would rather see his daughter remain single than marry a non-Greek.

"Angelique, if you lose your identity, you lose your soul."

"Baba, that's not true. My soul is right here," she said, placing her hand over her heart, "and you should know that better than anyone."

"He's English, my dear – a cold, blue-eyed kipper. Why would he want you, a warm-blooded Greek?"

"Because he loves me and I love him."

"Hrrumph. No, that's not possible. Ice and fire don't mix – and that's that."

"Well, Baba, I don't know where you get ice and fire from. We're people, not the elements. In any case, I am a chemist, and I know you can do a lot of good by mixing things together."

"No, *kori mou* (my girl), life isn't a chemistry set. This is your life you're talking about."

"Yes, Baba. *My* life! Exactly!" She twirled around with a "humph" and left the family patriarch standing there, too stunned to retort.

But with his charm and persuasive manner – and with the support of Mrs Kalonides, at the behest of Angelique – Neil was reluctantly accepted into the Kalonides family in a grand wedding attended by a handful of Neil's business acquaintances, including his attorney, Mr Landau. The rest of the party consisted of the Kalonides family and friends – over five hundred of them crammed into the majestic Sunnyside Park Hotel ballroom.

"I have only one child," her father explained to Neil, as he added another family he knew to the guest list.

There was no Jerry or Grace at that reception. It disappointed Neil and Angelique, but the Afrikaner-led government had begun to implement its policy of forced segregation that prevented races from mixing, even at weddings. The races were to be "separate but equal", or so ran the justification for the policy of apartheid.

Not to be put off, Neil arranged a special celebration for the black staff on the Sunday before his formal wedding. It was held at the big warehouse he had built as a storage depot for his motorcar stocks in Steeledale, east of Kensington. He arranged for the hundreds of Top Star African workers to be bussed in from wherever they lived – mostly the various black townships that had sprung up around Johannesburg.

He laid on copious amounts of roast beef, potatoes, cake, and beer. It was a celebration that started at eleven in the morning and had to be brought to a close at five in the afternoon to ensure the staff were transported home before they could be arrested for being in a Sunday "whites only" area.

Just before the food was served, Neil and Angelique got on the back tray of a large truck against the yard wall. A public address system had been set up for the occasion. He introduced Angelique, "my Greek princess", to his black staff. They all cheered and whistled loudly.

Jerry had organised a wedding gift from the African staff for the couple. At Jerry's signal, four tough mechanics hoisted a trolley onto the platform, loaded with a bulky shape covered by a black sheet. Jerry invited Angelique to unveil it. She pushed Neil forward, but Jerry stopped him, grabbed her hand and pulled her towards the sheet. "They want *you* to do it."

She stood there for a while and looked at Jerry, unsmiling. He, on the other hand, sported a huge white smile and nodded at the sheet. "You can trust me," he said, barely audible above the chanting guests.

She looked at the crowd, who by then were ululating and whistling loudly. Then they started shouting "Umfazi ... Umfazi ... Umfazi ..." (wife) over and over, until she took the sheet with both hands. She threw it with full force in one majestic swish up and over the high point and away.

The sweep of her movement revealed a magnificent large figurine of a lion and lioness cast in bronze. The lion pair lay playfully, body to body, with the maned head of the lion pushing into the lioness's neck.

The staff applauded. Jerry raised his hands for them to hush. "Boss and Princess Angelique, we chose this because you remind us of the British lion – strong and bold – who is tamed by the Greek lioness – beautiful and motherly. We wish for you both, many cubs." The audience burst into applause again. Jerry held up his hands again. He hadn't finished the presentation.

"This gift was made for you in our workshops by African staff. All the Africans knew about it and voted on the lions instead of birds, buck or people. All of us here today."

He pointed to the over three hundred black staff standing in front of them. Angelique burst into tears as she hugged one of the four sturdy mechanics, and the staff broke into song.

Apartheid was not strictly enforced both ways, and Neil and Angelique made a point of going to Jerry and Grace's wedding in the black township of Alexandra. This was also a grand affair, which lasted a whole weekend. Neil told Angelique that Jerry had exhausted his savings to ensure a display of wealth for the ceremony.

"He's even arranged for the attendance, at some cost, of Bishop J. J. Dhivani, head of the Trans-African Christian Church."

"Why?"

"Because that's the church Grace's family goes to. They're devout Christians, you know."

"Yes, and Jerry's bringing his family from some farm they live on."

They noticed a group of about a dozen who seemed out of place. "That must be Jerry's brother. They look so alike," said Angelique, pointing to Petrus.

Jerry had never mentioned to Neil that the farm owners were not invited. They were in the inner circle of Afrikaner politics, and Jerry didn't want them at his wedding. Not that they would have come, in any event. They firmly believed in separating the blacks and the whites.

Neil gave them his old Austin A40 as a wedding gift. "I feel a sentimental attachment to this car, my first," he had told Angelique. "I really don't want to sell it."

"But leaving it in Mrs Botha's backyard is a waste, Neil. It's just gathering dust. Giving it to Jerry and Grace will make their lives so much easier."

"I suppose it will make a big difference to them."

On the day he passed it over to Jerry, Neil was excited when he told Angelique how good he felt about giving the Ngubeni couple their first family car.

Angelique felt like something of an intruder at the wedding from the start, but not as much as she sensed Jerry's parents did. After Jerry introduced Thomas and Saleena to her and Neil, Angelique became acutely aware of their discomfort and empathised with them. She could see that they felt like strangers and were overwhelmed by the extravagance: mounds of food, unlimited alcohol, and Western music played live by the Jazz Apostles, Johannesburg's foremost African band.

She and Neil were treated like royalty and given pride of place ahead of Thomas and Saleena, in the centre seats at the front of the church and on either side of the bridal couple at the bridal table. But Neil charmed Jerry's father by exchanging seats with them, and after the meal Angelique moved to sit next to Saleena.

In striking up a long conversation with Saleena, she discovered a few secrets about Jerry. She learned that "Jeremiah" had been expected to marry a young woman, Rachel, from the farm compound.

"She is from the same people, like Jeremiah, like us," Saleena told her, "and she was his sweetheart before he go to Johannesburg. He didn't know it, but Rachel … she was expecting a child when he left the farm. Phineas is now nearly seven."

Angelique nearly choked on the wedding cake.

"This wedding with Grace," said Saleena, "it is big problem for us on the farm. We have to live with Rachel and her family."

"But Jerry hasn't seen her for years. Does he know about the boy?" Angelique was struggling to retain her composure and battled to keep her voice down. She forced the occasional smile at the crowd as she spoke and listened to Saleena.

"Aai, madam. We send letters to Jeremiah, and I send my brother to speak to him in Johannesburg. He just send us money, sometimes with news about his life in Johannesburg, but no reply to the question about Rachel. He never tell us his marriage plans until last month, and he never tell us no for Rachel. We think the money was for Rachel and Phineas. We give her the money he send. That make it worse, because she was waiting for him – with good signals from Jeremiah and us. Now she must find somebody else who will look after her boy." She paused in thought. "I suppose she will."

"Hmm," responded Angelique, not knowing what to say.

"Grace, she seems like good lady, and I think she doesn't know," said Saleena.

"Oh, I'm quite sure she doesn't know." Angelique was boiling with anger at Jerry. "I would've known if she knew. That poor woman there has no idea she's got a stepson. No idea."

"Miesies, please let it stay that way, otherwise another heart will break."

Angelique didn't reply and sat in silence.

"Miesies, please."

"I'm not sure. Surely she must be told."

"No, Miesies. No." Saleena took her by the hand and looked her in the eyes, her own eyes drawn into a frown of sorrow more fit for a funeral than a wedding. She said softly, "Please promise you will not tell Grace."

Angelique could do nothing but give in to this painful request from the heart. "I promise, Saleena."

Saleena's worried face relaxed with a brief smile as she patted Angelique's hands. "Please keep an eye on them for me. I am too far away. My son is like the young elephant. He is wild when there is no older one to control him. I know that Master and Miesies can control him."

"Neil is the same age and is not very sensible either. Who will control *him*? But Grace is good for your son. You will see. Maybe she will control him."

"I hope so, Miesies."

INTERLUDE

1957–1973

21

❖◈❖

Within three months of their wedding, Angelique had sold the pharmacy at Neil's insistence and was preparing for motherhood.

"There you are," she told her father. "You have your way now, Baba."

"Yes, kori mou. So do you and your good husband."

Six months later, Angelique chuckled as George Kalonides brought the biggest bouquet she had ever seen into the hospital ward. "For my grandson," he said.

She held her black-haired baby up and shook his right hand at her father. "Look, George is saying 'thank you'."

"Did you say 'George'? Is that his name?" asked Mr Kalonides.

"Yes, Baba. He has your name."

And her father burst into tears.

It was just two years before a second son was born. Although also dark-haired, his eyes were cobalt blue, just like Neil's. Neil wished he could have telephoned his parents to tell them the news.

He was sure he knew how that conversation would have gone. He could almost hear Mary's response: "I'm so happy for you."

"And we're calling him Milton."

Neil could imagine her shoes clunking down the passage and

then her voice, followed by a pause and the running back. "Oh, Neil! Your father is so happy."

He wasn't often given to daydreams, but the arrival of baby Milton brought his parents into his thoughts. He missed them.

❖

Neil insisted that they live in Houghton, the most expensive suburb in Johannesburg. "It's time to move on and up, Angie."

"But can we afford Houghton?"

"I think so. If not now, when? The business is expanding."

"But isn't the business backed by loans?"

"Yes, but that's my problem. Don't let my business worry you, darling. We should be near the best private schools in Johannesburg." And he knew that Houghton was not far from his new Top Star headquarters in Rosebank.

"Let's go for a drive," he said to her one day. "I want to show you something." Once in the car, he told her, "Oxford Road is just a couple of miles away from where we're going."

The large Georgian-style mansion he stopped at must have been the biggest of its kind in Houghton. A steeply sloped grey slate roof protected the brown-brick house. Three storeys and two acres of lush gardens maintained by two gardeners set it apart from its nearest neighbours – mostly two-storey homes on smaller parcels of land. Despite its mass, five dollhouse-like attic windows gave it a homey feel. Four chimneys punctuated the symmetrical edifice. Eight large rectangular windows were separated in the centre of the ground level by a white, plastered, rectangular portico leading to two wood-panelled entry doors. Above each ground-floor window, matching casements allowed the light of the highveld sun to flood into the roomy middle-level sleeping areas.

In a room on an upper floor, there was a doll's house in the same Georgian style as the main homestead. With two sons, Angelique had begun to wish for a daughter, and as she took in the doll's house, she imagined a little girl enjoying it.

The single-storey billiard room attached to the right side of the main house was balanced on the opposite side by a large home office. All the features of the home were well proportioned and balanced.

The setting was no less impressive. Parts of the garden were carefully manicured. Jacaranda, acacia and huge oak trees decorated rambling lawns. The gardeners ensured that the flowerbeds were constantly in bloom. Natural rockeries gave a flavour of the original Africa on the hillside at the rear of the property.

A tennis court and a Hollywood-style swimming pool added more opulence to the garden. The source of the swimming pool was a flowing waterfall that fed two square pools connected off-centre: one shallow, the other deep, both featuring dark-blue mosaic tiles with white Greek key inlay.

Angelique fell in love with the house at first sight – a feeling that grew stronger as they walked through it together.

It was soon theirs.

A little more than eighteen months later, Angelique was overjoyed at the arrival of a baby girl. "We'll call her Maria, after both grandmothers."

"What do you mean?" Neil asked.

"Mary and Maria, it's the same name."

"Oh. Yes. I see," he said, looking at the tiny black-haired miniature of his wife. Even though she was so young, he could see Angelique's eyes peering up at him through her long eyelashes and copious hair. "She's even stubborn like you," he said. "Look at her howling until you feed her."

Grace had become one of three domestic servants in the household. Angelique didn't want Grace to do housework, but preferred her to help with the children. The other two maids did the washing, cleaning, and kitchen duties like peeling onions and potatoes, washing the vegetables for salads, and setting the table. Angelique preferred to do the cooking herself.

The two live-in maids had rooms in the servants' quarters behind the three garages housing the family cars, which were set back from Neil's home office. Their rooms were adjacent to two storerooms, one of which accommodated the two gardeners. Although the maids were classified as Bantus by the government and therefore not permitted to live in the whites-only suburb of Houghton, Angelique got Neil to obtain permits to keep them on the premises, on the basis that their labour was needed by the white household. But Angelique did not require Grace to live on the Robertson grounds, away from Jerry, so Grace commuted every day.

Angelique insisted that the children attend the best schools. All three were placed in expensive private establishments run along the lines of the English public school system. George and Milton went to an exclusive school for boys in Houghton, and Maria was enrolled in one for girls nearby.

During the first twenty months of the Ngubeni marriage, Grace had two miscarriages.

She prayed and prayed.

"My prayers are answered in one," she said to Jerry after their twins were born. "He is a gift."

"Let's give him an African name. What about Sipho?"

"That's perfect. Sipho. A *gift* after my prayers. Yes. And the girl?"

"I don't know. What do you think?"

"Another traditional name."

"Yes, yes. Why should we choose a Western name?"

After almost an hour of speculation, she said, "I know … I know what to call her. Thandi. She who is loved."

"Oohh, that's lovely. I love it and I love her. That's it. Thandi.

My lovely Thandi. It's perfect." Jerry took Thandi from the crib. She almost disappeared in her father's embrace.

Grace smothered the beautiful open-faced baby girl with kisses when she smiled. Sipho, on the other hand, didn't want to be held. He pushed back with his determined fists until put down. As soon as he was strong enough he would take off on hands and toes at great speed, like a four-legged spider.

Within only a couple of years, there came a fat baby boy, Sylvester. She nicknamed him "little Buddha". He ate everything – even the sand when she put him on the ground.

After the fourth, a girl, Grace said, "That's it, now. She's the last."

Grace wanted to call her Angelique.

"But your madam doesn't even like me. How can I name my daughter after her?" asked Jerry. "I can't believe you actually want to name our child after her."

"She's been good to me. I feel she'll do anything for me, Jerry. Everything she's said is out of concern for me. She didn't like you because of what she heard about you. And what about the charge of murder?"

"That wasn't true."

"How was she to know? Besides, I like the name Angelique. Don't you? It's a beautiful name."

"But Grace—"

"Forget it's *her* name. It's our baby's name. You'll see. She'll be our angel."

Grace got her way.

Grace told her friends and loved ones how proud she was that Jerry had a good job, but Jerry saw it differently. His wages were only slightly more than the going rate for African labourers. "Even that alcoholic Prinsloo gets much more than me," Jerry complained.

"Why does Mr Robertson keep him on?"

"Why? I'll tell you why. Because the boss can't fire him. He says he's been there too long. He does nothing there. I have far more responsibility. I'm the boss's eyes and ears around the workers."

"You're lucky you've got a good job."

"No, Grace. The boss is lucky he's got me. Do you know my pay is even less than Brunelda's – that simple clerk who walks around with her pretty brunette hair and big empty eyes. She must be the most junior white at the business, and she gets more than me. And *she* calls me 'boy'. It makes my blood boil."

"That's the way it is. This is South Africa."

Although she tried to calm Jerry down, Grace knew he was right. His wages were barely sufficient for the family, and this meant that she had to keep working. Angelique had kept her position open for her after every miscarriage and childbirth. Grace took only two weeks off each time.

The Ngubenis shared a four-room shack with Grace's widowed mother, Eveleen; Grace's brother, Cheeky; and his children. The black township of Alexandra, where the shack was located – known to many people as just "Alex" – was a few miles north of the outer suburbs of Johannesburg.

Jerry had tried to find them a home of their own before moving in with his mother-in-law. "There's nowhere else to stay. I've looked at Soweto and Alexandra. I even asked the boss and then Uncle Samson to see if there's a place somewhere. Nothing."

"It's a pity we're too late to get one of the early houses built in Alex."

Eveleen spoke up. "I don't mind, Jerry. My late husband was fortunate to get this house. We happily shared it with his two brothers."

"Where are they now? Won't they come back?"

"No, they won't. They went to Soweto. Come move in with me.

We can save money if we all live together, and I'm so happy to be near Grace."

The young couple had little choice: there was no other available accommodation for a new family.

Eveleen's shack had no power or water. Grace recalled that when she was a young girl, it had had just two brick rooms with a concrete floor and a zinc roof. Another two rooms of rough zinc-sheet walls and roof, nailed and wired over timber plank frames, had been added by her father and his brothers. She had helped them carry materials scrounged from pavements and the veld. The surrounding homes were no better – anything was used to provide some protection from the weather.

The neighbourhood's brown-earth streets had been graded once. Now rutted and rough, they turned to sludge when it rained. Grace had to hop from stone slab to struggling tuft of grass or risk ruining her shoes in muddy puddles.

The Ngubeni shack had a coal stove, as did many of the other homes for the one hundred thousand plus residents. Clouds of black smoke nearly blotted out the Alex skyline. Like a rough, dirty blanket, this plume spread its smothering layers over Alex every day. It would begin to thin out during the late morning, but choked the sky again by the time dusk approached. Whether it was visible or not, the thick, bitter taste and smell of the smog clogged every pore and invaded every dwelling in Alex.

Grace left her children with Eveleen each day and went to help Angelique with hers. She commuted by bus, leaving her shack at six thirty in the morning and arriving at the airy Robertson residence just before eight.

She was very fond of the Robertson children; it felt natural when she knew them so well from seeing to their needs every day. She tidied up after the sporty George, who left a trail of barely used clothing on his bedroom floor. It was Grace who made snacks for him and his boisterous friends and then cleaned the table and washed the dishes when they left. George was hardly in the house. He spent most of his time playing with his friends in the garden, in the pool, or on the hill at the back.

Grace found Maria to be a bright little girl with an inquiring mind. She asked Grace many questions and was the only one of the three children to want to know about Grace's family. She listened when Grace spoke to Priscilla, one of the live-in maids, in their tongue, and she used the same greeting for Grace every morning. From a young age, the clever Maria had learned a few phrases in isiZulu. Grace also taught her African songs and dances. Grace admired the beautiful clothes Angelique bought for Maria, as she folded and stacked them neatly in the bedroom wardrobes. Maria had more cupboards in her bedroom than Grace had for her whole family.

But Grace had a soft spot for Milton, who was a gentle, shy, and sensitive child. She gave him special attention, and when he was sick – which was often – she stayed the night, sleeping on the floor beside his bed. She did not return to her own family until she saw that Milton was on his way to recovery.

Otherwise, she left work at half past four, arriving home just after six. Angelique often asked Grace to assist on weekends, when they entertained dozens of family and friends. On those days, Grace helped with the catering, serving and cleaning.

Grace was disappointed with the schooling for her children. Sipho and Thandi attended an overcrowded classroom where the children ranged in age within the same class, the difference often being three years or more. The teacher was rarely able to control the class, so different were the children's stages of development and so disparate their needs. He had few books to give them and very little to entertain them with.

It was Grace who provided her children with exercise books and readers. She insisted that they do their homework to the best of their ability, although she knew how much they preferred to play in the dusty streets of the township.

Soccer was popular among the boys. Sipho was so besotted with the game that Grace joked he was born with a soccer ball in his arms. She knew that he escaped the small home to kick the ball against the sidewall of Patel's general store on his own. She observed him once. He didn't know she was there. He aimed for the two o's of the painted Coca-Cola sign covering the wall, and was able to hit them from any angle, even when kicking over his shoulder with his back to the wall. *Goodness me. He's good.*

Grace sometimes gave the girls a doll that Angelique passed on to her when Maria lost interest in it. And once she mended a skipping rope that Milton had thrown in the bin. Grace laughed when Thandi got tangled as she tried to skip for the first time.

Grace felt blessed with Thandi, a popular girl who was always surrounded by her girlfriends. In her teenage years, she seemed to be the target of much flirting from the young boys of the neighbourhood. Grace observed regular gatherings of boys in their street on the weekends. They chatted and laughed on the path outside the house and dawdled between the house and Patel's store. On many occasions Thandi proudly returned with a lucky packet, gifted to her by some hopeful boy.

How could her children be so different?

Sylvester was nothing like Thandi. He was quiet and shy, and always happy to stay at home with his granny, Eveleen. He had one good friend. They spent hours and hours constructing a go-cart from scrap planks and broken bicycle tyres and then pushing little Angelique and her friends around the block.

But while Angelique enjoyed playing with Sylvester and his friend, she preferred the company of the younger kids in the street.

She also had a favourite doll that Madam Angelique had bought for her second birthday. She looked after her Poppie for years as if it were her baby. She hugged and kissed the beautiful, apricot-coloured, rosy-cheeked toy, admiring its long eyelashes that closed when it was laid down and opened when it was held in her arms, revealing glassy blue eyes.

❖

Jerry spent little time with the children, who grew up under the care of Eveleen and, when she was at home, Grace. Jerry chafed at the sameness of daily life, and at the way the weeks became months and the months years.

But there was one big difference from the early days. For a long time no one noticed the subtle change in his outlook. At first he was only half aware of it himself, until it loomed so large as to seize his thoughts. He was feeling more strongly than ever the frustrations of trying to feed his growing family. Increasingly he resented the lack of opportunities at work. Even though he had been with Neil for years as the boss boy and received raises in his pay, he couldn't advance further within the company.

The whites had the easy jobs. All of them owned cars and homes to go to in suburbs of their choice. He and his fellow black workers were denied these choices – and couldn't have afforded them anyway.

He could not understand how Prinsloo, of all people, had been kept on in the position of service manager. And Prinsloo drove a new Austin Cambridge. With the pay Jerry received, he couldn't afford a new car and was struggling to pay for basic needs like food and clothing.

He had felt very fortunate to have the old Austin A40 Jerry had given him as a wedding gift; very few blacks were that lucky. Yet, generous though the gift was, he would have preferred to buy a car of his choice with a higher wage.

He thought about the future. In the 1970s – another whole decade away – would his children still have the same limitations? Would the Prinsloos of this world always have it better than the Ngubenis?

And then he thought about the Robertsons. Neil was a migrant. Look what he owned. Jerry could not even buy a shack, even though – as his father had told him many times – he had the nose of an African royal family. What was the use of stories of royal blood when the government passed laws that would not let him rise above a servant? And the same would be the case for his children. What hope did they have?

Jerry often took his lunch breaks on the pavement near the Top Star side gate. During one such break in the middle of the crisp Johannesburg winter, he sat in the sun to soak up the warmth from above, with a Pepsi in one hand and a bun in the other. He bit into the sweet softness and was about to wash it down with his cool drink when a shadow blocked his sunlight. He looked up to see a man standing over him.

"Hello Jerry."

"Do I know you?"

"Not yet." He extended his hand to Jerry. "Jacob Madau."

Jerry held up the Pepsi and bun. "Hello, Jacob Madau. Do you want some bun?"

"No, no. I just want to show you something. I'm here for the day. From Top Star Pretoria."

"I see. Sit down."

Jacob lowered himself onto a worn patch of grass next to Jerry. "So, what do you want to show me?" Jerry asked.

Jacob handed Jerry a printed flyer. "What do you think of this?"

Jerry read it with interest. It was as though the author had read his mind and summarised his complaints and frustrations about employment opportunities. The flyer pointed to the lack of equality in the workplace and advertised a "freedom rally" at the Trades Hall.

He took it to Uncle Samson, who was by then working at Top Star. "Uncle, what do you think about this? Let's go."

Samson read the flyer. "Better not to go. Leave it to them. The police are hunting these people. The police break up the meetings with their *sjamboks* (whips), beating anyone in the way."

"But I want to hear what they say. What are their plans?"

"You must look after your family, my boy. Make your plans for them."

"Funny you should say that. It's just what I was thinking, and that's why I'm going to the meeting. You could come with me, you know. But I'm going anyway, 'cause I really want to hear what they have to say."

Samson frowned at Jerry. He shook his head. "No. And you also, you mustn't go." He scrunched the pamphlet up and put it in his pocket.

After work, Samson found Jerry. "You're really going to that meeting, aren't you?"

"Of course I'm going."

"Well, if I can't persuade you, I'd better go and make sure nothing happens to you."

"Thank you, Uncle."

Jerry and Samson went straight to the Trades Hall and stood on the side, near the podium.

A dynamic young lawyer spoke, impressing Jerry with his ideas and energy. He called for protests against the ever-harsher laws that brought more and more discrimination to the statute books. He said the people must oppose the government's laws and crackdowns, which denied land ownership to blacks, restricted their movement, and required the carrying of permits called "passes" for blacks only. He pointed to the struggles for work, for housing and for a fair wage. He decried the lack of opportunity. Samson concentrated on the doors and the crowd, whereas Jerry applauded at every pause.

Before the speaker could finish his message, Samson grabbed Jerry and pulled him towards the side door. "It's the police, look," he whispered. "Let's get out of here."

Jerry looked back and saw dozens of police lining the back of the hall. As the police marched to the stage to stop the meeting, Samson pushed Jerry out a side door, and they fled. "You see? I told you. They can't win. And it's dangerous for us."

But Jerry was not deterred. On the contrary, he was inspired. He attended more rallies organised by the African National Congress (ANC), whose leadership was in jail, in exile or on the run.

One night he attended a political meeting at the Odin Cinema in Sophiatown. As the meeting was proceeding, the police stormed in and arrested one of the speakers on the platform.

Jerry shook with anger. He felt like jumping onto the stage and calling for the audience to attack the police and free the young Indian man. But the charismatic chairman of the meeting, a tall and imposing, well-dressed black man with a strong, angry face, stood up. In a confident voice, he led the audience in a freedom song, bringing relative calm to a situation that was about to explode into violence. The song was sung defiantly and with vigour, but Jerry felt this wasn't enough. Songs wouldn't make the changes he wanted to see.

Jerry's eyes were opened by what he heard at the political meetings and from some of the leaders of the ANC that he spoke to. He noticed the day-to-day injustices more and more at work – low pay, high transport costs, high food costs, low pensions, long working hours and inconsiderate working conditions. It was even so at Neil's Top Star Motors, which he knew to be better than average.

He resented that the working conditions and advancement opportunities for him and the other black workers were so much worse than those for the whites. Even the toilets for the whites were better than those for the blacks, which had no toilet seats.

Uncle Samson had worked for years as a mechanic, yet his pay was far less than younger whites doing similar work. Where was the justice in that?

Jerry could see his life laid out before him. It would be just like Uncle Samson's. He would be living from day to day forever, with far too little left over to put aside for later. What kind of a future was that?

He thought about his royal father, who would never own his own home. And his mother, who would work for Mevrou Strydom until she no longer could. Would he and his family live in Eveleen's house until she passed on, and would he and Grace serve the Robertson family forever? He thought about the people he worked with every day. What hopes did they have for advancement – and for their children?

He took on the role of representing the workers, and this took precedence over looking after Neil's interests. He pushed Neil for more pay and better working conditions for the blacks.

"Boss, it's not fair. The differences between black and white here are unfair. Our blacks need a kitchen and a place to rest during their breaks, just like you have for the whites." He pointed to the alley along the side of the workshop. "Look there! Our people sit on the pavements having lunch. Is that right? And they need more pay. They have to travel to get to work. It costs so much to get to work, eat and get home. They haven't much left for their families."

Neil did a bit to improve those conditions, by putting benches in the backyard for the blacks and upgrading their locker rooms. But Jerry could see that his boss was unsure of how far outside the system he could go. Or wanted to.

The day came when he asked for higher wages for the workers.

Neil said, "Jerry, what's the matter with you? What you're asking for will cost me too much money. You must know that. Whose side are you on?"

22

As an influential member of the inner circle behind the government's new policy development, Jacobus Strydom knew and kept Marius informed of the activities of the security forces. These, he told his son with pride, had embarked upon an organised manhunt. They would seek out the leading dissidents who were agitating for rights for the blacks.

Strydom's farming interests grew, but he found time to drive regularly to Pretoria, the seat of government power, where he met with the policymakers. He was a major donor to the ruling National Party, and he seized opportunities offered by cabinet ministers who were indebted to him for his influence and campaign funds. By 1963 he owned many properties around the country, a number of which were leased to government departments. He sat on the boards of a bank and an insurance company established in support of the Afrikaner community and businesses.

One night in that same year, he was returning to the farm in his sleek black Buick Elektra sedan. As he approached Lydenburg, he noticed the lights of an oncoming vehicle and dimmed his own. It was a long stretch of about five hundred yards or so. The advancing vehicle appeared to sway from left to right, but then corrected itself. Strydom concentrated on the moving lights in the dark ahead. He slowed down, and the other car seemed to be behaving itself.

When they were almost upon each other, the nearing lights moved over to his side of the road without warning, aiming for a head-on collision. Strydom slowed down more, expecting the other vehicle to correct its path. It didn't. He flashed his lights on bright and dimmed again. The advancing vehicle raised the beams to bright.

"Oh, heaven!" he cried out. He sensed that if he went to the other car's correct side, it could go there too.

Not knowing what the other driver was going to do, he slammed on his brakes, pulled the steering wheel towards his side of the road, veered off and avoided the oncoming vehicle. The Buick bumped and glided over the loose gravel shoulder. He turned the steering wheel to get back on the road, but the car planed over the clearing beside the road. Strydom shouted, "God! God help me!" just before the collision with a massive bluegum tree that brought the Buick to a violent halt.

Strydom's momentum sent him forward. His chest crunched into the steering wheel, sounding the horn. His head whipped forward, and he screamed in pain as he shattered the windscreen. The back of the heavy car reared up some two yards off the ground and almost flipped onto its roof. Then it came crashing down, the roof slamming the 70-year-old Strydom to the floor.

The other vehicle kept going as Strydom lay broken, bleeding, and unconscious.

A black family living in a small hut not far from the scene heard the crash and the horn, and ran over to investigate. They recognised Strydom's well-known Buick, the only one of its kind in Lydenburg.

The woman sent her husband and teenage son to the nearest farmhouse to call for help and to get a message to Miesies Strydom. She held Baas Strydom's limp hand and, in a soft voice, sang to him until an ambulance arrived at the scene. This was the song her mother used to comfort her with when she was ill and the one her mother hummed to her father as he faded away.

❖

The ringing of the phone in the middle of the night woke Marius. He was surprised to hear the voice of the commissioner of police. "Advokaat Strydom, your father has been in a road accident and is very badly injured."

"What happened? How is he?"

"He's unconscious."

"Will he be all right?"

"I'm afraid you should expect the worst. He's still alive, but has bad head injuries and internal haemorrhaging. The doctors are very pessimistic. There is no better way I can tell you this news, I'm afraid. Mrs Strydom has requested that you come to the hospital without delay. He's been flown to Pretoria. My deputy in Johannesburg will pick you up within the next half hour."

A squad car arrived to collect Marius. He joined the commissioner's deputy in the back. The man appeared reluctant to add to what Marius had already been told about his father's condition. "The best we can do now is pray for your father and get there as quickly as possible. He's been under the care of the best in Pretoria."

"How did it happen?"

"We believe that some idiots were playing chicken. They've done it before."

"What do you mean?"

"I'm told that the damned Groenewald brothers from the liquor store are suspected. We've tried to catch them. They're a tough lot, and they make people too fearful to testify against them."

"You mean you know who it is and can't catch them?"

"Yes. Apparently they drive on the wrong side of the road as a car approaches them, and then they swerve back at the last minute – just for fun."

"That's criminal."

"I know. But we've been looking for witnesses to these incidents for a long time, and no one will give us a statement."

The squad car sped to Pretoria. Very early the next morning, Marius approached Strydom's hospital room. He stood at the door and stared, unshaven and still in shock. The private ward, painted a sickly light-green colour, smelt like disinfectant. He felt strange. Everything was so serene, yet he was well aware of the calamity unfolding.

Strydom lay on the single bed. A pale-green blanket covered his damaged body. His head was still and heavily bandaged. His eyes were closed.

Mrs Strydom sat on a chair, clasping her husband's hand. She held a handkerchief close to her nose. Hennie and his wife sat on the other side of the bed; he stared ahead from a face that was grey and drawn, while she looked at the floor, her hands resting on her knees.

Marius stepped forward into the room. Hennie looked at him and tried to speak, but his greeting choked. Martha Strydom turned to Marius. Her cheeks were moist with tears and red from the agony of the past ten hours.

She looked at her husband and squeezed his hand. "Pa, Marius is here." She turned and said to Marius, "Pa doesn't open his eyes, but he can hear us. I can feel him squeeze my hand when I ask him to. And look there." She pointed to his closed eyes as tears edged down his distorted and partially bandaged face.

There were no doctors. Marius assumed that they had given up hope of doing anything, so bad were his injuries.

His mother told him later that her cousin, Dr Christiaan De Wet, was the orthopaedic surgeon supervising the medical team. "Let Jacobus go to God with dignity," he had told her. "He deserves to depart this world in peace. We can allow that. You know, Martha, if there was anything that could be done, I would do it." Christiaan was also a powerful member of the Broederbond and a close friend of the ailing Strydom.

Now, as Marius approached the bed, Mrs Strydom got up. "Pa, here's Marius." She ushered him to her own chair and sat him down. She took Marius's hand and placed it over Strydom's.

Marius patted his father's hand and whispered in his ear. "Pa, I'm here. We shall pray …"

Strydom lifted the hand under Marius's and opened his mouth. His breathing became shallow, and a barely audible rasp came from his lips.

"Yes, Pa. I'm listening. Are you talking to me?"

Strydom nodded his head slightly and opened his mouth. Marius leaned closer to listen.

"Your … turn … lead … our people … our volk." He lifted his fingers and pointed them towards Marius. "Promise me … lead our volk."

Marius sat there looking at the fatally wounded lion whose soul was intact and who, to his dying moments, felt his mission and was still trying to execute it.

"Promise me … now," Strydom breathed. "Keep the … order … of … things. No mistakes. Promise … me."

Marius whispered into Strydom's ear. He could barely speak as his throat clenched stiff with emotion. "Yes, Pa. I promise."

Strydom's tears had stopped. He remained motionless except for his breathing, which was so shallow, it seemed not to go beyond his throat.

He died four hours later.

23

Top Star grew big. Very big. Neil added more and more British cars to his range and extended the second-hand car yards to another six locations along the busy arteries connecting Johannesburg to the satellite towns growing around it.

He loved British Motors' Morris Mini, the ingenious, trendy and nifty car that appealed to all age groups. It was fast becoming a good money spinner for him. And there was a neat little commercial vehicle that was popular with small businesses. He enhanced the commercial vehicle sales and service division of the business with the proven Leyland brand and then added the upmarket Rovers and sporty Triumphs.

He studied the motorcar trade market overseas and read good reports about Japanese-made vehicles. Then he got a tip-off from his contact in the traffic department: a Japanese manufacturer was looking for a dynamic dealership. They had sent cars for checking by the licensing department, and these had passed all the tests with flying colours. His contact thought it was a very well-made car. Other dealers wouldn't touch them. "They think no one will buy inferior Japanese products," he told Neil. "But I'm telling you, Mr Robertson, at the right price I'd buy that little car. It's solid and so well put together."

Neil thought about this. Businesses were cost-conscious. There must be a good market for the cheaper Japanese commercial vehicles that were receiving good reports from car critics. One wrote:

> *These vehicles are far from inferior to the British equivalent products. They are well engineered and manufactured, practical in design, and by all accounts they are very reliable. Their electrical systems work, which is more than can be said about some of our English cars! The commercial utility vehicles are solid and good value.*

Neil did not have to reflect long to come to a decision. *That's it! I can sell these.*

After doing some homework and reading up on how to conduct business in Japan, Neil flew to Tokyo with four older white members of his sales staff. He didn't care that they had no idea what their role would be. One of them had been taken on just the week before. The only requirement Neil looked for was that they have grey hair and look distinguished. They had to bow to him and his hosts, and otherwise keep their mouths shut.

He took them to his Italian barber and Indian tailor and had them groomed and dressed, fitting them each with two dark, tailor-made suits.

They arrived in Tokyo with dozens of African souvenirs: fluffy lions, elephants and monkeys; silver-plated sugar spoons; ten pairs of solid gold cufflinks with matching tiepins; a gold watch; and a large engraved silver tray.

The tickets were one-way, for the flight to Japan only. "We will book our return flight when we achieve our goal," he said to his team, "so tell your families they will see you when they see you."

At his first meeting, on the Tuesday after their arrival, his soft toys caused much discussion and resulted in much bowing and thanking, but no commitment on the main issue. They were asked to come back the next day.

The next day was filled with more discussion with another group of Japanese personnel, centred on his written proposal and the architectural perspectives of the proposed workshops and showrooms. There was also more appreciation of the next batch of stuffed animals and, especially, much examining of the colour photographs of his upmarket Rover showrooms that were modelled on London's St Hugo's Club for Gentlemen.

There followed another invitation to return the next day … and the next … and the next. Neil felt he was making progress, working himself up the line and passing the test each step of the way, but he was worried that he would soon run out of the souvenirs, as he was meeting new teams each day.

Finally, he was at the top floor of the Tokyoto Motors of Japan building and invited into a large wood-panelled boardroom. The long dark-stained cherry-wood table was smoothly polished and surrounded by lush royal-blue velvet chairs with gold piping.

He and his team were welcomed in a formal, businesslike manner by six senior, greying, impeccably dressed Japanese gentlemen in dark suits with white shirts and dark ties in shades from grey to black. In addition, there was a young interpreter.

They all deferred to the distinguished, tall, thin man who sat farthest from the door. Discussions were led by a stout, bespectacled man at the centre of one long side of the table. He had a pile of papers in front of him.

The interpreter listened carefully as the man in the centre spoke in Japanese. Then he looked towards the man farthest from the door and nodded. With a slight drop of the head, almost missed by Neil, the man nodded back. The interpreter looked at Neil and spoke in English.

"Robertson-san. Our chairman, Watanabe-sama, wants to express his appreciation for the effort you and your men have put in to earn his trust. He is satisfied that you have demonstrated much desire to represent the Tokyoto Motor Company in South Africa."

He paused as Mr Watanabe observed the proceedings, impassively it seemed, as there was very little expression in his face and no change in his demeanour. Neil realised it was not his turn to say anything and sat quietly. The spokesman spoke in Japanese again and the interpreter translated.

"Robertson-san. Watanabe-sama" – the translator bowed to the end of the table – "is willing to respond to your proposals because you have shown an ability to be a salesman." He bowed in the direction of Mr Watanabe. "Watanabe-sama has caused your showrooms to be investigated. Not only the Rover, but also the Austin. And the second-hand saleyards. And the service workshops."

The stout man spread some photographs of various parts of the Top Star business on the table. Neil smiled and nodded as though he were pleased that they had done their homework on him. He did not betray that he was worried – very worried – that they knew so much about him and he knew so little about them.

The stout man spoke again, and the interpreter continued. "Watanabe-sama wishes to tell you that if you can sell ten Austins, you can sell one hundred of his Imperial Crowns." The interpreter chuckled, but Mr Watanabe looked at Neil deadpan.

"Robertson-san. Watanabe-sama (bow) requires your honourable commitment to be given to the following, now."

They paused. Neil looked at the spokesman.

"Robertson-san. Number one. Tokyoto Motor Company of Japan will provide the plant and equipment to service our vehicles. It is important that all vehicles are properly checked because we want our reputation never to be blemished. You will comply with our presales servicing schedule. We will pay for your service staff to be trained. Number two. You must commit to employ six salesmen from the

225

first day of opening. Number three. For the first year, Tokyoto Motor Company of Japan will pay 75 per cent of the advertising costs. After that we will negotiate a lower percentage. Number four. You must construct a workshop to the plan on the sheet being shown to you now. We will match your cost, yen for yen, or should we say rand for rand."

The interpreter paused. This was the first time Neil had seen the Tokyoto plan; they had been examining his designs until then. In his proposal he had taken the chance of asking them to pay the full cost of construction, but he had a back-up plan. He glanced at their blueprint quickly. It seemed to have a streamlined design and practical set-out. He bowed in the direction of Mr Watanabe.

"Robertson-san. Number five. Here is the current supply price list with the current retail sale prices, which shows your mark-up. Watanabe-sama wants to entrench the market share before increasing your mark-up more."

Neil studied the figures. They were okay. In fact, the mark-up percentage was not bad compared to the British Motor Company.

"Now, Robertson-san. You will open doors and launch on the eighth of August. Do you agree with all these conditions?"

Neil had no idea whether he could achieve this schedule of just over seven months. He looked at Mr Watanabe. "Yes, I agree, Watanabe-sama. You have my word." He said this very confidently, and he saw that his words were translated with as much conviction by the interpreter.

Watanabe arose from his chair, and the other Japanese gentlemen all followed suit. They stood back as he walked to the middle of the table, where the contract documents were laid out, open at the signature pages. Watanabe signed two of the three documents on the table and sat back.

Then he said in fluent English with a hint of a British accent, "Mr Robertson, I do hope you can deliver on your promises. I know enough about you to believe that you will. It is not your words that have impressed or the gifts that you have given. We accept your determination, drive and enthusiasm, and the fact that you have not booked a return flight yet. We considered another week of meetings with our cleaning and maintenance staff, but then thought this unfair on your sales personnel." He pointed to Neil's team and grinned. "You see, Mr Robertson, we too can be theatrical."

One of the Japanese executives bowed and left the room.

"Now, Mr Robertson. Please sign the contract. There are two originals and one translation. You will have one original and the English version. We don't need the latter."

The previous spokesman brought the three documents to Neil and placed them before him.

"So now, Mr Robertson, we place our trust in you."

Neil looked at the documents and then at Mr Watanabe. He sat forward, placed his elbows on the table, and joined his hands at his fingertips, looking at his counterpart. "Watanabe-sama. And I in you."

He took the pen as the man who had left the room returned with a tray, a bottle of sake, and dainty pottery glasses. Neil signed the two Japanese documents. He carried one to Mr Watanabe and handed it to him with both hands, bowing at the same time. Watanabe's lips twitched with the suggestion of a polite smile as he took the contract from Neil and bowed in return.

Neil then handed each of the Japanese a royal-blue velvet case containing cufflinks and a tiepin, and also gave Watanabe the wristwatch. Then he withdrew the sterling silver tray from its wrapping with great ceremony and held it up for all to see. It had been engraved with the Tokyoto badge. He presented it to Watanabe. "This serves as a symbol of my positive thought for the future of your vehicles in my hands."

"My dear Mr Robertson. I was aware that you had brought a

silver tray with you, but had not been informed that you had been so presumptuous as to engrave it."

"Watanabe-sama, I had no intention of taking it back. But, I suspect you knew in advance that I wasn't going to leave here without an agreement."

"Yes. We knew that before we accepted your request for a meeting."

Neil set up the Tokyoto operation as a separate company, Tokyoto Star Motors, with separate premises and staff. As promised, he made sure the doors were opened on the eighth of August. Instead of the six promised, ten salesmen – all dressed in crisp uniforms with the silver Tokyoto badge embroidered on their shirt pockets – were eagerly waiting to promote the new Japanese "wondercar", a slogan created by Neil. The man who had been the spokesman at the Tokyo meetings came for the opening and approved of the catchy nickname. He took many photographs and notes for his chairman.

Neil made sure that all the mechanics working on these cars were properly trained. He wanted them to develop a reputation for reliability.

He took control of the marketing campaign and paid for expert road tests. Full-page advertising appeared in the newspapers, and large billboards looked down at motorists, who were mostly struggling with their more expensive European models.

Though he worked hard to achieve the outcome, Neil knew luck had a big part to play in the success of this new venture. The global fuel crisis of 1973 was one such bit of good fortune. Top Star benefited when the small, fuel-efficient Tokyoto brand became a car of choice, above the fuel-guzzling six- and eight-cylinder sedans that had been popular in South Africa.

The Tokyoto side of the business was soon way ahead of Neil's

Austin, Morris and Rover dealerships. And not only the sedans. In sale numbers, Tokyoto's utility vehicles, referred to as "bakkies" in South Africa, rapidly overtook the less fuel-efficient English and American commercial vehicles.

Tokyoto expanded its range, and Neil expanded his dealerships into smaller towns. He rebranded the Tokyoto business as Top Star Tokyoto, satisfied now that this division would not tarnish the lustre of his Top Star.

Neil detected a distinct shift in the way the public, and especially businesses, purchased vehicles. The Austin models were starting to look very ordinary in their designs. What used to be a respectable name, he now saw as a waning star. There was no point in wasting his resources on something that the Top Star brand could not afford to carry.

And the upmarket brands? Time to replace the Austin Princess and the uncertain Rover. He liked the Rover, but they just weren't selling so well any more.

Around this time, an idea occurred to him that gave him no small satisfaction. The feeling – the temptation – was too strong to ignore. He prepared a letter addressed to Mr Francis Harvey, Manager, Africa Division, British Motor Company, and copied it to Sir Julian Hackett, Chairman.

Dear Mr Harvey,

It is with regret that I have to inform you that Top Star Motors will no longer accommodate products of the British Motor Company. I have felt for some time that there has been a lack of faith in me. I know that I have been unfairly labelled, my honesty called into question.

The problem stems from your leadership (or lack of it), which is pedantic at best and, if I am to be honest, commercially negligent. You have failed to attract loyalty. This is most regrettable. As an Englishman, I took some pride in representing the British Motor Company, and I am sad that I have been spurned in return for my devotion over many years.

Yours faithfully,
Neil Robertson

❖

Identifying an opportunity, Neil flew to Germany and impressed decision makers at BMW. He persuaded them to give him one dealership in Rosebank, where he said he had ideal premises. He didn't, but then, wasn't Oxford Motors struggling to survive as a repair shop?

He offered the owner of Oxford Motors more than it was worth, and organised to replace the existing buildings with a custom-designed BMW showroom.

The day the site was sealed off for demolition, Jerry came to him in great consternation. "Boss, I must get into Oxford Motors before they break it down."

"Why?"

"Please don't ask questions. Can you tell them to let me in, please?"

It was arranged. Jerry walked around the demolition and excavation machinery with a shovel. He went to a spot in the backyard and started digging. Within a few minutes, he had unearthed his jam jar with twelve pounds and ten shillings in it, and walked away beaming from ear to ear. He held it up and yelled, "Safer than the bank!" as the team of demolition workers cheered him on.

The problem was that the currency of South Africa had changed to the rand. Even though he invited Dizzy and some of the old Oxford

Motors' crew for drinks at a shebeen in Alex that night, Jerry had to pass the hat around for rands.

"I'll pay you back when I change the pounds," he quipped.

◆

The BMW models appealed to affluent white South Africans. They sold so well that Neil could not keep up with the orders and had to resort to waiting lists. But his customers were prepared to wait.

He had cornered the high and low ends of the market with the BMW and Tokyoto dealerships. In the midst of all this activity, he managed to steal a few moments to smile at the thought of the way he'd selected and won over those manufacturers. How right he had been about them! As things turned out, he had dumped the British models just in time.

PART II

1974–1994

24

❖◇❖

Grace often found herself unable to draw her eyes away from her older son as she admired his good looks. In 1974 Sipho was a quiet 14-year-old, physically mature for his age. With the help of her mother, Eveleen, Grace had brought him up to respect his elders and authority. Soccer was still the love of his life, and, judging by what she had heard from his friends, he was a good player. Like his father, Sipho was athletic, and handsome.

He was not academic, but Grace imposed a strict regime that her mother helped to enforce. "Sipho, you have to be home by half past four. Then it's homework until you finish. Wash and be ready for dinner when I get home by half past six. At half past seven I'll check your homework with you. Then it's bedtime at half past eight. If you don't do this, you will help the girls do the cooking. Do you understand?"

"Yes, Mother."

"Don't laugh, Sylvester. This applies to you too."

She bought a paraffin-fuelled primus lamp especially for the children's studies and set up a small homework table in the bedroom she and Jerry shared with Thandi and Angelique.

Sipho and Sylvester slept in another room with two school going cousins and their father – Grace's younger brother, who was known by his nickname, Cheeky. Cheeky's wife had been run over by a car in Johannesburg and had died of her injuries.

Cheeky couldn't look after the children on his own, so Eveleen had told him to move in. Since then she had been the mainstay at home while Grace, Jerry and Cheeky went to work. Jerry got a job for Cheeky at Top Star Tokyoto Sandton, not far from Alexandra.

By half past eight every night, Grace was exhausted. Jerry came home later and later, and she scarcely noticed him slipping into bed next to her, often in the early hours of the morning.

Grace was aware of Jerry's frustration with the slow progress of change.

"It's not enough for the government to drop separate European and non-European entrances to some public buildings," he told her. "We continue to be denied access to sections of their parks, and to their new buses, their pretty suburbs, and their fancy jobs, just because we're black. Our kids will be grown up soon, and then it will be too late. We still have no decent freedoms."

"Well, *we* survived, didn't we?"

"I'm not talking about survival. I'm talking about living. We should be able to get equal pay, to live anywhere, to go to the same schools, to use the same buses—"

"Jerry, calm down, calm down."

"Why should I?"

Esther looked up at the autumn sun glowing gently over Johannesburg. It was a Sunday in May, and she felt happy to be here at Zoo Lake with Sipho and a few of his friends. A pretty and lively classmate, Esther had invited the boys to join her and her girlfriends on a picnic for her birthday. She was delighted by Sipho's excitement when he accepted overenthusiastically. *He is so cute, and I think he likes me.*

When she walked up the aisle of the bus, she had made a point of darting to a two-seater bench and shooing her friends away. Sipho ambled up the narrow walkway in her direction. She waved at him and patted the seat next to her. "Sipho, here. Sit here." He smiled, then sat next to her, folded his hands on his lap, and looked down. "Don't be shy." She took his left hand and held it. He looked straight ahead, not looking at her or his friends.

To arrive at Zoo Lake, they had had to change buses in the city. It took a long time. But now, here they were.

Set in extensive parklands that included Johannesburg's zoo and war museum, the beautiful oasis of lake and garden in the middle of white suburbia was many miles from any black township. It was unusual for lakes in white areas to be available to blacks, but Esther and her friends had selected this spot for their picnic. She knew that the Zoo Lake grounds had been gifted to the Johannesburg City Council on condition that it remain open to all races.

On this Sunday there were several families and groups lazing about, talking, drinking and enjoying the mild Johannesburg weather. Most of them were whites, but there were a few groups of blacks. Calm and still as a mirror, the bright blue lake reflected the sunny Sunday sky. Reeds and bushes lined parts of the waterfront.

The birthday Esther was celebrating was her fourteenth, and she had brought along her own homemade chocolate cake.

"Chocolate cake! That's my favourite," Sipho told her. "I can't wait to get stuck in."

"Later, Sipho. Later."

They took a spot near the water's edge, under a native umbrella thorn acacia. Their picnic blanket mapped the nucleus of their own little space as they lay around, enjoying their food and soft drinks, talking, eating and joking.

After digesting the snacks, the boys got up and kicked a ball around. Esther couldn't keep her eyes off Sipho, who was showing off his skills as he played with two of his friends, Vusi and Cyril.

He controlled the ball with his head and his right foot, and kicked it directly to his friends with grace and accuracy.

Nearby, a group of older Afrikaner youths – in their early twenties – also lay around. They had little to eat, but she noticed that they had much to drink. Beers. Many beers. As the alcohol started having an effect, they became louder and louder. They joked among themselves and then turned their attention to Sipho's group. Occasionally they hurled insults at Sipho and his friends. Esther sat on the blanket, admiring her athletic friend, but a look of concern replaced her smiles as she cast glances at what was going on among the white youths.

"Hey, you sissies. Soccer's a girl's game!" she heard one of the Afrikaner men shouting. His companions laughed out loud and heckled her friends.

That progressed a short while later to, "Hey, you kaffirs! This place is not for you – only for us, who play rugby!"

"Come, Sipho. Come sit down," Esther called. "Let's cut the cake."

Sipho turned, as if about to run to her. Just then Vusi kicked the ball to him. "Here, Sipho."

Esther was concerned that as a matter of principle, Vusi wouldn't shy away from the abuse. She hoped Sipho would see what was happening and force Vusi to sit down.

The whites had started a mini-rugby game of their own. They were kicking the rugby ball through Sipho's soccer game. The rugby players were well built and tough. They continued drinking beer as they played.

"Come, let's sit down," said Sipho. "I'm getting tired."

"Yes, come for some cake," called Esther.

"No," said Vusi. He spoke loudly in Afrikaans and within earshot of the white young men: "We are allowed to play here, and we were here first."

238

Esther could see Sipho hesitate, unsure and wanting to get out. He was kicking the ball towards their blanket and edging closer to Esther, away from the rugby players. "Yes, but let's have cake and Coke. I'm thirsty."

As he said that, the soccer ball collided with one of the bottles of beer that had been placed near the games by a burly member of the Afrikaans group.

"You fuckin' kaffirs! Now you've done it. Come, lads, let's show them!" The tough blond man ran over to Vusi. "Let's put these boys back in their place!" With full force, he threw a massive punch at Vusi's left cheek, knocking the shocked and unprepared boy to the ground. The other boys and girls scattered.

Sipho and four other boys ran to the water, hoping to get away, but the Afrikaners caught up to them in the shallows and punched, kicked and pushed the five black youths. They put up some resistance but were no match for the rugby players. Trying to evade their attackers and minimise their injuries, Sipho's group moved further into the water and away from the shoreline.

The shallows of the lake became muddy with brief pools of red blood from the black five. It felt to Esther as though the attack on Sipho would never end. She screamed as they pummelled him. He held his hands above his head. The kicking continued. He tried to support himself on his hands and knees and then tried to scramble away from them.

She had to act – the day was all going terribly wrong.

Esther ran to a group of picnickers about twenty yards away. Three older Afrikaner men who had been making a braai realised what was happening. They stormed over and got between the whites and the blacks, separating them. Shouting at the drunken Afrikaners, they ordered them to return to their blanket. They told the blacks to get out of the water, and went to the unconscious Vusi lying on the shore. A woman brought a flask of water, which they poured over

Vusi, and called to him to wake up. The others emerged from the water bloodied and exhausted, converging around Vusi to see if he was badly injured.

Esther had wet a handkerchief and dabbed it on Vusi's face, clearing the blood to see his injuries. "Vusi, Vusi. Wake up, wake up."

"He has a pulse. It's strong. He must have a concussion, but I think he'll be okay. Make sure he doesn't choke on his tongue," said the dominant one of the good Samaritans. He turned Vusi on his side, reached into his mouth, and loosened his tongue, making sure he could keep breathing.

They spent several minutes with Vusi as the others checked their injuries. Fortunately there were no broken limbs. But there were plenty of bleeding wounds and bruises, and a great deal of hurt pride. Their clothes were soiled from the lake and their injuries.

A two-man police patrol had been flagged down by someone who had seen the commotion. As the policemen approached across the lawn, the rugby players, who had sobered a bit, went straight up to them and started making accusations against Sipho's group.

"Those black ones, they swore at us and tried to steal our rugby ball," they told the police. They pointed to Vusi and the gathered group.

Vusi was stirring awake and was still not quite alert. The Afrikaner youth and police approached the black group, who were still being attended to by the three white adults.

Vusi opened his eyes and held his head. "Where am I? Sipho? What's happened? Sipho? Sipho?" They all turned to one another, looking for Sipho. "Where is Sipho?" Vusi asked, still dazed.

"He ran into the water where he was getting beaten up," Esther said. "When I came back, I didn't see him. I don't know where he is …" The concern in her voice turned to urgency even as she spoke. She stood up and looked at the lake. "Sipho! Sipho!" she called.

"Who is Sipho?" asked the police.

"One of our friends," Cyril answered. "He was chased into the lake with me." Cyril, who was sopping wet and muddy, also turned to look at the water.

"He must have run away," said a police constable.

"No," said Cyril. "He wouldn't go without us. Look, all the rest of us are here." He looked around him, making sure that all of them were there.

Esther was yelling for Sipho and walking towards the waterfront. She looked back at the policemen. "He must be here. Maybe still hiding. Please help me find him."

"Last time I saw him, he was being kicked in the lake by those men," said Cyril, pointing to the Afrikaners. He ran to the shallows where they had been beaten. He went in up to his knees and combed the water, shouting, "Sipho, are you still here? Sipho! Sipho!"

The others joined him, doing the same.

Then a young woman ran up to the constable. "There is someone in the water, over there." She pointed to reeds about a hundred yards to the left of the scene of the beating.

"Oh, God!" Esther looked in that direction and saw clothing tangled in the reeds, immobile. She realised it was not just clothing. "It's Sipho. It must be him. I think that's his blue shirt." She ran over to the reeds and tried to drag the limp Sipho out of the water.

The constable arrived beside her and pushed her out of the way. He lay Sipho on his side and hit his back to get the water out, harder and harder. There was no response from Sipho. The constable checked for a pulse and there was none.

He dragged Sipho out and laid him on the shore. "The kaffir's head was underwater. He's not breathing, and there's no pulse. He's gone," he pronounced.

The youths were distraught, holding on to and hugging each other, most of them in tears. "No, no. Try again," pleaded Esther. "Maybe he's just choking."

"No, he's not breathing and has been underwater too long." The constable grabbed the terrified Cyril, took him aside, and shook him until he calmed down. "Give me your names and the dead one's family particulars." He wrote the details in his notebook. "Where does – er, did he live?"

Cyril looked down as he answered the questions, doing his best not to cry.

"What's their phone number?"

"There's no phone, sir," Esther struggled to answer. Her aching throat felt as though it were being squeezed closed.

Cyril was unable to speak. With his red eyes, one of which was swelling closed; grey, bruised and wounded cheeks; bleeding and torn upper lip; and tattered clothing, he looked like a lost, helpless vagabond.

"No phone, hey? I'll send a kaffir policeman to tell his family what happened. Yous kids! Yous must give me your names and addresses. Then go home. We'll take statements from yous later."

Esther watched and waited as he went to the police van. She heard him radioing for Sipho's body to be collected. He came back with a pad of forms. Esther stood at a distance. Her hands were shaking as she dabbed her eyes.

The constable went around and asked for all their names. When he finally asked Esther for hers, she gave it and watched him write it down slowly.

"And the deceased. What's his name?"

"Sipho Ngubeni."

He looked at her blankly. "Spell that," he commanded as though he were instructing her to clean his shoes. She obeyed and looked on as he wrote Sipho's name on the incident report.

On the dotted lines at the bottom of the page, next to the words "Cause of death", she saw the constable write in shaky large print, like the print of a child, "Accidental death. Kaffirs attacked youths, who acted in self-defence."

25

Grace had bid farewell to Jerry early that morning when he left with Jacob for a meeting in Pretoria. Now she could not believe that the evening with its terrible news could belong to the same day.

When Sipho's friends arrived at the Ngubeni house in Alexandra just as night fell, they were so troubled by the tragic events that Grace had to tell them all to sit down and be quiet.

Then she looked at Esther. She knew the outing had been for Esther's birthday, and she saw at once that Esther was the most articulate of the group, more in control of her emotions than the others. She asked Esther to explain what had happened.

Esther was crying softly all the time she spoke, and soon tears were running down Grace's cheeks as she listened to the account of the day's events. Cyril broke in now and then with a bit of detail and context. "We were there first, enjoying our games and then these ... these Boers came and attacked us."

Esther developed the report in a shaky voice, but with precision and accuracy.

"We were trying to run away – we didn't attack!" he interjected again.

"Where is Sipho now?" asked Grace.

"I don't know," they said in unison.

"Esther, which police station were the police from?" she asked.

"I don't know. They didn't say."

"Does anyone know which police station they were from?" asked Grace.

"All we know is they were both white police officers, but they said they would get another black policeman to come over and tell you."

Grace spoke calmly, though her eyes were full of tears. "No one has come here. We've been here the whole day."

"I shouldn't have said we must play on." Vusi looked down at his hands and cried again.

❖

That night Grace waited for the policeman and Jerry.

And mourned.

The news spread quickly across the neighbourhood. Many Alexandrans came to express their sorrow. They brought food and prayed with Grace. Her friends made sure that there was always someone to sit with her to keep her company as they waited for Jerry, who did not know the news yet.

There was no way to contact him. Their house had no telephone, and in any event, she didn't know where to phone for him. They thought of asking someone with a car to go to Pretoria to try and find him. She knew there was a meeting but didn't know where it was.

"Jerry will be home soon. We will wait for him to return. If someone goes to find him and he is coming back, they will miss each other. What's the use? We'll wait. I don't even know where to start looking, except maybe at Jacob's house. But I don't know where that is."

Cheeky offered to locate a car in the neighbourhood whose driver would be willing to take her to a police station, any police station, to find Sipho and see what they could do.

"No, Cheeky. There's nothing we can do tonight. Jerry will be here soon, and then we can decide. And the police may still come."

She waited for Jerry. As midnight approached she realised that he would not come home until after work the next evening.

He had told her on other occasions that he didn't want to risk travelling in his tired state. And he once said that he didn't want to be stopped by the police and asked what he was doing out so late at night. "You shouldn't worry about me. It's better to just get up early in the morning and be back in Jo'burg before work starts. That's better than driving at night."

She had not liked the thought of him not coming home, but she knew that she would not change his mind.

Grace has come in earlier than usual, Angelique thought on entering the kitchen and seeing her there.

Grace stood up. "Madam, something very bad has happened, and I need to speak to the master."

The firmness in Grace's voice startled Angelique. She stood still and looked at Grace, whose face appeared surprisingly drawn and haggard. It looked as though she hadn't slept all night. Angelique felt the strangeness of the request. Grace hardly ever engaged with Neil and had never asked for his help before. In fact she had always been more reserved with Neil, as if a little scared of him. Neil's manner with her too had remained more formal than with Jerry. Now she was asking for Neil. Something was wrong.

"What's happened, Grace? What's the matter?"

Grace didn't look at Angelique, who could see the woman was trying her best to keep her emotions under control. Grace's eyes began to moisten as she dabbed them with a handkerchief. She looked as though she had aged.

"What's wrong? Is it Jerry? What has he done this time?"

"No, ma'am. It's Sipho. He died yesterday, and I must find him."

"What? Did you say *died*?"

Grace nodded.

"What do you mean? How?"

"At Zoo Lake. I need to find the policeman who was there, so I can see Sipho."

Angelique stared at her, lips slightly apart. Then she took a deep breath and yelled, "Neil! Neil! Come here! Something terrible has happened."

Angelique started shaking and ran to the staircase, where she called upstairs again for Neil. Tears, stalled for a moment by shock, blurred her vision. She returned to Grace.

Neil, who was still getting dressed for work, ran down the stairs, buttoning his shirt. "What's wrong, Angie?"

"Sipho is dead. Sipho is dead." Neil looked puzzled until she added, "Grace and Jerry's oldest son. He's dead."

"My God! How? When?" he asked, tucking his shirt into his trousers.

Angelique turned to Grace. "What happened, Grace?"

Grace had regained some of her composure. "He was killed."

"Killed?" Angelique heard her own and Neil's voices, which seemed to echo each other. Neil was agape, but then, she realised, so was she. "How?"

"He was with some of his friends having a picnic at Zoo Lake yesterday. Some" – Grace's voice was shaking again now – "some ruffians fought with them … and killed him."

"My God! My God!" Angelique cried. "That's awful, Grace. You poor thing …"

"Angie," said Neil, "perhaps you should get dressed. Your help will be needed here." Angelique looked at him through the tears that were flooding her eyes. She nodded and ran upstairs to change from her dressing gown.

Neil turned to Grace. "Where's Jerry?"

"I don't know, master. He didn't come home last night. He went to friends in Pretoria and must have slept over." She knew that he was involved in underground political activity but didn't want to be the one to tell Neil.

"You mean he doesn't know yet?"

"No, master, he doesn't. I don't know when he will be back. But I don't know where *Sipho* is. That's my big problem now. I must find the policeman who was at Zoo Lake yesterday. Can you help me?"

"Of course I'll help. Tell me what you know."

Grace told him all that Sipho's friends had told her. "We don't even know which police station to contact to find where Sipho is."

"Right. I'll see what I can find out."

"Thank you. Is the madam all right?"

"Yes, Grace. Are you?"

"Yes. I'll be fine." Her eyes were moist as she turned away from Neil.

❖

Neil telephoned three police stations near Zoo Lake and eventually ascertained that the Parktown station had reported a death at Zoo Lake the day before.

"Konstabel Swanepoel was the head of the patrol car. He is now off duty. You will have to call after three this afternoon, sir," he was told by the constable on telephone duty.

"No, sir. I will not call at three this afternoon. Who is in charge now? Because I must find out where the body of the dead boy is. His family is upset. They weren't even told by the police he was dead and have no contact details."

"No, Meneer. I cannot help you. Only Konstabel Swanepoel has the details."

"Who is in charge there? I want to speak to the officer in charge of your station," he insisted.

"Sorry, sir. I cannot give that information."

"Listen here. What would you do if the police wouldn't tell you where your son's body is? The police are supposed to help the public, not fight with us. If you don't put me on to the officer in charge, I'm going to come from Houghton and take you into his office. Now tell me. Who is it?"

"Kaptein Botha is the senior officer. But he isn't in yet. He'll be in at eight o'clock, Meneer."

"Is that Captain Koos Botha?" he asked.

"Yes, Meneer."

"That's good. Okay, I'll call back." He turned to Grace. "The head of the police station is the son of an old friend of mine, and I know him very well. I'll call him when he gets to work at eight. I'm sure he'll help us. Now, Grace. Have a cup of tea. I'll try and find Jerry."

"Where is the madam? I'll take her a cup."

"She's fine. She's upstairs and will come down soon."

Grace made a cup of tea in her work mug and left the kitchen. She and the black staff had never sat in the kitchen. The staff usually took tea and ate outside or in the servants' quarters.

She was grim and intermittently tearful as she fought to keep her emotions under control.

Neil made a few more calls to the various Top Star branches that Jerry might go to. He gave strict instructions that Jerry must be told Neil needed him urgently and that he should call without delay.

Then he went upstairs and found Angelique sitting on the bed. The small bin adjacent to the dressing table was overflowing with used tissues. She blew her nose and added to the pile.

"Pull yourself together, Angie. It looks like Grace is there to support *you*, not the other way around, as it should be!"

"This is tragic. I can't help it."

"Grace is so worried about you, she wanted to bring *you* a cup of tea."

"I'm okay. I just needed time."

"Then help Grace."

"Of course. You're right," she answered. "I must try and be strong for her. I'll come down soon."

Angelique soon appeared in the garden, having washed her face and put a little make-up on. She had grabbed a fresh handkerchief before going downstairs, but was still struggling to keep her composure when she found Grace in the courtyard with the other domestic servants and gardeners, some of them crying. They were speaking in an African language but changed to English as soon as they saw Angelique.

Seeing that Grace was in good hands, she said, "I'll make more tea and bring it here." She went inside and cried to herself quietly, but she was determined to be a support. She made a big pot of tea and took it outside with some *kourambiedes*, Greek shortbread biscuits covered in icing sugar, which had been made by her mother.

Angelique sat on the grass with the black staff, sharing the tea. At first she felt uncomfortable. She had never taken tea with them, an unthinkable event before then. But she wanted to do it now. It felt right sitting with them in this shared sorrow.

Just after eight in the morning, Jerry called Neil's house.

"Boss, you left a message for me to call you urgently. How can I help you?"

"Where are you?"

"I went to visit friends in Atteridgeville yesterday. You know – Jacob Madau, who works for us in Pretoria, boss. I thought, 'I will stay over and check out the Pretoria staff. A surprise visit.' It was a good idea because you know why, boss?" Before Neil could speak, Jerry continued. "Your service manager, who should be here at seven o'clock, isn't in yet. Yes, boss, your meneer Van Vuuren, who should be looking after your service department, isn't here. And it's after eight o'clock. But don't worry, because my staff, led by my friend Jacob Madau, *is* here."

"Listen Jerry, something terrible has happened. You just get back here immediately."

"What, boss? I'll come straight away. What must I do? Is it Madam Angelique?"

"No, Jerry. No. I am afraid it's your son. The older one."

"Who? What? What are you saying?"

"I don't know how to say this. It's Sipho. He's …"

"Sipho? What's happened to Sipho?"

"The worst … the worst news. I'm sorry to break the news this way, but he … he's passed away."

"What do you mean? I don't understand. What are you saying?"

"Listen carefully. It's the saddest news you can imagine." Jerry was quiet. "Sipho is dead. Grace is here at the house. Please come here straight away. Get Jacob to bring you in a company car to my house right away."

There was no response.

"Jerry … Jerry, are you there?"

There was no response.

"Jerry. Jerry."

"Yes, I'm here. What happened? What's happened to Sipho?"

"He drowned at Zoo Lake yesterday."

"What do you mean, he drowned? Was he swimming? There is no swimming there. He couldn't be in the water."

"Sorry, Jerry. It's true."

"How? What happened?"

"Just come to my house and Grace can explain."

Neil wanted to be there when Jerry was told what really happened. He knew that Jerry was becoming increasingly bitter against the whites for their exploitation of the blacks, and that Jerry blamed the Afrikaners for the oppressive laws. Neil had no doubt that he would not take the details well. With the wrong sort of encouragement, Jerry was capable of anything.

"Is Jacob there? Put him on the phone."

"It can't be true. Are you sure?" Jerry was breathing heavily into the phone and his voice was breaking.

"Yes. I'm afraid so. I'm so sorry. Give the phone to Jacob."

Neil explained to Jacob the basics of what had happened, without the details, and told him to drive Jerry straight to his house. "Jerry knows where the house is. Bring him here now, Jacob. Come straight here. Then we'll go and find where Sipho is."

By half past eight, Neil was able to get hold of Captain Koos Botha, Mrs Botha's son and officer in charge of the Parktown police station. He had to tell the policeman who took the call that he was calling as a friend, and this was a personal call to get through quickly.

"Hello, Koos. This is Neil. Neil Robertson."

"Hello, meneer Neil, what can I do for you?" He addressed Neil the same way his mother addressed him but with a lot more reverence, even though they were about the same age. Neil had become a successful businessman around town and was well known in police and licensing circles because of his businesses.

Neil explained what he had been told. "There must be a report by the attending police. I think they told me earlier his name is Swanepoel. But we don't know what happened to Sipho."

"I will have a look and get back to you within half an hour."

Neil called his office and said he was going to be late. He explained to his secretary what had happened. "If anyone calls for me, just tell them I'm in meetings, Mrs Hammond. I will let you know later whether I'm coming in at all."

In about twenty minutes, the telephone rang.

"Meneer Neil? Captain Botha here."

"Hello, Koos. Thanks for calling me back so promptly. What have you found out?"

"Well, I have checked, and there was a report of an incident that resulted in a death at Zoo Lake yesterday. Constables Swanepoel and Brink attended. I'm afraid they're both off duty. Constable Swanepoel must have done a report, but I can't find it. Someone is going to his house and will bring him here now. I also don't know yet where the body is. It is most probably at Baragwanath. If you come here to the station, I will have everything there is. It will take a little time. You should come by at ten o'clock."

"Thank you, Koos. I really appreciate your help."

"I am moving heaven and hell to help you."

"I know. Thank you again. I'll see you at ten."

Jerry arrived at Neil's house from Pretoria, alone in the old Austin.

Grace got up when she saw him come up the driveway and ran to him. Neil stood back, not wishing to be in the way. He couldn't hear what she was saying, but Jerry took her to a quiet section of the garden that was just within Neil's line of sight. He could see Grace sobbing. Jerry held her tightly. She stopped shaking and spoke to Jerry. He wrapped his arm around her shoulder and looked at her.

Then Jerry spoke. Grace answered and sobbed as Jerry held her tenderly and spoke.

They sat down on the lawn, alone and quiet for a while. Jerry dabbed his eyes with a handkerchief. He said something, and they both got up. Grace joined Angelique and the others again.

Jerry left them and came to the house. He knocked on the back door. Milton was in the kitchen. He shook hands with Jerry and then embraced him, tears gathering in his eyes as he did so. "I'm very sorry for your loss, Jerry," he managed to say.

Jerry patted Milton on the back, his eyes moist. He couldn't speak.

"I'll take you to my dad."

Milton led him to Neil's home office. Neil strode to the doorway and hugged Jerry. "What a tragedy. I'm so, so sorry for you. So, so sorry." He shook his head.

"Not for me, boss. I'm okay. What about Sipho? A young boy with his life ahead of him. Killed by the Boers." Jerry's eyes were wild.

"Tragic, Jerry. This is a big tragedy. Caused by a bunch of drunken idiots."

This was not the time to reason too much, but he instinctively felt the need to stress the influence of drink and the idiocy of the group's actions, not their ethnicity. He feared it would be of no help to Jerry to make of this a black and white issue. *Even though it is.* The stupid white hooligans had attacked Sipho because he was black.

"Drunken Boers. Where is the justice, boss?"

"Nothing can replace Sipho. But we'll see what we can do."

"I'll see what I can do. I know what I can do, and I will. Just you wait and see."

"Don't go and do something stupid, now. We must be there for Grace and the other children."

"I know where I must be and what my duty is," Jerry said. Neil felt the bitterness in his voice.

"Captain Koos Botha will help us. He's a good man and will make sure that justice is done. Come, let's go to the police station. He's waiting to help us there."

❖

Constable Swanepoel checked in with Captain Botha. His lean and small build did not give him an immediate air of physical authority. But Botha had seen him bully constables twice his size. His pink pit-bull terrier colouring, determination and sinewy toughness made up for his small stature. His long neck, scrawny hook nose and beady red-lined eyes gave him a vulture-like appearance that, together with his stare, usually ensured obedience.

He stood at attention in his two-piece safari suit. Light-green and speckled, its short pants revealed hairless legs that tapered to thin ankles. Thick, woolly khaki socks dared not dislodge from their fully extended positions just below his knees, the top immaculately folded over by precisely two and a quarter inches. His brown Bata shoes shone. His receding, mustard hair was combed back neatly and greased into place.

"Kaptein, why all the fuss about these kaffirs?"

Captain Botha glared at him. "Your duty is to keep law and order for everybody."

"They are animals, Kaptein." Swanepoel looked Botha in the eyes, his cold green-grey eyes not blinking.

"Is that why you didn't explain to the family what happened? Why you sent those children home and didn't go with them?" Botha remained calm. He felt uncomfortable because of his relationship with Neil. He remembered Jerry from two decades before these events, when Jerry sometimes dropped Neil off or picked him up from the Botha hostel. He liked Neil's driver.

"I never went there because they are kaffirs and I am not. These

254

are not my fellow men. In the Bible, the black man carried the cross for Jesus."

"Send some black policemen. Shouldn't you have arranged to tell the family?"

"There were no kaffirs at the station. In any case, the kids went to the family."

"Next time, Konstabel, make sure the family is informed by a policeman."

"God, Kaptein. What's all the fuss about?"

"Just give me your report."

Swanepoel passed it over. "You know that the kaffir boys provoked the whole fight. They tried to steal the rugby ball and then kicked their ball at the white people. What did they expect? They attacked our people first, and our people defended themselves."

"Who was in the water? The whites or the Bantus?" asked Botha.

Swanepoel hesitated, and then he stared at his senior officer, frowning. Botha looked at him without blinking. But Swanepoel concentrated on Botha's eyes with his unusual X-ray stare, which betrayed his lack of compassion.

The intensity of his gaze might have provoked disciplinary action for insubordination. Botha held his ground and maintained eye contact, forcing Swanepoel to blink and look away.

"I don't know what you're on about, Kaptein. The whites responded to defend themselves."

Botha sat in his chair. "That will be all. Leave your report. Thank you."

❖

Just then, Neil was ushered into Botha's office. He had arrived at the police station with Jerry and Grace, but left them in the car. This seemed to him to be the most prudent strategy, given Jerry's volatility and angry state of mind.

"Hello, Captain Botha." He addressed Botha formally in the presence of his staff.

"Good morning, Mr Neil. This is Konstabel Swanepoel, who attended the scene and recovered the deceased from the water. The boy was already dead and could not be saved." He turned to Swanepoel. "Konstabel Swanepoel, you may leave now." Neil could tell he wanted to dismiss the man quickly in case Swanepoel showed his contempt and lack of respect for Sipho and his family.

Neil addressed him. "Thank you, Constable. It will be a great comfort to his family to know that you tried to save him."

Swanepoel departed, not answering and not looking back as he strode out of Botha's office.

Botha gave Neil the information he needed and arranged for them to see the body straight away. "I've asked for an urgent post-mortem report."

"Will there be an inquest?"

"No, Meneer Neil. He was a Bantu."

"What do you mean?"

"We don't have an inquest every time a Bantu dies."

"Koos. Is this a cover-up?"

"It could become that."

"This was no accident. They didn't have to hit the kids in the water. No matter who started it, these youths went too far."

"I know that. I will get the post-mortem and finish the report with a recommendation to prosecute. I will send this all to the prosecutors. I must arrange statements to be taken from the friends of the deceased boy."

"Good. Thank you, Koos."

A large funeral service was held in Alexandra, attended by pupils and teachers from Sipho's school, and by his family and many of the Top Star employees.

Neil and his family wanted to attend to show their respect for the Ngubeni family. He wanted to support them. But Grace advised Neil and Angelique not to attend. "The mood is very bad, master," she said. "We cannot guarantee your safety."

"But they know me," Neil said. "I am not Afrikaans. I wasn't even there."

"It is not safe, master. I know you mean well. We understand, but it is better that you don't come," she said and left the kitchen.

26

Marius took nothing for granted. Though daunted by the challenge, he was determined to prove himself in Johannesburg, the business powerhouse of South Africa. Earn a reputation as an astute trial lawyer – that was the first step. Give his best in every case and draw on everything his master taught him.

His fear was being caught by surprise. It was better to go home late at night if need be, only when he was satisfied that he had examined every angle of his cases. He won them or made sure they were settled before they were lost. He knew he was achieving his goals when his mahogany desk filled up with briefs from the big commercial law firms, and their size grew.

Within a few years of commencing at the Johannesburg bar, Marius was basking in success. He was so sought after that he could select the briefs offered to him. He politely rejected those he didn't want. By now he knew that he was in the next gear of professional fulfilment.

It was six years after his father's death when he telephoned his uncle Eben one day. "I've been made senior counsel," he said, doing his best to keep his voice under control. It meant that he could put the suffix "SC" after his name and charge more per hour than most counsel at the bar. But it wasn't the money that mattered to him most.

It was the recognition and respect of his peers that this appointment represented, especially given his relatively short time at the bar.

"Well done, my boy. Your father would be so proud of you if he were alive."

"Yes. What a pity he's not here to enjoy this moment."

"And you know, this is such a sweet appointment because it means you've succeeded in Johannesburg. You must be one of the youngest SCs there. Congratulations, son."

"Thank you, Oom."

"I am glad to see you well settled in your professional life. Now, what about your private life?"

Marius was taken aback. "What do you mean?"

"Don't be bashful. When are you going to get married and have a family?"

"There's plenty of time."

"Don't leave it too late. Time will overtake you before you know it. How old are you now?"

"I'm only 40."

"Don't delay is all I can say."

"I'm looking. I'm looking."

"Look harder, my boy. She's there somewhere."

Marius changed the subject. But he *had* been thinking that he was lonely in Johannesburg. He had a few friends nearby, but that wasn't the same as having a family.

After the call with Oom Eben, his thoughts returned to a few months earlier. He had become aware of the graceful movements of his secretary, Letitia – the rhythm of her dress, the shimmer of her blouse. Her sense of clothing was conservative yet stylish. She had the looks of a model or film star with her blonde hair and blue eyes. He noticed how she spoke to the attorneys who briefed him – with a dimpled smile and friendly gaze. She oozed intelligence, confidence, and control.

He had thought nothing of the fact that she had been bringing him homemade beskuit for months. Even when she bought him new ties, he thought that was what secretaries did.

Then she remarked on his good looks and stayed back after work to chat, two or three times a week. At first she passed on the bar gossip, and then she asked about him and his family. It felt natural for him to talk to her about his past, something he had never done with anyone else. She seemed to understand him and his background.

During the drive to his flat in Killarney after one of these chambers chats, it dawned on him that *Miss* Letitia Viljoen wasn't married.

He had begun to invite her to dinner, the bioscope (cinema), and the odd social occasion, but the discussion with Oom Eben spurred him on. His uncle was right. Why wait? Within five weeks of the call, Marius had purchased a three-carat diamond ring.

The very next Saturday afternoon, he turned up at the modest Viljoen family home. The old cottage was in the whites-only town of Alberton, an industrial working-class settlement less than ten miles south-east of Johannesburg. He had been there before, to pick Letitia up and drop her off – before midnight – on their dates, but had never been invited in. He knew she wasn't expecting him; he had told her on Friday that they couldn't go out on the weekend as he had "something important to do". He knocked on the door, hoping she would answer. Instead it was Mrs Viljoen who greeted him.

"Good afternoon, meneer Strydom," she said in a shaky, high-pitched voice. "Oh, I don't think Letitia is expecting you."

Before he could respond, she turned around and in a raised voice said, "Meneer Strydom is here to pick you up, Letitia!" Then she turned back to him and smiled.

"I'm not here to see Letitia, mevrou Viljoen. I'm here to see meneer Viljoen," he said.

"Oh, I see," she said after a brief hesitation and knowing nod.

Just then Letitia came to the door. He could see the confusion on her face. "What are you doing here? I thought you said you had something to do."

"I do. That's what I'm here for."

"Letitia, ask meneer Strydom to come in," said mevrou Viljoen and beckoned Marius into the *voorkamer* (sitting room). "Come in. I'll get my husband for you." She ushered him to the couch. "Please make yourself comfortable." She whispered to Letitia, "He's here to see Pa. I think he wants to ask permission. Go get Pa, quickly."

Marius could hear the conversation and chuckled when Letitia frowned and edged towards her mother. "Permission? No, I don't believe it," she whispered.

"I think you should believe it," said her mother, winking at her.

Marius had never seen Letitia so unsure of herself, but he couldn't make out whether she was happy or not. He felt embarrassed and now regretted not giving her prior notice. He was confident that her father would say yes, but what if *she* said no? He hadn't actually asked her. They had spoken of marriage and having children in general terms, without referring to their own relationship. He had felt shy about posing the big question directly to her. He had thought it would be easier to broach the topic with her father – man to man – but now wondered if he had been foolish not to clear it with her first.

Marius rose from the faded maroon couch when Mr Viljoen entered the small, stuffy lounge room. He estimated that the portly, grandfatherly man was in his late 60s. Thick brown braces held up his baggy, coffee-coloured corduroy pants. A thin green necktie was neatly knotted up against his yellowing, frayed collar. His trimmed old Dutch-style beard reminded Marius of some Ossewabrandwag members who had visited the Strydom farm many years before.

Meneer Viljoen acknowledged the younger man with a firm handshake while engaging Marius with his eyes. "Gooie middag, meneer Strydom." His greeting was formal.

Suddenly Marius wasn't so sure Letitia's father would say yes. Maybe Marius had taken his acceptance for granted. Perhaps Letitia hadn't told them about his influential family – and his legal qualifications might count against him. He doubted that could be the case. After all, their daughter worked as his secretary.

Marius glanced over at Letitia in the hope of some support, but she wasn't looking at him. Maybe he should just have a chat and leave. They could talk about the National Party. Given the black-and-white photograph of Dr Malan on the passage wall, the old Afrikaner was clearly a Party supporter.

Mr Viljoen turned to his wife. "Make us some rooibos tea and leave us alone for a while, Ma." He then nodded to his daughter. "You too, *Meisie* (girl). Go with your mother." Then he waved his fingers up and down at Marius. "Don't stand there like a confused aardvark. Sit, man."

They both sat down. There was silence while Letitia's father took out his pipe, loaded it with tobacco, and lit up. The curtains trapped the hot, stale air in the close room. The ceiling light cast a dull beam over them that faded once it reached the browning cream walls. Marius felt uncomfortable and started perspiring. Pa Viljoen's thick tobacco cloud drifted towards him. He struggled to breathe and wished someone would open a window.

Meneer Viljoen sat back, rested his head against the high back of his arm chair, exhaled another stream of smoke, and looked over Marius's head. "So, meneer Strydom. What can I do for you?"

"Err … hrrm." Marius cleared his throat.

Meneer Viljoen drew on his pipe again and blew out a thick fog.

"I am here to … er … ask for your daughter's hand in marriage."

"I like that. No beating about the thorn tree. Yes, Marius. I would be delighted for my daughter to become a Strydom. I know she wants that too."

Marius was wet with perspiration by then and feeling nauseous.

He was afraid to cough again in case he released more than phlegm, and was relieved when the old man continued.

"You know, the most important decision I will ever make in my life is the decision to approve my daughter's husband. There is no better feeling than knowing she will marry the right man. A man who loves her and who will be good to her. She is our only child."

A needle of sharp pain behind his right eye affected Marius's concentration. He had to push his hands down on his thighs to prevent them from shaking as Pa Viljoen spoke.

"So, how are you boys getting on?" said mevrou Viljoen on entering the room with a tray of cups, saucers and a steaming teapot dressed in a green woollen tea cosy. Letitia followed with a plate of beskuit and a happy grin. Marius could see the excitement in her eyes.

Until she looked at him.

"Marius, are you all right? You've lost your colour. You look yellow."

He hoisted himself up and stepped towards her. "I'm not feeling too good," he coughed. "Let's go outside for a short while." He dashed past her and found a garden tap. After splashing some water over his face, he stood up and drew a deep breath.

"What's wrong? What's wrong?"

"Never mind that." He went down on his knees. "Letitia, will you marry me?"

They married in a low-key ceremony in the Dutch Reformed Church on Van Riebeeck Avenue, two blocks from the Viljoens' Alberton home.

A year later, upon the birth of their daughter, Annelise, Marius gave Letitia a pair of diamond earrings to match her ring. When he looked at their baby, he could see his father's frown and eyes, and Letitia's dimples and smile.

Marius was busy in his legal practice, but he maintained contact with influential family friends, especially after his father's death. He sometimes recalled the promise to his father to become involved in politics, but he pushed those thoughts aside. He was too settled in his career and in his family life. He knew that would change if he went into politics, and he would have less time for Annelise. Surely that was what mattered most of all.

Why, then, did he harbour these feelings of guilt, which rose to the surface whenever he thought of his father's last words?

Letitia's deeply religious Afrikaner beliefs fed Marius's determination to ensure the success of the Afrikaner government. He began to realise that he couldn't remain politically aloof forever. He now had a family to protect and felt spurred on by his wife's faith in him. It was as though a light had switched on in his mind, illuminating his father's pleading with him to lead his people. Letitia also reinforced his conviction that South Africa was best served with the National Party at the helm.

Thinking about the treatment of his ancestors during the Boer Wars, he felt a duty to honour his commitment to them. He was vaguely aware that this feeling pre-empted any guilt at dishing out the same treatment to those less fortunate than him. He remembered his father's bitter words about the heavy-fisted approach of the British Empire against his people, and did not see any basis for the blacks to view his family's party in the same light. There were differences. This was something so obvious that he didn't even need to think much about it. The blacks could not run a prosperous government, but his people could. And the British were foreign colonial landlords. *We Afrikaners, we belong in South Africa, our country.*

But the increasing successes of an international campaign against the government by exiled members of the ANC were beginning to concern him, as did protests against apartheid laws and campaigns of disobedience. For the first time in his life, he realised that, if the black power movements were not kept under control, the ability of the government to hold on to power would be threatened. He thought about how well trained and highly motivated the security police were. Surely they were far too effective to allow the government's power to be compromised.

Marius felt that his party had no option but to jail the black leaders who had not escaped into exile. How could their movement inspire international opposition to the government – the legitimate and elected ruling party? After all, didn't those black leaders belong to terrorist organisations? They were entwined with the banned Communist Party. They were challenging the laws of the parliament. They wanted to take the reins of power from the whites. Couldn't everyone see what would happen if the blacks got the vote? The country would disintegrate. Most of Africa was being let down by their leaders, thanks to the corrupt despots ensconced in a number of its countries – and, on top of it all, some of those were communists.

Now the pressure that seemed to be mounting against the Afrikaners was making some members of the Broederbond nervous. A number of his political bedfellows were anxious to hold on to power at all cost, whereas others wanted the government to make changes.

He had heard his Broederbond colleagues discussing the highly organised and well-equipped police force and defence capability. And security bureau was gathering intelligence through its network of spies. It had identified a number of organisations that the government then banned. Its informants had fingered scores of leaders advocating black power, who were then hunted down and arrested. Some were killed resisting, but Marius believed this was their choice – they could have surrendered. They could have lived in a prosperous South Africa that was wealthy enough to provide jobs for everyone.

Black majority rule was not acceptable. It was not an option.

The government would not let his ancestors down. They would not lose their grip on the power they had held for a little more than two decades. Was this all they could manage after so much suffering? Surely they could withstand the black demands, he thought. No, the Afrikaner nation would not give in.

Marius had taken his father's place in the Broederbond to ensure his family's influence. It had become time for him to make good on his promise to his father. He felt that he had fulfilled his ambition to become a respected advocate at the bar. He no longer went to his chambers with the same sense of enthusiasm as before. Perhaps it was because he was ready to become involved in politics. As a senior counsel, he had entrenched his position within the Broederbond in his own right and not just as the son of Jacobus Strydom.

Believing that God had given him a mission to support his people, he threw his support behind the Afrikaner government. He didn't like parts of the government's violent response to the non-violent protests against the pass laws. But he saw the need to control the movement of blacks into the whites-only areas, and was persuaded by the words of the prime minister at a dinner he attended: "They should come to the white areas only when we need them to work. If we need to be strict to enforce this, then that is a necessary consequence of our 'separate but equal' policy of segregating the races. We have reserved their tribal homelands for them to vote in."

What mattered was to ensure government for the whites and separate governments for the various black tribes. That was the correct way, one that simply followed the natural order: power to those with the capacity to govern. Allowing blacks to have a say in the parliament would mean that whites, outnumbered now by over five to one, would be swamped. Chaos would prevail.

No, the Afrikaner government had to keep a firm hold on power. He believed that the tribal homelands were adequate for those who were attached to their ethnic origins. And he felt that even those whose ties to their roots had been diluted in the human melting pots of Johannesburg and other cities and towns should exercise their political rights in the tribal areas, not in white South Africa.

His beliefs were a little shaken by what he regarded as the regrettable incident at Sharpeville, where the authorities killed sixty-nine and injured hundreds more protesting against the pass laws. Many of the people were shot in the back as they abandoned their protests, fleeing for safety. He reasoned that the government had had no choice. *The police felt threatened and had to shoot – that much is obvious.* And he made known his views: "If we give in to their demands, we let them govern. There will be chaos for everyone. Only *we* can keep law and order so that everyone can have jobs. This is best for the Bantus too."

In 1972 he decided to run for office for the governing party. He retired from the bar and stood for election for a seat in Parliament to represent the party of his father. The National Party, which had been in power since 1948, had every intention of doing what had to be done to retain that power.

As a trial lawyer with a formidable reputation for toughness, and with his impeccable conservative Afrikaner pedigree, Marius was quickly promoted to cabinet minister in the National Party.

He acquired his first cabinet portfolio, and the title: Minister of Tourism and Recreation.

Marius followed Jeremiah's life through his discussions with Neil's close friend and attorney, Mr Landau. He also saw Neil at events attended by business leaders and asked about "Jerry", his former client. He declined to look too deeply into why he took this interest and what it might mean. He had told no one that he had recognised Jeremiah when asked to defend him – that they had played together as children.

One morning, as he read official notes about the security issues facing the country, his attention was drawn to a report about the death of a young black boy at a recreation park at Zoo Lake, following a skirmish between black and white youths. The incident hadn't been mentioned in the newspapers, as the police hadn't released details to the press.

He noticed the surname Ngubeni and asked for details of the parents. Later that day, when informed of the deceased's father's name, he couldn't believe it. Could it be Jeremiah's child? It had to be.

Marius felt sick. He picked up the telephone and spoke to the deputy head of police. "Brigadier," he said after raising the matter, "this is very bad news for our country. We are trying to promote tourism and look what happens. I want a proper investigation. The people responsible for this attack must be prosecuted. I expect you to check on this personally."

"Yes, Minister. This is a tragic event. This will happen when the races mix. Black and white should be kept separate."

Marius recognised this policeman as one of the early members of the Broederbond. He had once boasted to Marius that he had been among the members of the Ossewabrandwag who had planted a bomb at a post office building against the government of Jan Smuts in the 1940s. Marius could feel that the police officer didn't seem to like the way he, a junior minister, was speaking to him. But Marius was not intimidated. As heir to the Strydom political legacy, he knew the extent of his influence.

"Unfortunately we can't allow and encourage these black and white conflicts," Marius pressed on. "The point is, Brigadier, this case must be properly investigated."

"But Minister, there are many deaths every day. What's so special about this one?" The brigadier was clearly getting irate.

"This one was at one of our lakes. One of our recreation spots. Families go there. Your family. My family. We can't let people turn our places of fun into battlegrounds. If you can't see that now, will you wait for the next clash? And, as minister of tourism, I can see the damage this can do to our country's reputation if this gets out. Don't you see it? As minister responsible for our recreational facilities, I will not have this incident pass without proper investigation." He wasn't sure if he was succeeding in persuading the seasoned party campaigner. "Next time, it may be a white child. Do you want me to say then that I warned you of this today? Shall I tell your minister that you agree or disagree?"

There was a pause. Marius waited.

"Yes, Minister. I will look into this, and I will get back to you." The senior policeman's words were mumbled and almost too quick to be understood.

"Thank you. I knew you would see what is best for the country. I expect that you will make sure that the right people are prosecuted."

As he put the phone down, Marius was surprised at his overwhelming sense of sympathy for Jeremiah. He couldn't concentrate on his work that morning and felt unwell. He told his secretary to cancel all his engagements and left his office well before noon. Usually a workaholic who was seldom home before eight at night, he went straight to bed, nursing a severe migraine.

As he lay there, he thought about Jeremiah and their past on the farm. He felt nauseous and downhearted. Jeremiah had been his closest boyhood friend. Jeremiah had doubted his honesty and judged him without listening to what he had to say. That was Jeremiah – act first, think later.

Only after Jeremiah's departure had Marius learned that it was his brother, Hennie, who had attacked Jeremiah's girlfriend. Jeremiah had obviously misunderstood Rachel when she said it was "Basie". It was the other "little boss". But Jeremiah had been so emotional about the matter that he hadn't given Marius time to explain. Instead, Jeremiah had called him a liar, even when Marius denied the charge.

At the time, Marius had felt betrayed. And he couldn't tolerate a servant lifting a finger to him or anyone at the farm, whatever the reason. It would have created a bad precedent if Jeremiah had stayed on. Jeremiah had to go. Reflecting on it now, he realised that they had both been the victims of Hennie's spinelessness.

Marius had not touched Rachel or torn her dress, and he regretted that Jeremiah would never know this. But he was surprised at the depth of his disappointment: Jeremiah should have known him better. *He should have known I would never attack his girlfriend.*

And he thought back to the time when he was called upon to defend Jeremiah on the charge of murder. Clearly Jerry had been innocent. Also embarrassed when their eyes met for the briefest moment. The recognition had been there, but no acknowledgement of their past relationship. Jeremiah might have had good reason to maintain his apparent anonymity, so Marius had left it to him to decide whether to disclose their connection. He respected that Jeremiah had chosen not to do so.

Marius had been taken aback when Jeremiah became hostile at the meeting. But on consideration, this was not unexpected; Jeremiah had always been confident and forward. After all, no one else on the farm had got on as well with any member of the Strydom family as he had done. That was unusual and showed that Jeremiah had something special. He had cheek, wit and intelligence – and self-belief.

Seeing Jeremiah's senior position among the black workers – he seemed to be a real leader there – Marius had been impressed. How lucky his boyhood friend was to have found a boss like Neil Robertson, who allowed him more liberties than any boss Marius knew. Others would not have tolerated the self-assurance, would have seen it as insolence and forwardness from a black worker. They would have fired him, if not beaten him.

Yet no one deserved to lose a son, especially in such a violent way. This tragedy should have been avoided.

A feeling of disquiet niggled at Marius, a sense of unease. Was there a chain of connection between this incident and his government's system? Surely not. These incidents could happen anywhere.

When Marius paid a visit to the farm after a long absence, it was a first for four-year-old Annelise. Hennie was now the baas, and even though it was still his mother's home, Marius felt like a visitor.

The Bantu staff fussed over Annelise, calling her fondly "granddaughter" and making cookies for her.

Thomas made her a life-size, carved-wood vervet monkey. Annelise gave this pride of place on her bedside table. That night Marius and Hennie ran with loaded shotguns into Annelise's bedroom as Letitia screamed, having mistaken the wooden carving for a real monkey when she entered to say goodnight to Annelise.

"It's only a toy, Letitia."

"How was I supposed to know that?" she said, still shaking. "It looks so real, and it was sitting there as if it was getting ready to jump on Annelise's face."

"Yes, I remember my mother chasing with a broom the one Thomas made for me."

"Well, I don't want it in the house. I don't want anything like it in the house. What if a real animal comes in and we think it's a toy?"

Marius laughed. "You know, there was a snake once in the workshop, and Hennie thought it was one of Jeremiah's wooden tricks. Luckily Alfred was alert. He drew the attack by jumping in front of Hennie."

"What happened?"

"He had a long pipe in his hand, and the snake came off second best."

"Well, that does it, Marius. No pretend animals and snakes in the house while I'm here. Please tell everyone."

❖

Marius took Annelise to the African workers' compound, which had hardly changed over the years. He spoke to Saleena and asked about Jeremiah.

"He's fine, baas. He's got a good job and family." They didn't say anything about the death of their grandchild.

"Is he happy in the city?"

"Yes, baas."

Martha and Hennie likewise hadn't mentioned the death of Jeremiah's child when Marius asked what they knew about Jeremiah. "That name has not been mentioned by anyone since you banished him, Marius," said Hennie with a chuckle.

"Yes, and you and I know why, don't we, Hennie?" Marius looked at Hennie, unsmiling.

No one said anything about the death of Jeremiah's child. It was as though Jeremiah and Sipho didn't exist. Marius seemed to be the only one who thought about him, but he knew that Thomas and Saleena were grieving. He could see that Thomas avoided him, always turning abruptly and walking away from him – appearing to be busy. Even though she was in the farmhouse for most of the day, doing her usual chores, Saleena also didn't speak to Marius and Letitia.

It upset Marius more that she didn't acknowledge Annelise.

He thought that they still blamed him for Hennie's attack on Jeremiah's sweetheart, Rachel. He wished he could tell them the truth but didn't want to sour things on the farm. Thomas and Hennie saw each other and worked together every day. It was better for Thomas that he didn't know Hennie was the culprit. Perhaps Rachel had thought the same and also decided to maintain her silence on the matter.

And there was the child Rachel had given birth to. If it was Jeremiah's, the feeling between them must have been strong. No wonder Jeremiah's anger had overtaken him.

But of all these things, it was Sipho's death that troubled Marius most. Every so often it would rise to his consciousness from what felt like some dark depth of his mind, where it remained embedded, a thorn he couldn't extract.

Annelise loved the Church of the Willows. She ran about freely in the fresh, grassy aroma of the willows and was delighted to get her hands dirty in the mud of the riverbank. Marius made clay oxen for her, just like the ones he and Jeremiah had made as children, which she lined up and played with every day for her entire stay. He remembered the times that he and Jeremiah had spent there – and the days of prayer that had saved his soul when he went astray during his university days.

On Sunday afternoon, he went to the Church of the Willows alone, before daybreak. He sat in the serenity of the trees, in contemplation for hours. Once again he searched his soul, meditating and praying for guidance, feeling that he was again at a crossroads in his life.

He could not help thinking of the impact that Sipho's death had had on him. The incident overpowered his thoughts. There must be some purpose to the tragic event, surely.

He felt sorry for Jeremiah, but how could Marius be so determined to prosecute the Afrikaner boys? Who was to blame? The white boys? They were part of the culture that he and his ancestors, especially his father, had disseminated, along with the doctrine of keeping the Bantus separate from the Europeans. Was he being reasonable with Captain Botha and the deputy head of police, expecting them to go against the white boys? They had families too. This would destroy many more lives if true justice were to be done. He had already applied some pressure to prosecute the white boys.

Surely that was correct. An innocent life had been taken. But on a larger scale, could this have been avoided? Was this a sign that the races should be segregated – as his government had advocated for over two decades? Or should the government be preaching more interaction, with tolerance and eventual acceptance of the rights of all races? That would result in a dilution of Afrikaner power, and risk the future of his people. But not to do so ... wouldn't that put the whole future of South Africa at risk?

Confusing thoughts tore his mind apart. He realised that his growing influence within the cabinet could affect the future of his people and the country. What was the right thing to do – retain apartheid and domination, or give in to the pressure and relinquish power? He knew what his father would have said, but that didn't give him a satisfied feeling.

This time he left the willows without clear answers to his questions.

27

Although he still worked for Neil, Jerry's role had been changing. Top Star had reached heights that they couldn't have imagined at the start, and the structural changes meant that Neil employed people with formal qualifications to help run the various parts of the business. Jerry saw much less of Neil, but this was hardly why they had drifted apart.

Though Jerry remained boss boy at Rosebank in name, he felt shunted aside when Neil appointed white managers to employ and train black staff. His new personnel manager didn't appreciate the history and treated Jerry like anyone else: with no respect. To him Jerry was just another Bantu worker. And Jerry had to report to him.

Resentment began to dominate Jerry's perceptions of the workplace. He felt more keenly the lack of power, and he often thought about this in the context of his belief in his royal heritage.

To make matters worse, Prinsloo was doing less than ever, but had the big title: National Service Staff Manager. He had been promoted due to his long service. Neil had told Jerry he wanted Prinsloo out of the workshops, where his drinking habits were infecting the real workers. At least at head office he would be isolated and couldn't diminish morale.

Prinsloo's sole task was now to make sure that each branch was properly staffed with mechanics if people didn't turn up for work: to control a pool of fewer than twenty roving mechanics, whom he could move around from branch to branch as required. The only black he came into real contact with was Jerry, who was in charge of hundreds of black workers. Yet Jerry could not arrange the movement of a few roving mechanics without instructions from Prinsloo. It rankled with Jerry that even this man, placed where he could do least harm to the business, could still give him orders. How could this unreliable drunkard still be his "superior"?

Jerry felt increasingly isolated from Neil and less loyal to the business. In fact his dissatisfaction with the lack of opportunity festered in him so much that he was rude to some of the white staff who, he thought, had overtaken him simply because he was black and they were white. He wasn't afraid to show open hostility to them.

After Sipho's death "at the hands of the Boers", he became even more bitter and angry.

"This is the next Boer war," he declared to some of his political supporters. "And this time we will win."

On a busy Friday morning at the Top Star head office, Jerry walked past Prinsloo, who was waiting for the lift with a group of the management staff. Jerry looked at the men and continued walking. Prinsloo pointed to Jerry and shouted, "Hey, boy! Come here. We need a mechanic in Kensington. Take one of your kaffirs there."

Jerry stopped and looked at Prinsloo. Then he walked towards him. "I … am … not … your … boy." Jerry stressed his words slowly and deliberately. Open-eyed and unblinking, he lifted his right hand and pointed his index finger at Prinsloo, almost touching Prinsloo's nose.

He'd been told that Prinsloo had warned Neil of his belligerence and asked for permission to fire him. Neil had said he would control Jerry.

"We'll see about that," Jerry had overheard Prinsloo say to another manager.

Glaring at each other now, they faced off, eye to eye, until Prinsloo diverted his gaze.

Prinsloo looked around him and at the burly sales manager next to him. "Yes, you are, boy. You're a dirty kaffir!"

"Am I a dirty kaffir? Am I a dirty kaffir?" Jerry stepped further towards Prinsloo, who wore a short-sleeved safari suit. They were now a few inches apart. Jerry rubbed the back of his hand on Prinsloo's cheek and on his bare arms.

Prinsloo sprang a foot back. "Voetsek! Fuck off."

Jerry's eyes were wild. "See? Are you dirty now? Are you black now, you white kaffir? Has my black skin discoloured your skin? Are you brown now? Are you a kaffir now?" Jerry lowered his arms, his hands moulded into fists. He wouldn't strike first, but he was willing to respond if Prinsloo was brave enough.

Prinsloo was ashen-faced. His jaw had dropped and his eyes were wide with shock. Jerry could see that he had no idea how to respond to this aggression. *He doesn't know whether I will hit him or not.* But Jerry knew Prinsloo was no match for him, and Prinsloo knew it too.

It surprised Jerry that the managers did nothing. They seemed stunned. As Prinsloo turned to leave, he shouted at Jerry, "You are crossing the line, Jerry. You are looking for trouble, and you will get it. Mr Robertson will hear of this. You'd better look out!" But Prinsloo looked afraid, and he entered the elevator shaking like a leaf.

Jerry yelled, "Fuck off, you Boer!" Jerry was also shaking, but in anger.

❖

Jerry wasn't easily scared now that his priorities had changed. Sipho's death made him feel that he had a higher calling. Keeping a job to support his family was no longer his primary goal. His agenda now, born out of a plan he was hatching with some members of the banned ANC, was to destabilise the "Boer power". And he felt resentment that he had few rights compared to Neil, an immigrant.

To make matters worse, Neil showed no interest in politics. Jerry felt he could see right through his boss, more than ever before. The man was in South Africa for one reason only: to make money.

"We have little to lose and everything to gain," Jerry preached. On a personal level, he believed this. He had already lost his oldest son. He was convinced that unless action was taken, the government would continue with its policy of apartheid.

The mighty police and military had a stronghold over the country. The struggle would take time. It would succeed. Wouldn't it? But when? The blood of Africa flowed through Jerry's veins, and had done so through those of his ancestors for thousands of years. Neil had first tasted the water of this continent less than three decades ago. Yet Jerry's people had become mere itinerant workers, and Neil's family enjoyed freedom and privileges. Would his remaining children see any of those freedoms?

It seemed unlikely that the underground campaign against discrimination could pose a real threat to the efficient and ruthless machinery of the state.

That didn't mean he should give up. He had to disrupt them, shake them, and scare them. Just like the operations of the ANC and other freedom movements, every bit that each person did chipped away at the foundations of the government's power. But to hit them high, where it was visible and could cause more damage – more like a crack through the halls of power – *that* was what he wanted. That was what Sipho deserved.

Every time he thought about Sipho, his heart hardened and his eyes pulsed with anger. An innocent child murdered. Murdered by apartheid. By the prejudices that the government had institutionalised. *They're all to blame. The Boers fought for their rights. We must fight for ours.* He refused to cry.

Still, he had to be careful. He knew that black political movements promoting freedom were quickly outlawed and their leaders thrown into jail. At times he could barely believe that it was 1974 and a whole decade since Mandela, now on Robben Island, had first been imprisoned. He thought again of the tall lawyer with the confident voice he had first heard so long ago.

The government's pursuit of black dissidents had continued relentlessly. How many were in jail? No-one knew. Mandela was not the only one. Images of other leaders flitted across Jerry's mind as he recalled how many they had been, and how they had kept coming – Robert Sobukwe, now under house arrest; Walter Sisulu, in prison; Steve Biko, banned. Then there was Oliver Tambo, who had avoided capture by fleeing the country.

Jerry felt pure admiration for them, but he was attuned to the warnings of their experiences. These strong men had become high-profile targets for the government. Other equally active dissenters were trying to remain anonymous and invisible to the authorities in the shadows of the black townships. They were all choking on the bitter smog of apartheid. Jerry was thinking of how he could maintain that balance and continue to be effective – without drawing too much attention from the wrong people.

On the advice of Mahmoud Lalla, an elderly and shrewd South African lawyer of Indian lineage who was helping the black freedom movement, Jerry refused to take formal leadership positions within it. Instead, he formed the low-profile Mechanics' Welfare Society, with a constitution that expressed objectives to care for the membership by providing support services, legal advice, and social assistance. They decided not to call it a trade union. Their goals could hardly be objectionable, especially because a clause of the constitution specified: *The Society will not partake in any political activity against the government of the day*. Mahmoud explained, "You don't need to get involved in politics if you carry out those objectives. We can use the 'no political activity' clause to defend you when they arrest and charge you. The government will make sure this society is illegal, but at least we can argue its activities do not amount to treason, which carries the death penalty. You will be arrested, Jerry. Mark my words."

"Well then, they must find me and arrest me."

"And you will be found guilty and sent to jail for being involved in an unlawful union or a banned organisation. But we may be able to get bail and give you a bit more time, possibly to escape. You must just try and accomplish as much as you can before that happens. Meanwhile, we will collect as many fees from the members as we can to give you some autonomy to achieve your objectives."

Although Jerry had decided some time back that he would become a leader in his Mechanics' Welfare Society for a purpose, Sipho's needless death now drove him on. His deep anger was fuelled by the silence concerning prosecution of the hooligans. He and Grace had heard nothing about it from anyone except Neil, who could only tell them that a trial was supposed to happen sometime in the future. Jerry saw the way Sipho had been killed as confirmation that he had a duty to campaign for equal opportunities for the black people and to fight for justice. His pain and grief festered as he began to feel that the killers would never be charged.

He knew that the interests of his family now took second place to what he saw as his primary purpose: the struggle for equality. What a different person he had become. He was no longer the fun-seeking, shebeen-hopping youth who had arrived in Johannesburg in 1951. He discussed this often with Mahmoud, who became a close friend and mentor.

Talking about it made the choices clearer, but not easier.

"I could be abandoning my family," he said in one of these conversations.

"These are choices leaders have to make," Mahmoud said. "Hard as it may be, we pray that your family will be proud of the bigger role you were born to play. But you must believe in what you are doing, Jerry."

"I believe, I believe. And Grace and her mother are good at bringing the kids up. I'll be there when they need me, and they'll realise why I wasn't there for them every day when they were young."

"They will understand one day, God be willing. It is important that you know this."

But there was dissent and further caution from Mahmoud when Jerry became involved in planning more radical anti-government activities. Jerry dropped by Mahmoud's office one day after work. Mahmoud was alone. He invited Jerry to sit down, offering him a cup of tea. Jerry steered the small talk to what was weighing heavily on his mind.

"We need to shake the Boers, Mahmoud. Talk is cheap, and this government ignores talk."

"What do you mean, shake them?" Mahmoud asked.

"We need to scare the whites. We need a stronger show of force. Maybe we can cause an explosion or two. Rattle the Boers a bit."

"I will have nothing to do with that. I think you will be more effective as a spokesman with the Welfare Society behind you. Not in jail. Don't go too far, man."

"The Welfare Society is going nowhere. The government just ignores us. Everyone ignores us. Even Mr Robertson is against us because every gain to us is a loss to him. We need to strike at them. Show them we can damage them."

"This is dangerous talk, Jerry."

"Others are doing it. Protests, strikes, and a bit of violence will start the changes."

"Well, leave it to the others."

"Who? Must I leave it to the schoolchildren? They're also unhappy. Do we expect them to rise up? I must play my role as much as I can."

"What do you want to do?"

"I told you. I want to shake them a bit. Cause damage to a government building or something."

"You know this has been done before. There is a precedent for blowing up government installations." Mahmoud sipped his tea, raising his thick eyebrows as he did so.

"Is there? What are you talking about?"

"The old Boers in the Ossewabrandwag used dynamite against Smuts in the forties," he said, shifting his cup and saucer to the side. He sat forward, his elbows on the desk.

"Really?"

"Yes. The same people later took political power. Some of them are now leaders in the government and the police."

"Well then. They should understand why we're doing what we have to do."

"No, they won't. They won't see the similarities."

"I'll tell them if they catch us."

"They'll shoot you first and then ask questions. It'll be too late then, my friend."

"I won't get caught. I want to make sure our targets are the military, not the public, not ordinary citizens."

They both sat silently for a while.

"Hah," Jerry exclaimed. "If we succeed, it will be because they have shown us the way."

❖

Jerry formed a team of people he could trust. Together they planned quick and small attacks on military offices in the city centres. These were easier targets than the more secure and remote military bases, where they would surely get caught.

One of the members of his team was Dr Albert Buthelezi. He had studied chemistry at Fort Hare University, where he became a lecturer and political activist. He was short in stature and wore thick tortoise-shell spectacles. His intellect and looks earned him the nickname "Prof". Through Prof's connections, a network of moles had been planted throughout the civil service. They were gardeners and cleaners in government facilities scattered across Pretoria. His spies could access many high-security areas in the military.

Prof suggested that the team's first target should be an army recruitment office in Pretoria. "It is not well guarded and is in the city centre. We can hit them in their capital city – the heartland of Afrikaner influence."

Jerry whistled. What a target! The seat of Afrikaner power and their military recruitment. "That's genius, Prof. When and how should we do it?"

"My sources tell me the minister of defence will visit there next month. He's going to make a speech to encourage recruitment for a bigger, more permanent army. It will be a huge event. It's a low-security office. A couple of lazy white soldiers guard the front doors just for show, but our spies are free to walk in and out. They make the coffees, clean the offices and empty the wastepaper bins. A small car bomb is quite easy. We can do it night or day."

Jerry was impressed. Prof had thought of everything.

"You've done your homework, Prof, but I don't want to kill anyone," said Jerry. "A small car bomb is exactly what we need. I want a big noise. I want the minister to be there – Mr Big Army Boots. And I want it in the daytime, when he visits with his entourage. Just a small explosion to give him a fright. He must realise we can get them anywhere. Will we be able to pull it off?"

"Yes, I think so," said Prof. "You get a car, and I'll find the fireworks. Not too big. Just enough to shake them."

Marius Strydom had become a power broker within the government. A fierce disciple of apartheid, he communicated to those around him that his people had to hold on to power. He was soon promoted to an important position and had a new title: Minister of Racial Affairs.

Soon after his advancement, he developed the theme of "ensuring the security of the nation". He encouraged the press to report on the state's security affairs. He was more than usually pleased one October morning to see in a daily newspaper the heading: "There is a communist behind every bush, Minister warns". He read on with satisfaction.

This morning the Minister of Racial Affairs, the Honourable Marius Strydom, spoke at a breakfast of party loyalists.

"We need to make sure that the pillars of government are not threatened by the undemocratic methods of a small minority of the black people of this country," he said. "There are misguided people who call themselves leaders, who want to cause harm to innocent people by violence; by using force against your children, my children and even their own children; by illegally throwing the country into chaos. That is to say, by terrorism."

The Minister told his audience that these were not South Africans, stating that many were from Mozambique, Angola, Zambia, and other communist countries. He issued this warning to South Africa and the world: "Make no mistake about it: they have brought people from outside our borders, and they are armed by the enemies of capitalism. Be alert. There is a communist behind every bush. The West expects us to fight their war and will not support us. We are the front line." He spelt out the resolve of the government to deal with the threat: "We will not give in. We will fight back harder than they can imagine."

The next day the government announced a series of security measures aimed at clamping down on anti-government activities.

Jerry was with his team, including Prof and Jacob, when they read these announcements in the *Rand Daily Mail*. He experienced a range of reactions on learning of Marius's role in extreme politics.

When the others had gone, Jerry sat alone in reflection. His thoughts about Marius were by then so intense, clear and articulate that he could have been declaiming them out aloud.

How wrong you are, Minister Marius Strydom. I am no communist, although I should be. But I am a South African. I want my freedom. You talk about democracy. What democracy? You are using undemocratic methods in your government of the minority. But you speak too loud, Basie. Like an animal making a noise when scared. You are scared and I am not. I have nothing to lose.

"Come and get me," challenged Jerry. And these last words he did give voice to, as if Marius were standing there before him.

❖

Jerry felt that the government was anxious. International support was wavering, and there were powerful calls for international sanctions. Large sections of the white minority in South Africa felt threatened by black power and expected the government to look after them. Jerry's idea was to show that the government wasn't as much in control as it thought. After all, blacks were employed in almost every white business and home. The whites had to be shown that their rule could be challenged.

In November he met with his small group of collaborators and urged them on. "These are words of desperate men. We need to be like the leopard: careful, concealed and mobile. Stealthy. We must turn them into little impala."

The group was worried, especially the Prof. "I think we should slow down. The police are all over, and they have informants everywhere. We can't be sure who is on our side any more. I don't know that my informers are still loyal to us. They're scared of being jailed, and I can understand the pressure they're under."

But Jerry was determined that as blacks they needed to show their power and induce panic in the white people of South Africa.

He did not want the government to feel secure. "No," he said. "We go for the Boer stronghold. Pretoria. The army recruitment office is a perfect target, especially when the defence minister is there. There is no reason to stop now."

"The minister will definitely be there next Wednesday at ten," Prof confirmed. "There's also a morning tea to send off Brigadier Steenberg. Lots of the top brass will be there."

"Good," said Jerry. "I will be nearby and give the signal for the car bomb. I've arranged for someone to buy a cheap Beetle for cash, and the registration hasn't been changed. No one can trace it back to us. Are we agreed about Wednesday then?"

There were murmurs of assent.

"Then Wednesday at ten it is."

When Wednesday dawned, Prof turned up at Jerry's house well before the arranged time. Jerry was up having an early breakfast, and Eveleen ushered Prof in.

"Let's go outside, Jerry."

Prof looked anxious. Jerry took his sandwich and coffee, and followed him out the door.

"What's the matter?"

Prof grimaced. "The minister of defence is ill."

"Is the event cancelled then?"

"No. The minister of racial affairs will attend in his place. I don't suppose that makes a difference."

"Who's that?"

"Strydom," said Prof. "Marius Strydom."

Confusion followed the shock of this news. Though unsettled, Jerry had to give a reply. All the preparations had been made. There was no way he could call the attack off.

Basie Marius was going to be in the building. They did not

intend to kill. Just a bang and maybe some splintering. He was determined not to show any uncertainty. "You're right, Prof. It makes no difference."

◆

At 9.30 am Jerry was waiting around the corner from the army recruitment office in Kerkstraat (Church Street). His stomach was all tension, and he felt a little shaky. The target was a modern building in the centre of Pretoria, a multistorey office block. Three flagpoles at the entrance, bearing the flags of the army, navy and air force, announced its connection with the military.

Between 9.40 and 9.45, the large official cars of defence force generals with multiple stars on the number plates drove slowly into the building basement.

Finally, at ten minutes to ten, Jerry saw a long black Mercedes Benz with a bonnet flag approach the building. Marius was in the backseat.

Prof had found out that the minister would be taken to the underground parking lot and would then walk in through the front door and say a few words. Jerry and his team planned to explode the bomb a few minutes later, when the minister was in the front recruitment shop. The idea was not to assassinate him, but to shake him up and terrify him. Jerry had a concealed walkie-talkie under his loose jacket and would give the signal for remote detonation.

As the ministerial car drove past, Jerry had a clear view of Marius looking out the car window directly towards him. He thought he saw Marius do a double take. Their eyes met briefly. It was as if Marius recognised him.

Surely not. Marius hadn't recognised him when briefed to defend him a few years ago.

He could give the signal to explode the bomb here and now, as Marius passed the main entrance, or he could wait as planned for the minister to go inside the front shop. In either case, Marius could be injured by flying debris.

Marius's car turned slowly and disappeared into the secure underground parking lot.

Should he wait for Marius to reappear or give the signal now, when Marius would be safe? *I can't risk injuring him. It has to be now.* His trembling hand could not press the walkie-talkie transmit button to issue the signal. *Steady.* He took a deep breath and forced his hand down and shouted, "Now! Now!"

The innocuous-looking old VW, parked near the shop-front entrance, exploded. The noise was louder than he expected. He ducked instinctively but saw and heard parts of the Beetle flying in all directions. A door landed in the middle of the street. Windows shattered in first two floors of the building.

Jerry made his way quickly to his Austin, which he had parked three blocks away. He got into it and sped to Top Star Tokyoto Pretoria. He parked his car at the back of the yard, walked into the garage and immediately set about work, as though this was one of his usual inspections. Although shaking inside, he forced himself to look calm. When he saw Jacob, they nodded. He drew strength from Jacob's cool demeanour.

When the report of the attempt on the minister's life hit the newsstands later that day, the country seemed on a war footing. The news dominated the headlines. "Minister of Racial Affairs escapes bomb by seconds," said the *Pretoria News*. "Bomb aimed at Minister of Racial Affairs explodes too early – Minister safe," announced the Afrikaans daily, *Die Vaderland* (*The Fatherland*).

Jerry listened to a radio news report: *"Today a bomb was planted in a car outside Defence Force Recruitment Headquarters in Pretoria. Its explosion was apparently meant to assassinate the minister of racial affairs. Two army personnel entering the building at the time died from injuries sustained, and extensive damage was caused to the building. The bomb detonated too early to cause any injury to the Honourable Marius Strydom, Minister of Racial Affairs. Minister Strydom was due at a farewell ceremony for retiring Brigadier Johan Steenberg. The minister for defence had been scheduled to talk about recruiting for a bigger permanent army force, but could not attend due to illness. Both ministers were unavailable for comment, but a spokesman for the Ministry of Racial Affairs said, 'The minister has been warning for some time of forces external to South Africa who want to dismantle law and order and cause chaos, to the detriment of all our peoples. Because the minister has been so successful in opposing them, he has become a target. This was clearly a bungled terrorist attempt on the minister's life. The government will turn over every stone to find the foreign culprits who plotted this failed assassination attempt.'"*

"Bungled terrorist attempt," Jerry repeated in disgust. "Foreign culprits." His mind was abuzz. If only Marius knew! Jerry had saved him but not the others – an unintended consequence of the last-minute change. Two other men had lost their lives. Jerry played the scene over and over in his mind – where had the others been, the two who died? He hadn't seen them.

I saved you, you bastard. For old times' sake. You don't know it, but I could have taken your life there and then. This is your war, Marius. You declared it! My son has been taken from me, and there has been no justice. But that will come. Just you wait and see.

Jerry picked up the telephone and called Neil. "Boss, have you heard the news? I'm at the Pretoria branch, and my car's in the yard. I can't get out. All the streets have been blocked and I can't get home. I'll just stay here today."

"What are you doing in Pretoria? I thought you were in Sandton."

"No, boss. I told you I was going to check on Jacob, to see if he's still on the ball. Don't you remember?"

"Oh, yes. Was that today? I thought you said you were going there next week."

"No, boss. It is today. Now I can't get out of here. The roads are closed."

"Okay. You stay there. This bomb attack has caused a lot of panic. It's not safe and we're all worried. Bloody terrorists. Maybe the government is losing control over them."

"I don't know. Maybe. I'll see you tomorrow then. I'll call you in the morning."

"Okay. Watch out, because it's dangerous on the streets. The police will shoot anyone they suspect is up to no good. Stay put. Come back to Jo'burg as soon as you can tomorrow. Call me if there's a problem getting back."

"Boss, can you please get a message to Grace? Tell her I'm okay and I'm staying in Pretoria at the office tonight. Otherwise she'll worry."

"Sure, Jerry."

❖

The next morning Neil was at the office early. He had to be there to deal with any impact that the panic over the Pretoria attack might have on his business. Staff would be late, and some would not turn up at all. If the unrest spread, he might have to close some of the branches.

As he was dialling the Sandton manager, Mrs Hammond came in. He paused his dialling and looked in her direction.

"Mr Robertson, Jerry called you. He said to tell you there's a problem with his car. He said Jacob will take him home after work, and he will see you tomorrow."

Neil thought nothing of it. His day was busy enough. Fearing that the trouble would escalate, he instructed that all branches be closed early. He stayed late to make calls to all his branch managers to find out how their areas were coping.

He finally got home at eleven o'clock that night.

Shortly after midnight, Neil heard the dogs bark and a car stop at the driveway entrance. He had just got into bed. He jumped up and looked out the window. One of the car doors opened and someone got out. As the car sped off, a figure came running up the driveway.

Neil grabbed his 9mm Browning Parabellum pistol and went to investigate. He pushed the lounge curtain slightly and looked out the window again. He recognised the gait and saw that it was Jerry walking up the path. Neil ran and opened the front door and stood on the porch.

"Boss, I'm not here. I just need to use the backyard for a few hours and I'll be gone."

"What do you mean? What's happened?"

"Nothing, boss. Some misunderstanding. I'll sort it out tomorrow, I promise."

"What? What are you talking about?"

"Goodnight, boss. Go to bed. Remember, you didn't see me. I never saw you."

Jerry disappeared into the backyard, and Neil went to bed again. He was puzzled as to what Jerry meant but decided he would discuss it with him in the morning. He hoped Jerry wasn't going to unsettle the servants in their quarters.

Neil fell asleep. But he was disturbed again.

At about four in the morning, he heard someone running down the driveway towards the gate and the hum of a car engine. He sprang out of bed, pulled back the curtain, and looked towards the driveway entrance. He saw the car door close and the car drive off with no lights on.

What the hell is Jerry up to?

28

Neil woke again, this time to the dogs' wild barking. Then he heard loud banging on the front door and voices shouting. He sat up, bewildered, and looked at the alarm clock. It read 6:08 a.m. The banging continued, violent and unrelenting.

Angelique was also jolted awake. "Neil, Neil, what's happening? Are we being robbed?"

"Call the police. Quickly!" he yelled to her. He was shaking with fear. He jumped out of bed, fumbled for his pistol, and ran to the children's rooms, shouting to them to wake up and lock themselves in the en suite bathroom with their mother.

"Dad, you can't go alone," said George. "I'll come with you."

"No, George. Go with them."

"Milton and Maria should go with Mommy."

"No. You look after them!"

"They'll be fine upstairs. The danger seems to be down there." George pointed to the staircase.

"Okay, okay. Get the others into the bathroom and then come down," he said. The athletic George was hurriedly pulling on a tracksuit. Neil went downstairs to investigate.

Three heavy bangs rattled the front door on it hinges. "Mr Robertson!" Bang. Bang. Bang. "Mr Robertson! It's the police. Open up!"

He looked out the window and saw a posse of about twenty men. Some were in bulky, dark riot uniforms and bulletproof vests. Others wore plain clothes, also with bulletproof vests. All were armed with big black automatic machine guns and ready for action. There were four marked and two unmarked police cars in the driveway.

Neil hid his firearm in the half-round entrance-hall table drawer and switched on all the lights, even though day was breaking. After opening the front door, he held his hands in front of him where they could be seen, palms turned towards them to show he was unarmed and not a threat. He didn't want any trouble. He judged they would not hesitate to use their fierce arsenal.

Just then George stormed down the stairs, armed with the shotgun his grandfather had bought him.

Neil turned around and shouted at him. "George! Put your gun down. It's the police."

The unclipping of safety catches all round sounded like a pack of photographers. Twenty deadly weapons, each of which could have ripped him apart, were pointed at George by men ready and willing to use them.

Neil didn't like the police response. George wasn't going to shoot. Why the hell were they getting ready to attack?

Neil changed the tone of his voice. He grabbed George and spoke calmly and slowly. "George. These are the police. Put your gun down. Down on the floor. Here." Neil pointed to the Persian carpet on the floor between them.

George looked at his father and saw the panic in his eyes. It didn't correspond with his quiet tone of voice.

"They … are … the … *police*."

Neil kept his eye on George, who now looked at the men and the barrels of twenty or so guns. Did his son know enough about shotguns to recognise that these were big? He could see with some relief that George had realised from his father's own reaction that things were on a knife-edge.

"Okay, okay." George kept looking in their direction. "Gentlemen. I'm putting my gun down. I thought we were being attacked by robbers. Here. Look." He held his gun out in front of him horizontally, his hands far away from the trigger, and placed it slowly on the floor in front of him.

One of the policemen shouted. "That's a good boy! Now we can't shoot you. Well, maybe not." He laughed.

Neil looked at him. He was in plain clothes and closest to the front door. "I recognise you." Neil extended his shaking hand to break the tension. "You're Constable Swanepoel, the policeman who attended the attack on Sipho at Zoo Lake. I met you with Captain Botha the day after."

"Yes, sir. That's me. Or was me. You got a good memory."

"Good morning, Constable. You've scared me out of my bloody wits. I thought we were being attacked by a gang of … *criminals*." He spoke the last word loudly and pointedly.

"I was a normal cop when we last met, Mr Robertson. I am now with the … Bureau of State Security. You know? BOSS." He stood erect as though coming to attention, puffing his chest proudly, but there was a smirk on his face.

Neil was careful to react as though this was something people told him every day, as though someone had mentioned that he had a good job as a librarian. By now he had his fear well concealed. "Oh, I see. Why are you here then? How can I help you?"

"We have information that Jerry Ngubeni, your kaffir boy, is involved with the failed attack on Minister Strydom. And, sir, we have reasonable grounds to belief that this person is here on your grounds." He chuckled and his grin grew wider with his pun. He lifted his head higher and frowned. "Yes, sir. We have reasonable grounds to belief that this person" – and he smirked again – "he is here on these ... premises."

"Oh. Really, Constable? I don't know what you're talking about." Neil looked at him confidently.

"Well, sir. Since I am with BOSS, I'm now Lootennant. You can call me Lootennant."

Just then there was a scuffle as a gorilla-like policeman shunted Jacob Madau towards Neil. Jacob was bruised, bleeding, shaking, and clearly terrified. Neil saw that one of his eyes was swollen closed. He stood uncertainly on his feet, and his hands beside his inflamed left cheek were chained together with handcuffs.

"Well, then, Mr Robertson. We'll see who's a liar. You ... or this man, also your kaffir boy, who we catch going to Pretoria. Do you know him?"

"Of course I know him. This is Jacob Madau, who works for me in Pretoria. He lives there and is in charge of the black staff in one of my divisions. What have you done to this poor man? Jacob, what have they done to you?"

"Haai, master," Jacob mumbled through his bloody mouth.

"You have beaten him. Maybe he told you what you want to hear to stop the beating." He looked at the cuffed man, who had been forced to kneel. "Jacob, you are safe now. You don't have to say anything." He said these words before Jacob could speak. Neil then turned to the other man. "Swanepoel." He wasn't prepared to address him as Lieutenant. "I presume you have the house surrounded?"

"Yes, I does, and we is going to search the premises."

"Where do you want to search first?"

"I know your types. You Jewish comminists. You makes your money, help the kaffirs, but you go to your churches and pray for our Christian government so that you can live safely in houses like this. We let you sleep peaceful." He waved at the high ceilings of the entrance hall and the stairwell behind Neil.

Neil decided that he wasn't going to point out the many errors contained in that statement. "Just get on with your search." Neil was impatient, making it clear he wasn't going to engage in any political discussion and just wanted to get it all over with. He was relieved that Jerry had left early that morning. Whatever he had done yesterday, at least he was off the property and out of range of these dangerous men.

"Under the Terrorism Act, numburr 83 of 1967, section 3, any person hiding or assisting a terrorist will go to jail for a munumum of fife years ... or even ..." he paused and looked at Neil, "get the death penalty." He cleared his throat and stood at attention, upright and rigid, as he said the last two words. "Mr Robertson, I got good grounds to belief that a wanted terrorist is here, and I can search without a warrant." He said this as if it were a formal declaration of Swanepoel officialdom.

"Swanepoel, I am giving you permission to search. You don't need a warrant. Look for whoever you want ... under one condition."

"What's that?"

"You instruct your men that no one – and I mean no one – is to be hurt by them. I have a family in the house. And four servants on the premises. And I have permits for them all to reside here. My family is upstairs, and I presume they are not sleeping peacefully, but are all now awake and terrified, thanks to you. We are cooperating, and if anyone gets hurt, I will report you to Koos Botha."

"Your pal Kaptein Botha has no power here, meneer. I am the BOSS now." Another pun – he chuckled again. "But we will be careful, as we always are. We only uses force when we have to, like when we deals with terrorists." He looked at Jacob as he said this. "But we'll leave this one here for you to clean up. He's no more use to us right now."

Then he turned around and issued instructions in Afrikaans. His men split up into four teams, two of which had sniffer dogs, to search the grounds, the servants' quarters, and the house, for Jerry.

They searched in vain.

Once they had gone, Neil sent Jacob to the servants' quarters with a message for Priscilla to try to tend to him. He hoped that Jerry was at least four or five hours' drive away.

It seemed that the police had departed, but there was an unmarked car stationed in the road outside – obviously BOSS operatives. Neil decided he would work at home that day. He felt shaky and tired from the night's events, and he could not stop worrying about Jerry.

While talking on the phone, he looked out the window and saw Grace walking slowly and with some difficulty up the driveway. She was arriving for work much later than usual. As she came nearer, he could see that she wore a scarf around her cheeks. He went to the kitchen to open the back door and noticed that she had bruises on her face. Her upper lip was swollen, and when she opened her mouth, he saw that some of her front teeth were missing.

"Oh my God, Grace! What happened to you?"

"Last night at midnight the police bashed down our door, looking for Jerry. He wasn't there, so they asked me where he was. I didn't know …"

"What did Jerry do?"

"I don't know, master. I don't know what he did or where he is. They hit me – they hit the children too."

"God! Are they okay?"

"Yes. A lot of bruises but nothing is broken. Those men, they hit my mother too."

"Why hit an old woman?"

"They hit her face. Like me. But she's walking around. She's sore, but she says I mustn't worry. She said I must come here and tell you. Maybe you know where Jerry is … what he did …"

"And Cheeky? Where's he?"

297

"He was there with us, master. They hit him hard and took him away. I don't know where."

"Do you know what Jerry did?"

"No, master."

"They say he was behind the Pretoria bomb."

"Oh, no! It can't be." Grace covered her mouth with her shaking hand.

"Why not?" asked Neil.

"He knows nothing about bombs. But I don't know what's happened."

"They'll hunt him down, Grace. Well, at least they haven't got him yet, but they do have Cheeky. I'll see what I can do. I'll make some phone calls to my contacts to see if we can find out what is going on. God, I hope he is not involved in this Pretoria bomb blast. What is he thinking?"

Grace swayed on her feet and didn't answer. Neil realised that his question was unsupportive. He regretted asking it, and called Angelique to attend to Grace.

He went to call his lawyer, Mr Landau.

"My dear Neil." Landau paused, and Neil could almost feel him thinking about what to do. Then Landau spoke slowly and deliberately. "This is not my area of law. I am out of my depth here. But as a friend, let me tell you that this is just the beginning for Grace and her family. She will be hounded, even though she may know nothing. If Jerry has something to hide, he will stay underground for as long as he can. They will wait for him to make a mistake and then they will pounce. The police – and especially BOSS – are a well-oiled machine. They are bloodhounds."

"Yes, but they can't go around like dogs, attacking innocent people just because Jerry was there at some time. And Cheeky? Where is he? He works for me too. We can't just let him disappear."

"I will make some enquiries about Cheeky and will get back to you. You may remember that I used to brief Minister Strydom when he was a young trial lawyer. I'm not sure of him now. I don't know if he'll help us, but I'll try. I'm sure that he'll at least take my call. I know he has the power to find out what happened to Cheeky, but he'll do that only if he's so inclined."

"I'm not sure you'll get anywhere. After all, the bomb was meant for him."

"I can ask, and he can answer as he sees fit."

Later that day, Neil's secretary called Neil at home. "Mr Robertson, I received a most unusual telephone call from a man who said his name was Sipho. He asked to speak to you, but I said you weren't in. He said to tell you that you should open a branch at Komatipoort. He has been there recently, and it's a very good town for salesmen. He said he couldn't leave a number but to make sure I told you."

"Thank you, Mrs Hammond. If he calls again, please let me know immediately."

What the fuck is Jerry doing now?

In spite of his suspicions, Neil was still shocked. Jerry *was* involved! How clever to use his late son's name. Clearly, Jerry had crossed the border post at Komatipoort into Mozambique. Could he have been behind the attempt on Strydom's life? It was looking more and more that way. Neil wondered how he could not have seen this coming – not suspected a thing. Even though Neil had mixed feelings, he hoped Jerry would find safe refuge in Mozambique.

Neil told Angelique about the message, and then they went together to break the news to Grace.

Grace pondered for a while. "I have thought about this, and now I know it – Jerry is a leader. He is very angry, especially since Sipho's death. He feels he has a duty. A mission for Sipho."

"What mission?"

"Freedom for all of us blacks. I don't know. He has a mission."

"But what about your family?" Angelique said. "What will happen to them?

"They need a father," Neil added, "and now they need school, university, clothes, food …"

"You know Jerry. Family is important to him, yes. But he is for more than us." She sighed. "I'm just glad he's alive. I am scared for him. I don't want to bury him. And now I see that he must have known something could happen to him, because he left me a bit of money. It's not much, but I will still work. Cheeky will work, and soon the children must work. They will have to leave school."

"No, Grace," said Angelique. "We'll pay for the school and for university too, if they get in. You should go home to your family now. I'll take you to the drop-off point outside Alexandra so that you can be with your family. Don't come in this week unless you need something."

"Is it safe to go home, Grace?" asked Neil.

"They've done what they've done, master. Jerry's out of the country now, so they can wait outside my house every day if they like. Nothing's going to happen for a long time."

"I hope you're right."

Angelique loaded the car with provisions from her kitchen and took Grace to the outskirts of Alexandra – as far as she dared go. It wasn't safe to be driving along some streets in a BMW. She had brought one of the gardeners along to help Grace carry the bags of groceries and the first-aid pack she had made up. She gave him money to catch a taxi back when he was done.

29

The oldest Robertson child graduated from senior high school. His results were slightly better than average. Angelique was relieved. She had been a little concerned about George's commitment to schoolwork – he didn't spend much time on his studies. He much preferred to be on the sports field, yet he seemed to achieve respectable grades. She knew he was a born leader. At the St Luke's School for Boys, he had been the head prefect, chosen for his all-round abilities and leadership qualities.

He was a good mix of the two of them, she thought. His charm and height – all six feet of it – came from Neil. His looks were more Greek – black curly hair and olive skin, like her father. And he had her own strong nose.

Engaging and articulate, with a wicked sense of humour, George was the practical joker of the family and led the conversation and play of his siblings. He was full of energy and didn't like to spend too much time thinking. He made decisions quickly. What failings he had, if she could call them that, came from impetuousness. He always chose action over reflection.

His palate was definitely Greek, she thought, with his passion for olives. *Pappou* (Grandpa) George prepared them especially for him. George downed olives the way his friends ate peanuts. She knew he was the old man's favourite grandchild. Maybe it was because he was named after Pappou George, or was it because they had much in common and loved everything Greek?

Angelique wasn't happy when, right after graduating from school, George was conscripted into doing his compulsory national service at the Heidelberg army base of the South African Defence Force. That meant he would serve for two years – until 1976 – unless he went to university first.

Neil didn't want George to go into the army any more than she did. If only George could see, like her, the wisdom of Neil's arguments in trying to persuade him out of this choice. More than once Neil told him, "If you must join up, then do it later at least – as a skilled professional and not directly from school, as a foot soldier."

It made no difference that she backed Neil up when he took every opportunity to raise the matter with his son. She wished they could manage to bring about a delay. They didn't see the point of a young man wasting two years of his life.

But this afternoon's discussion was typical, she thought.

"George, you want to be a doctor," Neil had said. "With your school results, you can get into a university here in South Africa. You can postpone your national service."

"No, Dad." George waved his hand dismissively.

"But you never know. Things are changing in this country. There's talk about national service being reduced. Who knows? It could even be abolished by the time you finish studying. Or you could go in later as a qualified doctor. Work in a hospital. That's much easier. And safer too."

"But all my friends at school are going now, and we have been posted to the same training camp."

"If they don't want to study first, that's their choice," said Angelique.

"Don't make this mistake," Neil pleaded.

"It's expected of me to do my duty in the army. I'd feel a fraud ducking out."

"What duty? The army is in South West Africa – fighting in Angola, for heaven's sake! What are you going to do up there, and for what? That's not even in South Africa!"

Angelique thought that Neil was being too forceful.

George shot back. "I've discussed it with my friends. They could also study first. But they've decided to go – because I said *I'm* going!"

"Well, tell them you've changed your mind," Angelique put in. "Tell us who they are. We'll call them. I'll call their parents."

"I've seen what happens," Neil persisted. "Most of the young guys come out of there and don't want to go back to the discipline of studies. They get lost or they don't reach their full potential."

"That won't happen to me."

"George. Please study first. It's the right thing to do." Neil was trying hard, she thought, to sound calmer. But it wasn't working.

"Dad, you don't understand." George got up and walked out, ending the conversation.

Later that night, when they talked about the discussion with George, she told Neil, "George doesn't want to be a doctor. He just thinks he does. He likes the idea of walking around importantly in a white coat and stethoscope. He's more suited to business – making and spending money, leading a team in a corporate environment. I predict he'll change by the time he gets out of the army."

"Why didn't he tell me?"

"He doesn't know yet. He doesn't know his mind. He's young. But the army will mature him, you'll see. It's become obvious to me now that nothing we say will change his decision. At least he will be with some of his friends."

❖

Angie was right, Neil thought. That last exchange, with its stridency on his part and George's deafness to their pleas, had gone nowhere. If anything, it had entrenched their son's position.

Neil sat there glumly. A feeling that he had lost control at home, where he thought he was in command, came over him. He was confused by its unfamiliarity.

In January 1975, Angelique accompanied Neil and George to the military camp near Heidelberg, some thirty miles south of Johannesburg, where George would do his basic training. All they could see of the training camp was a rambling tent city extending across a range of dusty hills, and dozens of young men lined up at the entrance to one large military-green canvas tent. The rookies were still dressed in civilian casual clothing or "civvies". A number of military personnel in brown bush-fatigue uniforms walked about purposefully and issued orders to their new charges.

Notwithstanding her earlier bravado and her philosophising about how good this would be for George, Angelique sniffed and cried the whole way to Heidelberg. Neil said nothing; she knew that he was still bitterly disappointed that George was wasting two years of his life.

"You're to stay in the car, Mom and Dad. I'll say goodbye right here. I'll see you in three months anyway. Apparently, we'll get leave after our basic training."

Neil drove towards a roadblock. A soldier whose red MP armband labelled him as a member of the military police directed Neil to stop. "Sir, this is as far as you can go."

The MP looked inside the large BMW and saw George. He pointed at him. "Sir, you can get out here and go to that tent over there." He waved in the direction of the large green tent. The queue seemed to have doubled in the last few minutes. "Join the line, please, sir." He was polite but firm. He also seemed to notice the queue had grown. "Don't worry, it's moving quick. Just go, because there are lots of soldiers still behind you."

"Right. Bye." George hopped out of the car and grabbed his sports tog bag with the few essentials he was allowed to bring, as spelt out in his call-up papers. Angelique understood that he was choosing to pre-empt any lengthy, tearful separation when he slammed the car door shut and left them without further words of farewell.

She watched her young man walk off with his duffel sack over his shoulder. Neatly dressed in well-fitted designer jeans, his athletic body filled his new shirt, tailored to show off his broad shoulders and well-built torso. During the six-week Christmas break, he had overindulged, so his shirt was a little tight. He was leaving her behind. She felt the tears welling again.

He looked back briefly and waved at his parents. He gave that endearing wide, white smile, highlighted by his olive skin and dark stubble – even though it was barely four hours since he'd shaved. He turned around again and went to the queue, his short black hair shining in the sun. He immediately shook hands and spoke with those around him. Angelique saw that he must have cracked a joke, as the strangers burst out laughing.

"Go around that loop, sir, to go back," the MP told Neil, and he obeyed the order.

❖

On her son's first weekend pass after three months, Angelique waited anxiously outside the camp with Neil at her side. Boys streamed out past the gates, all looking the same in their brown, baggy field uniforms and floppy hats. Each one appeared thin and scrawny. Unable to tell them apart, Angelique almost ran up to every olive-skinned boy.

She was shocked when George came up to her. "Hi, Mom, Dad."

His face was thin and small under his brown, limp hat. She hugged him. "Okay, okay, Mom." He pushed her back.

"Let me see you." He was so dark from the outdoor training that he looked Indian. His baggy uniform hung on him.

But his eyes looked happy, even though she found them larger than before. His big white smile, too, dominated his thin face with its sunken cheeks.

"What have they done to you?" she cried.

"Nothing, Mom. I'm fitter than ever, and I'm going to do an officer's course when I get back," he said proudly.

Neil groaned at the news.

Upon his return to the army camp, George began the officers' course. He telephoned Angelique one morning with excitement in his voice. "I've been fast-tracked, Mom. I'm now Lieutenant Robertson."

30

For a long time after the visit of Swanepoel and his men to the Robertson home, nothing more happened on the Jerry front. All appeared to have quieted and settled down. For Neil, the house felt emptier with George off doing his national service, but little else had changed. In fact it was as if no unusual events had ever taken place. Life continued at its customary pace. Angelique told him that she had asked Grace a few times whether she had heard from Jerry, and Grace had said that she didn't expect to be contacted because it would place both of them at risk.

Nearly a full year went by. It was late in 1975 when Neil opened the newspaper one morning to find a headline on the third page: "Four killed in terrorist 'safe house' in Mozambique". All his attention suddenly focused as he read through the article in intense haste.

The Ministry of Internal Security announced that reports have been received of an unexplained explosion at a safe house used by terrorists in exile in Maputo, Mozambique. The cause is not known.

The house, which was the home of Dr Jonathan Levine and his wife Sarah, was totally destroyed. Dr and Mrs Levine, both card-carrying members of the banned Communist Party and ANC, absconded from South Africa four years ago and have lived in exile in Mozambique since then.

They were at home at the time and are believed to have died from their injuries.

Also believed to have been killed were Jerry Ngubeni, the militant general secretary of the banned Mechanics' Welfare Society, and Albert Buthelezi. Known as 'Prof', Buthelezi was a former lecturer of chemistry at Fort Hare University. Both are believed to have masterminded the failed assassination attempt on Minister Marius Strydom at the Army Recruitment Headquarters in Pretoria last year.

A government spokesman said that, although not confirmed, the explosion is believed to have been caused by a bomb planted by a faction within the ANC, as there is panic within its ranks following the government clampdown on recent unlawful activity.

'They don't know who they can trust and are in disarray. Our campaign to enforce the law is working,' he added.

"My God!"

Neil could barely take in what he'd just read. He called to Angelique and passed her the report.

"Oh my God! It's Jerry – they got Jerry!" She stared at Neil. "What is Grace going to do? We must tell her. Oh no … What will happen to Grace?"

"The same as is happening now, except she knows not to wait for him. She's strong and has been expecting this – never to see him again. In fact, she won't even recover his body." He turned around and walked towards the window. "It was probably one of the BOSS undercover hit squads that did this. And in another country, too. Instead of seeking peace, making changes, they have become brutal."

He heard Angelique leave in a rush. Of course. Her thoughts were with Grace. It was understandable.

He stood looking out, though he saw nothing. He was surprised at the tears that started to run down his cheeks as he recalled Jerry's bold, insubordinate grin and his unbreakable spirit. That was what had first attracted him to Jerry. His spirit. Always up – using his survival instincts to cash in the empties and to engage Grace to heal him. It was no coincidence that he had landed in a pharmacy yard after his injuries.

Neil went to a chair in the corner. He sat there in thought, and the reality hit him. *He* wouldn't see Jerry again. Jerry, that spunky young man. Jerry, the boss boy. Jerry, the matchmaker who had led him to Angelique.

And again Neil marvelled, as he'd often done, at Jerry's inspirational leadership of the black workers. It wasn't only the staff at Top Star. Neil could see clearly now that Jerry had always had the confidence and self-belief to be a future leader of his people. Why had it taken his dramatic death to bring Jerry's real potential properly into focus for him?

But must that mean that Jerry had been involved in an assassination attempt? He had already long suspected Jerry of being politically active. He had seen this at work. But he would never have believed Jerry to have blood on his hands. And, of all people to choose to assassinate, how could it possibly have been Strydom, the lawyer who had got him off a murder charge?

Angelique had still not returned. He thought of how she tolerated Jerry – she believed that Jerry had been unfair to Grace for some time. Neil had reminded her – damn! How many times had he reminded her? – that Jerry's family *did* matter to him. Jerry's commitment to a cause had come as a result of Sipho's death: the manner of it and the way prosecution of the case had been delayed. She could not agree with Neil whenever he brought it up – her allegiance lay with Grace.

Neil's recollections of Jerry kept returning to the work environment, where he'd seen him most. He remembered Jerry's visible contempt for Prinsloo. Of course Jerry was a better leader than Prinsloo. But the situation was sensitive and complicated. Vehicles had to be sold to Afrikaner-run municipal councils and government departments. He couldn't get rid of the most senior Afrikaner member of staff because a black staff member was doing a better job. Yet Jerry just wouldn't contain his scorn for Prinsloo. Neil had decided not to be involved and to let them find their own equilibrium.

Neil found himself sobbing quietly. He should have done more for Jerry. What a waste! Still so young ... so much potential. He could have engaged with Jerry more and guided him better, helped him to become a leader without becoming an outlaw. He could have been fairer and given Jerry a better position. *Why didn't I? He might have been alive now.*

Neil got up again when Grace entered with Angelique. As he had predicted, when they told Grace the news, she took it tranquilly and philosophically. "I'm not sure if he made a difference," she said. "I hope he did and hasn't gone for nothing." After a pause she added, "I'd like to go home and tell my family."

"Yes, of course," said Angelique. "I'll drive you to the entrance to Alexandra."

Grace wanted to hold a memorial service.

"I have thought about this," she said to Angelique. "I am a follower of the Trans-African Christian Church. Jerry never joined. He never had a church, but he spoke a lot about his Methodist teacher in Lydenburg. I am thinking to take the family to Lydenburg and we can have it at his school."

Angelique hesitated to reply. She wasn't sure that Saleena would want the political activities that led to Jerry's death to be raised in the community. "Leave it to me to make enquiries. I know you have a lot to deal with."

She decided to write to Saleena Ngubeni immediately. Sitting down with a plain writing pad, she thought about how she should address Jerry's mother. Then she remembered that she had addressed her as Saleena at the wedding. It had seemed so natural then. She didn't want to be more formal now. She wrote:

Dear Saleena,

Our family is deeply shocked and saddened at the loss of your son, Jerry. It will be no comfort to you, but I thought you should know we knew him as a good man who cared for his people as much as his family. I can say that he made a big difference in our lives and has been Mr Robertson's African guardian and right-hand man from the day they met.

I am afraid that we have failed in your request that we look after him, and for this I am very sadly sorry.

I send you and Mr Ngubeni our sincerest condolences. As a mother, I have some idea of what it is to love a child, but I cannot imagine what it is like to lose one.

Jerry lost a child. You have lost two – Sipho and, now, Jerry.

Grace has lost her child and her husband. She is strong, but sad. She wishes to honour him as he would want and has suggested a memorial service at the mission school he went to in Lydenburg.

Will such a service have your blessing?

Please let me know if there is anything we can do to assist you and Mr Ngubeni at this difficult time.

With heartfelt condolences,
Angelique Robertson

The next week, she received a letter on yellowed exercise paper, very neatly written:

Dear Miessies Angelique,

Thank you for your letter. Mr Ngubeni and I are in deep sadness from the early departure of Sipho and Jeremiah. Our hearts are very heavy.

You cannot blame yourself. We knew Jeremiah too well. He could not be controlled and would always do what he wanted to do. We knew that.

Life for us goes on as usual. One day is the same as the next. But it is the knowledge that he will never see his family grow up and he will never see his grandchildren that is heavier. What people they will become? He will never know that.

The memorial service nearby is a problem for us. We think you do not know that we live on the farm that belongs to Minister Marius Strydom's family. The news that it was our Jeremiah who nearly killed Baas Marius has been kept very quiet by us in the compound. There could be unpleasantness for our people if the Strydoms find out who Jerry Ngubeni really is. He is still called Jeremiah here.

As you can imagine, we beg the understanding of you and our daughter-in-law, Grace. We will visit if a service is held in Johannesburg.

We thank you for your careful thoughts for our feelings and pray that Grace and the family can lift their hearts with time.

We are thankful for your wisdom and support,
Saleena

Angelique read the letter a few times before taking it to Neil. "Read this."

He read it. He stretched out his hand, giving it back to her. "Yes, I think it can't be held there, can it?"

"Did you know they worked for the Strydom family?"

"Yes, of course I knew. Jerry told me he and Mr Big-Shot Marius grew up together."

"Oh? When did you know this?"

"He told me after the charges were dismissed. And he explained that's why he didn't want his baas on the case. He didn't want Strydom to be hailed a hero. Above all, he didn't want his family to be in debt to the Strydoms. Jerry felt awful about his antics, even though he didn't kill anyone at that shebeen. He felt he had let his family down. It galled him to think his family should feel they owed Strydom when he got him off. As far as he was concerned the Strydoms were in their debt, because his people had been in the area long before the Afrikaners arrived."

"Oh, I see." Angelique frowned.

"Yes, his honest, hard-working family live on the Strydom farm under sufferance. But he swore me to secrecy because he didn't like their politics. He didn't like them, yet he wanted to preserve his family. It's all very strange, you know, because Jerry saved Strydom."

"What?"

"Yes. Jacob Madau, one of my people in Pretoria – the one Swanepoel brought here that morning – he told me Jerry accelerated the time of the bomb blast. He thought it would cause damage, maybe some injury, but not death. To be sure it would not affect Strydom, he made it go off before Strydom was in harm's way. How do you think Strydom wasn't injured?"

"Oh … my … God! And Strydom got Jerry killed and doesn't even know Jerry saved him?"

"Yep. It's ironic, isn't it?"

"It's more than that! It's a fuckin' tragedy, Neil!"

That was the first time Neil had ever heard his wife swear.

"You sit there and tell me this as though we're talking about your day at the office! And you've known this – I don't know for how long – and haven't told me anything? How could you keep this from me?"

"Angie, I was sworn to secrecy. Imagine if you knew. You're not good at keeping secrets, you know. I can read you like a book. Everyone can. Your heart jumps from your chest to your sleeve every time it gets a whiff of something to feel passionate about."

She stormed out of the room. Neil thought he saw her clutching her sleeves.

Grace arranged a small family service in her congregation. Mr and Mrs Ngubeni came down from the farm. They were accompanied by a woman in her early forties and a tall young man with a familiar face who appeared to be in his twenties. Thomas and Saleena Ngubeni introduced them as close friends.

Angelique's mind was churning at high speed. Goodness! The son! Her thoughts went directly back to what she'd learned from Saleena at the wedding. She stole a longer glance at the young man. Surely this had to be Jerry's illegitimate son. The likeness was there. And that meant the woman was the boy's mother and the wife Jerry had never taken. They'd obviously been long under the wing of the Ngubenis.

Angelique couldn't stop looking over at him. Handsome and innocent-looking, with the distinctive Ngubeni nose, he was the spitting image of Jerry when she first met him. Even his walk was the same as Jerry's. He strode confidently, firm buttocks swaying as his weight shifted. He swaggered up to the Ngubeni children and spoke to them, quite self-assured.

Saleena whispered to Angelique. "Phineas is very good at school. He reads plenty of books but works on the farm too. He is a fixer of everything, like his father. And he is good at school. Reverend Michael says he is a gifted child. He is good at 'rithmetic."

Neil and Angelique left the ceremony in Neil's car. As soon as they were on their way, Angelique spoke. "Do you know who the Ngubenis had at the service?"

"Family and close friends, farm friends," he replied.

"So you think you can read me like a book, hey?" She sat there and looked at Neil as though he were a child and she had a big lollipop. "I have a secret, Neil, one that I'm sworn to secrecy about. Do you want me to tell you?"

"You will? Remind me not to tell you any of my secrets."

"I'll tell you a secret. I think you should know this one. Not that I can't keep one."

"Oh?"

"Yes. The mother and son at the service were not just farm friends."

"So who were they then? Family?"

"I'll say. That was Jerry's first child and the wife Jerry was promised to and didn't marry," she said coolly.

"No ... I don't believe you."

"It's true. Saleena Ngubeni told me about her and the child at the wedding."

"I don't believe you."

"It's true. It *is*."

"What? And you've known this all this time?"

"Yes. And Jerry has refused to acknowledge the child exists, but he's been sending them money. And when I saw the boy today ... well, it was like Jerry twenty-five years ago when we first knew him."

"Can this be true?"

"Of course it is. I had a good look at him, and he looks like the

315

Ngubeni men. And guess what? Saleena told me deliberately that he is a mechanic on the farm. Just like Jerry was. I think she's scared for him if the Strydoms put two and two together and get the full picture."

"Well, blow me down! Come to think of it, he does look like Jerry." They were quiet for a time. "So Jerry sowed more oats than we knew of."

"Yes, and we have to do something for those poor people. They've all lost a father."

"What about Grace? Does she know any of this?"

"Nooo, no! And she mustn't. She would feel awful! We need to help Phineas."

"Who?"

"That's the boy's name. Phineas."

"But how can we keep this from her?"

"Please let it stay that way. We can't tell her; otherwise another heart will break," she said, remembering Saleena's words at the wedding.

"I need to think about this, Angie."

"There's no need to think about not telling Grace. I have promised Saleena. But you *can* think about helping them."

❖

The following week, while the senior Ngubenis got to know a bit more about Grace and their grandchildren in Alexandra, Neil arranged to see Rachel and Phineas a couple of times. He took them to the workshop in Rosebank and said that Phineas could work there if he wanted a job. "Mrs Ngubeni's brother Samson also works here, although he is getting on in age. He could do with a full-time assistant, and Phineas would get training from the best in the business."

They thought about it overnight, and the next day a tearful Rachel stood next to Phineas in Neil's office. She told Neil how good Phineas was at schoolwork. "He's very good at arithmetic," she added. She had wanted him to go to college, to be a teacher. But she could not afford it. They had made a decision.

"Yes, master," said Phineas, "I'm ready to work for you. It's time for me to make a change." Phineas was articulate and sure of himself.

"I cannot be responsible for your behaviour, so if you take the job, you must promise your mother that you will behave."

"Boss, my mother knows me too well for any promise to make a difference. Even a promise to you. But I'll take the job. You won't be disappointed – that *I* can promise *you.*" With these last words he gestured first to himself and then to Neil.

Neil did a double-take. It was Jerry standing in front of him again!

31

❖◇❖

In his second year in the army, George – now a lieutenant at 19 years of age – was feeling overwhelmed but excited. He had been given the command to head a platoon of infantrymen at Oshakati in the far north of South West Africa. He knew that the area around Oshakati, a short distance from the border with Angola, was the scene of intense fighting with the South West Africa People's Organisation (SWAPO), the nationalist movement fighting for Namibia. Its members were hunted by the South African Defence Force.

His military instructors drummed into him that, by fighting SWAPO, they were repelling the communists and forces of evil. SWAPO was a threat to white rule in South West Africa – and South Africa was next.

He studied his briefing notes assiduously and absorbed all the data about SWAPO: they had infiltrated the local villages and had teams ready to attack the defence force's military installations. They were also effective in planting land mines. He read reports of attacks by agile SWAPO squads who quickly fled across the border, taking refuge in the Angolan bush.

George led his men on reconnaissance missions to monitor the movements of the enemy. His missions took him through little settlements in remote areas of South West Africa and over the border into Angola, on sand tracks and often through the bush.

Milton, in his last year of school, was aiming for straight As. He was not quite the gregarious person that George was, but teachers saw in him a smart young man with a keen intellect who was thinking about his future. It was March 1976, and he had thought about compulsory national service which he was due to be called up for commencing in January 1977.

"I want to delay the army. I want to study law," he told Neil one day. "I will do it differently to George. I want to go to university first."

"That's a great idea. Which university? You know, if you maintain your present grades, you could even get into Oxford."

"That's exactly what I'm aiming for."

Milton wanted to avoid the army altogether if he possibly could. He had never fancied the idea of the gruelling physical training and war games. And the thought of fighting a real war, especially one he was completely against, was even more repellent.

Neil was relieved at Milton's decision. And he was doubly pleased to learn that Milton had taken up a volunteer leadership role at a camp organised by his school for underprivileged children. All this coincided perfectly with the completion of George's term of national service due to end in December. He would be home for a fortnight's leave soon after an absence of over six months. Neil was looking forward to seeing George, though he was less keen on the party that Angelique was preparing. Everyone would ask what George would do next.

Even at work, where the day's activities usually gave little time to worry over personal matters, Neil's concerns for what George would do after his army service, made him uncharacteristically pensive. It bothered and confused him that although he had raised the subject a few times when George he wrote to him, the young soldier that his son had avoided responding on the issue. Neil made his offers of a job in the business sound as attractive as possible, with only the proviso that George obtain a university degree first. He could try commerce, for instance, "or maybe economics … even medicine if that's still what you want". Nothing he wrote seemed to have any appeal.

He was deep in such thoughts one day when Mrs Hammond's voice over the intercom on his desk broke the silence. "There's a Colonel Grobler on line one for you, sir."

Neil's mind was still filled with George's career choices. "I don't know a Colonel Grobler, but put him through."

When the colonel introduced himself, Neil thought he must be a colonel in the police force – something to do with licensing his stock or maybe they had finally decided on prosecuting Sipho's killers. "What can I do for you?"

"I'm George's commanding officer." The man spoke clearly. "There's no other way to tell you, sir. He's been involved in an accident. He's alive but critical."

Neil wanted to cry out, but had to control his emotions if he was to fully grasp whatever the man had to tell him. "What? What happened, Colonel?" he asked in a steady voice. He knew he had to be calm.

"His vehicle went over a landmine near Oshakati."

"How bad is … he?" Neil could barely say the last word as he battled to hold his emotions in check.

"All I can say is he's alive and we're arranging the best medical team in the business. He's on a plane to Waterkloof as we speak. I suggest you come to Pretoria with Mrs Robertson immediately, sir."

Neil swallowed hard. "Wha—," his voice faltered.

"What did you say, Mr Robertson?"

"Wh … what are his injuries?"

"His legs are bad, but we are more concerned about shrapnel that has penetrated his skull."

Neil rubbed his moist eyes with his left hand. The colonel remained quiet. "Colonel," he said forcing strength into his voice. "I want the best that money can buy. If the best surgeon is in Cape Town, London, New York, bring him here. My son cannot be paralysed ... I don't care if the army doesn't pay. I'll pay. He is not coming out of hospital in a wheelchair."

The image of his father, broken and shattered from shrapnel wounds, loomed in Neil's mind as never before. Paralysed. Bound to a wheelchair. How could the very same thing that had happened to his father now happen to his son? He felt the blood drain from his face, and he started perspiring. Surely a stake was being driven through his chest – the pain was so intense.

"Mr Robertson," the colonel said, "we have the best facilities for war injuries in Pretoria." He spoke calmly and with a slight Afrikaans accent. "I can assure you that we will do everything that is necessary for your son."

❖

Neil and Angelique were at George's side as he was stretchered off the aircraft and whisked away in a waiting military ambulance. Angelique sat beside him in the ambulance, which was led by a convoy of flashing lights and sirens. She heard nothing as she held his limp hand and took in the blood-soaked bandages covering the damage to his beautiful body.

At the hospital, Neil rushed to see the officer in charge. "How is he, Doctor?"

The doctor squeezed Neil's left shoulder, trying to reassure him. "I cannot lie to you, Mr Robertson. Your son has serious injuries. But if anything can be done, he is in the best hands in the world. A team of the top consultants from Jo'burg and Pretoria is here already. They are prepared to do whatever they can."

"Let me speak to the head surgeon. Who is he? Tell me his name."

"Mr Robertson, we cannot disturb them now. They are with Lieutenant Robertson. What we must do is pray. That's what we must do. And tend to Mrs Robertson. Shall I call the hospital chaplain?"

"No. No, thanks."

"Can I get anything for Mrs Robertson?"

"No. We will wait here for news."

Angelique was in the arms of Mrs Kalonides, who had arrived with Mr Kalonides and Maria. But Neil felt the absence of Milton, who was at the charity camp.

"I need to contact our younger son. I need a telephone to call his school."

"Yes, of course. I'll get the adjutant to bring a telephone here, sir."

"Thank you. I need to call … to tell Milton. He doesn't know yet."

Within five minutes a young soldier brought a telephone to the lounge, plugged it into the telephone socket, tested it for a dial tone, and placed it on a small coffee table against the wall. "Sir," he said to Neil, "the colonel asked me to give you his extension number in case you wish to call him. Here is the telephone number and extension for this room. You can now call your son or get him to call you."

"Thank you … my son to call me? My son?" He looked at the young orderly hopefully.

"Er … the son you are trying to contact, sir."

"Oh," Neil's voice was soft and broken. "Yes, my son. Thank you."

The Robertson and Kalonides families kept vigil for almost eight hours. They huddled together or paced up and down in the lounge for the families of injured soldiers.

At one point Neil tried to put his fears for George out of his mind by examining the lounge. It was a functional room with government-issue chairs. The old magazines and journals on the coffee table were of a military nature. Faded beige vinyl covered the floor, which was softened with an orange-brown, regulation-sized carpet. The dark-brown curtains had been pulled open. The windows, with their aged ivory enamel-painted frames, overlooked a neat garden two storeys below, criss-crossed with immaculately swept concrete paths.

From above a sideboard, a wooden-framed photograph looked down as if guarding the room. Neil recognised the chief of the defence force smiling grimly at them. Staring at the image, Neil thought about how this strong-willed, intelligent soldier was following government orders to fight on borders he knew he couldn't hold forever.

The image gave no comfort to Neil. His family sobbed, asked for news, dozed, cried, questioned, prayed ... and waited. Neat sandwiches were brought in and left untouched. Strong coffee and rooibos tea were what sustained them and boosted their wakefulness in case there was news.

In the early hours of the morning, the telephone rang. Neil ran to it. "Hello."

"Dad? Dad?"

"Yes, Milton, is that you?" he said, forcing out the words through his hard, dry throat, which felt as though a thick tube had been pushed down it.

"Yes, Dad."

"Thank God. I asked your principal to fetch you. They're operating on George. He's badly injured."

"Yes, I know. Mr Kroes told me what happened. He's bringing me to the hospital now, but it'll take us about four hours."

"Tell him to hurry." He put the telephone down and looked at Angelique, and tried to hold back his own tears as she sobbed.

❖

Another three hours passed. Then two men in green medical robes approached them.

The family stood up. Neil rushed forward.

One of the men said, "Mr Robertson, Mrs Robertson. Please, sit down." Despite their obvious exhaustion, his eyes conveyed understanding and compassion.

Once the family had all sat down, he sat next to Neil. "My name is Nathan Schloshberg. I head up the neurosurgery unit at the Johannesburg General Hospital. About twelve hours ago, while your son was being flown here for treatment, I was called in by Colonel Hercules Klopper, head of the neurosurgery unit at this hospital. The colonel is a professor at Highveld University." He directed his fine long fingers towards the man in uniform who had come in behind them.

Neil felt as though the energy had been sucked out of him. He was helpless as Schloshberg spoke. He looked at Klopper, who nodded in acknowledgement of Schloshberg's introduction. Then Klopper said, "If Lieutenant Robertson were my son, I would want Dr Schloshberg to be the surgeon. I tell you this because your son has received the best care there is."

Schloshberg looked into Neil's eyes. "We all did our best for him. I am afraid—"

Angelique cried out, "Nooo," and her mother followed with, "What's happened? What?"

"I am afraid we weren't able to help—"

"What do you mean, Doctor?" asked George Kalonides. "What do you mean, 'help'?"

"Sir, I'm deeply sorry, but George passed away on the operating table as we—"

"Oh my God! Oh my God ..." Neil dropped his head and cried. He sat forward in the lounge chair, his elbows on his knees, head down. He slowly lifted his forehead and dropped it against his fists, repeatedly. Angelique and her mother held on to each other and Kalonides stood up, lost for words … lost.

Maria wept quietly on her own.

"No, Colonel," Neil shouted into the telephone. "George will *not* have a military funeral, and he will not be buried in uniform or in the flag!"

Neil felt guilty because he couldn't explain how both his father and son had received war injuries that were similar. That couldn't be just coincidence. He thought he must be cursed. Inwardly, even though he missed George dearly, there was a sad sense of relief that George was not going to live his life out in a wheelchair.

His memories of his father haunted him. He had no recollection of what his father had looked like before the war, only a vague outline of a large and bear-like figure. He had the abstract knowledge, but no memory, of how handsome his father had been. All he could recall was a disfigured man who suffered mentally as well as physically. More persistent now than ever was this image of his father – emaciated, doubled over in his wheelchair, unable to eat, drink or do anything by himself.

His memory of George was of a healthy, tanned, athletic, well-groomed young man. As Angelique had said, he was a charmer who got on well with the girls. Neil pictured the George he'd always known: full of enthusiasm and the promise of life, yet in control of his faculties – though unfortunately not of his destiny. Neil was troubled by the tragedy of his thoughts that it was better that he should remain with that mental image of George, young and smiling. He couldn't conceive of George dribbling and unable to talk properly or smile. Yes, it was better this way.

On the heels of Neil's anger came the guilt. He should have insisted that George go to university and study medicine, even if

George were to change his mind later. He couldn't understand why George had disagreed so strongly when he suggested putting study first. He blamed himself for not recognising the signs that George was not really committed to a medical career. Maybe if he had been more aware of what George preferred, he might have been able to persuade him to do a business degree and his national service later.

George's funeral was one of the biggest that the St Constantine and Helen Greek Orthodox Cathedral had ever seen. Neil wanted the service there to honour George's Kalonides roots. At Neil's insistence, no mention was made in the ceremony of his service in the "defence" of South Africa.

Milton took several days off school for the funeral and hung around his mother, both of them weeping intermittently. Maria seemed dazed as though drugged. Neil stared straight ahead, his eyes thick with tears.

Kalonides wept uncontrollably in church as he placed an olive-laden twig on George's chest before the coffin was closed. "There will be plenty of olives where you're going, my child," he said.

32

Angelique did not understand Neil's feeling of responsibility for George's death. Like her, he was shattered by the loss, but his sense of guilt did not diminish with time.

She worried about him. He seemed to have no energy or ambition. The old desire for success and hunger for power had been extinguished in him, and he withdrew into himself.

She accompanied him to the office, but he did not go every day. When there, he walked around aimlessly, trying not to engage in conversation with anyone in case George was mentioned. He told her that he couldn't bear that. Nothing anyone could say would make a difference to him.

Angelique was relieved that the business managed to keep going on automatic because of the structures Neil had set in place over the years.

She felt that she should be with Neil most of the time. It helped her to cope. After setting up a desk next to his secretary, she became his unofficial mouthpiece. Slowly she took charge of the business and made sure that the staff knew someone was watching over them.

Occasionally she brought Maria in and they met with the bookkeepers and managers. Although not yet 16, Maria showed a keen interest in the business. She spoke to the staff, and Angelique noticed that she developed a quick understanding of who did what at head office. Angelique's instinct had been telling her for some time that Maria had a shrewd business brain. Her savings were larger than those of her brothers, and her way with people made them allies.

Neil stopped going to work. He sat in front of the TV for hours and hours in between sleeping restlessly.

Angelique attended on the business without him and spoke to all the managers. She gave much the same message at each branch of the business: "My husband has built up a business with your help. Everyone is an important part of the success of Top Star. You have been a critical part of this division, and we need to work together to keep the standards high, so that we retain profitability. We have a responsibility to the people working here, and to their families who depend upon us, to maintain the success of this division. If we can't, we fail them, ourselves and our families, who will suffer. Mr Robertson needs a bit of time to recover from the tragedies of the last few weeks. I'd like your help. He'll be back soon. And when he does come back, I want you to be able to present your division to him and say with pride, 'Mr Robertson, I've made the following improvements'."

They all responded enthusiastically, especially when she announced bonuses based upon the performance of their divisions. These bonuses were sweeping and were shared with all the staff within a profitable division. She figured that if they increased the pie, she could share a piece of it with them and still have a bigger piece for the family.

She also kept an eye on Phineas, who seemed to be a popular young man among the black staff. He joked with them, and his enthusiasm was contagious. Even the old workhorse, Samson, smiled more than he used to and seemed to get a new lease on life from teaching Phineas his skills. No one knew about the relationship between Phineas and the late Jerry, but many remarked on the similarities. "It's like Jerry's back," they said. Angelique thought Samson may have suspected something, but he didn't say a word.

Phineas matured quickly and, like Jerry, was a born leader. People were drawn to his zeal and touched by the interest he took in them. Angelique often noticed Maria in deep discussion with Phineas; she didn't have to wait long for Maria to come to her with suggestions on making practical changes in the business.

Although Grace had lost both her son and husband, she kept her sorrow to herself. She realised that there were many mothers and wives in her position who didn't have the support she was receiving. Soon she was using much of her energy to set up an informal association of mothers who had lost children, and of widows. She accepted financial support and passed it on to others in need. The movement grew, and soon she could count on scores of black women of all ages to support others who had suffered tragedy.

She continued to care for her children with her aging mother's assistance, but never mentioned Jerry's name.

On 16 June 1976, a cold winter's day, Marius was meeting with his department head when he received a telephone call from the prime minister's secretary. "Mr Minister, we are receiving reports of protests by a group of black school students in Orlando West that are spreading through Soweto. Two white officials have been killed."

"When did this happen?"

"Today. The prime minister wants to meet."

"I'll be there within half an hour."

He rushed to his car and had the driver turn on the radio. During the short trip to the Union Buildings, he heard that the police had wasted no time in responding and had moved into Soweto with armoured vehicles and riot gear.

But the schoolchildren of Soweto were angered and frustrated by the government's refusal to heed their pleas to be taught in a language other than Afrikaans. They boycotted their schools and marched in protest.

Marius had warned his colleagues about forcing the language issue and had suggested backing down some weeks before. But the relevant cabinet minister had insisted on adopting a hard line. As a result, now they had to deal with demonstrations by students.

The black community's anger had spread. Following the initial peaceful protests and the police response, enraged blacks were on the rampage. Marius was shaken by the reports of the deaths of the two white people, one a doctor.

Surely the highly trained and heavily armed security forces would be able to contain the black community's rage. Marius felt frustrated knowing that this problem could have been avoided.

He arrived at the prime minister's office. With other ministers there, he waited all through the day. There was little they could do but receive reports of the measures being taken by the security forces and of the scores of blacks killed in the crackdown.

The official report released long after the event gave the figure as 176 dead, but Marius knew that many more black protesters and young students had been killed. Thousands were injured. Most of the dead and injured were black children, as their schools had been the centre of the outcry. To halt the growing, desperate demonstrations of black power throughout the day, the government continued to unleash the full force of its military might wherever it was deemed necessary.

Political unrest spread to other townships, including Alexandra. The cabinet received reports that the security forces had blockaded streets and towns and imposed curfews, a news blackout and other severe restrictions, such as on the movement of blacks into the white areas of Johannesburg and other towns and cities. In this way they hoped to stem the growing tide of discontent sweeping the country.

Marius also heard that whites were flooding to the gun shops. He knew they would take refuge in their homes in fear, expecting general civil conflict.

A cabinet minister read aloud the police report about the protests at the liberal Wits University on Jan Smuts Avenue. The students had carried banners, marched and chanted until they were attacked by police, who chased them through the campus and beat them with batons. As he read this outcome, the minister chuckled. Marius looked the other way and rolled his eyes.

Neil's Rosebank headquarters were not far from the university. Hearing the news on the radio, Angelique kept a skeleton staff at the businesses and sent the rest home to their families. She also left early to be at home with Neil. The day's events worried her. Could the government lose control if the protests spread as they seemed to be doing? With its military might, surely not.

Once home, she stood staring out the window, deep in thought and feeling insecure. The ringing of the intercom to the gated Robertson compound startled her. It was well after dark, almost eight o'clock. Who could it be?

She switched on the sweeping garden lights and looked in the direction of the gate. Grace stood there, waving. *Something's wrong. Maybe she couldn't get home, what with all the trouble. The poor woman.* She opened the remote-controlled gates and went out to find Grace walking up the path with Thandi, Sylvester and little Angelique.

"My God, Grace! You look ten years older than you did this morning."

"Madam, I'm sorry to come here. I have nowhere else to go."

"Come, come. Don't be sorry."

"Our house is not safe. The police came today and bashed the door down. Only Mother was there. They left her alone but said that they would be back for me and the children. Apparently they think I am dangerous to them. That I am a troublemaker."

"You! Why on earth would they think that?"

"It could be because I'm Jerry's wife. Or maybe it's because I lead the Mothers and Widows Movement. I don't know."

"Oh, that doesn't make you dangerous."

"Who knows what they are thinking? They are looking for me, and I'm scared for the children. Can we please stay the night? We'll go to the shed."

"Of course you can stay. Why ever not?"

"It's not safe, madam. The police will try and find me. They will make trouble."

"I will speak to Mr Robertson. In the meantime, come inside. Go to the kitchen and make the children some sandwiches." She looked at the Ngubeni children, who stood beside their mother. "Hello, children. Follow your mother to the kitchen." She didn't wait for them to return her greeting but hurried off to locate Neil. He would know what to do.

Neil was sitting in his darkened home office, doing nothing. He had remained lethargic, disinterested in the world around him, unable and unwilling to come to terms with George's death. He hardly ever went to the office now. In stark contrast to his previous obsession with neatness and good clothes, he didn't dress up to go out, neglected his appearance, and started smoking again. He shaved every few days, and then only because Angelique nagged him to do so.

When she found him to discuss Grace's arrival, he had a three-day stubble and looked old and tired.

She explained what Grace had just told her. "I said they can stay the night."

"The police could come here, you know. Grace and her children don't have permits to be here. This is pretty dangerous stuff, Angie. Her children aren't little kids – they're nearly adults." Neil looked around as though the police were in the room. He seemed frightened.

"But the roads are closed and she works here. They can't get home!" said Angelique forcefully.

"If they're looking for her, they'll come here. What about us? What about Maria? If they find Grace here, we'll have a lot of explaining to do. They could even arrest us, and then what?"

"We'll just call Mr Landau."

"They're a bloody law unto themselves. If the police take anyone out of here, we might never see them again. Old Landau won't be of any use."

"Then we can't let them take anyone. We must hide Grace from them."

"Where? We are taking a risk, you know."

"If they find her here surely they will accept that this is where she works. We're not hiding a terrorist."

"They may not see it that way."

"Come on, Neil. You can't be serious. This is Grace we're talking about."

"But her husband is a terrorist."

"She's worked for me for over twenty years!"

Angelique kept silent to let him think. After a few moments she asked, "Should we put them up in the servants' quarters?"

"I don't know. I don't think that's a good idea. The servants are all locked up and scared, and there's very little space there."

"You're right. And that's where the police will look if they come here."

"Where then?"

Angelique hesitated. "Wouldn't it be better if they're somewhere in the house? We can hide them somewhere."

"Yes, I agree." Neil tapped his fingers on the arm of the chair. "Take them to the billiard room. They can sleep there for the night." He stood up. "But I want lights off very soon. I'd prefer the house to look as though no one's home. There's no need to attract attention."

Perhaps alerted by the tone in his voice, Angelique looked more closely at Neil and noticed that his eyes had changed in those last few moments. They were coming alive again after almost four months. He seemed to be rising to the occasion, to its challenge.

Angelique, Maria and Grace transferred mattresses, blankets, towels and food to the billiard room. They showed the children the bathroom adjacent to the billiard room.

Angelique saw the Ngubeni offspring survey the luxury of their surroundings. She overheard Sylvester whisper to his younger sister that the billiard room was larger than their home in Alexandra. It embarrassed her that the tiled bathroom seemed to flaunt an opulence beyond anything they had probably ever seen.

In all the years the parents had known each other, the Ngubeni children had never been inside the Robertson home. Grace went there only to work, and Jerry if Neil asked him to. But they had never visited with the children.

Within an hour they were all settled, having eaten leftovers and sandwiches that Maria and Thandi had assembled. The Ngubenis were sitting on the floor in a corner of the room. Angelique and Maria also came in and sat down against the wall.

Neil did a tour of the house and made sure all the windows and doors were locked and the lights were switched off. He wanted the house to look deserted.

Then he joined them in the billiard room and sat next to Angelique. "It's time now to close the curtains and switch the lights off," he said. "With any luck we can get some sleep, and all will be well tomorrow."

Angelique shuddered. "Let's leave the curtains open. At least we won't be in total darkness. I can't sleep now."

"Okay."

When the lights were off, they could see each other in the glow of the night, but could not be seen through the lace sheers.

Neil looked at the grown-up Ngubeni family. He and Jerry had been close when these near-adults were born, and now he didn't know them. *I wouldn't recognise them if I walked past them in the street.* He felt ashamed.

Neil studied Jerry's Angelique, 12 years old, tall for her age, almost as tall as Grace. He saw the whites of her scared eyes as they searched her mother's shadowed face. The son's name he couldn't remember – an unusual name – Salvo, Silver … oh yes, Sylvester, like the cat in Tom and Jerry. Sylvester was quiet and a little overweight. He had Jerry's nose.

Then there was Thandi, beautiful and well groomed. At 16, she looked like a young lady. She and Maria were close in age. Thandi had a warm, reassuring smile and spoke confidently. Against the tension of the events outside, she had a calming effect on the Ngubenis, making them feel as though they were doing something quite ordinary, something they did every day. She was very capable and seemed to get things done without much fuss, arranging the mattresses and linen efficiently, guiding her brother and sister – but without ordering them – on what they could do to help serve the food.

Neil couldn't tear himself away from them.

Angelique or Maria turned on the radio. They sat and listened to reports of the day's events. His wife and daughter were in their pyjamas and dressing gowns. He was still in his untidy day clothes, and Grace, Thandi, Sylvester and young Angelique sat in the clothes they had arrived in. They had taken off only their coats and jerseys.

The mood was sombre as reports streamed in of action taken by the government in response to the violence spreading in the major cities. No one in the room said anything. The radio had a life of its own – except that it seemed to be stuck, repeating the same message over and over again: "The students and disruptive forces have caused riots and deaths, but the government is restoring order." It was the same message, but the events were happening at dozens of locations throughout the country.

Neil had heard air force jets fly past and wondered what they were going to do. Drop bombs? On whom?

He was concerned about the security of the country. In financial terms, he had much more to lose than most. But he was becoming increasingly irate at the thought of the spark that had set the issue alight.

How could the government be so stubborn about the language used in the schools, insisting on teaching the blacks in Afrikaans? *The bloody Boers want to save their language, and in the process we're all going to lose the country!*

And surely there was a better way of dealing with the protests of school children. The country didn't need to go to war against its children!

Neil didn't want the mood in the house to dip any lower. The radio reports felt as if they were invading his home. "That's enough," he said. "We're safe here, and that's all that matters. Maria, switch off that bloody radio."

But the sudden silence was worse. He had to say something.

"Thandi, how's school?"

"Oh, well, sir … I'm trying to get good grades to study at university."

"That's great. What line of studies are you thinking of?"

"Law."

"Really? That's what Milton, my middle child, wants to do next year. I'd love you to meet him, but he is staying at a friend's place at the moment. They're studying together."

"Yes, I know he wants to do law. Mother told me."

"Do you enjoy school?"

"Well, it's been hard because we don't have many facilities at our school. We have been very unhappy at school, sir. That's why we have riots today. And then we get home and we struggle there too. We have bad light at home." She glanced hesitatingly at her mother, as if asking if she was speaking out of turn. But Grace gave her a reassuring look.

"Oh?" Neil said. He had never thought about the fact that Alexandra was without electricity. Of course it lacked the infrastructure that white South Africa took for granted.

"Yes, sir. We use candles or paraffin lamps."

Neil looked at Grace. He knew she had been under strain since before Jerry left Johannesburg, but hadn't fully appreciated the many problems that Grace was forced to take care of. She had to provide for her family, including her elderly mother, and then there were her community activities. This all took place as she reported for work by eight every weekday morning.

He had seen Grace crack only twice: when she lost Sipho, and on the dark night when Jerry went missing and she was beaten by the police. Even on those extreme occasions, Grace had maintained her dignity, keeping her composure far better than his Angelique, whose heart and sleeve worked overtime.

Later, when news of Jerry's death came through, Grace could have lost her equanimity and fallen apart. She could have blamed the vicious forces of apartheid. Or she could have blamed Jerry for leaving her to pick up the pieces.

Instead she had responded calmly and accepted that she could not let his death pull her down. She had stood with her head high, he thought, and shown that she could not be beaten. *And that's what she's done ever since.*

Neil turned to the other son. "And you, Sylvester?" he asked.

"I'm still at school." Sylvester didn't look at Neil when he spoke, and he mumbled shyly.

"How old are you?"

"I am 14, master." He looked at his shoes.

"How's school? Are you enjoying it?"

"There haven't been enough teachers at his school," explained Thandi, "and it has taken Sylvester eight years to do six school years."

"The schools are unreliable, and many children don't go," Grace added. "At least Sylvester goes to school to see if there are lessons."

"That's terrible. Do you have an idea of what you want to do after school, Sylvester?"

"I want to be a teacher," Sylvester said softly, "but I don't know now. Maybe I'll look for another job."

"It must be hard to learn without teachers and proper schools." Neil spoke softly and tried to be reassuring. "Your father would have wanted you to be happy, whatever you choose." He tried not to sound critical or patronising. "Angelique, what keeps you busy?"

"Me, I'm also still at school," answered the awkward 12-year-old, looking at Grace for approval, her white teeth glistening in the night light as she spoke.

"And what do you want to be?"

She looked again at Grace, sank her head into her neck, chuckled, and said, "A mother." She looked at her hands, lifted them to her mouth to hide her smile, and looked again at Grace.

"Angelique helps me a lot with the Mothers and Widows Movement. She loves to look after the children in the playground. Sometimes she has twenty to thirty children to look after while we look after the mothers."

"Good heavens! When do you do this?" asked Neil's wife.

"During the week, when I'm at work, there are other ladies who give their time. I am there mainly on the weekends. Sometimes, in an emergency, I will help at night. But Angelique helps with the children even when I'm not there."

"My goodness, Grace, how do you keep up?"

"We manage, ma'am. We manage."

They spoke for a couple of hours, going through events that affected them all, avoiding the serious ones like Sipho, Jerry and George.

Then the intercom system chimed from the front gate. They all kept quiet. Neil got up, went to the kitchen and answered it there without switching a light on.

"Yes, who is it?"

"Meneer Robertson. It's Majoor Swanepoel from State Security here."

"Ahh, Major Swanepoel. You're not the same man as Lieutenant Swanepoel of a short while ago, are you?"

"Yes, Meneer, one and the same – Majoor Swanepoel," he confirmed loudly, the pride in his voice palpable.

"Congratulations on your promotion, Major," said Neil in a friendly tone, feigning an uncontrollable cough. He knew better than to antagonise Swanepoel when he might have to negotiate about the presence of the Ngubeni family in his house. "How can I help you tonight?"

"We arr looking for illegals. Can you please open the gate because we got reasons to believe there is illegals on your yard?"

"Oh?" asked Neil, coughing again and battling to hold back his contempt. Swanepoel's broken English was spoken with the formality and mock precision of an old slapstick comic show. It might have been funny if Grace were not in Neil's house.

"I'm sure I would be aware if anyone came in," he said, choosing his words carefully. "I'll open and will see you at the front door. Just give me a minute. I need to put some warm clothes on (cough, cough). I'm recovering from the flu, you see, Major." He spoke reverently, using the major's title with all the charm he could muster.

He pressed the remote button to open the automatic electric gates and then ran to the billiard room, where he told Maria to close the curtains very slowly in case they shone torches in. He ran up to his room, put a dressing gown over his clothes, took a handkerchief from his cupboard, then flicked it open and scrunched it up. He switched on the lights in the bedroom, the stairwell, the hallway to the front door, and the porch light outside the front door. His heart was beating fast as he prepared to face the major.

Neil opened the front door to find Major Swanepoel and three men with him. The three were tall and strong, dressed in riot uniforms and armed. Each had a pistol loaded with a magazine, spare magazines appended to their uniforms, and a machine gun firmly held across the body, ready for action. Their faces, Neil thought, had that deadpan look associated with professional killers. *Hell! They may as well be hit men.*

"Good evening, Major, gentlemen," Neil said, recovering quickly and nodding to the four visitors with a forced smile. He performed a thespian sneeze and a dab of his nose with the used-looking handkerchief. "I'm so sorry. As you can see, I am recovering from the flu. I haven't been to work for three days now." He rubbed his three-day unshaven cheeks.

"God, man. You *does* look terribal," said Swanepoel. "And white like a spook. You need a *klippie* or two." Neil recognised the affectionate nickname of a popular cheap brandy that Prinsloo frequently drank and, no doubt, Swanepoel too.

"Good idea, Major. Now, I presume you don't believe I have illegal blacks in my house. Come in if you want, but I suspect you have better things to do. Maybe you prefer to check the servants' quarters? I'll switch the lights on the path. But, Major, please. Can we make sure there's no violence? I don't want any trouble."

"Yes, yes, Meneer. Come, men, let's check the kaffirs' backrooms. Even meneer Robertson won't have kaffirs in his luffly clean house."

Neil couldn't believe his ears. He coughed and sneezed again. Who did Swanepoel think kept the "lovely clean house" clean?

"Major, I hope you don't mind if I don't come with you. I'm not feeling very well." He knew they wouldn't find anyone to assault there – the so-called illegals were in the house itself. "I'll wait here for you, though."

"*Ja-nee* (Yes-no). That's fine, Meneer. Maybe you can pour you a dop of brandy now. You will be good right away," said the major, uncharacteristically friendly to Neil.

After a short while, he heard a bit of shouting from the servants' quarters. The lights went on, and he could hear the maids screaming, woken unexpectedly by formidable-looking officials. There were no more sounds.

Neil quickly ducked into his liquor cellar and came out with four bottles.

As the four swashbuckling soldiers strutted towards the front door, Neil heard one say in Afrikaans, "Major, we should check the house out. They must be in there somewhere."

"I don't think that's necessary," Swanepoel replied.

"We should, Major. Where else could they be?"

Before they stepped onto the porch, Neil called out, "Hey, Major. Come in. Look here," he said, pointing to four bottles of seven-star Greek Metaxas brandy. As they entered the entrance hall, Neil sneezed near the officer who wanted to search the house.

"I haven't got your klippies, but my father-in-law gave me six bottles of his favourite Greek brandy. You can each have a bottle."

"Ah, yes. Your father-in-law. George the Greek." Swanepoel's expression then became solemn. "Meneer, I'm sorry about your son George. He was a rreel heero. I know what happen. I reed his file. A rreel heero, man."

Neil went paler and started shaking. He turned around and coughed. And dabbed his eyes. "Excuse me."

"*Gesondheid*," replied Swanepoel. "Yes, rreel heero. Such bad luck. May the Lord bless his soul." Swanepoel handed a bottle of

Metaxas to each of his men and took one himself. "This is good medicine. If I durrunt recommend it to you, I would have think you arr trying to braaib me, Meneer."

"Major, this can't be a bribe because I called you in when you were on your way out, after you had finished your work," said Neil, forcing a charming smile.

"Yes … er … right. Let's go, men, so that this sick man can go back to bed. Good night, Mr Robertson. If any illegals should come here, plees call me. Here is my card. You doesn't want any trrubbel at your house."

Neil took the card, his hand trembling. "Yes, Major. I'll certainly call you if any illegals come here. Thank you."

They got into their unmarked Chev Commando and fishtailed out through the gates. Neil pressed the remote control button to ensure the gates closed behind them.

Neil looked up at the ceiling. "Thank you, George." His whole body shivered as the hairs on his arms and neck stood on end.

33

The morning after the night in the Robertson billiard room, Angelique saw that Grace had not settled down. As the minutes and hours passed, the radio reported that the security forces were dealing with the unrest as it spread to many townships. Angelique knew that Alexandra would be a tinderbox. Grace told Angelique that she had hardly slept during the night.

"I should be with my mother and my movement in Alex," she said. "The ladies there need me."

Only the week before, Angelique had been told by Priscilla, one of the live-in maids, that Grace was revered as a strong leader by the women in the township. "She lost her son and her husband. It's like being shot twice in the heart, madam," said Priscilla. "But she stood up again, and looked around to see what help she could give to others."

"What does she do?"

"She gathers women who have big troubles in their families, and her Mothers and Widows Movement just grew. She gives the women help and hope. They meet at the churches and talk. And they help each other."

"Grace arranged this?"

"Yes, ma'am. They follow her. They collect food and clothing too and pass this around. They look after other peoples' children when the families can't. Grace has made a very big family."

Angelique realised why Grace was concerned about the security police: it wasn't only because of her late husband, but also because she had become a matriarchal figure. Angelique recognised Grace's internal conflict. The woman wanted her children to be safe, yet she didn't want to let her community down. Grace must surely feel that she was deserting them by seeking refuge in the safe white haven of Houghton.

Around noon, Grace approached Angelique. "Madam, we're going back to Alex," she announced.

"What about the police? Swanepoel and his army are looking for you. They've threatened you and your children. Remember what they told your mother."

"I think they'll forget about me. After all, they have much bigger problems on their hands than a mother and her children."

"It certainly feels like the entire country's become a pressure cooker about to explode. That doesn't make it safer for you and your children, though."

"We'll be fine, ma'am."

Angelique frowned as she thought about the news reports she had heard. It seemed to her that the security forces trying to put a lid on the unrest were going about it in the fiercest way. The whole nation was overheating – some people wanting revolution, and the whites fearing revolution.

Marius's South Africa was quaking from the pressure and threatening to come apart at the seams. He saw the unarmed student uprising as ominous, the first event to really crack the foundations of apartheid and the granite-like determination of the Afrikaner people. Marius knew that the government would respond to the rising threat in the best way they knew how: they would fight with guns, teargas, curfews and anti-riot armoured vehicles. They were arresting any black student leader who could be identified as a troublemaker.

The activities of Swanepoel had come to Marius's attention in the security reports he monitored. He read that Swanepoel had arrested over two dozen school children and sent them to a police lock-up. The reports also stated that he and his subordinates had fired shots into the crowd to bring them under control, but they did not mention injuries or worse.

This was not the order Marius and others had envisaged. It had all gone horribly wrong. Now the government had to ban all gatherings and protests.

Marius knew the people were waiting to see whether the white rulers were going to be toppled.

But there was never really any doubt. The security forces had planned for this eventuality for many years and were able to cordon off the black townships and isolate the turbulent areas. Under the control of the tough heads of the security forces, the protests were stamped out and the agitators removed, through arrest, injury or death. Some fled into exile. The government and its forces did their best to repair the fractured house of Afrikaner order.

Yet the policy of teaching blacks in the Afrikaans language was soon abolished. Strangely, he felt, this simple language issue showed how they couldn't go on governing as before. He no longer thought of blacks as "natives" or "Bantus", and in his heart he knew they could not be called "kaffirs". He recalled the discussion many years before between his father and Oom Eben and now understood what his uncle had been trying to tell him. The thoughtful advocate had been ahead of his time. He knew that now.

The time had come for change.

On the night Grace and her children spent at his house, Neil had sensed himself responding more to the world around him. It was too soon to say that he had begun to rejoin the living; it felt more like drawing back from a precarious edge.

In the morning he woke with a pressing sense that he should take an interest in his business again. Angelique couldn't go to the business while the Ngubenis were at the house. He knew he had to as someone needed to be there to lead. He shaved and showered and selected his newest suit.

As he drove into the garage at Rosebank, he saw Phineas sitting on the stairs that led to the building's entrance. Phineas got up and followed him as he parked his car. The young man's expression was grim and worried.

"Hello, Phineas. Is something the matter?"

"Boss, have you seen Grace and the kids? I've been trying to go to Alex to see if they're okay, but the transport is shut down and the police are everywhere."

"They're okay, Phineas. They're at our house."

"Thank God. And the girls? Are they with Grace?"

"Yes, they're also at our house. And Sylvester too."

"Both of the girls?"

"Yes, both of them. They were there when I left."

"Good. I feel much better now."

"We should go and see what's happening inside."

"Yes, sir. There's a lot of confusion. Many people haven't turned up for work. The black townships have been shut off. Buses aren't running."

"How did you get to work?"

Phineas coughed into his hands. "I didn't leave yesterday. I knew there would be problems today, so I stayed in the back storeroom."

"Oh, I see. And tonight?"

"I'll wait and see what happens."

346

"Yes. Let's speak later. Come to my office at two."

Neil rushed to his office and was busy on the telephone for most of the morning, calling the branch managers and getting updates from them. Shortly after noon, Angelique called him. "Grace has decided to go to back to Alexandra."

"Is that a good idea?"

"No, it's not. But she's determined and is going soon. She feels for her mother and her supporters in the township."

"And her children?"

"They're going with her, of course."

"It's risky."

"It is, but I do see her point. She can't live with us, and she needs to be home. She also needs to be there with her people, not in a posh white suburb."

"But the police have said they're coming for her."

"She's willing to take the chance. What would you do?"

At two o'clock, Phineas was let into Neil's office by Mrs Hammond. "Phineas said you wanted to see him at two, sir," she said.

Neil looked at his watch. "Yes. Is it two already? Come in."

"I'm going to stay here again tonight," Phineas said. "There are no buses again."

"Hmm. I suppose you have no choice. I need to make a few calls." He dismissed Phineas and picked up the phone. "Phineas," he suddenly called out as the young man was just outside the office door.

Phineas came back. "Yes, sir."

"My wife called me earlier to tell me that Grace and the children have gone back to their house."

"What? No, they cannot be so careless! Have the girls gone with her?"

"Yes."

"Boss, that's a mistake. The children should have stayed and

347

Grace should have gone on her own. There's no need for them to be in Alex now. It is no place for young girls. They can be attacked or arrested. For nothing." Phineas was fidgety and appeared genuinely anxious and concerned.

"Has Cheeky come in? Have you spoken to him? He should know if they'll be fine," suggested Neil.

"No, boss, Cheeky hasn't arrived. He probably can't come in to work either. The whole of Alex is shut down. No one can move without being arrested. People aren't going outside their houses."

"Grace has many friends there. She should be okay."

"It's dangerous. This is a mistake."

"We'll just have to wait and see. I'll let you know if I find out any news. We must hope that Grace and her family are safely locked inside their home."

Phineas turned to go, frowning and visibly uneasy. "Boss, if Grace wants to stay in Alex, that's her decision. But, you know, it's not safe for her and the girls. They must get out."

Neil was impressed by Phineas's anxiety for Grace's children. Even though Angelique had told him that Phineas did not know who his father was, Neil had not expected the young man to be so distressed about the plight of his stepsisters, whose safety he spoke of with extreme concern.

❖

Phineas shook his head in frustration. He told himself to stay calm. How could the boss be expected to understand? Hardly anyone knew how well he and Thandi had got on since their first introduction at the memorial service for Jerry. When their grandparents visited, he and Thandi had crept out for walks. Then they made arrangements to meet secretly at Patel's General Store, where they hung around with some of her friends. He thought of how this had added to the attractions of the city, how it was part of the reason why he had embraced life in Johannesburg, away from his mother and the farm.

He looked forward to seeing Thandi. He started meeting her on the weekends, when they spent many hours together.

Thandi and Phineas hadn't told anyone of their new relationship except Sylvester. Thandi needed her brother as an accomplice to their secret courting. She coerced him into promising that he would not tell on them until she was ready to let her mother know. She guessed that Grace wouldn't be too enthusiastic about a farm boy turned mechanic; not after Grace had given so much to educating her children. For years Grace had stressed to them, especially the scholarly Thandi, the importance of education. "That is the only way you will get better jobs than me and your father."

They hadn't yet discussed what Grace hoped for in a husband for her oldest daughter, but Thandi knew that, ironically, Grace would not be happy if Thandi married a mechanic like her father. When she left the house in the company of the complicit Sylvester, she told Grace they were going out with their friends. Her accomplice went his own way when they met up with Phineas at a prearranged meeting spot. Later, when brother and sister had had their separate nights of romance and fun, she met Sylvester at the same spot and they returned home together, completing the subterfuge. But Thandi was beginning to wonder how long she could keep it up.

With the government measures to isolate trouble spots, most of the staff had not turned up for work. Neil closed up early and sent all the workers to their homes.

But Phineas could not be satisfied by Neil's response to him earlier, and he remained distressed for Thandi. He decided that he would walk to Alex to find her. He wanted to get her out of there. Stories of the heavy-fisted reaction of the police forces were doing the rounds. Many more people would be killed or maimed if this continued. He didn't want her to be in the middle of one of the hotspots.

Phineas skulked along the backstreets of the suburbs between Rosebank and Alexandra, avoiding the main roads as much as possible. The streets were teeming with police and army patrols – on foot, in armoured vehicles, and in marked and unmarked cars. Everyone was so jumpy that any wrong move could get him arrested, assaulted, or even shot dead. Almost everyone was armed – police, army, and residents, white and black.

As he made his way to Alex, he scoured the surrounds for anyone who might pose a threat to his safety. He was ready to run. He predicted that the main entrances to Alex would be manned, so he walked through the veld and found a remote path that led to an isolated, unpatrolled way into the township.

Once in Alexandra, he was careful to steer clear of crowds; he knew the threat they posed, even to the innocent. Alert for trouble, he crept from wall to wall to the Ngubeni neighbourhood, aware that at any time he might have to hide or run for cover.

Disturbing scenes of burnt car carcasses, smouldering shacks, and red-brown pools of dried blood on the streets confirmed that danger was everywhere. Pedestrians made their way to their destinations briskly, trying not to be noticed or attract attention. Occasional groups of young men, some little more than boys, sat on the verges – talking, but alert to danger.

As he approached the Ngubeni home, he saw Sylvester and four young men sitting on the low front wall. Like Jerry, Phineas could present a formidably imposing figure at six feet tall and broad-shouldered. He straightened up and loosened a few extra buttons of his shirt to reveal his taut upper chest. Like Jerry, he could swagger and appear unafraid and arrogant.

The young men saw him and stood up in unison, revealing

lethal-looking metal rods, pangas, and knives at their sides. Some raised their weapons to rest on their shoulders.

Phineas walked up to Sylvester. "Hey, Sylvester. How's it going here? Is everything all right?"

"Yeah, I suppose so. No school again."

Phineas was aware of Sylvester's friends staring at him. He figured they were considering whether to challenge him or hold off. "So, introduce me to your friends." Phineas oozed confidence as he drew his windbreaker to the side and put his left thumb in his pocket to reveal a shiny bone dagger-handle tucked into his jeans. That, together with his big frame and obvious toughness, had the intended effect.

"It's okay, boys. He's a friend," said Sylvester.

They shuffled and coughed into their hands as Sylvester introduced them. No one made a move that Phineas could interpret as aggressive. They covered their weapons.

"This is Phineas. He's a friend of the family, from a farm."

Phineas smiled and the others relaxed. "Is your mother here, Sylvester?"

"No, she's out with the Movement, but Granny and Thandi are at home. I'll let you in."

As they entered the house, Eveleen was boiling water over a primus stove. "Hi, Granny. We have a visitor." Sylvester pointed to Phineas.

"I'm glad you came in, Sylvester. It's not a good idea to be out in the streets." She paused when she saw Phineas, frowned, and examined him from head to toe. Phineas felt self-conscious and buttoned up his shirt. "Oh, hello. I remember you."

"Yes, *Gogo* (Granny). This is Phineas, my friend. You remember? He came from the farm with his mother, Rachel, for Father's memorial service."

"Yes, I thought so. I remember him well."

"And guess what?"

"What?"

351

"He works where Father used to work – as a mechanic. Isn't that a coincidence? He's from the same farm and worked in the same workshop where my father learned his skills. Now it's like he got Father's job."

Eveleen looked Phineas up and down again. "Yes, that is a coincidence. I remember he spoke a lot to your big sister after the service."

Phineas greeted Eveleen respectfully.

"Thandi's working in that room," said Eveleen, pointing to a doorway. Phineas wiped the beads of perspiration from his forehead with the sleeves of his windbreaker. *I hope my shirt is not showing my nervous sweat.*

Sylvester opened the door and said, "Thandi, guess who's here?"

"Who?" she asked as Phineas peeped into the room. She saw him and pushed her chair back to get up quickly – too quickly – and fell over the chair. Phineas reacted just as fast. He caught her and held her, their eyes locking together.

Then he helped her up and turned to Eveleen.

"Hello," they both said simultaneously, and then kept still.

Eveleen broke the awkward silence. "I'm going to see Primrose next door, Thandi. If you need anything, call me." She hobbled out the front door, relying heavily on her walking stick.

Phineas looked out the window. Eveleen lifted the stick and walked perfectly upright without any limp or difficulty. She even held the stick six inches off the ground as she hopped down the two front steps, seemingly to make sure the stick didn't get in the way.

Sylvester ducked out the back, leaving Phineas and Thandi on their own.

Before Sylvester had slammed the kitchen door, Phineas hugged Thandi tightly. "I was so worried about you."

"I'm fine. I was worried about you, Phineas." She kissed him. "I'm so glad you came to see me."

He responded by squeezing her harder against him and prolonging the kiss until she pulled back a bit. "How'd you get here? All transport is stopped."

"I walked."

"Really? That's far. And dangerous."

"Actually, it was fine. I was just about the only one walking the streets."

They kissed again. She stroked his back and his chest, down to his belt, then pulled back. She pointed to his belt. "What's that?"

"Oh, sorry. That's my knife. Just in case."

"Oh."

"But I never use it. I wouldn't unless I had to. I'm not a tsotsi."

"Yes, I know."

He pulled out his dagger and placed it in the inside pocket of his windbreaker, which he then removed and hung over a chair in the kitchen.

"Oh, that's better. You could cut something there," she said, pressing into his crotch and giggling.

"Stop joking. Everyone is scared. Some people out there are scared and dangerous – very dangerous." He held her shoulders and looked her in the eyes. "You cannot stay here in Alex. It's not safe. There are plenty of bad people. They are attacking anyone they want."

"There's no need to worry. It's okay. There've been no threats against us. I must be here with my family."

"No one can control what's happening." Phineas held her shoulders.

"My mother and sister are out there now. They're okay."

"How do you know? In any case, it's so mad out there that things can change in a second. Haven't you heard about the police shooting at schoolkids? If they can do that to them, imagine what they'll do to crowds. They'll just shoot. Never mind who's in the way."

"Phineas—"

"And it's not only the political attacks. The tsotsis are there to take advantage of the confusion."

Thandi pulled back from his embrace and held his head in her palms, forcing him to look into her eyes. "Listen to me. I can't leave my family. I live here with them. If it's not safe for them, how can I leave them? That's when I need to be here."

"But what about your safety?"

"This is my home. Where should I go? Nowhere is safer, and at least we are all here together." She moved to the other side of the kitchen table.

He thought about this for a minute. He walked around the tiny shack. She watched him.

"Fine," he said after a while. "But only if we tell your mother about us and if I stay here too. In the house. Or I'll camp outside; I don't care. At least until the danger is over."

"Oh … I'm not sure." She paused and seemed to be thinking. But she only shook her head slowly and repeated, "I'm not sure. Not sure. Mother will not take this well."

"Now is as good a time as any."

"It's not going to be easy going. But maybe … well." She hesitated. "Do you really think so?"

"Yes, I do."

"Okay, why not now?"

Phineas could see that Thandi's eyes smiled at him, almost as if she was amused by his anxiety. He felt she was flippant about the threat to their well-being. But when she looked at him again, smiled, and gave him a big hug, he shivered. He felt her love.

"Let's tell her together." She kissed him quickly. He could tell from the look on her face that she had reservations and didn't know how this would go.

❖

Grace could not hide the look of shock on her face when Thandi told her the news, with Phineas standing right there beside her. "When did this all happen?"

"Since the service for Dad. We connected straight away. It was as though we'd known each other for years and had a lot in common."

"Why was I never told?"

"Mrs Ngubeni, I am sorry you were never told, but it just happened. We didn't realise we were … falling in love. Even later, we just enjoyed talking to each other and taking walks." Phineas's soft baritone washed over the words.

Grace could only see before her, in shards, the hope that she and Jerry had built up for a more secure provider for Thandi. They had struggled long enough in life to know that it was better to have an education than to work, as she did, as a domestic maid. Jerry had been lucky to have a good job with Mr Robertson, but it hadn't provided enough to live well and raise children the way they deserved. She wanted a better future for her Thandi.

Grace looked Phineas up and down. She saw in him a quietly confident young farmhand who reminded her of Jerry when she'd met him. Could he be even more handsome than Jerry had been? Something about his gait and build seemed familiar. But didn't all farmhands have the same muscle? She could see why Thandi was taken by him.

Thandi was always top of her class and wanted to become a lawyer. What did she see in him intellectually? Thandi might be attracted physically and not realise until too late that he hadn't the intellectual depth that would make her happy. When she mixed with her professional group, would she be embarrassed by Phineas? It would get worse as he got older.

No, this could not work in the long run. Thandi shouldn't choose him. And if the attraction was mostly physical, they were courting disaster.

355

But then Grace had another thought. Perhaps it might be better for Phineas to be around them so that Thandi would see his inadequacies early on, before the affair went any further. The political turmoil had reached boiling point. This could be just the right time to find out how he would stand up to the pressure. Would he show himself up as a protector, or would he be a burden – someone in need of assistance? She felt she could engage with Phineas and expose his shortcomings. She knew Thandi. Phineas wouldn't last if, in spite of his mechanical skills, he turned out to be just another naive farmhand.

And she and Eveleen could supervise them in the house rather than let them carry on "out there".

Grace nodded. Yes, being under the same roof might be a good idea so early in the relationship.

But not under the same blanket.

She didn't know Phineas well, but there was the added factor that another male in the house could be useful. Things were on the edge in South Africa, and many forces were pulling in different directions. There was no doubt that her family could get mixed up in the unrest without looking for it. She was expecting the security forces to seek her out eventually.

Moreover, Phineas's imposing and tough look would provide a deterrent against the criminal elements taking advantage of the political instability. Even if all he did was accompany Thandi when she went outside, it would be worth having him around.

"Okay. He can stay with us. He will sleep with the boys in Cheeky's room. But as soon as Alex settles down, he goes back to his own home."

Phineas thanked Grace respectfully. Eveleen stood up without the aid of her *knopkierie* and said, "Now, young man, go and bring some coal for the stove."

34

Through the fog of pain, Neil was vaguely aware that he was beginning to cope. He was back at work and managing his battle with grief.

The time came for his remaining son's departure. He felt the pride when Milton excelled at school in his final year notwithstanding the family tragedy, and again when his son was offered a place at Oxford. It was a relief that Milton was more determined than ever to avoid military service. Unlike his older brother, he had shied away from sports and much preferred to read books, especially non-fiction.

Whenever they had spoken about it, Milton expressed his views on South Africa strongly. Besides finding abhorrent the ideas of physical training and mixing with boys he did not know, he was convinced that this war was *not* one they had to have. "Yes, the communists are in Angola, but SWAPO are fighting for their freedom," he said.

"The communists killed your brother."

"It's a war I don't want to be in. It's not my war. George shouldn't have been there either. It wasn't his war."

"Yes," said Neil after some hesitation. "If only George'd kept out of it too. He'd still be here."

Milton seemed not to understand the complexity of the problems in South Africa. To him, the solution was simple and obvious. "Get on with opening up opportunities for everyone," he said to his father. "Give the blacks the rights they want."

Neil did not agree. He wasn't a supporter of the National Party, but as a businessman, he was conscious of the benefits of a white government and cheap labour. He was worried about how a government elected by the majority would protect business and the white community. *It won't.* He said as much to his son.

"But Dad, can't you see? There are millions more customers out there if you pay the blacks better."

"Yes, but if you upset the status quo, you never know what will happen."

During these father and son discussions, what hovered at the periphery of Neil's thoughts was a concern that he had barely acknowledged, even to himself. He tried not to think that Milton, once gone, might never return to Johannesburg to live. He began to regret encouraging Milton to go to England to study.

Every time they saw each other, he could tell that Milton was maturing. Still very thin and of average height, with his dark, thick hair, Milton seemed to have plenty of Kalonides in him. But his skin was light and his eyes were Robertson blue. Neil sensed Milton's stare penetrating deep into his soul, as though he could read Neil's feelings – even his thoughts.

Neil raised the topic of Milton's future career with him on many occasions. Each time, Milton said, "I'm not going to do my national service. I'm not tough like George. I'll live in England if need be."

Neil's heart sank. "You can go if you promise to come back. You can do your national service after your studies – in the legal corps. You won't be in the front line like George."

"No. I'm not going to help them fight this stupid war of theirs. It's time for the blacks to get the vote."

This argument always reminded Neil of how deeply Sipho's murder had affected Milton. Then had come the utter futility of

George's death. In these moments, Neil had a glimpse into Milton's logic. How could he expect his remaining son to see it any other way? To Milton, his brother had had no choice – had been made to fight for a cause that was not his.

But the understanding was brief, and Neil felt no better when the time came for Milton to leave.

Milton did return unexpectedly for a period of a few weeks.

It came after another year without much alleviation of grief for Neil and Angelique. In 1978 the long-delayed prosecution of the hooligans who had caused Sipho's death was at last under way. Milton, in his second year at Oxford, interrupted his legal studies and flew from England to follow the proceedings.

"Grace, would you like me to take you to the court? I'm going to attend every day until it finishes."

"No, master. The young men's families will be there."

"But they are the criminals. Why should that worry you?"

"I know. But they will be sad."

Milton was awed by Grace's acceptance and her sadness for the parents of the boys who murdered her son.

Grace waited for him after he returned from each day's hearing. They sat on a bench in the garden as Milton summarised the evidence. Looking at the ground in front of her, hands on her lap, she listened to Milton's every word. When he got to the evidence about the last minutes of Sipho's life and the police response, he saw tears in her eyes.

Four of the white youth were convicted and given prison terms ranging from four to ten years.

Milton was fuming when he arrived home that day. He told Grace the sentences. Milton was disgusted. "Four years for a life! How ridiculous! They should have got fifteen to twenty."

Grace's response was calm. "Shame, master."

"What do you mean?"

"I feel sorry for their parents. They must be very sad."

"What? What about you? What about Jerry?"

"They are parents too, and many hearts are heavy today. Nothing can bring Sipho back. More people are broken today."

She went to a quiet part of the garden, and Milton could see her head in her hands and her shoulders shaking.

Neil's pride grew when Milton gained honours and progressed to his master's degree. But his hopes for Milton's return to Johannesburg faded when, at the end of his masters, Milton took a part-time job as a law tutor and deliberately delayed returning to South Africa. To Neil that meant he would never live in South Africa again.

While Milton was at Oxford, Maria dutifully did her schoolwork. She had been deeply moved on the night in 1976 when Grace and the Ngubeni children hid with them in the billiard room.

She thought a great deal about what she learned on that frightening evening – about the lives of the Ngubeni family. Grace was so strong and courageous, as a mother for her own family and in helping the other women in the township. Maria felt embarrassed that this was all happening around her and, growing up in her Houghton cocoon, she had never given any thought to how others were living. Was it that she did not need to or was it that she did not want to look beyond the luxuries of her life?

Maria made up her mind to find out more. She asked Grace about Alexandra. She read the newspapers and listened to the radio. For the first time, she realised that many blacks had no political connection with the remote Bantustans that the government had set up to assuage their ambitions for equal rights.

She was piecing together the bigger picture like a jigsaw puzzle, and began to find many parts she had not previously seen. Even with the knowledge that the picture in her mind still had gaps, she realised that it was not all golden-green and leafy like their garden. There was dust and mud, grit and grime, and there were impoverished populations.

She was determined to change her own outlook. But beyond that, what could she do? She was just a high school student and had no illusions about changing the world.

After finishing high school, Maria enrolled in an accountancy course and began to spend much of her spare time at Top Star. When Neil gave her a small BMW for her twentieth birthday, she went around to the branches and reported back to her father. She could see that this was one thing he was truly pleased with – her growing participation in the business.

Neil tried to pull tighter the loose threads holding him together. He and Angelique had reversed roles again.

She withdrew from the business and spent more time with her ageing parents. He became concerned when he saw that this allowed her to think more about George and to grieve. Allowing her hair to go grey and foregoing make-up, she looked older than her age.

Neil immersed himself back in the business but he involved Maria in some of his activities. She embraced the opportunity.

For their twenty-fifth wedding anniversary in 1981, Maria bought her parents first-class plane tickets to England and arranged with

361

Milton to book accommodation in Oxford and Guildford. It was Neil and Angelique's first trip to England together.

Neil hired a vintage Mini Minor to drive to Guildford. He was excited to show Angelique where he grew up. Many of the old landmarks were still there. Robertson's Garage had been converted to a dry-cleaning factory. Hidden next door, wedged in between the progress of the sixties and seventies, was the old house. Mrs James was still living there. Neil had been paying the rates, taxes, and utilities since his mother's funeral. Mrs James was keeping the place alive, barely. She maintained it exactly as it had always been and hadn't even painted the front door. But it was clean and tidy.

Neil knocked on the door.

"Oh, Neil … Neil. Is it you?"

"Yes, Mrs James," he told the heavy-set, aged woman who peered from the darkness of the entrance. He had expected to find her getting on, but still felt the shock. He coughed and managed to recover quickly. "And this is Angelique, my wife."

"Oh, dear. This is the beautiful Greek goddess." She winked at Neil and took a long look at Angelique, from her permed hair to her white patent-leather shoes. "Oh, yes. She is, too."

Neil stepped aside so that his wife stood on her own. Angelique looked striking in a crisp royal-blue slack-suit with silk white trim along the lapels and pocket edges. The silver buttons seemed to match her hair, completely grey even though she was just over fifty. Her engaging eyes, which always reflected her moods, warmed as she gazed at the older woman. "Hello, Mrs James. I'm very pleased to meet you." Angelique hugged her and kissed her on each cheek.

Mrs James looked at Neil with a big smile.

"Neil has told me how good you were to his parents," said Angelique.

"Oh no, my dear. They were so good to me after I lost Alf in the war. But enough about that. How long are you staying?"

"Mrs Ja—"

"Neil, I moved out of your parents' bedroom. I've done it up for you and your bride for as long as you need it." She turned around and shuffled in her torn slippers to the sitting room.

"No, no. That won't be necessary. We're staying in a hotel nearby, and then we're going on to Oxford, where our son is."

She stopped at Mary's favourite couch, let herself down with great effort, and then looked up at Neil. "Oh, yes. Milton. What a lovely boy!"

"Oh, do you know him?"

"Why, yes, of course! He visits me often. He comes here at least once a month and stays in your old room."

"Are you sure?" asked Neil. He and Angelique were sitting on the two-seater couch like visitors.

"Of course I'm sure. I think he feels at home here. He loves our pies. I must confess I spoil him with Mary's recipes. I'm slower nowadays but can still cook."

Neil couldn't conceal his surprise. "Well, blow me down! I had no idea. How did he find the house? He never asked *me* about it."

"Why wouldn't he find it? He said he just looked up his name in the telephone directory, 'Milton Robertson', and found it. No one changed the telephone listing, and you're paying the telephone account."

"Of course. And he comes here often?"

"Oh yes. He says he does some of his best thinking here and often walks to the cemetery, spending time at the graves. Oh, silly me! I've sat down without offering you a cup of tea."

"Thank you, Mrs James," Angelique put in, "but Neil wanted to go to the cemetery, and we'd better go there before dark. We'll come by again before we leave Guildford. Maybe we can have some tea then."

"Yes, you'd better go to the cemetery. But you're staying here, and you're not leaving without having meat pie. Milton is on his way. He

363

knows you're here for the night and asked me to bake Mary's meat pie. We're having it for dinner, right here in the dining room." She pointed to a dark doorway across the passage. "He'll sleep here in the lounge, and I've set up in your room, Neil. You have the main room for as long as you need."

"Well, well," said Angelique. "Surprise after surprise. These kids keep such secrets from us. I wonder if we can ever trust them again."

Neil turned to Angelique with a look of amazement that mirrored her own. "Mrs James, we'll be back in an hour," he said.

They drove to the cemetery, where they found the gravestones of Milton and Mary, side by side. The graves were well kept and clean. The stones had clearly been wiped down recently. Neil noticed a rose bush between the two graves. There was a heavy concrete bench alongside them, the only one of its kind as far as Neil could see. His eyes moistened as he stood there thinking of his father and mother.

Angelique made the sign of the cross and walked away to give Neil some space. He stood over the graves and whispered, "I hope you've met George. You'll love him." And then he wept.

Angelique came back and guided him to the bench, where they sat. She held him. "I didn't even come to see them before they died, Angie. After all they did. They let me go. They did it for my own good." He wiped his eyes with his handkerchief. "I never felt abandoned because I knew they loved me. All I can think of in the house is the shadow of my father. Could you also smell his pipe tobacco?"

"No. There's no tobacco smell."

"I could smell it. It's like he was lighting up in the room next door. I can't get rid of the guilty feeling that I abandoned them."

"You didn't abandon them, love. You sent them money."

"But that's not what I really regret. I was in London. Just before she died. And I was too busy to come and see her."

"She didn't want you to see her. She was ill. She wanted you to remember her the way she was when you left."

"And they never met you. Or the children. Their only grandchildren."

"Yes, that's true. That *is* a shame."

"You know, I've come back to England a couple of times on business, but I never felt my roots here. Not until coming with you. And now more so through Milton. I'm amazed at what Mrs James told us. Can you believe it? The roots are still there for him, stronger than they were for me."

In South Africa, Maria was finding the roots and branches of the Top Star tree and was tending them.

The organisation boasted almost three thousand staff across fifty branches in twenty cities and towns. To entrench her position, she convened meetings for all levels of management. She printed a newsletter for the Top Star family and made sure there were many photographs of white and black workers. She sent the managers regular messages of praise and encouragement.

Maria made visits to branches unannounced, often when she knew the managers were away. She spoke to the black staff to see that they were getting their share of the bonus that Angelique had introduced.

In many instances she got Phineas to drive her. She perceived that he had a keen interest in people. The black staff he met warmed to him immediately. He became Jerry's successor as the leader of the black workers.

A few weeks after Neil and Angelique returned, he went into his office one day and was greeted by Maria. "Dad, Mom seems to be feeling George's absence more now that Milton is away. The trip has helped her escape a bit, but she shouldn't go back to where she was before you went away."

He raised his eyebrows. "I'm not sure I understand."

"Look at her. She doesn't go out and doesn't have people over. She just stays at home in the garden. And then she worries about her parents so much she hardly thinks about herself. She sees Pappou and *Yiayia* (Grandma), who are also sad and getting old very quickly. It's like she's waiting for something to happen, waiting … for what? What's she waiting for?"

"Hmm. In England we just couldn't stop thinking about George. He had never been there. He never met his English grandparents, and they didn't know him. Yet they all dominated the trip."

"Oh?"

"I didn't help either. I feel so guilty that I abandoned my parents. I was the one who fell apart. Mommy helped me through this voyage to my past. We had our ups, but boy did I spoil it all with my melancholy."

"Oh, I didn't know. The trip was supposed to give you both a boost."

"The problem is I felt as though George was right there with us, looking over us. And I'm afraid I may have made Mommy feel the same. Thank heavens Milton was there to pull us out of it occasionally. He went out of his way to be with us."

"Well, Milton's not here. I don't spend much time at the house now that I have my own apartment. You should try to be there for Mommy."

"Of course I'm there. I see her every night."

"And during the day? Why don't you take more time off? You don't have to come in to the business as much as you do. I'm managing. If you really want, you can come in for an hour and leave again. You've set the business up well. I'll tell you when I need your help."

"Oh … well, I'll see. There are some issues with the financing that will come up soon. I need to tidy them up, but I'll see," he repeated.

❖

Neil reduced his hours at work. He and Angelique began to spend more time together. He tried to lift her spirits, but he could hardly manage this when, almost in spite of themselves, they began visiting George's graveside each week. Now that Neil was at home more, each pulled the other down more.

They spoke many times of how they had both felt George's presence watching over them in England, but this sharing seemed to offer no consolation. For Neil, it did not help that he thought often about his parents and the way he had abandoned them.

And even though they had seen Milton settled, they talked of feeling the separation more than ever. Neil had long given up hope that Milton would return to live in South Africa. For the first time, Angelique mentioned her fears about this too.

They both fell into a black hole of self-pity.

35

On an overcast summer's day in 1985, Phineas came to Maria as she was about to enter her office. She called her work space the fishbowl, because it was walled with glass except on the side facing the secretary, Mrs Hammond. That side was completely open. If she needed to be private, she would go into her father's office.

It was shortly before knock-off time, and Mrs Hammond was still there. Phineas was not dressed in his greasy workshop overall but in clean, casual clothes – very neat and trendy. Phineas really was rather spunky, Maria thought.

He approached her, waving an envelope as if he had won the lottery. His face beamed, but he said nothing as he handed it to her. It was addressed in neat cursive: *Mr and Mrs Neil Robertson, Milton, and Maria.*

"What is it, Phineas?"

"Open and see."

She tore open the envelope and slowly withdrew a bought invitation with a 1930s-style bridal couple embracing, the bride's veil flowing in the breeze. She looked at Phineas, puzzled. "Who's getting married?"

"Look." He pointed a long index finger at the invitation.

She opened the card and was surprised to discover that it was an invitation to the wedding of Phineas and Thandi, four weeks away.

Maria shrieked with excitement. "You and Thandi! Thandi!" She threw her arms around him. Some of the white head-office staff and Mrs Hammond looked on at this display by the white boss's daughter – no, the boss – and a black mechanic from one of the workshops. "When? I had no idea. I'm so happy for you both," she shrieked and kissed Phineas on the cheek. Mrs Hammond and others gaped.

"It's been a long time. Since the first time I saw her, actually."

"I can't wait to tell Mommy." Maria reached for the telephone and dialled. "Mom, Mom … yes, it's me. You'll never believe the good news here!"

"What, what?" Angelique said, picking up on the hint of excitement. Given Maria's tone, it must be fantastic news.

"Phineas and Thandi are getting married!"

There was a short silence, then a "Whaat?" uttered in a quiet voice.

But the shock in her response did not register with the exuberant Maria. "Yes! Phineas and Thandi, in four weeks."

"How do you know?"

"I've got the invitation here. We're all invited. Milton too. I've got to call him straight away so he can make plans to come over from England. I'll bring the invitation to you tonight."

Angelique sat down, stunned. What should she do? Should she do anything? The two were brother and sister and didn't know it. Surely someone had to do something. *And I didn't even know they were courting.*

"Neil … Neil …" She ran into the family room, where he was

watching the cricket on the TV. She looked around. They were alone. "Disaster. It's a disaster."

"What's a disaster?"

"Phineas and Thandi – they're getting married."

"Oh, shit!" He lifted the remote and switched the TV off. "When did this all happen?"

"I don't know. It's the first I've heard of it. I didn't even know they were together."

"Nor did I. Phineas certainly kept that rather quiet."

"So did Grace. I had no idea this was happening. What can we do? They can't get married. They're brother and sister. I'm sure they don't know."

"Of course not. Grace probably doesn't know either. But who expected this to happen?"

"Surely we must tell her."

"Must we, Angie? We're not supposed to know, and you've promised not to say anything."

"But that was before this happened! I can't keep this from Grace any longer."

"Why not?"

"No, Neil." Angelique frowned at him. "She has to know. Jerry's not here. He would have stopped it if he were around. We have to do the right thing."

He was still for a moment, in concentrated thought. "I suppose you're right, Angie. You need to tell her."

❖

"There must be a mistake, ma'am." Grace seemed taken aback when Angelique said someone had told her that Jerry was Phineas's father. But she didn't respond with the shock they expected. In fact she seemed to have made up her mind that the wedding should go ahead. "I'm sure it is fine for them to marry."

"Can't you see that you were not told, but this is the truth? They are brother and sister."

"No. I don't know who told you that, but it's not true. There is a mistake. I'm sure there is no problem for them to marry," she said obstinately.

"Grace! How can we confirm? We must be sure."

"I am sure, but I will check again. Thank you, ma'am. I know you mean well. I will check."

Grace turned and continued with the housework.

The next day Angelique stopped Grace as she was dusting the dining room table. "About our discussion yesterday. Have you checked?"

"I have asked and will have confirmation soon."

The next day Angelique enquired again, and was answered again in the same way. Every day for a week the same question was met with the same response.

"I must write to Saleena," Angelique said to Neil. "Grace is giving me the run-around. Something's not right. Saleena will be frank with me."

"No, Angie. You've told Grace. That's enough. Leave it to them to do what is correct. Maybe they don't mind a brother marrying his sister."

"Don't talk nonsense. Phineas and Thandi clearly still have no idea they are brother and sister. And Grace doesn't seem to want to believe it."

A few days later, two and a half weeks before the wedding, Grace approached Angelique. "Madam, I have confirmed. Phineas isn't Jerry's son."

"How do you know? Have you seen the birth certificate?"

"Ma'am, no. But I am sure." Grace looked at the floor when she spoke.

"How can you be sure?"

371

"I am, ma'am." She walked away.

Angelique wasn't satisfied. She wrote to Saleena and within ten days received a reply, in neat handwriting.

> *Dear Madam Angelique,*
>
> *I received your letter. The news about the couple is well known here, and everyone is very happy. Even Phineas's mother is very happy.*
>
> *I don't understand this. She has kept very quiet that Jerry is the father. Only we know. She say nothing about this since we first learn many, many years ago. It is a subject that no one speaks about. But Thomas and I are confused because we can't let brother marry sister. That is not right. Yet, when we mention this to her, she says it is no problem and we can relax.*
>
> *But we cannot relax, Miessies, and are very worried like you. We are coming with her to the wedding, and Jerry's big brother and his wife are also coming.*
>
> *I hope more hearts will not be broken. Please see what you can do.*
>
> *I greet you,*
> *Saleena*

This did not make Angelique feel any better. In fact, she felt decidedly ill. "Here, Neil. See. There *is* something fishy. Something's very wrong. What should we do?"

"I don't know. But Grace wouldn't be so naive."

"She's a mother. She's desperate."

The next day, Grace came into the kitchen while Neil and Angelique were having breakfast. It was three days before the wedding.

She stood there quietly, slightly behind Neil, but within full view of Angelique. She looked at Angelique.

"Morning, ma'am."

"Hello, Grace. How are you? Is there something you want to tell us?" Grace seemed a little fidgety, almost nervous. "Is anything the matter? I knew it. I *knew* it. The wedding can't go ahead. See, I told you." Angelique pointed at Neil.

"No, ma'am. It's not that."

"What's the matter, Grace?" asked Angelique.

Grace looked at Neil. "Master, Jerry would have wanted master to give Thandi away in church, if he was still alive."

"Oh, my God!" exclaimed Angelique. "How can he do that when they are brother and sister? Grace, that's very wrong, you know. I may stand up at the ceremony and object."

"Angie! Shut up!" barked Neil. He turned around to face Grace and said gently, "Are you sure it's okay?"

"Yes, master," she said quietly, avoiding Neil's gaze.

"Are you sure you want me to?"

"Yes, master."

"And Thandi and Phineas? What do they want?"

"They want it too."

"Okay, then. I'll do it for you and my late friend."

"Yes, but I'll still object. This cannot go ahead. It is unlawful, it is immoral, and it is wrong," said Angelique emphatically.

Just then Maria walked in with Milton, who had come for the wedding. She had picked him up from the airport. They all greeted him fondly.

He went up and embraced Grace, who still had a soft spot for him. "I'm so happy for you, Grace. Some good news at last for your family. It's about time you have some good news."

Then he looked around at his family and sensed the tension in the air. His mother sat with a deep vertical frown, fidgeting with a serviette. "What's wrong?"

"Tell Milton. He's a lawyer. He'll know what to do. Go on, Neil, tell him."

"Angie, shut up! It's none of your business."

"It is. And it's yours too. You're now acting for the father! *The* father! Of them *both*!"

"What's going on?" asked Milton.

"You don't want to know. And it's none of our business," said Neil.

"You do, and it is our business!" said Angelique.

"Master," said Grace quietly to Milton. "Madam has heard from someone that Jerry is Phineas's father. But I am told he isn't."

"Mom, who did you hear that from?"

"I can't say."

"Are they in love?"

"Yes," said Grace. "Very much."

"Are they happy?" asked Milton.

"Very happy," Grace and Maria both said at the same time.

"Well, unless you can prove they're brother and sister, what's the problem? And even if you could, are we going to stand in their way?" asked Milton.

Angelique held her head. "My God! Am I the only sane one here? At least we need to tell the couple. How can we go ahead with the marriage without them knowing? I'm going to object, and we'll see what the priest says."

"You will not, Angie. Or you'll be uninvited," said Neil.

Angelique noticed greying clouds break over the Saturday afternoon sky on the wedding day. Polished and gleaming for the occasion,

Neil's sleek silver BMW, now the bridal car, was dressed with ribbons over the bonnet.

Cheeky had come early in the morning and driven it to Alexandra to collect Thandi and Grace from their home. He brought them to the Robertson residence.

Angelique stood back when Thandi rose out of the car. Even through Angelique's disapproving eyes, Thandi looked magnificent in a colourful, flowing African costume.

"My God, Thandi! You look exquisite," said Neil when he saw her. Angelique said nothing.

Grace had told her that Phineas paid for the dress. She knew Grace was paying for the food. Maria had wanted to help pay some of the costs, but Phineas refused. The reception was to be nothing fancy, a simple spread of roast beef and vegetables in the hall adjacent to the church, for a small guest list. A church ceremony and a meal. That was all the couple wanted and could afford.

Angelique was adamant that she would make no contribution. She made it clear to everyone around her that she still felt the same way as she had when she heard the news of the wedding. The obstacle would resurface, she was sure, and no doubt at the worst possible moment. She didn't want to be seen to support this union.

When everyone was ready to depart for the church, Neil got into the bridal car with Thandi and her sister Angelique, who was her bridesmaid and wore a simple white dress. Each of them had a small bouquet of white carnations set in a cloud of delicate baby's breath.

Neil had told Angelique that Maria had helped behind the scenes. Apparently she had arranged with Jacob, the late Jerry's friend, who was still working for Top Star in Pretoria, to make sure that the guests arrived at the church first, in one of the staff buses.

Angelique, Grace and Maria were driven by Milton in Angelique's BMW, also dressed with bridal party ribbons. On the way there, Angelique expressed her objection again, alternating with a prayer in Greek for guidance to do the right thing and a threat to ruin the ceremony. "Saleena's going to object. And if she doesn't, I will," she said.

"Mom, stop that now," said Milton and Maria from time to time.

"I can't. I can't let your father carry on as though there isn't a problem."

She had such mixed feelings about this marriage. If only she didn't like Phineas and Thandi so much … or feel so close to Grace. It wasn't just that Grace had worked for her since the pharmacy days. Hadn't she been right there when Grace went through those difficult times? And hadn't Grace been a solid support for her when she lost George?

Angelique wanted to be loyal to her. Was it loyal to let this ceremony go ahead when the young couple had no awareness of what they were getting into?

"I can't bring myself to accept that brother and sister can marry without knowing of their relationship. They must be told. If they were my children, I would want them to know the truth," she said.

"You're sounding like a broken record," said Milton. "You have no right to destroy this ceremony."

"How can you say that? If I was in Thandi's shoes, I would want to know. You're supposed to be a lawyer."

"Yes, and as a lawyer, I say you can't prove anything."

Grace said nothing. Angelique could see she was nervous. She was hiding something.

Milton arrived before the bridal car, and they all alighted. They stood outside the church and turned to face the road, waiting for the bride to get there. Angelique looked around and saw Saleena, who frowned and shook her head as though she did not want to speak to Angelique. But Angelique went up to her. Saleena's eyes were red and moist. Angelique realised that she had been crying and was trying hard to hold back the tears.

"Saleena," she whispered. "Are you okay?"

"Yes."

"What will we do? This is wrong." She looked at Saleena, who turned to look in the direction of a long black Mercedes Benz limousine with its engine running. Angelique saw that the car had a government number plate. The windows were so heavily tinted that the occupants could not be seen. The mysterious limousine was parked at the side of the church and was partially concealed from the road.

The bridal car approached at a snail's pace. Angelique saw no other vehicles in the street as Neil's BMW drew up slowly in front of the church.

Saleena seemed to be about to say something to Angelique, but instead she walked towards the bridal car.

The doors of the Mercedes and BMW opened simultaneously. Neil alighted from the BMW. As he guided Thandi out of her seat, Angelique noticed a tall black man with a greying beard and heavy sunglasses approach. The man was dressed in a dark suit, dark shirt, and light-grey tie. He struck an imposing figure and was a little overweight. His gait was familiar to Angelique, but she couldn't place it.

He was surrounded by what appeared to Angelique to be a gang of black thugs, all thickset, their jackets bulging with badly concealed weapons.

Neil was looking at Thandi and didn't see the man swaggering towards him. Angelique panicked. He could have a gun. It was an assassination or kidnapping, she thought. Everything was happening in slow motion, like a bad dream – a nightmare – where something evil was going to happen, but she could make no sound when she tried to scream out and warn Neil.

The big man tapped Neil on the shoulder, and Angelique let out an incomprehensible cry, trying to alert Neil to the danger.

"Boss, I'll take over now," said a familiar voice casually as though offering to wash the car. A voice from the dead. Jerry's voice.

Neil turned around in disbelief. Angelique let out a high-pitched scream. She looked at Maria and Milton, hoping they would help, but they stood motionless, apparently confounded. Thandi stared with a mixture of shock and delight before uttering the words, barely above a whisper: "Daddy? Daddy, is it you? Is it really you?"

Jerry hugged her closely. Tears runnelled down his cheeks and were lost in his unfamiliar beard while Thandi's tears marked his shirt with a big wet patch.

Grace came up to Angelique and hugged her. "Madam, I couldn't say anything because Jerry isn't supposed to be here."

"How can he be alive?" Angelique said in a tone that was an octave or two higher than usual. She pointed as if she were looking at a ghost, still shocked by this scene that did not correspond with the reality she knew.

Grace held her arm. "He wasn't killed, ma'am. He wasn't in the house when the Levines were killed."

Jerry greeted his children one by one, then Eveleen, Cheeky and Cheeky's children. Saleena told Angelique there had already been a meeting with Phineas inside the church, and Jerry had given his blessing for the marriage. Jerry had also spent some time with Thomas and Saleena in the church. They were still coming to terms with the resurrection of their son and looked with awe at the church and the priest. Saleena was unable to control her emotions.

Jerry then greeted Neil with a close embrace. "Thanks, boss." That's all he could say without becoming emotional.

He then went to Angelique. "I wasn't killed, as you see. Something happened that saved my life. Yes, I was spared, but the others were killed."

"So why didn't you say so? Why all the secrecy about your

death – er, your non-death? And there was your wife and your family. They mourned for you."

"I had a lot of things to do for the cause. I had to fulfil my purpose."

"And your family?"

"I have already explained to Grace. We have been communicating for several years now."

"And Phineas?" she asked before Neil could stop her. "Is he your son, Jerry?"

"No, he's not. But that's for later."

In the church, Jerry led Thandi down the aisle as Angelique sat there, confused and disconcerted.

36

❧◆◇◈

Neil and Angelique were late risers the next morning. The lace curtains filtered the sunlight, which cast speckled shadows across the breakfast table. Neil sat down at the head of the table, his steaming coffee waiting for him.

Their kitchen intercom buzzed. He got up to speak into the wall-mounted speakerphone. He looked back at Angelique, who was cutting whole-wheat bread for toast. "Hello?" he said.

"Boss, it's me."

Neil pressed the remote to open the driveway gates. He went to the front door and stood at the entrance as the black limousine sailed up the driveway to the entrance and stopped a few feet from Neil.

Jerry and his bodyguards got out. "Wait outside. I'm safe here," he said to them.

He approached Neil, shook his hand, spun it shaking the thumbs, and repeated the handshake again, in a peaceful and friendly greeting.

Neil showed him in.

"Boss, this is the first time I've come in through the front door." Neil saw that Jerry couldn't resist making the point as he looked up the majestic timber stairwell and then through the large doorway to the formal lounge room. His gaze rested for a moment on the luxurious blue velvet cushions of the gold-edged couches, and then on the backdrop of heavy gold drapes. They walked past the copper lion and lioness statue which had pride of place on the entrance hall table.

"I never stopped you before. You always came to the back door, Jerry."

Neil showed him to the kitchen, where Angelique was seated. She remained sitting. "Hello, Jerry," she said without emotion.

"Morning," he responded.

Neil waved for him to sit down. Jerry sat on a green melamine chair at the kitchen table, directly opposite Angelique. Neil sat between them at the head of the table. "Well, what happened?"

His left elbow on the table, Jerry was turned slightly towards Neil. "Boss, I'm sorry I couldn't tell you earlier, but it was better for you not to know. The Boers would have only made you a target too." Jerry shook his head slowly. "How I escaped with my life that day, I really don't know. But I suspect someone didn't want me dead."

"Oh?"

"Yes. It's funny. I was going through the Levines' front gate, and this man stopped me. The way he stood in front of me and wouldn't let me move … I thought he wanted to hit me. But then he asked me politely for very strange directions. He wanted to know if there was a willow tree nearby, as he had to meet a friend at the willow in that suburb." Jerry paused, frowned, and shook his head again. "For directions to a willow tree?" he exclaimed and gazed at Neil.

Neil sipped his coffee.

Angelique sat motionless, her arms crossed, but she stared at Jerry as he continued.

"I have a soft spot for willows, boss." He ignored Angelique. "There was a cluster of them at the farm where I grew up where I passed many hours. And I knew there was a willow tree just up the road and around the corner from the Levines. It's an oasis, and I sometimes spent time lying under it. It was the only one that was near the Levine house. So I walked up the road to show him this willow sticking up above the roofs. And then the explosion went off."

Both Jerry's elbows were on the table. He looked down at his clasped hands, fingers entwined. He cleared his throat. "I was safe, but poor Jonathan and Sarah ... they had no chance. It was a big blast. There was nothing left of them." His voice was soft. "They were so good to me."

Angelique's eyes shifted from Jerry to the table between them.

"Good heavens, Jerry!" said Neil. "That's awful. But ... good God! That was lucky for you." He sat back in his chair.

"Well. You could call it luck. I wasn't sure then."

"How did you survive in Mozambique? It was a Portuguese colony back then. The rebels there – FRELIMO – they wouldn't have had time or energy for you."

"The Portuguese were distracted by their own battles. But I didn't stay in Mozambique all the time." Jerry sat back with a smirk. "I met up with ANC operatives in Zambia, Kenya, and Libya. We had support in many countries, you know. I even went to Sweden. And I met with trade unionists in London. I moved around a lot."

"And no one knew who you really were?"

"I grew a beard and assumed a new name. I also went grey."

"So why did you go back to Mozambique?"

"After Mozambique's independence, we had support from there too. I'd been gone a while, so I thought being close to South Africa could give me a chance to get in and out of the country and maybe see my family. That was wishful thinking," he added with a chuckle. "I hadn't been there long when the safe house was bombed. I realised I couldn't put Grace and the children in danger."

"So, the few years became more," said Angelique with a frown. "And all this time your family thought you were dead."

Jerry looked at her squarely, paused and said, "I am accountable to *them* for that."

Neil felt embarrassed at Angelique's response. He was quick to ask Jerry, "Do you think the government planted the bomb?"

"I have no doubt about it. The security police has hit squads with orders from high up the chain. When we take over, we will find the evidence. You'll see."

"You can't be sure," challenged Angelique, still frowning.

"I am sure." Jerry's voice was emphatic.

"Why didn't you tell everyone you were alive?"

"I thought of that. But, you know, I heard the radio reports almost immediately. They said I was dead. Killed by the ANC. Before they even checked the bodies." He looked ahead of him and pointed his right index finger towards the window behind Angelique. "I knew then that this had to be government agents. I hid in the house across the road with a friend of mine. He had a radio. They announced I was dead." He was speaking louder again. "I thought maybe it's better that they think that. It will be easier to go underground. So I took on a new name and did just that. The ANC knew, but the government didn't, and I've been safe."

"Well, blow me down!" Neil glanced at Jerry and then at Angelique. She fidgeted with a napkin.

"Just as well, because I'm part of the team negotiating a new South Africa with the government." He pushed his chair back. "And guess who is very high up in the government team?"

"Who?"

"The Honourable Minister Marius Strydom." Jerry slapped his right thigh. "He knew that I wasn't dead. That thing with the willow tree. It goes back to the farm. He saved me."

"Really?"

"Yes. And when I saw him recently, he said to me, 'Hello, Jerry.

How is my client? Keeping away from the railway tracks?'" Jerry paused. "He knew all along."

Angelique got up and refilled the kettle.

"He's foxy. That's for sure," said Neil.

"Yes. He is," Jerry replied.

"So, Jerry. What's this about negotiating a new South Africa?" Neil asked.

Angelique sat down and listened while the water heated.

"Well. I am one of many on our side. I'm a small player, you know. There are many giants on our side. Mandela is the big lion. There's no doubt about it. On the government side, they're confused." Jerry chuckled. "Marius is quite strong. And it's funny. He has his head screwed on the right way. I wouldn't have thought so with his father's strong influence. But there you go."

Neil got up. "You know he found Cheeky for us when you left?" As he spoke, he placed his cup next to the kettle and extracted another cup and saucer from the cupboard. He stood next to the kettle, leaning against the kitchen counter. "He got Cheeky released."

"Oh, I didn't know. So he was the one who did that." Jerry looked thoughtful. "Anyway, he is a strong persuader and is having plenty of influence in the background. And if there's a problem in the talks, we meet privately. It's odd. I'd say we've picked things up where we left off thirty years ago. We talk as though we're in the veld, chatting about how to trap the dassie. Marius told me he recognised me when he took the railway line case. But he said he wanted to leave it to me to make the first move. He understood why I didn't want to reveal my identity. He's a pretty good poker player. Better than me. I've learned that now, so I think I'm getting smarter where it counts."

Neil pointed to the extra cup and saucer. "Coffee or tea, Jerry?"

"Another first in your house. Tea, thanks. White, with two sugars."

Neil poured boiling water over a tea bag and placed the milk carton and sugar bowl in front of Jerry. "Help yourself." He then placed a fresh pot of plunger coffee between himself and Angelique and sat down. "Why all the secrecy? Why haven't you come out about the fact that you're alive and part of the ANC team?"

"Well, that's where it gets difficult. Marius tells me there are a few Boers who are out of control and want me dead. He says he can't guarantee my safety yet. That's why I have a government car and bodyguards. They think Swanepoel is one of them. I believe you know Swanepoel. He was the one on Sipho's case. Apparently he has also lost someone through the war. Up near Angola." He extracted the tea bag, placed it on the saucer, and filled the cup with two heaped teaspoons of sugar and some milk. He stirred slowly. "There are others too. Marius says they're trying to identify and neutralise them, but haven't yet. I said to Marius, 'I *will* go to my daughter's wedding.' I told him I wouldn't hide away for that. Until now, only Grace has known about me."

Angelique placed some of Mrs Kalonides's icing sugar-coated kourambiedes in front of Jerry, together with a cake plate and a paper napkin. "How long has Grace known?" she asked.

"About six months after the bomb. I got word to her. But she couldn't tell anyone. I didn't want anyone to know. It wasn't safe for her or the family to know. I was better dead, for their safety.

"The worst thing for me was to keep the truth from my parents. I have been an embarrassment for them since I hit Marius. I hid the business about the railway murder charge from them. I had been sending them money and news but had to stop after the bomb. They must have felt I was truly lost to them. But they were never far from my thoughts. My father's lesson that I have royal blood inspired me too. This gave me a kind of belief that I was chosen. Then Sipho's death was a message to me that I had to do something."

Angelique nodded slowly, as if in thought.

But it was Neil who spoke next. "Did Marius know you weren't killed?"

"Of course he did. Marius said he got wind of the security operation and heard my name. He hasn't admitted that he saved me. That would be like treason for him. But who else would arrange for someone to ask for directions to a willow tree? A willow tree! Our favourite place on the farm. He knows I know, but he won't admit anything. The bomb was meant for me. When I think about it now, somehow ... that man who diverted me ..." Jerry shook his head again. "I don't know. He didn't just ask me. He stopped me. I told you I thought he was going to push me. It seemed he was looking for trouble. But when he asked me for those silly directions, I relaxed. I stopped, walked back a bit and showed him where to go. Then boom. He ran off when I turned and looked back at the house. I never saw him again."

"They were saying it was infighting in the ANC," said Neil.

"Bullshit! Sorry." Jerry looked at Angelique sitting opposite him. "Nonsense. That makes me so angry! Marius has told me it was them – the security forces. The truth will come out one day."

"It is very intriguing," Neil commented. "Whew. That was a close shave. So now what?"

"I'm sorry about using you to lead Thandi to the church. We had to throw them off the scent. I was worried they would come. You know they saw you leave the house."

"Who saw me?"

"These other people who want me dead. Swanepoel and his gang. He was in your street when you left the house. They know of me now and are seeking me out. I'm a target. Marius had them followed, but they went away soon after you left your house in your car." The teacup seemed to shrink when he lifted it with both hands and took a long sip. He exhaled loudly and dabbed his wet lips with the napkin.

"What? You mean Marius had spies on the people spying on you?"

"Yes. We think they wanted to make sure I didn't appear at your house and get in the car with my daughter. They expected me to turn up." He took one of the crescent-shaped biscuits and looked at it.

"Well, well. So many people spying on me … and I had no idea," said Neil. He shivered at the thought. "Just as well you didn't turn up here. We could have had a real shootout, what with your bodyguards, Swanepoel and his spies, and Marius's spies."

"Don't worry. I wasn't coming out if it wasn't safe for my daughter." He put the biscuit on his plate.

Angelique piped up. "So, Jerry." She paused and looked him in the eyes. "Is Phineas your son?"

"No." He didn't call her Angelique or madam, but his eyes engaged with hers, showing they had nothing to hide.

"So why was I told you are?"

"Who told you?"

"I'm not saying. I have made a promise." She tapped one of the kourambiedes on her cake plate to shed some of the icing sugar and took a small bite.

"Okay. I would like to keep this secret. It's a very sensitive situation, you see." Copying her, he tapped his biscuit on the plate. "Well, it's like this. Phineas's mother and I thought we loved each other. But Petrus, my older married brother, had liked her and … well … you know … they weren't careful. He couldn't say it was him. He was promised to be married to Harriet. I agreed with him and Rachel that I would accept the blame among the families because it wasn't a big deal to me. My parents were okay with this … mistake … coming from me. They would have been shattered if they'd found out it was Petrus's child. And so would Harriet, his wife-to-be."

He took a small bite, looked at the remaining biscuit, held it up and looked at Angelique. "Mmm, nice." He sipped his tea again and continued, "I was angry with Petrus. Rachel began to like me, but then I had to leave the farm. Petrus wrote to me when they found out Rachel was expecting. I agreed I wouldn't say it was Petrus. That would cause too many problems on the farm. I suppose we all thought I would come back to her. But I never promised her." He waved the hand with the cookie in it. "They kept it quiet, so people think it's me." He shoved the rest of the cake in his mouth.

Angelique sat in silence as the cookie crumbled in his mouth and he swallowed it with a satisfying gulp of his tea. Then he licked his lips. "I don't think anyone else knows who Phineas's real father is. Only his mother, Petrus, and me – we're the only ones who know. No one else. Oh … and now you do. And I told Grace recently – after you opened your mouth – and my parents just before the wedding. They thought it was me, but it isn't."

Angelique hid inside her cup as she drank the coffee.

"The people at the farm must be stupid, because the resemblance to me and my brother is there, isn't it? Phineas is handsome and cute." He chuckled and looked at Angelique. "Just like me … like I was. Good-looking, isn't he?" He wore his big white smile as he teased Angelique.

"Jerry. You're a real actor, aren't you?" she responded.

"But so is my brother. That's who Phineas really looks like. Not me. I was more worried that he might fall in love with one of my brother's kids! Any girls there would have been his sisters. But they're all boys, so we were lucky."

Angelique was cross. The agony she had gone through leading up to the wedding was still raw. "My God, Jerry! You could've told us."

"Why? It's none of your business. You wanted to get involved."

"Really? We thought Neil was going to be jailed for giving Thandi away to her brother!"

"Yes. Sorry about that." Jerry looked at Neil.

"Sorry. Sorry! That worried me so much I didn't sleep for four weeks." Angelique wasn't going to make it easy for Jerry.

He shook his head ruefully. "Poor Grace asked me a hundred times in the last four weeks to tell you. She was getting messages through to me, and we met a couple of times. Every time you asked her, I received an urgent message. But I couldn't break my promise to my brother, and had to tell you personally. That's why I came here today. I knew I owed you an explanation. I hope you will understand. I had to come and explain myself. And by the way, I think that Swanepoel knows I'm here. There was a car parked outside. I've now blown my cover. They saw me come in."

37

"Jeremiah, I can't guarantee your safety. You must keep a low profile while I try to find out what they're brewing. I'm confused because they tell me that the security police aren't after you, but there are rogue elements who have an agenda of their own. I can't prove it, but Swanepoel is one of them. You must be careful," pleaded Marius.

"But Swanepoel knows where I am. He could have killed me."

"Yes, exactly. He must know we've got him under surveillance too. Him I can control. I know where he is. But there are others – not even in the security forces – who see it as their mission to stop the change that we have begun. The Afrikaner Weerstandsbeweging, for example. They're not very organised, but their people are fired up. Some are also motivated by the fact that they have had family killed on the borders and in the ANC attacks, and they blame leaders like you.

"You have seen the footage of people who think we're still living in the fifties and sixties. They can't accept the change that will come. I'm getting Swanepoel's cabinet minister to transfer him to the Cape for your sake. I want him far away from you."

"Good. I'll be glad never to see him. The way he treated my family, from Sipho to today … If I see him, I'll kill him. I'm telling you."

"Listen here, man. He's not the only one looking for you. There are many more who will want to see you dead if you go public. I'll have to give you a bodyguard bigger than the pope's, and you still won't be safe. Listen to me. It is better to keep your head down. Don't make statements. Don't give interviews. Make sure you get a good job in the government later. But, for now, keep your big black head down!"

Jerry laughed. Marius was baiting him with the racist taunt that recalled their earlier closeness. "Listen, you bloody boor! You can't say those things anymore."

"I don't, except to idiots who I care for … and who won't listen to me."

"I'm back now. I am part of the process. I have a future and ambitions after free elections. I need to have a profile, and I'm not giving in to those Nazis."

"What do you mean, Jeremiah? What do you have in mind?"

"Thanks for your advice and your concern. I am not a criminal who needs to hide. I am not the one who has done wrong. I will look after myself. But Jerry Ngubeni is back in town!"

That day Jerry issued a press release saying that Jerry Ngubeni was alive, had returned to the country, and would hold a press conference at three o'clock. He knew it would be in time for the evening news broadcasts, and he wanted to be the headline.

He stood on the steps of Top Star Motors HQ with Grace, Thandi, Phineas, Sylvester, young Angelique, and Maria at his side. A barrage of journalists stood in the square below the stairs.

"There were evil forces in the government who tried to get me killed, but I managed to avoid the bomb with my name on it. I have since then worked hard in Africa and Europe to advance our freedom. Yes, I made contact with anti-apartheid movements in many countries and spoke to many governments, trade unions and banks to step up the sanctions. This was necessary to make the apartheid government see reason. For the good of the whole country. We now see this has worked and reason will prevail. The country *will* change. I want to be part of that change." He waved his right index finger in the air to emphasise the point. "I want to live where we can all have the same opportunities in life. This won't happen overnight, but I want to help make it happen. In a peaceful way. We all need each other now." He held his hands out as though about to lift the heavy air between him and his audience.

The cameras clicked, popped, flashed and whirred. Microphones were thrust at him. Over twenty journalists asked questions at the same time. He raised his hands. "One at a time. One at a time. Yes, you over there." He pointed to a black woman journalist.

"What do you mean 'you're back'? What are you going to do now?"

"I'll take up my position as secretary general of the union I represented before I left. I will serve the interest of the workers of this country."

The loud voice of a white male journalist swamped all other questions. "Were you involved in the bomb attack in Pretoria? The one at the army recruitment office?"

He held his hands up, seeking silence. A hush filled the square before he answered. "Let me say this loud and clear. And I want every black person who is asked questions like this to give the same answer." He paused for effect and attention as the whole audience went silent. "Until the Boers and their collaborators account to us for everything they did to attack our people, we don't need to account for what we did to resist them."

An Afrikaans journalist stood up quickly. "Did you intend to kill Minister Strydom?"

"You heard my answer."

"Are you in contact with Minister Strydom?"

"Ask him that question. He has my permission to answer it."

"How did you avoid the bomb with your name on it?"

"I don't really know. But I think a guardian angel who was with me when I was young was there too, somewhere."

"How do you feel about the death of your son Sipho?"

He froze. He tried to open his mouth to say something and couldn't.

Grace stepped forward. "We still grieve for Sipho. It's a tragedy for South Africa that he and many like him will not live to see the changes that are coming. That's all. Thank you. Thank you."

She shunted Jerry into the building.

Neil's empire was beginning to suffer the effect of the political uncertainty in the country.

Neil tried all sorts of measures to maintain some profit, but his overheads were high. He soon realised that nothing he had done was working. Maria had also brought up the decrease in sales in discussions with him. What could they do?

His business hadn't been under this kind of pressure since he bought Top Star from mevrou Van Tonder all those years ago. Thirty, wasn't it? Even though he borrowed the full price then, he'd felt more relaxed about that first investment, knowing he could improve the business and that it could pay for itself. Now the future was not so clear.

He had been forced to risk everything, even the family home when his bank took a mortgage over the Houghton house.

He didn't sleep much now. It was pure luck if he managed three hours a night. That wasn't enough, and he felt tired the whole day. Unable to relax in the evening, he paced this way and that, in the house and then in the garden.

Angelique got irritable. "Don't do that, Neil. Sit down and watch the TV."

This exasperated him even more. He felt he couldn't burden her with his financial problems. He could see that she was battling to deal with her own thoughts about George, Milton, and her parents who seemed to depend on her more and more. But her reaction to his inability to be calm aggravated his anxiety and restlessness.

"What's the matter, Neil? You can't carry on like this. You have to sleep, you know."

He and Angelique weren't working together to overcome their sadness. He was fully aware of this, but the knowledge made no difference. It seemed they couldn't help feeding off each other's gloom. They even looked for more reason to worry.

"I'm concerned about Maria. She's not even looking for a husband. You need to speak to her. That's what my father did."

"And you listened?"

"That's not the point. Show an interest in her future."

Neil didn't eat well and increased his smoking, a habit he had once almost got rid of. He lost weight. His eyes were sunken in, and the skin around them went black. His cheeks sagged and he started stooping, looking a foot shorter. His clothes hung loosely as though made for someone else. He shuffled around like an old man.

He didn't tell Angelique that his blood pressure had increased, aggravated by his stress and increased smoking. He said nothing about the pains up his left arm.

On a hot and humid January night, the high-altitude air of Johannesburg felt heavy and oppressive. Although he went to bed just before midnight, Neil couldn't sleep. He got up, put his dressing gown on, and paced the house. The whole world was pressing down on him, and a vice gripped his chest and was forcing his lungs closed.

The huge, airy house seemed like a prison. It was closing in on him. The air felt stale, thick and soupy. When he tried to inhale deeply, he couldn't. *I have to get out.*

He disengaged the security system for the house, flung the front door open and stepped out into the garden. The trees seemed to be falling in on him.

He tried to take in air. But even the outside felt close and stuffy. Thick grey clouds, gathering like a stifling fog, smothered his nose and mouth. He thought he inhaled the stale smell of his father, of his bitter pipe tobacco. It was suffocating.

Now the very heavens were invading his space, invading his lungs, invading his mind.

❖

At just before seven in the morning, Angelique heard screams outside. The kitchen door banged shut, and the maid Priscilla shouted, "Madam! Madam! It's the baas. He is sick. Come, come. Call an ambulance."

Angelique was already out of bed and looking for Neil in the en suite.

She ran down the stairs, grabbed the kitchen telephone, and dialled for the ambulance. "Priscilla. Here, take the telephone and explain what you saw carefully to the person who answers. Tell them to send an ambulance, and give them the correct address. Here. I'm going to see to the master."

She ran outside and saw Neil lying on his side, groaning, one leg twitching.

"Neil, what happened?"

He mumbled something, and she saw he was drooling and couldn't talk. She realised it must be a stroke.

"He is cold and wet. Get a few blankets and two pillows, quickly," she said to the other maid. "Neil. You'll be okay. You passed out. Are you in pain?"

He groaned and mumbled unintelligibly.

"If you're in pain, blink."

He opened his eyes wider.

"I can't see any injury. But we won't move you, just in case. An ambulance is coming." She said to a gardener, "Tell Priscilla to phone Maria to come here now. She's at her flat."

Angelique held Neil carefully, trying to warm him without moving him. She could see his eyes were confused. They were open. They looked around and fixed on her. He looked vulnerable and scared. He moved his lips to speak, but she couldn't understand his mumbling. He tried to move, but only his right leg twitched.

Definitely a stroke, she thought. "Your breathing seems okay. That's a good sign," she said, masking her concern and encouraging him. "You fell, Neil."

"No! No!" he grunted and then repeated a sound that she realised was his attempt at saying "Stroke … stroke … stroke."

"Yes, love. I think you have had a mild stroke. Keep still. Here are some blankets. We'll keep you comfortable until the ambulance arrives. It's on its way."

A tear coursed down his cheek as he looked at her, his blue eyes pleading.

38

Angelique sat at Neil's bedside in a private ward at an exclusive clinic in Johannesburg. He slept for hours, with brief, intermittent periods of waking up and grunting. Talk was impossible. His very limited movement made him bedridden – he was able to move only his right leg.

Neil mumbled unintelligibly in his sleep and became teary when awake. Angelique held his hand continually, making sure he knew she was there when he was conscious. The clinic brought a bed into his ward for her. She insisted on being at his bedside twenty-four hours a day.

Angelique dismissed Maria's concern about her.

"I must be here for him. This is when he needs me. You look after the business. My place is here."

"We'll get a nurse to sit here if you want. You need to go home and rest. We don't want you to get sick here too."

"No. I want to be here if he calls for me. I just couldn't live with myself if he called for me and I wasn't here. Or … worse still. No, Maria. I'm staying here until he comes home."

The doctors told her that he could recover from the stroke, but they could not say whether there would be any permanent incapacity. "There may be damage, Mrs Robertson. Sometimes it affects one side of the body. Sometimes movement comes back. It is impossible to predict how far he will recover. All we can do now is wait and see."

Angelique skimmed through the newspapers, seeing little more than the headlines about protests, unrest and threats to the peace talks. She wasn't interested.

Nothing had been revealed to Angelique about the growing cracks in the Robertson empire as she kept up her vigil next to Neil's bed.

Grace, who had stopped working for the Robertsons upon Jerry's return, visited her at the hospital frequently.

The two women spoke about the past as they sat in the darkened ward, huddled together.

They discussed Jerry's father, Thomas, who had recently passed away. "No-one really knew how old he was," said Grace. "He never suffered any illness. Saleena found him lying on his back next to the fire outside their hut, with his eyes open as though admiring his beloved sky."

They reminisced about Jerry and Neil, hoping the two husbands could remain friends for life – and would have many years to do so. The discussion was wishful, given Neil's semiconscious condition in the bed next to them.

They shed tears again about Sipho and George. How they missed them. Comparing notes, they discovered that they both thought of their dead boys every day. They thought about what the boys could have been – the kind of men they would have made. The mothers knew their sons and were convinced that they would have been good husbands and good fathers. How unfair life was!

And they spoke of the uncertain future as they felt South Africa boiling around them.

"We have each other," said Grace, optimistic that things would improve for her, Jerry and her children.

"Yes, we do have each other," responded Angelique, less hopeful about Neil and whether the country could be held together.

Throughout the days when Grace and Angelique were sharing their thoughts in this way, the bright Top Star, a business they and their families had relied upon for decades, flickered and almost went out.

Maria knew she had good cause for concern about the Top Star business. Revenues dropped by 70 per cent. It was from these revenues that a living was provided for the families of the three thousand staff. Many of them were no longer needed and would have to be made redundant to keep the business afloat.

Here, Maria's thoughts went to Phineas. From behind the tinted office windows, she observed how the black staff looked up to him. This was partly because he was Jerry Ngubeni's son-in-law, but mainly because he had proven himself to be astute, confident and willing to speak up for his co-workers. They trusted him and followed his lead at workers' meetings. They had made real gains in pay rates and working conditions under his leadership.

Many of the men were much older than Phineas. But then she realised that he exploited this farm-boy image. He became one of them with his childlike smile and non-threatening approach. She detected that some even felt a fatherly duty to look after him.

Like many who'd grown up on the farms, Phineas had known poverty and lack of opportunity, and fully appreciated the value of having a job.

It was now Maria's hope that Phineas would understand the pressures of the business and that he would help.

"So you see, Phineas, I have shown you the full picture, and it's not good. The drop-off in sales has put everything under pressure."

"You want us to take a pay cut. What about you?"

They were seated at the boardroom table in Neil's large office. He put a spreadsheet down.

"I won't draw my salary for six months."

"What about the properties? You can sell them."

"Who will buy? You can see what's happening on the streets, in the newspapers. Until there is peace and the first proper election, no one will buy anything. Let's hope that Mandela can keep the country together. Otherwise, we'll lose the lot."

"But why cut *our* wages? Why the black workers first?"

"I'm doing the same to management. Everyone will take a cut. We must all take a risk for the new South Africa."

Phineas leaned back in thought. "This is the time for risk," said Phineas. He paused. "This is the time for history."

After some haggling, she struck a deal with Phineas that she could take to the bank to demonstrate that the business could survive if the bank extended the loans.

Maria prepared a handsome briefing package for Top Star's bankers. It was carefully crafted to show the long-term impressive performance of the group. She made an appointment to see the new manager who had recently been allocated the family's accounts.

Maria went to see him with the group's senior accountant. She wore a power-black pinstriped dress-suit with a white, collared blouse. She introduced herself.

"Pleased to meet you, Miss Robertson. Francis Harvey's the name." He did not offer his hand in greeting, but stood with his left hand in his pocket and his right hand clutching a folder that bulged with papers.

"Pleased to meet you, Mr Harvey."

He sat down, and she followed uninvited.

Mr Harvey looked straight at her. "Well, Miss Robertson. I have looked through the accounts for your family and the business, and it doesn't present a good picture. In fact, you are very much in the red." He spoke without hesitation.

"Mr Harvey, the borrowings are small compared to the assets of the group. As you can see, the projected income is easily able to service the debt."

"Projected income? South Africa may have seen all its good days, Miss Robertson."

"The way we see it, whatever happens in the future, more people will want to buy cars in South Africa." Maria tried to remain dispassionate.

"So, what's the problem? Why do you need more money now?"

"Well, Mr Harvey. I would like to retain our staff and not create unemployment. My father has been a visionary entrepreneur. Three thousand families rely upon the business and we must do our best to keep them on. I—"

"That's neither visionary nor entrepreneurial," he interrupted. "That's simply stupid and suicidal. That business will burn in the chaos of the 'new' South Africa, Miss Robertson, and your family with it." He mockingly drew the quotation marks in the air.

Maria felt her face heating in anger. She cleared her throat and drew shallow breath. "With respect, my optimism is a show of faith and commitment to the future of this country."

"We cannot bank on your visionary, entrepreneurial family's faith and commitment, Miss Robertson." His flat facial expression remained constant.

Maria sat forward and this time drew a deep breath. "Mr Harvey, we want to invest in our staff as an investment for the future."

"That's no investment, Miss Robertson. That's expense. As for investing in the future – well, what future?"

"Your bank is not at risk, Mr Harvey. The buildings are worth much more than the loans."

"I'm afraid that's not good enough. You see, your father is a dishonest man. I know that for a fact, and I will refuse any extension of the loans." He leaned his elbows on the table. Maria could see his right cheek being pushed out by his tongue. "Not only that, I must thank you for coming to see me, as I had intended to come and see you. I have discussed your accounts with the board, and the board has decided to call up all your loans. You have sixty days to pay – otherwise the bank will foreclose. Read this letter. It explains everything. Good day, Miss Robertson."

He got up and walked out, leaving them with a sealed envelope.

As they drove back to the office, the accountant, who had been with Neil for many years, broke the silence. "You know, I think I've heard the name Francis Harvey before. Some years ago, he was with Austin when they decided to give a dealership to someone else. Your father was very angry and said something about Harvey trying to steal some nuts at a bar that he used to work at. There's clearly a history here that we're not fully aware of. Harvey has a vendetta against your family."

"That's all very interesting, but what are we going to do about it? I can't see any other bank funding the lot. Let's face it. We owe the bank a lot of money."

When she got back to Top Star, Phineas was waiting. She took him to her father's office, shut the door, and explained the details of the discussion, including Harvey's comments that South Africa had had its best days. Phineas stopped her. "Repeat that. What did he say?"

"I think he may have said 'South Africa has seen all its good days.' And that our land and our family would 'burn in the chaos of the new South Africa'."

"Excellent, Maria. We got them. Listen to me. You will have your loans."

A week later, Maria took a call from Mr Harvey. "Miss Robertson. I have something I need to discuss with you urgently. Will you be available tomorrow morning?"

"Umm. What time do you have in mind?"

"Shall we say ten o'clock? I'll come to your office."

"Oh. Are you sure?"

"Yes."

"I see. That will be fine." She knew she had no prospect of repaying the bank's loans and wondered whether Harvey was coming to see which office he would occupy after the bank foreclosed.

The next day, Mr Harvey marched into the head office of Top Star Motors in Rosebank and asked for Miss Robertson. Mrs Hammond led him into Mr Robertson's office, where Maria was waiting. He stood erect and glared at her coolly. She was apprehensive but didn't show her nervousness. She was ready for him to sit in Neil's chair, request her to leave, and say the bank was taking over.

She had Mr Landau on standby in the staff lunchroom in case she needed help.

"Good morning, Mr Harvey. How are you?" She extended her hand to shake his.

He sat down uninvited and without shaking her hand. He stared at her. Without smiling, he placed his leather attaché case on Neil's desk and took out a wad of papers. "Miss Robertson, the bank has reviewed the proposal that you submitted and is now willing to accept your application. And the board has agreed to remove the mortgage over your father's house."

"Sorry. I'm not sure I understood that, Mr Harvey. Could you repeat that please?"

"Miss Robertson, please don't play games with me. I have said very clearly that you get what you asked for and more." He flinched as if in pain when he said this. He avoided her gaze and shuffled the documents officiously. "I am informed that the bank is taking a positive outlook on the future of South Africa and that the best days are still to come. I have been told to tell you that the bank would not want businesses like Top Star to burn down in flames before the new South Africa is born. We also feel that now is the time to support your staff and not lay people off. The bank wants to make sure no jobs are lost."

"Well. Thank you, Mr Harvey. This is good news. Please leave the forms there, and I will arrange for them to be signed. Good day, Mr Harvey."

He got up and, without any farewell to Maria, stormed out.

She called for Mr Landau and Phineas to be brought to Neil's office. Landau was there within minutes, and Phineas walked in about ten minutes later in his work clothes. She was sitting at the conference table in Neil's office with a bottle of champagne and three glasses.

"Phineas, I don't know what you did, but we just got more than we asked for."

"I know."

"You know?"

"Yes."

"Why didn't you tell me?"

"I wanted Harvey to come here and tell you himself."

"What do you mean? What did you do?"

"Well, I arranged for the secretary-general of our union and his assistant to meet the chairman of the bank. Jerry and I explained to Mr Coetzee what his staff were telling its customers. We said it doesn't look too good – when his bank intends to be part of the future of the country – to have a senior manager telling customers that the good days are over and that their families and assets will burn.

"We also said that our union has its funds with his bank too. And we expect to have a director on the board soon. He was rather taken aback, you could say. We told him that the bank had refused to extend the loans of a major employer of our members. The bank appeared to be prepared to put the jobs and the livelihood of three thousand families at risk because the bank had taken the view that South Africa has seen its best days. That was very un-new South Africa, we suggested."

Phineas paused theatrically and took a sip of the champagne.

"You would have been proud of me when I rattled off the financial summary of the Top Star group we went through the other day. I could see even Jerry nearly fell off his chair. I ended with a statement like this: 'In short, Mr Coetzee, the properties give you a cushion of over several million.' Then I went in for the kill."

"How?"

"I asked him, 'What car do you drive, Mr Coetzee?' Guess what he said?"

"No! He didn't."

"Yes. He drives a BMW. Of course I knew that before I asked the question. And guess what else I said?"

"I don't know. What?"

"I turned to Jerry and asked, 'Mr Ngubeni, what car will you buy in the next two years?' He was quick and said, 'BMW.' I said, 'Me too. That means, Mr Coetzee, that business will get better for Top Star, wouldn't you say?'"

Maria burst out laughing.

"Guess what he said then."

She shook her head.

"He said, 'What is your name, young man? We may need you for our board. Please send me your CV.' Well, at first I was hopeful, but my CV won't stack up, so that's the end of that."

"I'm not so sure, Phineas. I'll help you write one. I could easily make you look better than the governor of the Reserve Bank."

39

"We celebrate a man who built an empire from the smell of an oily rag, who took me in when I was hiding from my enemy, and who gave me a job when I was down and out. Not only was he my boss, he became my counsellor when I strayed. He forced me to make the best decision in my life, and the result is the family I have today. He was there for them in very difficult times. Of course, I counselled him too, and that led to his lovely family. He is a man who understands people and brings out the best in them. He did so in me – at least *I* think so ..." The gathering of Neil's family and friends laughed.

Jerry went on, "Please raise your glasses to my friend, Neil." They all sang "For He's a Jolly Good Fellow" and cheered Neil three times.

Neil turned beetroot-red with embarrassment, the one side of his face smiling, the other drooping. He waved in appreciation with one hand; his other hung loose over Angelique's supporting shoulder.

It was his sixtieth birthday. He hadn't wanted a celebration. What was there to celebrate? He felt half a man. Having survived the stroke, he was determined not to be like his father, a prisoner in a wheelchair. At times he tried to will his heart to stop.

When he realised he would not die, he doggedly struggled through the rehabilitation, pushing himself harder than his medical team requested. He refused to lie in bed or sit in his chair. He walked the corridors of the clinic, holding the wall with his good hand and dragging the lame half along. He ignored the pain caused by the tightening of the muscles on his weak side. Frustrated by the fact that he couldn't be understood, he practised speaking in front of the mirror, then recorded his grunts and played them back.

Images of his father haunted him. *I will not be like this forever.*

He regained the partial use of his bad leg and hobbled on both feet, the one pointing inwards. Angelique could understand him, but he preferred not to speak in public, leaving the conversation to her. She never left his side.

At his request, he was discharged from the rehabilitation clinic before they wanted to let him go. He put himself on a strict exercise regime at home and spent hours and hours with a speech therapist. He struggled to eat and lost more weight. He had his clothes tailored so that they fitted without appearing to hang. He refused to accept the sickly pale face he emerged from the clinic with. Instead he meandered through the Houghton grounds and sat on a bench in the sun, topless, so that – apart from his drooping eye and bent mouth – he looked tanned and healthy.

He came to realise that there *was* something to live for. Then he cast his thoughts back to his injured father, a war hero and war victim. How could he have abandoned him when he needed him most? Of course he should have supported his father. He *could* have made a difference.

And what about George? It suddenly struck Neil how selfish he was when he felt it was better for his son to die than to live. Even though a part of him knew he had no influence over George's death, he could not bring himself to believe that he was blameless. His shame tormented him.

His stroke was not punishment enough for his callous past.

These thoughts were not far from his mind as waiters served

cocktails and snacks from laden trays to almost two hundred guests spread around the pool patio of his Houghton home. But Neil was not ready to speak at his birthday party. Maria gave the thank-you speech while he stood next to her, in profile, his good side facing the audience and the photographer. Afterwards, Neil circulated amongst the gathering, shaking hands with deliberate firmness, using his strong hand, patting guests on the shoulder and nodding.

He was patting Marius Strydom when Jerry walked over to them and held out his hand to Mrs Strydom. "I'm Jerry, Mrs Strydom."

Neil noticed she hesitated and then shook Jerry's hand. "I know who you are, Mr Ngubeni. Marius has told me a bit about you."

"All good, I hope."

"Well, let's put it this way," she said, and paused. "We know change must take place. My husband says we can trust you. I pray he is right."

"Your husband is a very clever man," said Jerry with a smile.

Neil nodded at them and shuffled on.

When he saw Koos Botha, his eyes filled with tears. He embraced him to acknowledge the recent passing of Mrs Botha. Neil had been in hospital when she suffered a heart attack. He tried to tell Koos how sorry he was to hear the news, but couldn't. He hugged Koos with his firm arm and held his cheek against Koos's for a long minute. Koos responded and half hugged, half held Neil up, sobbing.

Neil thought of how courageously Mrs Botha had suffered at the hands of the British, and then picked up the pieces when her husband died; of how she had taken him under her wing and opened her family to him, a young Englishman. He shook his head at the crowd of memories. It was Mrs Botha who had guided him to Top Star. That was what led him to Jerry and, of course, Angelique. It was as though God had sent him to Mrs Botha so long ago to set him on his path. And Koos, a man with power to abuse, had proven to be compassionate and willing to help when needed.

Neil regained his composure and separated from Koos, wavering briefly on his feet until Angelique moved in so that he could lean on her. She handed him a handkerchief, and he wiped his face. He squeezed Koos's shoulder and shuffled on to the next ring of guests, nodding and patting them on the back. But he said nothing, ate nothing, and drank nothing. Those things he did in private.

Although polite with all the guests, he longed for the event to end. At some stage, exhaustion overtook his determination to please his family. He knew they wanted the celebration for him, even though he had protested. But he felt he could no longer put on the brave front.

He pulled Angelique aside and pointed to the bedroom upstairs. She wanted to announce his retirement from the party, but he dragged her away, nodding to those they passed, waving for them to continue, as though his exit were temporary.

After a slow struggle to climb the stairs, he fell onto his bed, fully clothed. Before Angelique could remove his shoes, he was fast asleep.

For a period of five years following her schooling Thandi had dedicated her time to reading law. She followed that with tutoring and going for her honours degree.

Three months after achieving that distinction, she met Phineas at the bus stop one evening as he alighted. At first Phineas thought there was something wrong, but then he saw her excited smile. "What? What?" he asked.

"I'm expecting."

Phineas looked confused.

"We're going to have a baby!"

He whooped with joy and did a little dance around her. "And guess what. Our child will be born just before the first free election in this country. Your timing is perfect, my love."

Phineas, Eveleen and Grace treated her like a princess for the next few months. Then Phineas arrived home one evening to find Eveleen on her own. "Where's everyone, Grandma?"

"Grace and Jerry have taken Thandi to hospital. Your little boy is on his way."

"How do you know it's a boy?"

"I know, my child. Believe me, I've seen this before. Let's go."

At the hospital, Phineas could not take his eyes off his wet offspring with perfect features. "It's a boy, Thandi."

The nurse handed the baby to Thandi, who held him close. He fitted perfectly under her neck. Phineas stepped forward and pushed a finger into the baby's palm. The little hand locked tightly over Phineas's finger and shook it.

There was no discussion about a name. They had long ago agreed that if the baby was a boy, they would call him Sipho, after her late twin brother.

Jerry had become a participant in the negotiations that were taking place between the Pretoria government and the ANC. Jerry prayed for peace to last during the time leading up to the first truly free elections in South Africa under a new interim constitution.

He was a public figure – a union leader who spoke up for the rights of workers. To his expectant black supporters, he gave messages of hope and the promise of jobs without restrictions or discrimination. But he felt that their jobs would be more secure in a climate that encouraged responsible business. He promoted the continuation of private ownership of businesses and mines, and he gave messages of comfort to the worried white community.

"But," he warned, "we must legislate for compulsory involvement of black leadership in businesses. No longer will the whites have a monopoly over the boards of business corporations. No longer will the best jobs be reserved for the white minority."

Jerry met Marius once a week, and sometimes twice, to discuss the public statements made by the unions and the government. It concerned him that there were elements on both sides that polarised the country. Marius warned him that there would be enough vitriol in the months to come.

Jerry sometimes digressed from current issues and reminisced on the times at the farm, commenting on how things had changed. They spoke about Marius's father's strict management of the staff. He stopped short of commenting on Hennie, who still ruled the farm.

He asked Marius about the battles fought by the Afrikaners against the British Empire, and he pointed out the similarities he saw to his own people's struggle. Marius didn't respond to that. Instead he referred to Neil and the opportunities he had been able to exploit. They both agreed that Neil had done well. Marius commented that Neil was happy to take advantage of the apartheid system without taking responsibility for it.

During one of the meetings in Marius's office, shortly before the first free election was to be held, Marius's secretary burst into the room. "Mrs Strydom has telephoned to say you must look at the TV immediately, sir. There is a civil war."

Marius switched on the TV in his office. Jerry gaped at the replay of news reports from the puppet "independent" state of Bophuthatswana, where black police had returned fire on a convoy of armed right-wing Boers dressed in military-style khaki uniforms. The convoy of white militants had been firing into roadside huts. The TV reported that police had shot in the neck the driver of a blue Mercedes Benz at the end of the convoy. Another passenger had been shot in the arm, and a third in the leg. The car had come to an abrupt halt, and the three men had faltered out.

Jerry groaned as TV footage showed a black police officer relieving one of the men of his weapon and another policeman attempting to fire on nearby journalists. His rifle jammed.

"Oh, no!" Marius exclaimed when one of the Afrikaners admitted he was a member of a notorious Boer supremacy movement and pleaded for the lives of his two co-conspirators. A policeman responded by shooting two of the three wounded men at point-blank range. Then he shouted angrily, "Who do you think you are? What are you doing in my country?" Jerry sat at the edge of the chair with his eyes locked on the TV.

The shooting had been captured by the nearby journalists and broadcast worldwide. The final moments were replayed again and again. The images showed two Boers lying next to their Mercedes Benz, and then the third pleading for mercy before he was also shot.

The mood in Marius's office was grim. Jerry glanced at Marius. For the first time, his boyhood friend's eyes betrayed his feelings. They revealed his concern about these events and fear of what might result from them. Jerry saw in them the grim mood that was surely spreading throughout the country.

Jerry was not giving up hope. He continued to canvass for the ANC in the upcoming elections and sighed with relief when the Bophuthatswana conflict failed to spread. He had slotted back into his role of secretary-general of the union, which was no longer a banned organisation. The position had not been filled since his exile. He changed its constitution, converting it openly into a trade union. From that pedestal he spoke on behalf of millions of workers. He used his power to his advantage and that of the black movement negotiating for a new South Africa.

He and Marius agreed to encourage toning down the rhetoric, but Jerry refused to keep out of the spotlight, even though his safety was at risk. This worried Marius. "There are still people with elephant memories who have not forgotten and not forgiven, Jeremiah."

"They should be asking *our* forgiveness for making us suffer all these decades."

Jerry sought and used every opportunity to express an opinion, make demands for workers, and claim land rights for blacks. He did so in the workshops of the factories, in the overcrowded accommodation rooms at mine hostels for men, in the squalid streets of the townships, and in the five-star hotels where international groups were considering their future dealings with the country.

As his stature grew, he was quoted more and more. His face appeared regularly in newspapers and on television. Journalists asked for his opinion on a range of issues. He was aggressively impatient for changes at a social level, insisting upon open schools, neighbourhoods, and transport. "Reserving parts of these for whites only is the continuation of apartheid. This must be stamped out *now*."

He warned of big changes to the civil service, in which the whites monopolised managerial positions. Marius was relieved when he spoke against nationalising the mines but shivered when he said the farmlands should be redistributed.

"Listen here, Jeremiah. The country is riddled with uncertainty. You cannot claim the farms *and* the government jobs of the whites."

"Why not? You did. Our people have been disadvantaged far too long. They have expectations. Why should only the whites be wealthy?" Jerry paused and Marius looked down. "How do you expect to reduce crime if the poor get poorer?"

"We are battling to keep this political process in check. You guys are demanding too much change too quickly. We are trying to prevent a complete collapse of law and order."

"You can't hold the wave of change back. You've built a dam to keep all the water to yourselves instead of sharing it. We have lived on the dry riverbanks for too long. Your dam is cracking and breaking. You can't stop the water."

"Yes, but see how the whites are arming themselves. They will defend their schools and homes."

"It's too late."

"Well then, you can be careful. Step back. You are a target," said Marius. "You may think that your speeches are moderate. But there are those who don't see that. They hear what they want to hear. Some of those people out there hate you."

"Don't talk nonsense. I'll be fine." Jerry sat back in the armchair.

"I'm worried. Swanepoel lost a nephew in the army, and he moves around the country with stealth. And then there is your big mouth. Even I think your talk about giving the farms to the blacks goes too far."

"Yes, I expect you do. But then, that's what my people felt when you took our land. Don't worry about me. I am surrounded by so many bodyguards, my grandson doesn't know who his grandfather is."

"He's a baby. Of course he doesn't know you yet. You need to stay alive so that he gets to know you when he's older."

"I'll be okay. We have the advice of your security. Since you interfered, we drive as part of a convoy of three cars. I change cars frequently. I don't know where the hell I am most of the time because we never take the same way home. I don't even know whose car I'm getting into sometimes. One of these days I'm going to get into Swanepoel's car by mistake!"

40

◇◆◇

Jerry felt ready for the inevitable changes to his life. He was itching to step up to the national political stage and was no longer afraid to use the welfare society, renamed the Mechanics Trade Union, as a platform. His concerns about how he would make a living after so many years away from the workforce were answered: his salary as secretary-general provided enough for the family to live on comfortably.

He thought about trying to use his influence to find a new home, but felt that would be a betrayal of all he stood for. Instead, he insisted that the family remain at Eveleen's place. They had already been cramped in the four-room house and Marius's insistence that Jerry be guarded by a team of hand-picked minders twenty-four hours a day only added to the crowdedness.

And it unsettled Jerry. Although he didn't want an entourage of bodyguards, the security forces had received word that his life was in danger. Marius had told him this, but had been vague about where the threat was coming from. "You have made many enemies," Marius warned.

Jerry resented having so little choice. How could he feel like the father at home if he was constantly surrounded by security? Sure, his family could adapt to having him around again, but it would mean a bigger adjustment if he came with a mini-army. And if he really was in danger, wouldn't maintaining guards be giving in to intimidation by radicals, preventing him from living a normal life?

The barrage of questions kept coming. What was the origin of these threats? He knew that some right-wing Afrikaners wanted to disrupt the election and bring down black radicals who had committed gruesome attacks. But why should they go after him?

Maybe Marius was right. His old friend wouldn't be so persistent unless he genuinely feared for him. The passionate plea from the usually demure Marius finally persuaded him. He arranged for a quick extension to be built on Eveleen's shack, and for eight weeks of construction, the bodyguards slept in cars and the family squeezed into the two front rooms.

He was pleased with the result. The extension was compact and functional. The original bedrooms became a large kitchen and dining area, while the security detail took over the rest of the old front section.

A large opening along what used to be the back wall of the shack led to the new lounge room. Sliding doors could close it off. Two doors from there opened onto a bedroom for Eveleen and Angelique, and a new bathroom. He added an upstairs: four small bedrooms and a bathroom. Sylvester and his cousins occupied one, and Jerry and Grace another – the first bedroom they had ever had on their own. Cheeky had his own room, and Jerry was pleased that Thandi, Phineas, and baby Sipho occupied the fourth upstairs bedroom.

The kitchen/dining room was the centre of activity. When Jerry was home, he avoided this area. He preferred to be away from Eveleen and Angelique at work, catering for the family and for the bodyguards. He overheard one of the bodyguards saying to Eveleen one day, "Mama, you don't have to cook for us. We can buy our own food."

He could hear the horror in Eveleen's voice. "Don't talk nonsense. You're our guests."

Jerry smiled to himself.

Between union business, ANC campaigning, and his meetings with Marius, Jerry spent little time at home during the day, and he had something on most nights of the week. He tolerated the security arrangements for his commuting: four bodyguards accompanied him everywhere, and there were three drivers for the convoy of three cars. He felt the need to keep two guards at home to protect his family and the house.

It was unusual for him to spend time with Grace at home. He enjoyed those rare occasions, even though they were never alone.

One hot and muggy Tuesday night in 1994, Jerry was relaxing after dinner. His political campaign to be elected a member of parliament in the first free elections had kicked up a gear, and he sought out as many opportunities as he could to increase his profile.

That night he was to have addressed a public meeting at a football stadium. He had been rehearsing his speech in the late afternoon when Grace called him to the phone. It was Marius, who went straight to the point. "The security police received a tip-off that you're going to be attacked tonight."

"What do you mean?"

"We've searched for bombs in the stadium and found nothing. But it's too risky."

"I'll take the risk. I can't let my supporters down," said Jerry.

"The tip-off is too strong to ignore. We think there might be a sniper." Jerry heard the tension in Marius's voice. "There are too many dark hiding places in the stadium. We cannot assure your safety. We have closed down the venue and cordoned the area off."

"What?" Jerry shouted. "We can't stop our lives just because of rumours. I'll never be able to run an election campaign."

"This is different," said Marius, keeping his voice calm. "The source is reliable, and the police are sure someone would have tried to take your life at the meeting. In any case, it's too late to change. We've cancelled the buses scheduled to go to the meeting."

"If the information is so credible, why don't you catch them? Who are they? Who's after me?"

"Er …" Marius cleared his throat. "We think it's from within the force. That's why we're so sure. But we haven't been able to get the whole story. Something was overheard. And it was enough to be taken seriously. I can't give you details yet."

"Do you mean to tell me your security people are after me, and you can't find out who it is?" Jerry's voice was raised. Marius did not answer. "What's happening, Marius?"

"I warned you before of rogue elements. We know they're there. We're close to getting some names, but at this time we need to be careful. We had no choice. We had to cancel your rally."

If Marius was taking these steps, then the threat was real, but there was something Marius was not telling him. Still, he couldn't run his campaign like this. "Cancelling my rally is giving in to *them*. This is against my principles. Next time let *me* decide," he said almost shouting.

So, there was a one-night pause in the feverish campaign for the approaching election. This was the first time he hadn't had an evening engagement for almost two months, and he didn't know what to do with himself at home.

Eveleen had been unwell, with a temperature. He went to her room to see how she was. Grace and Thandi were there, fussing over her. "She'll be fine," said Grace. "There's nothing you can do to help." So he left them and returned to the dining room.

Angelique and Phineas, with little Sipho on his lap, were sitting at the table, peering at that day's *Star* newspaper spread out in front of them. They were discussing an article, and Sipho was sucking his thumb, looking content. Cheeky was out, and the other children were milling about upstairs and downstairs.

He went to the front of the house. Two bodyguards were patrolling the street, three were sitting on the stoep, and four were resting in the front rooms. None of them were interested in his company.

He went into the kitchen, made himself a cup of coffee, and retired to a couch in the lounge. He stretched his legs out in front of him and rested them on the coffee table. He sipped his coffee, but it was too hot and burned his tongue. He placed it on the side table and leaned back. He didn't really want the coffee.

His eyelids were heavy, and he let them close. His limbs felt weighed down. He stopped resisting the calm that took over, that started in his mind and seeped into his muscles and bones. He felt his pulse slow down and his body sink deeper into the soft couch.

His snoring jolted him awake once or twice. Then he closed his mouth, shifted his position, and dozed off again, barely aware of the argument between Phineas and Angelique in the next room.

Suddenly Jerry's sleep was shattered by a loud bang. Where was he? He followed his instincts and fell to the ground.

Raising his head, he realised he was at home. A thick cloud of dust filled the lounge. The source appeared to be from the front of the house. He looked around and then ducked quickly. Another violent explosion rocked the kitchen. Splinters and debris flew over him. Everyone screamed, and baby Sipho howled. Rapid shooting followed. A bodyguard fell upon Jerry and yelled, "Down! Down! They're shooting. Get down!"

Jerry lay down and looked towards the dining room. Where was the baby? He saw Phineas on the floor. Their eyes met. Where was Sipho? *There he is: little Sipho is under Phineas, well protected.* Jerry felt relieved.

Angelique crawled into the lounge to get away from the front. "Come, Phineas," called Jerry. "Take the baby to the back. To the bathroom at the back. That's the safest room." Phineas crawled on one arm, keeping baby Sipho under him all the time.

Another bodyguard ran to Jerry as bullets punctured the walls and ceilings. Machine-gun fire, screams and the shouts of the guards filled the air. There was another explosion. Jerry ducked as another force of dust-filled smoke engulfed him. He looked towards the front of the house. The bodyguards' room was destroyed.

The two guards steered Jerry to the back exit. He shouted for Phineas and Angelique to follow. There was a prearranged escape route through the yard of the neighbour who was diagonally behind them. A getaway car was kept there at all times, just in case. It was ready for this kind of attack. The car was guarded by the police.

Shielded by the two men, Jerry ran towards the neighbour's gate. Then one of his bodyguards shouted, "No, this is an ambush! Get back! Get back! Something's wrong!" He raised his arms and tried to screen Jerry.

Two clear cracks – sniper shots – confused Jerry. He didn't know what they were. They seemed soft and far. He felt something impact his back but couldn't understand what had happened. His head hit the ground.

❖

Grace had seen Jerry being escorted out the back door and heard the shouts and shots that followed. She ran outside to see if Jerry was safe.

A bodyguard covered in blood lay lifeless two feet from another body. She recognised the shirt. "Jerry!" she screamed and rushed to him. "Jerry! Jerry!" She looked up when another shot was fired, and she heard a flat thud on the ground beside her. She saw two white men in military fatigues just before they turned and fled. She could make out the vulture-face of one of them in the bright moonlight.

Four other bodyguards joined them and fired into the dark.

"They've gone. Help me!" shouted Grace. "Jerry's been shot."

One of them ran over to her. There was yelling, orders being given by a senior bodyguard to secure the scene and get Grace into the house.

But Grace knelt next to Jerry. His eyes were open and his face was calm. She looked down and saw a dark pool bloom just below his chest. Grace eased herself under him and cradled his head in her arms, leaning him on her. He said something she couldn't hear. She put her ear next to his lips.

"Yes, Jerry. I'm here. You'll be fine. Just stay still."

"Grace ..." he said softly. "I think it's ... over now ... I know ... I love you."

"Stay quiet. Help is on the way," she said. She held his head and closed her eyes and prayed.

Paramedics arrived. "Mama, please, you must let us have space."

"No. No. He's dying. Leave him. Leave us alone."

"Please, we must get him to a hospital straight away. We may be able to save him."

A bodyguard helped her up. "Come, let's go to the ambulance. You can go to hospital with him."

"But he's not going to make it. I must be with him now."

"Please wait, Mama." They put him on a stretcher.

The family and bodyguards parted as they carried Jerry through the front of the house and to the ambulance, where they started working in earnest to stabilise his condition.

"Mama, you may get in. Take that seat."

She sat next to Jerry, took his hand, and looked him in the face as they worked on him from the other side. His eyes were closed.

"He has lost consciousness. He has lost a lot of blood." They worked on him, connecting him to tubes and machines. They tried to stem the bleeding, applied bandages and administered intravenous medications.

Before the ambulance drove off, Grace saw the paramedics glance at each other. The urgency seemed to ease from their efforts, and their expressions were grim.

Grace looked at Jerry. His chest had stopped heaving.

Grace cried, "No. No. I didn't say I love him. Jerry, Jerry … I love you too … I love you too." She stood over him and squeezed his hand. "Can you hear me? I love you, Jerry. I love you." She thought she felt a faint twitch in his finger and turned to them. "Don't give up. Don't give up. His finger held me." She grabbed the paramedic. "He's still alive. Don't give up."

They tried to revive him.

Grace closed her eyes at the nucleus of the chaos and prayed. She became aware that something new and strange was happening outside the ambulance – there was singing. Quietly at first, then louder, stronger. To her it sounded like heaven. The voices of Jerry's supporters opened up in song and joined in unison to ask God to bless Africa, to bless this son of Africa in the bosom of his wife, Grace. She felt their sorrow and their hope.

A police convoy led the way for the ambulance to speed to the hospital. She watched from behind her moist handkerchief as Jerry was wheeled down the corridor to the operating theatre.

The shrill ring of the telephone jolted Marius awake shortly before midnight. He picked up the receiver and recognised the sombre voice of the head of state security: Jerry had been shot and was undergoing surgery. The attackers had not been apprehended. "They wore uniforms but used unmarked cars," he said. "My people believe police weapons were used."

Marius struggled to breathe as the shock of this news sank in.

The gravity of the attack brought with it a painful understanding. "This could be the spark that ignites the country," he replied, almost to himself.

"I know," said the general. "We've cancelled all leave."

"Let me know if you hear any news at all about Mr Ngubeni's condition. Let's pray he lives."

He got out of bed on trembling legs and went to the lounge, where he switched on the TV. The incident was already dominating the media reports. He flicked from channel to channel. All reports speculated about whether Jerry had survived the attack.

Marius could not go back to bed. He missed Letitia. Her father was in hospital, and she and Annelise were staying at the Marais cottage to support her mother. Marius paced the room, made coffee, let it go cold, and returned again and again to the television. He also kept the wireless on in the background and listened intently to the news every half hour.

When he turned again to the screen and watched the footage taken shortly after the attack, he knew he was witnessing something he had long anticipated.

He watched intently as the scene unfolded.

Crowds had gathered around the Ngubeni house. The family, neighbours and guards formed a ring around the ambulance, its red light pulsing as urgent medical attention was given inside. The guard of honour became larger as scores of people arrived and stood in silence, their faces and bodies illuminated by fires and vehicle lights.

In a very short time the crowd became dozens … and then hundreds.

Some raised their fists in a spontaneous gesture of the freedom that had yet to come. Marius saw them conferring with hushed respect about the terrible attack. Every detail was caught on camera, including the sound of soft sobs, which then escalated into wrenching wailing and the powerful ululating of the women. He gripped the arms of his chair and his thoughts spun from Jerry's condition to the possible consequences. The hairs on his body stood on end.

From out of the chaos, from the wailing and chanting, a lone and pure voice rose in song. Another joined in, and then another. Even with the many voices, the words remained clear and the timing sure. The more voices there were, the more they became one. Raw emotion gave power and strength, and the number of singers swelled, united in the strong and stirring African hymn, "Nkosi Sikelel' iAfrika". Sorrow was giving way to something new.

Marius was riveted. As a police convoy led the ambulance away, the passion of that powerful anthem throbbed through his veins, filling him with a new and strange understanding. Tears coursed down his face.

The crowd became one whole, breathing, seething country at the dawn of a new birth, painful yet exhilarating. Marius felt this new life wail and swell and rise up to meet its destiny. All across the nation, the huge mass of people that grew hour by hour could be seen singing the anthem on every TV station.

The camera kept zooming in to focus on the young, bloodstained, and tearful couple at the centre. With wet cheeks they sang. Hope rose into the dark, smoke-filled night.

The woman's voice grew stronger as she punched defiantly at the sky with her right fist while she held her baby tenderly in the crook of her left arm.

End

GLOSSARY

Although some of the words listed below may have more than one meaning, they appear in the text with only the meaning given in this glossary.

Advokaat (Afrikaans) — trial lawyer

Baba (Greek) — Dad/Daddy

Babaton (Zulu) — alcohol brew served at shebeens and made of sugar cane, yeast, cooked potatoes, and brandy, sometimes with pineapple skin, whisk carbide, or other secret ingredients (possibly from the Barberton daisy) to distinguish a shebeen owner's special recipe. The word could also be a corruption of 'Barberton'.

Baas (Afrikaans) — Boss

Basie (Afrikaans) — Little boss (an abbreviation of *kleinbaas*)

Beskuit (Afrikaans) — rusks – a chunky, dry, dunking biscuit

Biltong (Afrikaans) — dried, salty meat sticks

Bioscope (SA English) — cinema (a word used among English speakers from the UK, currently still used in South Africa)

Blerrie (SA English)	bloody
Boer (Dutch and Afrikaans)	farmer (later, used specifically of the group of European settlers in South Africa from which the Afrikaners are descended)
Boerevrou (Afrikaans)	Boer lady, farmer's wife
Boom (Afrikaans)	tree
Braai (Afrikaans)	barbecue
Broederbond (Afrikaans)	Brotherhood (society of Afrikaners with shared ethnic and political values and goals)
Dankie (Afrikaans)	thank you
Dassie (Afrikaans)	hyrax or small-hoofed, rodent-like mammal native to Africa
Domkop (Afrikaans)	dumb-head (blockhead)
Dop (Afrikaans)	shot (of alcohol)
Duku (Nguni)	cloth head covering
Heiligdom (Afrikaans)	sanctuary (literally 'holy place')
Gogo or *Ugogo* (isiZulu)	Granny
Gooie middag (Afrikaans)	greeting: good afternoon
Ja (Afrikaans)	Yes
Kaffirs (Arabic origin)	indigenous Africans (literally 'non-believers'; became the generic term in SA, later derogatory)
Kleinbaas (Afrikaans)	little boss
Klippie (SA English and Afrikaans)	brandy, from Klipdrift, a popular cheap SA brandy
Knopkierie (Afrikaans from Nama)	African walking/fighting stick
Koffie (Afrikaans)	coffee
Koppie (Afrikaans)	hill
Kori mou (Greek)	my girl
Kraal (Afrikaans)	compound-like village in southern Africa

Kudu (Khoikhoi)	kind of antelope
Meisie (Afrikaans)	girl
Meneer (Afrikaans)	Mister
Mevrou (Afrikaans)	Miesies (or English Mrs)
Mielie (Afrikaans)	corn
Miesies (Afrikaans)	madam
Nee (Afrikaans)	No
Oom (Afrikaans)	uncle
Oubaas (Afrikaans)	old boss
Ouma (Afrikaans)	Grandma
Oupa (Afrikaans)	Grandpa
Panga (Swahili)	broad African knife, machete
Pap (Dutch/Afrikaans)	African maize porridge
Pasop (Afrikaans)	beware
Rondavel (Afrikaans *rondawel*)	thatch-roofed circular hut
Shebeen (Irish Gaelic)	tavern (in SA, serves illegal alcohol to Africans)
Sjambok (Afrikaans, from Malay)	thick, tough whip, made of hide
Skelm (Afrikaans)	cheat
Skokiaan (possibly Zulu)	an illicit alcoholic brew made from a basic recipe of sugar, yeast and warm water. The Zulu word *isikokeyana* (small enclosure) could be the origin, as the practice was to hide the liquor in holes in the ground.
Skomfani skokiaan (Zulu?)	a particularly strong skokiaan with a higher percentage of alcohol
Stoep (Afrikaans)	veranda
Theio (Greek)	uncle
Tokoloshe (Zulu)	mischievous dwarf-like bogeyman in Zulu mythology
Tsotsis (Nguni or Sesotho)	young black South African urban thug or gangster

Twak (colloquial Afrikaans)	nonsense
Umfazi (Nguni)	African married woman/wife
Voetsek (Afrikaans)	Aggressive admonition to 'go away'
Volk (Afrikaans)	people
Voorkamer (Afrikaans)	front room
Vuilgoed (Afrikaans)	dirty goods
Weerstandsbeweging (Afrikaans)	resistance movement; specifically, the far-right nationalist Afrikaner resistance movement formed in the 1970s
Yiayia (Greek)	Grandmother

ACKNOWLEDGEMENTS

I owe a great deal of thanks to many for helping in the making of this book. I refer to them here in the sequence in which they became involved.

My wife, Athena, suffered from beginning to end. I was so obsessed that I was uncommunicative almost every night and every weekend for over four years. She was my first critic, telling me, "It's a good story – now convert it from a legal pleading into a novel." She set me on the path of getting there and guided me throughout the full journey.

Rosemary Penman read the first version of a couple of chapters and said "I want to read more." That's just what I needed to hear.

My son Phivo was the first reader of the complete first version. He told me he enjoyed the story and diplomatically presented me with pages and pages of comments.

Then, dinky di Aussie and close friend, Ian Anderson, and very serious South African Greek, Nick Mastrandonis, read the initial draft. I waited impatiently to hear what they had to say. Although frank, their views were reassuring and helpful.

But the novel really started taking shape after my editor, Michèle Drouart, got involved. Of course, I felt I didn't need an editor, but I was fortunate that a mutual friend, Di Dixon, suggested meeting with Michèle. My reluctance was replaced by humility as Michèle taught me that there are ways to write a story that don't make the reader shiver as though listening to glass scraping on glass. I can testify as to her patience and professionalism in the face of a very impatient lawyer who thought he was an author.

I also thank South Africans John Linnegar and Kenneth McGillivray, who both put much time into a careful reading and gave me an early reality check on aspects of the story when I had some doubts.

I gave a draft to my mother, Marina, to check some details. She read it overnight. The next day she told me that she had been very moved by the story in a number of places.

Much later, I received excellent feedback from the following group of readers: Tim Barrett, Richard Brophy, Mark Delahoy, Carly Drew, Chris Edmonds, Robyn and Ed Heyting, Hilary Hunt, Jenny Kennedy, Helen Mastrantonis, Andrew Paizes, Di Raymond, Julie Scanlon, and Tineke van der Eecken. Each of them gave a very thoughtful response, and their input resulted in much cutting and changing.

Then, Balboa Press gave the writing and story another thorough reality check and contributed insightful and valuable suggestions.

The whole process flowed because of the support Marion McLaren provided in my day job, in her ever efficient way. My gratitude is also due to my partners and the team at Jackson McDonald.

I thank them all from the bottom of my heart and I hope you have enjoyed reading the results of their work.

BG
2017

lia
60917
I00002B/8/P